Anonymous

Memorials of the life and ministry of the Rev. John Machar, D.D.

Anonymous

Memorials of the life and ministry of the Rev. John Machar, D.D.

ISBN/EAN: 9783337260316

Printed in Europe, USA, Canada, Australia, Japan

Cover: Foto ©Raphael Reischuk / pixelio.de

More available books at **www.hansebooks.com**

MEMORIALS

OF THE

LIFE AND MINISTRY

OF THE

REV. JOHN MACHAR, D.D.

LATE MINISTER OF

ST. ANDREW'S CHURCH, KINGSTON.

EDITED BY MEMBERS OF HIS FAMILY.

TORONTO:
JAMES CAMPBELL & SON.
1873.

TO THE CONGREGATION OF

St. Andrew's Church, Kingston,

THESE MEMORIALS OF THEIR LATE PASTOR ARE,

IN MEMORY OF THE UNBROKEN HARMONY

AND STRONG BOND OF ATTACHMENT ALWAYS SUBSISTING

BETWEEN HIM AND HIS PEOPLE,

AFFECTIONATELY DEDICATED.

PREFACE.

EVER since the removal by death of one who had been, for so long a period, the pastor of St. Andrew's Church, Kingston, it has been felt that some record of his ministry among them, as well as of his connexion with the history of the Presbyterian Church in Canada, should be preserved.

Feeling, on his death-bed, deep concern for the spiritual well-being of the congregation he was so soon to leave, he said, " I am conscious of having preached the truth to my people, though in much weakness, and I wish them to remember it when I am gone." The feeling that a short memoir should be written of his life and ministry, accompanied by as many of his sermons as could be conveniently contained in the volume, has been more and more strongly felt as time has passed on. Many changes and sad events have occurred in his congregation since he was taken from it, and if some record of the past years be not preserved, many circumstances well worthy of remembrance will soon be totally forgotten.

Many of those who had sat long under his ministry are now seen no more in their wonted places, and lie near their former pastor in his quiet resting-place. Many whom he baptised, and who are now grown up, can have but an indistinct remembrance of their old minister. Others who were attached members of his congregation, during his sojourn here, are widely scattered throughout Canada and the United States, while many of them are settled in adjoining townships, continuing steadily attached members of the Church of their fathers. Such will doubtless welcome a volume which will bring to their remembrance how he walked among them, and the words of life which they heard from his lips.

It has not been desired unduly to eulogise his memory, or to give the private experience of his inner-life, but simply to present a true, unvarnished history of his faithful and incessantly laborious life among his people, during the long period of thirty-five years.

KINGSTON, June, 1873.

TABLE OF CONTENTS.

CHAPTER III.

(1827—1832.)

FIRST YEARS OF CANADIAN PASTORATE.

CHAPTER IV.

(1831—1832.)

MEETING OF THE FIRST PRESBYTERIAN SYNOD IN CANADA, AND PASTORATE DURING 1831-32.

CHAPTER VII.

(1844.)

DIVISION OF THE PRESBYTERIAN CHURCH IN CANADA.

CHAPTER VIII.

(1844—1849.)

PRINCIPALSHIP OF QUEEN'S COLLEGE—THIRD VISIT TO SCOTLAND.

CHAPTER IX.

PASTORAL AND PERSONAL TRAITS.

CHAPTER X.

LADIES' MISSIONARY ASSOCIATION.

CHAPTER XI.

(1849—1860.)

RESIGNATION OF PRINCIPALSHIP—LABOURS CONNECTED WITH QUEEN'S COLLEGE—LAST VISIT TO SCOTLAND.

CHAPTER XII.

(1860—1863.)

CLOSING YEARS.

CHAPTER I.

1796–1813.

CHILDHOOD AND EARLY YOUTH.

THE life delineated in the following pages, although its general character was that of quiet, unobtrusive ministerial usefulness, has, yet, a special interest attached to it, in having been, throughout most of its course, closely linked with the early history of the Presbyterian Church in Canada, and with events and circumstances which have had and must still have, an important bearing on its progress and development.

To those who look only, or chiefly at "things seen and temporal," the life of a faithful pastor can seldom seem one of striking interest. The aims which he follows are far other than those which usually lead to earthly distinction, and his time and strength are absorbed in constant labours whose arduousness few can appreciate, and in a round of daily duties, which, however important in their results, must, often, to a superficial observer, appear small and unimportant. And yet, to those who feel that, of all the varieties of work which it is given to men on earth to do for God,—that of winning back to Him souls wandering in the wilderness of this world,—of nurturing and caring for the tender plant of Christian life, amid the checks and dangers to which it is constantly exposed, is, beyond measure, the highest and most important,—the record of a life of earnest, faithful labour for these ends will scarcely, even in itself, be devoid of interest. And in a time when, more perhaps than ever before, doubts and mists cross the spiritual vision of men,—when the path of simple faith is often difficult to find, and men wander far from it in wistful search for the light which can only be found there ;—the history of an active Christian life kept safe and unshaken by a simple and steady realization of the faith from which it sprang, and happy and healthy in its growth because engaged in happy and healthy Christian work,—may have its lesson for all.

As, however, the subject of this memoir was one who never courted public notice, the personal history will be, for the most part, merged in that of the pastor, and his private life and character traced chiefly in connection with the public events with which it was associated, and the work he was privileged to do.

JOHN MACHAR was born in December, 1796, in the parish of Tannadice, a quiet, secluded part of Forfarshire, Scotland, a few miles from the ancient burgh of Brechin. Owing to the retired situation of his childhood's home, at a time when the absence of railways made country life more secluded than it is now, his earlier years were filled up with the simplest rural interests and pleasures, and he never lost the love of green fields, and trees, and running brooks, which had been implanted in his nature by happy early associations. He recalled vividly in after years, the gratification of being taken to a "distant wood " which had long been the goal of his childish desires, and a visit to the little county town of Forfar was looked back to as a wonderful and exciting event. His father, an intelligent, active, and proverbially *honest* man, was always busily occupied with his farming concerns and the supervision of his flax-mill. As the youngest son of a family

2

of nine, of whom the eldest alone still survives, and a child of remarkably sweet and amiable disposition, John was the favourite companion of his mother, whose cultivation of mind and high tone of character exercised a strong influence over the formation of his own. Her father had been a follower of the unfortunate Charles Edward, and had participated in the ruin in which his adherents had been involved. Being a thorough classical scholar, he had become, when overtaken by adversity, the parish schoolmaster of Tannadice, and had given his only daughter a most careful education, much beyond what was usual for girls in the age in which she lived. She was a woman, also, of a tenderly affectionate heart, and of high religious principle, and her memory was always regarded by her son with love and veneration. He cherished, to his last days as a relic of her, a little ancient Sternhold and Hopkins' Psalter, which she used to carry to church, whose old English characters and angular musical notes are as antique as its embroidered satin binding. The early impressions made upon his heart and conscience by her Christian example and instructions moulded and influenced his character and life, and it was from her strong desire to devote him to the ministry that his mind received its first impulse towards the profession which he afterwards chose.

His sisters remember him as always a most affectionate brother, and a younger one describes him at eight years old as escorting her to school and tenderly carrying her over the rough places of the road. He was early taught to feel and sympathize with sorrow, for, during his childhood, the family was repeatedly visited with heavy trials. Three of the children, one of them a youth of much hope and promise, were removed by death,—a bitter cup of sorrow for the affectionate mother. Far from being engrossed with her own griefs, however, she was always ready to relieve and sympathize with the woes of others, and Dr. Machar often used to speak of a characteristic instance of her quick and warm feeling for others which

3

had made a deep impression on his childish heart. This
was the vivid recollection of seeing his mother's tears
flowing out of sympathy with the grief of a poor old man,
who had been driven by a series of misfortunes to leave
his farm and beg from door to door;—and the impression
which the scene left on the child who witnessed it was
never effaced.

He had from childhood a very tender conscience,
which, being afterwards spiritually enlightened, was a striking feature in his character. One summer day, while
wandering alone in the fields, a leveret chanced to cross
his path. In a momentary impulse of childish wantonness
he threw a stone at the little creature, which, unfortunately
struck and killed it. The moment he saw the poor animal lying dead,—deprived of the life he could not restore,
—an overwhelming fit of remorse took possession of him,
and he felt as if he were a murderer. He carefully took
up the leveret, which he would have given anything to
bring back to life, and buried it under a heap of earth,
stones and withered grass; but for months afterwards, he
could not pass the spot without a keen sense of remorse,
and a haunting fear lest his evil deed should be brought
to light. To the deep impression which this little incident left, may be partly traceable the horror of all cruelty
to animals, which was through life one of his most striking characteristics.

He was always disposed to study, and eager to acquire
knowledge. At four years old, he set off by himself, book
in hand, to the neighbouring village, *to look for the school*,
to which he found his way. It was holiday-time, but the
master,—amused no doubt by the zeal of the little student,
—goodnaturedly gave him a lesson and invited him to return. His ardour did not flag when brought to the test
of regular study, and, as he was naturally persevering, his
progress was rapid, both at the school at Tannadice, and
at the grammar-school of Brechin, where his family, about
this time, went to reside. It was no small grief, even at

4

that early age, to leave a place endeared by so many associations which, throughout his after life, continued to cluster round that secluded early home. When visiting Scotland, for the last time, in 1860, he thus wrote,—describing a visit he had paid to it. "Two days ago my nephew drove me to Tannadice, where I visited my mother's grave, and many of the haunts of my early boyhood, along the banks of the South Esk. The river flows on still as it did of yore, and some of the rocky precipices still stand, but great changes have taken place. I went to the house where we were all born and dwelt till I was about eight. I asked to be allowed to go in. To this the good-wife very kindly and heartily acceded, and I stood in the room where I first drew breath. Having taken from her hand a drink of water, I said, 'In this room I got my first drink.' She looked up seriously and wistfully, saying' 'That must be *langsyne !*' I wandered over the farm, and felt almost surprised to find how many were the associations I had with those pleasant fields. I had wandered over them with my mother, the last year we were living there, and I could still recall how she looked, when she surveyed, with almost a breaking heart, scenes where she had been so happy, and which she was so soon to leave."

At the grammar school, at Brechin, he continued a regular scholar for several years ; his diligence and proficiency making him a special favourite with his master, a somewhat stern yet kindly "*dominie*" of the class described in Goldsmith's Deserted Village, from which Dr. Machar was wont to quote the following lines, in reference to him :

> " Full well the boding tremblers learned to trace
> The day's disasters in his morning face,—
> Full well they laughed, with counterfeited glee,
> At all his jokes, for many a joke had he ;—
> Full well the busy whisper, circling round,
> Conveyed the dismal tidings, when he frowned,
> Yet was he kind, or if severe in aught,
> 'Twas that his love of learning was in fault ! "

5

Mr. Linton was indeed one of the best teachers and most accurate classical scholars of his time, aud Dr. Machar, in after years, was wont to speak with gratitude of a master under whose careful tuition he laid the foundation of his thorough classical attainments, and of the extreme accuracy which in after life characterised his scholarship and manifested itself in everything he did.

Brechin, where these early school-days were spent, and which has lately had a wide-spread interest connected with it, as the birth-place of the late lamented Dr. Guthrie, is an ancient, quaint little town, most picturesquely situated in the midst of a rich, undulating pastoral country. Though not large in extent, it is, like all old Scottish towns, very densely built, and the grey slated stone cottages of which it is chiefly composed, resound still, as they have done for generations past, with the busy hum of hand-looms for linen-weaving, by which most of its inhabitants earn their subsistence. The narrow, steeply-slanting streets slope downwards to the Esk, which, spanned by the arches of a noble bridge, "winds about," now deep and still, between wooded banks, now spreading out over pebbly shallows- -

> " With many a silvery waterbreak
> Above the golden gravel ;—"

and overhung to the right by the rich woods and picturesque old turrets and gables of Brechin Castle. Near these rises the massive, weather-beaten tower of the old Cathedral, part of which is now used as a parish church, and the broken arched windows of the choir behind, draped with ivy, remain a picturesque ruin, suggestive of associations from ages long gone by. Close to the church, and in the same beautiful old churchyard, thickly planted with mossy gravestones, sculptured with quaint devices, rises an ancient round tower, whose origin is lost in antiquity, but is supposed to date at least from the time of the Roman occupation. To ascend its worn, spiral stair was

6

a favourite feat of the school-boys in their play-hours, and long afterwards Dr. Machar would vividly recall the pleasurable excitement, not unaccompanied with danger, of feeling the time-worn and battered edifice tremble slightly under the influence of a high wind, when he and his companions had mounted to the top. The influences of these objects surrounding his boyhood, acted very strongly upon a temperament peculiarly susceptible of such impressions, and tended to nurture and strengthen the love with which he always clung to the old poetic associations of his native land.

The dark shade of sorrow, however, soon again descended upon his home. His father was attacked by a painful and tedious disease, which, after several years of suffering, terminated his life. The bereavement was deeply felt by the family, especially by John, who was the youngest but one, and who long afterwards, in his own last illness, spoke of the instruction he had received from his father's death-bed, and the sayings he had treasured up in his memory. He deeply sympathized, too, with his widowed mother, who was left with very slender means of support for herself and her three daughters, and determined to observe the strictest economy and to use every exertion in his power, in order to be as little burdensome to them as possible in passing through his college course ; for he had, even then, set his heart upon entering the ministry. He often, in later life, expressed his thankfulness that he had been called to bear " the yoke in his youth," and early to feel his dependence on the providence of God, which was ever with him a deep reality. The self-reliance which he was thus taught, and the self-denial which he was called to exercise, he considered a most valuable part of his education, as it obliged him to think of others before himself. He entered King's College, Aberdeen, when only a little past thirteen, and in his first session obtained a bursary by competition, which opportune success greatly encouraged the young student.

King's College, Aberdeen, is one of the most ancient universities in Scotland. Its massive, crown-shaped dome,—its irregular quadrangle, its chapel richly decorated with antique carvings,—all associate themselves with the first rise of literature and education in Scotland, and with the lustre of many celebrated names that tend to quicken the ambition and stimulate the diligence of the youths who study under such influences. Contrary to the usual custom in Scottish universities, the students had their lodgings in the quadrangle itself—a pleasant and quiet residence, highly conducive to thought and study. The parapet of the walls, and the square tower which rises from one end,—surmounted by the crown and the cross,—command a noble view, including the picturesque vicinity of the Old Town, with its massive antique cathedral, the winding course of the Don and the Dee, the fresh modern buildings of New Aberdeen, and, over a wide expanse of broken ground or "links,"—the white curling waves of the German Ocean, and the distant sails it bears on its bosom. At this time-honoured university John Machar passed several busy years of pleasant student life, diligent, and successful in the studies which deeply interested him, and by his industry and exemplary conduct gaining the approbation and favour of all his Professors. Many note-books still remain, filled with ʰabstracts of the lectures he attended,—written out in the beautifully-formed and regular hand-writing of his earlier days, and proving that he put in practice a maxim of Lord Bacon's, which in after life he was wont to impress upon students ; " *Reading* makes a full man,—*writing* makes an *accurate* man." Without the quality of accuracy, indeed, he did not consider *any* knowledge of much value.

During his Arts course at Aberdeen he formed some friendships which lasted unbroken, and with undiminished strength, throughout his life. One of these early friends

8

—the late lamented and revered Dr. Urquhart, of Cornwall, who before his death was looked upon as the *Nestor* of the Synod—became in after years his neighbour and fellow worker in his distant field of labour, and the two closely-united friends enjoyed frequent opportunities of renewing the familiar intercourse of their youth, and recalling the pleasant memories of their college days. With another, also lately called to his eternal rest, the Rev. Dr. Simpson, late Free Church minister of Kintore, in Aberdeenshire, his friendship was always of a peculiarly close and confidential nature ; and neither the changes of succeeding years nor separation by distance, nor even the unfortunate " Disruption question," which awakened so much bitter feeling and broke so many ties,—and of which they took different views—had power to weaken the strength of the bond which made them one in Christ Jesus, or to diminish the delight with which, at distant intervals, they enjoyed the renewal of personal intercourse. The pen of this much loved and valued friend has furnished some reminiscences of the formation of their friendship, which are given in his own words :

" At the time when I first became intimately acquainted with Mr. Machar, he had been one session a student at King's College, Aberdeen, whereas I, though a few years older, was then but preparing to enter the same ancient University. Previously, we had known each other only by name, as we had attended different schools in Brechin. And I well remember the day on which I first called on him, in order to obtain information concerning College matters. Out of this simple and casual interview sprang an intimacy and friendship which proved to both of us the source of much true enjoyment; and, as I believe, of mutual benefit. From that day we became almost inseparable companions, and during the three succeeding college sessions we had much agreeable intercourse. But it was in the summer recesses of these years that our friendship was fully cemented. In the providence of God we were

9

then thrown upon each other more exclusively, and our tastes and habits were thus gradually assimilated. At this period Mr. Machar lived at his father's house in the immediate neighbourhood of Brechin, and prosecuted his studies in private, free from all other engagements, while I attended the public schools, partly as the pupil and partly as the assistant of my esteemed friend Mr. Alexander. My time was consequently fully occupied, except on Saturday afternoons. And in these circumstances, we met week after week in my leisure hours for reading and conversation. These happy seasons were chiefly spent in perusing the Latin classics, for which Mr. Machar, from his teacher, Mr. Linton, had imbibed a strong parpartiality, and were generally ended by a walk amid scenes of a neighbourhood to me always interesting and dear, as being my native nook,—scenes now ever vividly associated in my mind with fondly-cherished recollections of my friend's lively converse and buoyant humour."

CHAPTER II.

1813–1827.

STUDENT LIFE AND ENTRANCE ON THE MINISTRY.

AVING completed his fourth session at Aberdeen University, Mr. Machar took the degree of Master of Arts with great credit. As he was still so young, only seventeen, —and wished to do something for his own main-tenance, he was employed for a year in teaching the parish school of Inverury, as a substitute for its regular master. Inverury is a solitary grey moor-land parish in Aberdeenshire, and his life there, at an age when a young man's mind is generally in a transition state, does not seem to have been one of the happiest periods of his life. Old papers, dated Inverury, 1814, containing Latin and English ver-ses, and dreamy imaginative fragments of a diary bear traces of a morbid depression and restless self-dissatisfaction — a phase of feeling through which so many thoughtful minds have passed. These feelings find expression in such passages as the follow-ing :—

"'*Nihil est annis velocius ;*'—we sport away our time, and ere we can reflect upon it, 'tis fled and lost to us forever ! Well may I say that every passing day has brought 'near to little but my last !'—There is a vacuum in my heart—a something I cannot describe ; will my soul never be satisfied ? " In a letter to his mother about this time, he expresses a deep sense of the unsatisfying nature of the things of this world, and of the necessity of fixing the affections on things unseen or eternal. His friend, Dr. Simpson, already referred to, thus speaks of his " becoming impressed with the paramount importance of Divine things : "—" I am inclined to think that in his case, as in the case of many eminent Christians, the change was gradual. But still there was a period at which the life of God in his soul became visible to me. At Inverury, however, he was not placed in favourable circumstances for religious progress. Some of his acquaintances there were not serious persons, and his best friends were afraid of their adverse influence on his mind. In my opinion, it was after his return to Brechin and while living quietly at home in the summer of 1815, that a decided gracious change took place. At that time I certainly observed a marked difference in his religious character. His views of divine truth became deeper and clearer, and the whole tone of his conversation was more spiritual and experimental. His personal piety was more manifest, and were I to state what I considered to be the means which, under the operation and blessed influence of the Holy Spirit led to the happy change, I would ascribe it to the single-minded earnestness with which he at that period gave his heart to direct preparation for the ministry. He had, indeed, previously, in the ordinary sense, made choice of the sacred office, and even attended a partial session at the Divinity Hall at Aberdeen. But he had never previously, so far as I know, considered the matter in the same anxious and prayerful spirit. And it was, I think, when he was humbly seeking to see his warrant for undertaking the solemn responsibility of the Gospel Ministry, that the light of the Truth, as it is in Jesus, broke in upon his soul with new clearness and power. He asked and received. And henceforth his path became as the shining light, shining more and more unto the perfect day. "

Of their happy mutual intercourse a little later, Dr. Simpson thus writes : " On returning from his temporary engagement in the North, Mr. Machar, after a short interval, became tutor in the family of Captain Allardice, of Murlingden, while I entered a neighbouring family in a similar capacity. We had once more frequent opportunities of meeting—the distance between us being only eight or nine miles. We now, as before, occasionally met at Brechin in the houses of our friends there. But such casual, brief interviews did not satisfy us, and we soon contrived to establish stated meetings, for the purpose of mutual improvement. With this view we found means to arrange our avocations so as to meet from time on a wooded knoll in the intervening parish of Stracathro. At this trysting-place, weather permitting, we duly appeared according to appointment, to give reciprocal accounts of our reading studies. Here we not only held discussions, but also read essays on various subjects, chiefly connected with theology, as we were now both students of divinity. For several successive years, too, we accompanied each other to Aberdeen, to attend the Theological Hall, for what were called " partial sessions," —our tutorial engagements not allowing us a longer absence than a few weeks at Christmas. But, before this period, I had attended one full session in Edinburgh, and Mr. Machar one, if not two, there."

It was at this period, also, that he made the acquaintance of another gentleman, with whom he formed a close and intimate friendship—the Rev. George Alexander, who was then, as he still is, the able and highly respected teacher of the Brechin Grammar School. Mr. Alexander, and in after days his wife also, were always counted among his kindest and most esteemed friends, and with the former he maintained a steady correspondence during all his after life.

An incident, bringing out a characteristic trait of his character, occurred about this time. His mother, with some difficulty, prevailed upon him to visit with her a very wealthy relative, whose aid or influence might, she thought, be of use to her son, but he was so completely repelled by the cold-hearted, narrow-mindedworldliness manifested by this gentleman, that he could never be induced to repeat the visit.

In 1816, he went to Edinburgh University, where he spent two sessions, thus completing his Divinity course, while he employed in private teaching as much time as he could spare from his studies. Here, also, he was a most diligent student, and wonby his zeal and faithfulness the favour and approbation of his professors, whose friendship he retained in after life. It was a very happy time, to which he often looked back with pleasure. He went through his college work with the eager zest of a mind fresh and vigorous, and keenly enjoying the pursuit of knowledge for its own sake ; and while deeply interested, also, in the special theological studies which principally claimed his attention, he voluntarily kept up his beloved classical and mathematical studies and attended classes in Natural Philosophy and Chemistry, to supplement his previous course in the Arts. To show how fully and profitably his time was occupied with his various studies, a few extracts are given from a diary of study kept by him at this period. Some of the entries also indicate the keen enjoyment of natural scenery and of the historical and romantic associations which cluster so richly about Edinburgh and its vicinity :

March 1st, 1816.—Mathematics. Called on Dr. Buchanan. Walked out by Merchiston Castle, where Napier discovered the Logarithms. I contemplated it with a feeling of mathematical enthusiasm. His discovery might have indeed admitted a double *Eureka!* Teaching from five to six. Attended the Theological Society. Essay on the Evidence of Prophecy.

March 6th.—Mathematics. Attended College as usual. Teaching from five to six. Read sixty pages of Horne on the Psalms—a very fine preface. Consulted Poole's Synopsis on Psalms, cxxi, and other passages. Read forty lines of Homer.

March 13th.—Mathematics. Attended the usual classes. Dr. Brown—refutation of ' fitness or utility the reason of the morality of certain actions.' Teaching from five to six. Read fifty pages of " Tytler on Translation, etc." Forty lines of Homer.

March 14th—Mathematics. Attended the usual classes. Teaching from five to six. Read fifty pages of "Tytler on Translation." Forty lines of Homer.

March 15th.—Mathematics. Attended College as usual. Teaching from five to six. Attended the Theological Society (Question, " Ought all sorts of Religion to be tolerated? ") much discussed. Read a portion of " Tytler on Translation."

March 19th.—Mathematics. Attended the Hebrew Class and the Hall. Walked from twelve to four, during which time I ascended Arthur's Seat, saw the ruins of St. Anthony's Chapel and the well that also bears his name. Teaching from five to six.

March 20th.—Mathematics. Attended the Hebrew Class. Closing of the Class. Attended the Hall and Church History. Teaching from five to six. Read fifty pages of Prideaux and forty lines of Homer.

March 29th.—Mathematics. Examined part of the first Book of the Iliad. Attended the Hall and Church History. Walked during the afternoon. Teaching from five to six. Attended the Theological Society ; Essay, " Canon of the Old Testament "—Question, " Has the British Government any right to interfere with the French in regard to the persecution of the Protestants ? " Debated with much keenness and ability.

April 4th.—Up at six o'clock. Saw my friend, R. Simpson, just leaving town. Mathematics. Read a part of second Book of the Iliad. Attended the Hall. Read 130 pages of " Paley's Evidences."

In May he was attending, with all the keen interest of a theological student, the meetings of the General Assembly, the great ecclesiastical event of the year in Edinburgh.

"May 16th.—Teaching as usual. General Assembly met to-day. Saw the procession and the Commissioner, Lord Napier. Heard sermon by the last Moderator from the text—" The Lord, the Lord God, merciful and gracious." Some preparatory business. Could not get to attend Natural History. Read thirty pages of Eustace, completing Vol. II., and eighty-six of Thompson's Lectures.

May 17th.—Teaching as usual. Read eighty lines of Third Book of Iliad. Heard Dr. Chalmers, now of Glasgow, preach from Acts xx., 35 ; "It is more blessed to give than to receive ; " an eloquent sermon and in some parts highly wrought up. Read a hundred and twenty pages of Thompson's Lectures. Attended the General Assembly. Read some of Cicero, Horace, etc.

May 21st.—Teaching as usual. Completed Vol. III. of Gibbon. Attended the General Assembly. Considerable discussion on the rejection of a minister by a parish without the assigning of any reason for so doing, and on the Presbytery agreeing with them. The proceeding of the Presbytery disapproved of. Began the fourth volume of Gibbon, and read Cicero, Horace, etc.

May 22nd.—Read part of Gibbon and eighty lines of Third Book of the Iliad. Attended the General Assembly from ten to eleven at night. Grand question of the Pluralities. Many fine specimens of eloquence.

May 23rd.—Teaching as usual. Attended the General Assembly. Little of importance. Dined with some clergymen and others at Mr. ———'s. Read a part of the "Antiquary."

May 26th. Heard Dr. Chalmers preach before the Commissioner from two verses of eighth Psalm—"When I look up unto the heavens;" &c. (Then follows an abstract of the sermon, since widely known as the first of Dr. Chalmers' "Astronomical Discourses.")

May 29th. Read a hundred lines of Homer; seventy-four pages of Gibbon. Attended Jameson. He was on "Fogs, Snow and Hail;" in Meteorology. Teaching from four to five and from six to eight at Leith.

June 3rd. Teaching inthe morning. Accompanied an agreeable party on a very agreeable jaunt to a very agreeable place—Roslin. Was much pleased with the many fine views the river Esk presents from Roslin to Buccleuch, or rather Dalkeith House. Saw Hawthornden and Lasswade. Dined at Dalkeith, supped at Mr. ———'s, and home in good time.

July 2nd. Teaching in the morning. Read a page of Herodotus; ninety pages of Gibbon. Finished Chalmers' Evidences. Read a second time part of Moncrieff's Discourses on Miracles. Read in Juvenal, Plautus, &c.

July 17th. Teaching in the morning. Read a hundred and forty pages of Gibbon—Articles of Edinburgh Review—Sixty pages of Juvenal, with some parts of Anacreon—Plautus, &c.

While in Edinburgh, the late Dr. Guthrie, his fellow-townsman, and some years his junior, was sent to college with him, and committed to his watchful care by the family of Dr. Guthrie, who had the fullest confidence in him, and expressed their entire satisfaction with his guardianship. He often reverted with pleasure to the time when the brilliant talents which were afterwards to win a world-wide fame, were developing under his own eye. He used to enjoy describing, in after days, Dr. Guthrie's first essay at original composition, in the shape of a letter home, in which the future popular author was sorely per-

C   17

plexed by the not uncommon difficulty of finding nothing
to say. Though their lots were cast far apart, Dr. Guthrie
and he kept up their early formed friendship by occasional
correspondence, and, on Dr. Machar's visits to Scotland,
renewed with pleasure their former kindly intercourse.

He enjoyed, also, the close companionship of several
pious and estimable young men, who had been his school-
fellows, as they were now his fellow-students, and who
afterwards became devoted and distinguished ministers of
the Gospel. One of these, with whom his friendship was
closest and most intimate—afterwards Dr. Simpson, of
Kintore,—has already been mentioned. Another was the
Rev. James Martin, the youthful minister of St. George's
Edinburgh, whose early promise of great usefulness to the
Church was buried in an early grave at Leghorn, whither
he had gone to recruit his failing health.

After the completion of Mr. Machar's theological course,
he became for a time tutor in the family of Captain Allardice, of Murlingden, a few miles from Brechin, where he
was much esteemed as a faithful and successful teacher,
and regarded as one of the family, to whom he was much
attached, and between whom and himself there ever afterwards existed a strong interest and affection.

In October, 1819, he was licensed to preach the Gospel
by the Presbytery of Brechin, and preached his first sermon in its ancient church. During his residence at
Murlingden, he assisted the Rev. Mr. Mollison, of Montrose, for six months, preaching once every Sabbath. He
was afterwards assistant for eighteen months to the Rev.
Mr. Whitson, of Brechin, preaching every Sabbath with
much acceptance in the same old Cathedral Church already
mentioned.

He was privileged at this time to enjoy the society and
friendship of several of the most able, devoted and useful
evangelical ministers of their time. One of these was the
Rev. Dr. Brewster, of Craig, whose praise is still in the
Church. Another was Dr. William Burns, then minister

of Dun, who afterwards removed to Kilsyth, where he died in a ripe old age ; and both in Dun, where he spent the earlier years of his ministry, and in Kilsyth, where he closed it, his memory is held in love and veneration. He was the father of the late Rev. W. C. Burns, the devoted and self-sacrificing missionary to China, and of the late Prof. Islay Burns, of Glasgow. With the Rev. James Burns, minister of Brechin, and father-in-law to Dr. Guthrie, Mr. Machar lived in intimate friendship, warmly appreciating his deep piety, his great simplicity of character and singleness of heart. He was colleague to Mr. Whitson when Mr. Machar was his assistant, and they walked to-gether in unbroken fellowship. He has long since gone to rest, but his memory is still fragrant in the Church.

In 1823 Mr. Machar left the neighbourhood of Brechin, and the scenes of his early joys and sorrows, his early friendships and early labours. He had already been twice disappointed in his hopes of an early settlement. The aged minister of a parish in that neighbourhood, for whom Mr. Machar had often preached, was very desirous to have him as his assistant and successor, and he was also very acceptable to the people. But it was in the days of high handed patronage, and when application was made to the gentleman in whose hands the presentation lay, the reply was that it was already promised to another. In another similar case, a like cause produced the same result. The memory of these early days of ministerial labour and changing hopes and fears, remained deeply engraven on his heart throughout his after life, and he often spoke of them with tender sadness.

He entered at this time the family of Sir William Ogil-vy, of Inverquharity,—then living at Bank House, near Dundee, again in the capacity of tutor. On the death of Sir William, not long afterwards, Lady Ogilvy removed with her family to Edinburgh, where Mr. Machar continued to superintend the education of the younger members of the family until January, 1825.

19

While in Edinburgh, in the autumn of 1824, he had experienced a severe trial in the unexpected death of his beloved mother. Though summoned to attend her dying bed, he was too late to see her alive,—a circumstance which greatly aggravated his sorrow. To his sister he thus wrote after his mother's death,—alluding to it and to other simultaneous trials.

" If we could uniformly realize the presence of God with us, and his ever watchful care over us, we should never be unhappy. We should see many of those things which we call evils, of which you and I have had our share during the eventful year just elapsed, to be in reality blessings, and though the severe loss we have experienced must be deeply felt, we should consider that we have consolations which many in like circumstances have not; for we trust what is loss to us is gain to our dear mother.——It is now more than ten years since a father on his deathbed bade me be kind to my sisters, and although my mother, to my never-ending regret, had not the opportunity of giving me the same charge under the same solemn circumstances, yet she has often given me the same command; and ever sacred to me will be the will of those whose memory we must ever cherish and revere."

Faithful always to this trust committed to him by his parents, he continued, during his whole life, to take a most affectionate interest in all that concerned his sisters, sympathising with them in illness and trial, and counselling them and aiding them in perplexities and difficulties. As one of them expressed it after his death,—" Never was there a kinder or a better brother ! "

In January, 1825, Mr. Machar accepted an invitation to become the assistant of the venerable Dr. Clason, minister of Logie; and left with much regret Lady Ogilvy, with whom his connection had been a most harmonious one, and his pupils, to whom he had become much attached. The parish of Logie is a lovely spot, in a beautiful part of the country, at the foot of the Ochill hills, a short distance

20

from Stirling and from the Bridge of Allan. Opposite to it rises the Abbey Craig, upon which now stands the national monument of Sir William Wallace. The time of Mr. Machar's residence in this parish was a very happy period of his life. He entered into new relations, and came under new and what he felt to be solemn responsibilities. He lived in the Manse, and thus was much in the society of Mr. Clason, who was a man of deep and unaffected piety, and had been a faithful and devoted pastor. Mr. Machar's relation with him was one of unbroken confidential intimacy and Christian fellowship. He regarded his aged friend with almost the love and veneration of a son for a father, and it was his constant aim to please him and to walk in his footsteps. In a letter written about that time he says :—"The more I see of Mr. Clason the more I love him, and I trust I shall ever account it among my greatest mercies to have been so intimately acquainted with him." He often spoke of Mr. Clason during his last illness, and expressed his sense of the benefit which it had been to him to witness the deep and and earnest piety visible in his life, both as a Christian and a pastor. In Divine Providence he had here a preparatory education for the future faithful labours in the pastoral office, which won for him the epithet bestowed in the address given at his funeral, of a "model pastor." He was very happy in his work, of which he thus wrote :

"I have plenty of employment to keep me busy, but not so much as to overburden me. Besides preaching on Sunday I visit from house to house at least once a week. I also visit the sick and assist Mr. Clason in instructing the young communicants. I find the exercise of visiting not only profitable to myself, but most useful in making me more intimately acquainted with the condition of the people to whom I am appointed to minister. And now that I have had a short trial of most of the duties of a parish minister, I can truly say that I think no life so delightful, if he steadily seeks the glory of God and the salvation of the immortal souls committed to his care. Would that I had a deeper and a more abiding sense of these great objects !"

There also he enjoyed the society, and occasionally, on sacramental occasions, the pulpit ministrations of several most estimable and earnest ministers, well-known in the Church—the late Dr. Patrick Clason, son of his esteemed friend ; Dr. Macfarlan of Greenock ; Dr. Binnie, of Stirling, afterwards of Lady Yester's Chapel, Edinburgh ; and others. With them he corresponded and remained on terms of friendly intimacy, until it was terminated by death. In a letter of this period, he says :—

"I have been preaching a great deal of late, up and down. I was with our common friend at Kilsyth, on the fourteenth, and spent a delightful day with Mr. Burns* On the first Sabbath of the month, the Sacrament of the Lord's Supper was dispensed here, when we had the presence and society of several excellent ministers, as well as the pleasure of listening to their edifying public instructions. Among others, we had a gentleman whom I much admire—Mr. McFarlane, of St. John's, Glasgow. How well he spoke in the General Assembly you know. All in all, I think he is not unworthy to be the successor of Dr. Chalmers. We enjoyed his society much during the short time he stayed in the manse, and very sorry were we to part with him. I hope to see you soon. You will think of me sometimes, and remember me where it is of especial importance that I should be remembered."

While at Logie, he had also the pleasure of frequent intercourse with Sir William Abercromby, brother of the celebrated Sir Ralph. He was an excellent Christian man, an elder of the parish, and took a deep interest in the spiritual well-being of the congregation in which he held office.

But while Mr. Machar was peacefully and happily

---

* The father of the missionary to China.

labouring in this beautiful spot, enjoying many pleasant friendships, and faithfully discharging his duties of preaching and teaching and pastoral work, a great change was, in the providence of God, preparing for him—a change which was to bring him into entirely new circumstances, and to direct his future life into a very different channel from any which he had previously contemplated or desired. Like many others, he was led to experience the truth that "a man may devise his ways, but the Lord directeth his steps."

CHAPTER III.

1827–1832.

FIRST YEARS OF CANADIAN PASTORATE.

THE sphere of labour to which the providence of God seemed now to direct Mr. Machar's course was one which his intense love of country and attachment to home associations, would have prevented his voluntarily choosing, except under the constraining influence of Christian duty. The charge of St. Andrew's Church, Kingston, Canada West, had just become vacant through the sudden and deeply lamented death of the Rev. John Barclay, its young and beloved pastor, after a short ministry of only five years. The son of the Rev. Dr. Barclay, minister of Kettle, Fifeshire— Mr. Barclay, who was the first Presbyterian minister in Kingston, had devoted his energies and abilities, which were of a high order, to the work of his ministry, as well as to promote the interests of the Church of Scotland in Canada, then in its infancy. He was a pious and amiable man, and much beloved by his congregation, especially by the young, in whom he took a deep interest, and some of whom, now grown old, still affectionately remember him. He had been ordained

over St. Andrew's congregation by the Presbytery of Edinburgh, who had been requested to make the appointment,
on the 26th of September, 1821, and he died on the same
day of the same month five years later.

The trustees and elders representing the congregation
so unexpectedly left without a pastor, again applied to the
Presbytery of Edinburgh to appoint and ordain a successor
to the late minister, guaranteeing his stipend, and promising all obedience in the Lord to him whom they should
select. The staff of elders nine in number, who had
applied for their late minister, was the same as that which
now applied for his successor, their number havingbeen
left entire, while their young pastor had been removed.
But the successor now appointed outlived by a year or two
the last survivor of their number. An extract from their
communication to the Presbytery of Edinburgh, on this
occasion, will show how much their departed pastor 'had
been loved and appreciated by his people. It is addressed
to the Rev. W. Ritchie, D.D., Professor of Divinity,
Edinburgh University.

"It is in the depth of affliction and sorrow that we submit to you the again destitute state of this congregation,
earnestly praying that you will have the kindness to lay
our case before your venerable Presbytery, that the vacancy
be filled up with all convenient speed. The success which
attended the ministerial labours of our late lamented pastor, induces us to state that the greater number of points
in which the gentleman whose name you may determine
to insert in the accompanying call, resemble him whose
early removal from among us we so deeply and so justly
deplore, the more acceptable will he be to us, and the
more likely to promote the interests of this congregation."

An extract from a letter written by the Rev. Harry
Leith, then minister of Cornwall, C.W., which accom-
panied the one from the trustees and elders, refers to
Mr. Barclay's services toward the Church in Canada, as

well as throws some light on the state of ecclesiastical matters in the Province at that time. It runs as follows :

" As no Legislative Act of the Imperial Parliament has yet secured to the Scotch Church in Canada, and imparted possession of those rights and privileges which justly belong to it, from its connexion with an established Church of Great Britain, the Episcopal Church frequently lays claim to *exclusive* rights and privileges, as *the* Established Church in Canada (and hitherto with too much success,) which a Scottish clergyman sometimes finds it difficult to concede. In this situation of affairs, difficulties not unfrequently occur, and we are often subjected to inconveniences not less than those arising from the want of pecuniary support. These collisions have been most frequent in Kingston, and have on some occasions excited very strong party feelings, which are unhappily still far from being allayed. The late most lamented incumbent maintained with much firmness the rights of the Church with which he stood connected, and effected much toward the peaceful establishment of our church in that place. Matters are not, however, in such a situation as will preclude the occurrence of some trial of the ecclesiastical knowledge and prudence of his successor."

The Edinburgh Presbytery felt the great responsibility of so important a trust, and chose a committee of their number, who endeavoured faithfully to execute the trust committed to them. While Dr. Gordon, the Moderator of the Presbytery, and the others associated with him, were anxiously looking for a suitable minister to fill the appointment, Mr. Machar was warmly recommended to them by a number of those pious men and faithful ministers, who had the best opportunities of knowing him thoroughly. A few extracts are here given from their recommendatory letters. The following is written by the aged minister of Logie, Mr. Clason :—

" Mr. John Machar, preacher of the Gospel, was recommended to me as my assistant by the Rev. Dr. Andrew

Thompson. He has assisted me for two years, much to my satisfaction and comfort, and with great acceptance to all in this parish of every rank. He has prepared uniformly impressive public Gospel discourses, has assisted me in pastorally visiting and catechising the parish, has attentively visited the old and the sick, has assisted me in instructing young communicants for weeks, and in a word, has shown all along that he delights in every part of his ministerial work. On all which accounts I feel warranted with truth and confidence to recommend Mr. Machar as a most promising labourer in the work of the Gospel."

His son, Dr. Patrick Clason, after adding his testimony to the " zeal, assiduity and diligence," with which he had discharged his ministerial duties, says, " I am aware that the judgment of his preaching rests not with me, but with those to whom judgment in the matter is committed, yet I think it quite right to say that his views of the Christian religion always appeared to me clear, correct and Scriptural. His preaching is plain, forcible and practical ; no parade of sentiment about it, no straining after effect. I am satisfied that he has the work of the ministry deeply at heart, and wherever his lot is cast, that people will be fortunate which receives him as its minister."

Dr. Brewster, of Craig, characterises him as " a young man of very superior talents, pious principles and pleasing deportment, and his preaching as " scriptural in doctrine and delivered with much earnestness," and expresses himself as " persuaded that in any situation he will approve himself, under the Divine blessing, a faithful and useful Christian pastor."

His friends, Dr. James and Dr. William Burns, sent equally satisfactory expressions of their esteem. Dr. James Burns, one of his oldest friends, thus wrote :—

I have had the pleasure of knowing Mr. J. Machar for many years. His conduct has been uniformly exemplary, his talents highly cultivated by diligent study. His preaching is eloquent, discriminating and Scriptural, fitted to be

27

acceptable and highly useful to any congregation. This testimony I feel great liberty and pleasure in giving, having very frequently heard him and conversed with him, especially during the last eighteeh months, while assisting my colleague, Mr. Whitson. He was also in high estimation, while he acted for several years as tutor to a gentleman's family in the neighbourhood."

The Committee having received these and other testimonials to Mr. Machar's Christian character and usefulness as a preacher, and having themselves heard him, took him on trials for ordination. The Presbytery, being fully satisfied with his fulfilment of the prescribed exercises, his scholarship and theological qualifications, " the Moderator, Dr. Gordon, leaving the chair, did by solemn prayer and imposition of the hands of himself and the brethren present, ordain Mr. Machar as Minister of the Gospel and Pastor of St. Andrew's Congregation, Kingston, Upper Canada. After which Mr. Machar received the right hand of fellowship from the brethren present, and was suitably exhorted by the Moderator."

This event, to which he always looked back, as the most solemn in his life, took place on the 27th of April, 1827. It was, perhaps, rendered more solemn by the reflection that, six years previously, on the 28th of September, 1821, Mr. Barclay had been ordained over the same charge by the same Presbytery, and with the same warm expressions of satisfaction as were now given to his successor.

Mr. Machar had now to prepare for leaving his native land, and proceeding to Canada, then a more unknown country in Scotland than Japan, or the Sandwich Islands is to us now. To his nature it was a very severe trial to leave the country of his birth, the home of his youth, with which all his friendships, associations and sympathies, which were very deep and lasting, were so closely bound up. He had also the prospect of being settled over a parish at no distant period in case he should remain in

Scotland, but he felt that the providence of God was calling him to this distant sphere of labour, and at whatever sacrifice of inclination and feeling, he would not resist the call.

Having made all preliminary arrangements, and paid farewell visits to the friends from whom he parted with deep mutual regret, he sailed in June, 1827, for New York, by one of the New York sailing packets; for in those days there were no steamships. The voyage was a very tedious one, and he did not reach Kingston until the beginning of September. He had been entrusted with the important documents relating to Church matters connected with the Government, in consequence of which he had to proceed to Quebec to visit Dr. Harkness, and afterwards had an interview with Lord Dalhousie, whom he found very favourably disposed towards the Church of Scotland. On his arrival at Kingston, he was met and most affectionately welcomed by the elders and trustees, as well as by the people generally, who had been anxiously awaiting his arrival. Their cordiality made him feel at home at once, and he often, in after life, recurred with pleasure to the pleasant memories of the kindness he had received from his people on his arrival among them. He always took a deep interest in all the families which at that time composed his congregation, with many of whom he continued in intimate friendship, during the whole course of his ministry.

The following extracts from letters written immediately after his arrival, give interesting particulars of the *nearly two months'* voyage, and of his first impressions of the New World :—

" My voyage, you will hear, was long, but it was otherwise far from being unpleasant, although it was a little depressing to be looking out, day after day, upon the same wild waste of waters, without ever seeing a single bit of green earth. I arrived in New York on the 23rd of August, having been fifty two days at sea, a voyage far exceeding in length the average passages made. (Mr. Canning's death, for instance, was known in Kingston exactly twenty-nine days after it happened). Our vessel, the *Manchester*, an American packet, was fitted up in the most convenient and superb style, and was well commanded and well manned. I had a state-room to myself; and when wearied with gazing for hours, over the blue interminable deep, towards Scotland, or perhaps, with following the elevated fin of the shark sweeping around the ship at a respectful distance, or the nearer gambols of the shoals of dolphins that were playing close to us, I used to dive beneath to my books and amuse myself with reading or writing *solus*—my fellow passengers sitting down the while to whist, sometimes on deck, when the weather was fine, and sometimes below, when it happened to be surly. Our passengers, on the whole, were agreeable—some of them superior people. Among others was the Prince of * Musignano (Prince of the Holy Roman Empire), a nephew of Napoleon, and a son of Lucien Bonaparte, a clever and well informed young man, very like what his uncle once was. We had just got the life of his uncle, by Scott, and he was kind enough to give the volumes to me as he read them. We had many contests on this subject, he almost always running down our countryman as partial and unfair, and I endeavouring to defend him. Another passenger was a young American Unitarian minister, or rather, as he loved to be called, an "*Eclectic.*" The truth is, he did not know well what he was. He was asked to preach to us on Sundays, but chose to decline, on the plea that we were all of such varying creeds, that preaching would neither be edifying nor agreeable to the generality of the passengers. Not viewing the matter in the same light with my Eclectic friend, I did not refuse my services, but preached regularly, and as a Trinitarian, too, during the voyage. I know not whether my fellow-passengers were much the better for my sermons, but I wished much to mark the return of the Lord's Day on board, where I find it is often lost sight of.

"It would not be easy for me to describe the delight with which, after so long a voyage, I set foot on the American soil. I could hardly contain my joy; it was so delightful to gaze

---

* Charles Lucien Bonaparte, Prince of Casino and Musignano, and father of the present Cardinal Bonaparte, said to have been recently nominated by the Pope as his successor.

again upon the green earth. I was much pleased with New York, and indeed with every part of the United States which I had occasion to pass through. Having business at Montreal and Quebec, I took the Montreal route by the Hudson river, Lakes George and Champlain, and never, on any route, have I seen so much in scenery to delight me as on this. The sail up the Hudson is beautiful beyond compare. That occupied one day. The next, I plunged deep into the American forest, passing many a beautiful lonely lake, many a rugged mountain, and many a magnificent river. Day third was spent on Lake Champlain, again travelling by steam. The scenery here was most beautiful and interesting. Its banks are, almost everywhere, classic ground, having been the scene of well-remembered encounters between the British and the French, and between the British and the Americans at a later period. Rock Putnam,—Ticonderoga,—Crown Point,—all these famed places are on Champlain.

"I arrived in Canada on the last day of August, and was very glad to be once more under the sway of King George. I went to Quebec, and afterwards to Sorel, where I spent part of two days with the Earl of Dalhousie, and where I met Captain Maule. I preached both at Quebec and at Montreal, finding it utterly impossible to get away from my Canadian brethren, without giving them a 'darg.' Kingston is a pretty large place, and contains some fine public buildings. There is, beside my church, an Episcopal, a Methodist and a Roman Catholic church in Kingston. I have been very kindly received by my congregation, the most numerous Protestant one in the place. I was met by my trustees and elders at the landing-place, and everything has been done to make me comfortable. I have already preached three Sundays, and seen a good deal of my people. Last week the pews were let, and I learned from one of my elders on Saturday that they were all let except three. I have been using my predecessor's pulpit-gown, but I am, this week, to be presented by my people with a new one. I expected I should have got one of my Canadian brethren to introduce me to my flock, but I found this impossible, and I had to introduce myself. I began my labours by preaching on the 16th of September, in the forenoon from 1st Corinthians ix., 24-27, and in the afternoon from Romans xii. 1. I find I shall have enough to do. Last week I was as busy as it is possible for man to be."

In July, 1828, he writes to his sister :—" I have not much to communicate, nor have I much time. I have not now the vacant hours I had at College, or even during my residence at Murlingden and Logie. I am not unhappy, however, that it should be so. I feel that I shall be then only happy when every portion of my time and strength is dedicated to the duties of my office. On the first Sabbath of March I dispensed the Sacrament of the Lord's Supper for the first time, when everything was conducted with as much solemnity as I ever witnessed at home. I preached twice on the Sabbath, forenoon and afternoon, and we have a Sabbath School in the evening, which I teach myself, attended by between seventy and eighty scholars. Externally, things go very well as respects the church. The congregation is steady, rather on the increase. Several officers of the army and navy attend St. Andrew's. I visit from house to house, and am very kindly received. On Sunday week I assisted at the Communion at Williamsburg, a hundred and fifty miles distant, and preached on Saturday, Sunday and Monday. I trust we shall soon have Presbyterian churches more thickly planted in the colonies, and then I shall not have to make such long journeys. I am sorry that Lord Dalhousie, the Governor of Lower Canada, is going home. Our Governor in Upper Canada is an Englishman, and not very friendly to Scotchmen. The country is a good deal split into political parties as with you. There has been a good deal of controversy between the Episcopal and Presbyterian churches for some time past, in which I have not been much engaged, and anything I have done has been rather from a desire to close than to widen breaches. Many emigrants are arriving now. Poor people ; their difficulties are often great on their first arrival. This will be a fine country some thirty or forty years hence, but the emigrant who goes into the woods has at first much to struggle with, though, if he is industrious, his family will, by-and-by, find themselves in very comfortable circumstances."

In October of the same year he writes again : " I had a pretty severe fever at the end of July, when the heat was very great, but I soon recovered, so soon that I was able to preside at our Communion on August 17th, and to go through the usual course of duty. Since then, although I have had a good deal of fatigue, and have travelled more than a thousand miles, I am quite well. Indeed, I never was in more vigorous health than this autumn."

On October 7, 1829, he writes : " The present season in this country has been comparatively cool and very healthy, and I have for several months enjoyed excellent health. This season, owing to the residence here of the 79th regiment, to whom I act as military chaplain, in addition to my other duties, I preach three times every Sabbath ; but even in the hottest weather I have been enabled to discharge this duty with considerable benefit to myself. The Sacrament of the Lord's Supper was dispensed here on the last Sabbath of August. There were forty new communicants. Everything about our church prospers externally, and I would hope internally also. There is much religious coldness and deadness here, as with you, but there are also some favourable symptoms. May the Lord prosper His own work ! My sentiments are changed in some points since I came to this place, but upon one thing they are more confirmed, that one thing is needful. Oh, if we only chose this one thing, other things would not grieve and depress us as they often do. My correspondence both here and with Great Britain has become so great of late that I have been utterly unable to overtake it. We are getting out a few more ministers from time to time. I expect a Mr. McGill from Glasgow this week, who will preach for me on Sabbath, and I shall have to accompany him to Niagara, two hundred miles and upwards from here, to introduce him to his people on the following Sabbath."

D

The circumstance that there was then no Presbyterian minister between Kingston and Niagara, will show something of the state of matters in those days, when ministers were so few and far between, that much time was necessarily occupied, and much fatigue endured in the journeys which they were obliged to take, in order to discharge the numerous public duties which devolved upon them in the infancy of the Church.

To a sister, who had been passing through a season of trial, he wrote in June, 1830 : "I know that what you have met with is very grievous to flesh and blood, but the hand of God is in it. Man can do no more than God permits, and you must not murmur against God. Woe is unto him that striveth with his Maker ! I have felt something of this woe myself, for when it pleased the Lord to afflict me very grievously, I did not bow under His chastening rod as I ought, and the longer I strove the darker and fuller of sorrow my path became. Oh, let us earnestly pray that He would enable us to say, ' It is the Lord ; let Him do unto us what seemeth to Him good !' Good is the hand of the Lord, though we in our shortsightedness often think it is evil. He afflicts us not willingly, nor grieves us causelessly, but for our highest good. Let us not think it strange that we are afflicted. 'Our sins afflict us, and the Cross must bring us back to God !' Trust in God then, my dear sister ! Seek the Kingdom of God and His righteousness, and all other things shall be added unto you."

In the summer of 1830, in consequence of impaired health, Mr. Machar visited his native land, and enjoyed exceedingly the temporary return to home scenes, and the re-union with many dear friends. He endeavoured also, as far as possible, to make his visit of use to the Church in Canada, by endeavouring to excite an interest in it among the people of Scotland, and drawing attention to its spiritual destitution. This visit was a deeply important one to himself, events which occurred to him in the course of God's providence exciting deeper spiritual feelings in his own soul, and giving him a more vivid sense of eternal realities.

While crossing the Atlantic on his return, a terrible thunderstorm burst over the ship's course, and a thunderbolt, striking the vessel, killed instantaneously two of the crew who were on deck. Among the passengers there was a sudden transition from careless merriment to awe-struck terror. With pale faces and trembling nerves, they had just believed the danger past, when smoke was seen issuing from the hold, and the cry was raised that the ship was on fire. Happily the exertions at once made to quench the smouldering fire were successful, and the terrible calamity which at one time seemed imminent was providentially averted. But the solemn and startling experience through which he thus passed, left a very deep and lasting impression upon Mr. Machar's mind.

The following letter was written to a very intimate friend in Scotland, in March, 1831 :—

" Your letter came to me in the evening after our Communion. I was sitting alone, musing over many things. I was not assisted by any minister at the late solemn season. Most of our ministers had preached for me when I was at home, and I could not think of so soon bringing any of them so far again. The duties were arduous, but I was enabled to go through them with more than usual refreshment to my own spirit, and also to many of my fellow-communicants. I had twenty-nine new applicants, and with not a few of them I had many pleasing conversations previously, particularly with some of the younger ones. One, especially, is now rejoicing in Jesus as the portion of her soul, and already earnestly seeking the salvation of her nearest relatives.† Oh, it is a very awful thing to be a minister—to think that we may be guilty of the

† She was cut off by cholera in 1832, and several years afterward her prayers were answered in the conversion of her nearest and dearest relatives.

blood of immortal souls! God has spoken to me of late in a way I cannot mistake, and I must—and through Christ I *will*—spend and be spent in His service! Surely the Lord's voice was in that thunderbolt, which had well nigh buried me in the deep. I know you would have wept for me, but through the tender mercy of God I have been spared, and I trust we shall meet again, and rejoice that Jesus has been revealed in us. I see a greater glory in the Scriptures than I ever saw before. To save man far more is necessary than many think. Far more is necessary than to remove the judicial penalties attached to sin, to shut the gates of hell or even to open the gates of heaven. To save man, his spiritual health must be restored, the power of inherent corruption must be subdued, the work of the devil in him must be destroyed, his hard and stony heart must be broken, and he must be renewed in the spirit of his mind, so that he can rejoice in the *righteousness* of God, as well as in His *mercy*. Not only must he have access to the privileges and joys of Heaven, but he must have that meetness in his own soul which alone can make them privileges and joys to him. The love of God must be shed abroad in his heart, enabling him to delight in God, and to enjoy fellowship with Him. When man was happy in Eden he was in the image of Him who created him, and when he shall be happy in a yet fairer Eden, it will be when he is renewed in that image again, when he shall have perfectly put on the new man, which after God is created in righteousness and true holiness. This is a high and blessed calling, and *nothing less* is our calling in Christ, in whom God hath given to us all things pertaining to life and to godliness, through the knowledge of Him who hath called us to glory and virtue.

" Several affecting events have of late taken place in my congregation. One of my elders has lately lost his wife. She was a very amiable person, and, I trust, a true Christian, and I esteemed her very highly. She longed to see me, from day to day, during her last illness, but I

36

arrived only to attend her funeral. Though young, she has left several children ; one—a little daughter—has since followed her mother. Another of my elders has just lost two blooming children by whooping cough, and a third is not expected to live. If he be taken, a whole family—except one—will have been swept away within a a few weeks. Hardly any one of the families of my congregation has been unvisited by sickness and bereavement since I came here in 1827. Oh, may such sad events come in aid of the Word! May they break down the hard heart, and, by showing it how easily God can dry up every fountain of earthly comfort, lead it to say— 'And now, Lord, what wait I for ; my hope is in Thee.' "

The following extract from an entry in a private MS. book, was written about the same time :—

" I have often said that I would be Thine ; I now record this resolve. I give myself up to Thee ;— O Lord, truly I am Thy servant ! This day I flee unto Thee for strength to enable me to subdue my corruptions, and to triumph over my spiritual enemies. I have been a fool, trusting in my own heart, and not trusting in Thee,—therefore have I to deplore so many broken vows, and so many declensions ! I have experienced much of Thy loving-kindness of late, particularly in being protected by Thee amidst the dangers of the deep, and from the stroke of the thunderbolt, in being restored to better health, and brought back in safety to the flock committed to my care ; and yet, in the very midst of these mercies, I have sinned against Thee ; I have forgotten Thy goodness, and *my own* vows. But I desire this day to flee to Thee for strength. 'What I know not, teach Thou me !' Oh, give me to see that there is a fulness, a complete fulness, in Christ for me, out of which I may receive grace for grace ; and oh, grant me grace to draw out of it, daily and hourly,—to live continually as seeing Thee, who art invisible,—seeing Thy will respecting me, and seeing that there is enough in Thee to enable me to conform myself to this will. Surely, Thou wilt 'perfect that which concerneth me !' "

CHAPTER IV.

(1831–1832.)

MEETING OF THE FIRST PRESBYTERIAN SYNOD IN CANADA, AND PASTORATE DURING 1831-2.

THE year 1831 was marked by an ecclesiastical event of much interest to the infant Presbyterian Church in Canada,—the meeting of its first Synod. Hitherto the Canadian branch of the Church had existed only as an aggregate of far scattered congregations ; it was now to acquire some consistency and organization. The first Presbyterian Synod of Canada was constituted at St. Andrew's Church, Kingston, on the eighth day of June, 1831. It was a small band that met, numbering not quite a score, fourteen being ministers, and five lay commissioners or elders, but this little band had the privilege of laying the foundations of the now flourishing Presbyterian Church in Canada, several hundreds of whose ministers and representative elders now meet at its annual assemblies. The ministers then assembled, enumerated in the Minutes of Synod, stand as follows :—the Revds. Alexander Gale, George Sheed, John Machar, John Cruickshank, Alexander Ross, Robert McGill, Thomas Clarke Wilson, William McAlister, William Rintoul, Alexander Mathieson, Henry

Esson, John McKenzie, Hugh Urquhart, Archibald Connel. The laymen were George McKenzie, John Willison, John McGillivray, Alexander McMartin and John Turnbull. Those founders of the Canadian Presbyterian Church have nearly all now passed away. Of the fourteen ministers, two only survive :—Dr. John Cruickshank, now of Turriff, Scotland, and the Rev. T. C. Wilson, who still preaches in the old cathedral church of Dunkeld.

At the first meeting of the Synod, Mr. Machar being chairman, the Rev. John McKenzie, of Williamstown, was chosen the first Moderator, and the Rev. Robert McGill was appointed Synod Clerk. It may be mentioned here that the Moderator of the second Synod, also held at Kingston in the following year, was the late Rev. Dr. Mathieson, of Montreal, and that Mr. Machar was Moderator of the third, which met at Toronto, then York.

After lengthened and mature deliberation the Synod of 1831 unanimously resolved :—"That this convention of ministers and elders in connexion with the Church of Scotland, representing their respective congregations, do form themselves into a Synod, to be called the Synod of the Presbyterian Church of Canada, leaving it to the Venerable the General Assembly to determine the particular nature of that connexion which shall subsist between the Synod and the General Assembly of the Church of Scotland."

The Synod then proceeded to divide the charges under its care into four Presbyteries :— those of Quebec, Glengarry, Bathurst and York (Toronto) ; Bathurst consisting of the charges of Kingston, Bytown, Perth and Lanark. Kingston, which was far separated from the other congregations, was afterwards formed into a separate Presbytery in 1833. Committees were appointed to draw up the memorial to the General Assembly, a petition to the King in regard to the Clergy Reserves, and an address to Sir John Colborne, Lieutenant-Governor, all of which were approved and signed. The ministers were enjoined to draw up a report of the state of religion in their several congregations and neighbourhoods, to be transmitted for the information of the General Assembly; and the different Presbyteries were directed, within their bounds, to see that sessions should be regularly organised and records kept of their proceedings. A Standing Commission was appointed to watch over the general interests of the church. The Synod also appointed a Committee on Missions, with power to collect funds, and appoint one or more missionaries to labour within their bounds. Of each of these committees Mr. Machar was appointed a member, and the work that devolved upon him in connection with them added much to his ordinary labours, and entailed upon him the large amount of correspondence to which he alludes in one of his letters.

Towards the close of the summer of 1831, Mr. Machar was attacked by a severe rheumatic fever, which lasted for nearly two months. It was a season of intense physical suffering, the more trying in his solitary position, separated by so great a distance from all his near relatives. He had friends around him, however, and he often, in after life, gratefully referred to the kindness which he received, during his painful illness, from many members of his congregation, few of whom now survive. In a letter of October 3, 1831, he says :—" I have been very ill, having been confined to bed for seven weeks by rheumatic fever, and for some weeks I could not turn myself, but through the great goodness of God, I have recovered my health, and am better now than I was before."

Towards the close of the year occurs the following entry in the MS. book before quoted from, in which he again refers to his merciful preservation at sea :—

" What reason have I to exclaim, 'What can I render unto the Lord for all his benefits unto me!' Twelve months ago, this day, the Lord redeemed the life of myself and my fellow-passengers from destruction. I might then have been taken away. Thou might'st then have said concerning me, ' Cut him down,—why cumbereth he the ground?' But at the intercession of the great vine-dresser, Thou didst let me alone for a space, and give me an opportunity to bring forth fruits to the praise of the glory of His grace. But, alas ! alas ! I have not improved this season of merciful visitation, no, not although Thou hast poured upon me many a precious influence from on high. ' Create, I beseech Thee, a new heart within me. Cast me not away from Thy presence, take not Thy Spirit utterly away from me ! ' "

These entries, made at a time when he was faithfully and diligently discharging the manifold duties committed to him, manifest his great sensitiveness of conscience, and his deep and realizing sense of the inward sinfulness of the heart. In September, 1831, he wrote to his sister :—

" You will, I am sure, rejoice that my health is greatly improved. I have not been so well for two years. Bless the Lord, oh my soul, and forget not all his benefits ! The last month has been a season of much refreshment to me, and yet a season in which I have seen much of the sin that is in my own heart. How dark were the times before that, I have been taught, and I do rejoice that I have heen taught, though painful the lesson, that man has no life in himself, that there is *no* life except *living in the light, seeing and understanding and receiving the mystery of Christ, the truth as it is in Jesus.*" I dispensed the Sacrament of the Lord's Supper last Sabbath to a numerous body of communicants. The season was a solemn one, and several who enjoyed it will, I trust, long remember it. I was assisted by a young minister who left Scotland last summer, the Rev. T. C. Wilson, of Perth, Upper Canada. He preached three delightful discourses, and our private intercourse was very pleasant. Mr. Wilson is quite a young man, and very candid, and notwithstanding the use which has been made of Confessions of late, he looks for his faith in the Bible. I can this day look back upon all the ways by which the Lord hath brought me, and can say He hath done *all* things well. It is blessed to say with the Apostle that we are ' chastened of the Lord that we should not be condemned with the world.' He might have with-holden chastening from us ; He might have given us the desires of our hearts, and sent leanness into our souls ! Yet I am not able at all times—nor at any time aright—to glorify God by justifying His ways to me. Evil is often present with me. May we give glory to Him by practically acknowledging that of Him are all things, and that to Him alone doth power appertain to make us altogether what He would have us to be!

" It seems almost selfish to be writing so much about myself when the Church of Christ requires so much all our thoughts and all our care. Pray for us, for an out-pouring of the Spirit of grace upon my congregation, and for me, that I may *know* the truth more, and deliver it more fully and faithfully to my people. There is much indifference among many of my congregation, but I trust there is a seed serving the Lord. The wife of the Arch-deacon* is an estimable Christian lady, and notwithstand-ing the jealousies that sometimes divide Episcopalians and Presbyterians, they do not divide us. I have expe-rienced many kind and loving attentions from her. She was very kind to me, and ministered many a comfort to me during my long and painful illness. My visit to the dear Andersons last Spring was very delightful. I had much Christian intercourse with them. Captain Ander-son much regrets that the General Assembly has dealt so harshly and injuriously with Mr. Campbell."†

The Captain Anderson here referred to, was in after years well-known both in England and Scotland as Gen-eral Anderson, R.A. He was a man of large and loving

---

* The venerable and well-known Archdeacon Stuart, son of Dr. Stuart, the first clergyman in Upper Canada. With him and his excellent wife Dr. Machar always maintained a close friendship.
† The Rev. John McLeod Campbell, of Row.

heart, a faithful soldier, and a devoted Christian, and was honoured in bringing many souls to Christ. During the long period of his active service in the army, his sunny Christian character and loving genial influence made him much beloved, and helpful to many, especially to young soldiers entering upon the Christian warfare. Miss Marsh, in her Memoir of Major Vandeleur, says of his " frank and friendly kindness,"—" It was offered to all who were within his reach ; and to how many that Christian and fatherly influence has been made the means of the beginning of a new life, or of the stablishing, strengthening and settling of that life already begun, will never be known until the day when it shall be revealed, how much of the living water has been permitted to flow through human channels." While Captain Anderson was stationed in Kingston. he attended Mr. Machar's ministry, and between the two, like-minded in Christian simplicity and earnestness, there grew up an affectionate intimacy, and a strong and lasting mutual attachment. After the removal of Captain Anderson from Kingston, they continued to correspond by letter until the death of Dr. Machar terminated their earthly intercourse. General Anderson survived him only about two years. He died peacefully at his residence near Edinburgh, in a good old age, but still in the midst of active and happy Christian and benevolent labours. The following extracts from a letter written after the death of his friend, in which he recalled some of the circumstances of their pleasant early intimacy, will help to fill up the portraiture of this period of Dr. Machar's life and ministry.

"At that time," (the time of Captain Anderson's arrival in Canada,) "the state of religion in both the Churches of England and Scotland was in a very low and dead condition. There were some godly and devoted ministers in both Churches, but they were the exceptions. It was in 1829 that my company was ordered to Kingston, and I well remember the heartfelt joy and delight with which I heard my dear friend preach on the first Sabbath after our arrival there, on Hosea xi. 8. There was a genuine tone and power in his sermon that gladdened our hearts, and I lost no time in forming his acquaintance. I fondly trust we were both of us in earnest in seeking to know the Truth, and enquiring the way to Zion. There was a savour and unction in all his pulpit ministrations that betokened a living man of God, and one thoroughly in earnest to discharge his duty.

"As his health was by no means robust, he was seldom able for much ministerial work on the Monday, except visiting a few sick people, and he generally spent the greater part of the day with us. We mingled very little in the general society of the town, and were all the more closely drawn together. The chaplain of the dockyard, a truly excellent clergyman of the Church of England, was frequently with us, and there was much endeared confidential intercourse between him and Mr. Machar upon the grounds of a common Christianity. I well remember their proposing to exchange pulpits, and they were pleased to submit to me the propriety of doing so ; but, as I expressed my apprehension, however I would individually rejoice in seeing such an exhibition of Christian oneness of spirit, lest it might awaken unnecessary hostility on the part of the ecclesiastical authorities, without a corresponding benefit, they gave up their cherished desire, while ever maintaining the warmest regard for each other.

" It is my conviction that there was a manifest growth in the Divine life, even during the time that we enjoyed the privilege of sitting under his ministry, and that, each succeeding Sabbath, his sermons were more and more full of matter, and there was a great expanse in his religious views and experimental acquaintance with the truth. Just as his own soul prospered, he was made the blessed means of feeding the souls of his people, while his holy life and daily walk and labour of love more and more endeared him to the affections of his attached flock. It was a mournful day for us when we were removed from Kingston, but my company was sent to the Lower Province in 1830. He kindly visited us several times at St. Helen's, where we remained for three years, and we recollect to this day, a most striking sermon which he preached just after the fearful visitation of cholera, with which it pleased God to visit Montreal, from the text,—" Shall a trumpet be blown in a city, and the people not be afraid; shall there be evil in a city, and the Lord hath not done it ?"

" Many letters were exchanged between us while we remained in Canada, which I deeply regret have been destroyed, as I am sure they would have shown rhe gradual and yet the most decided enlargement of his mind to the truths of the Gospel. He paid us a short but delightful visit, some years after our return to England, and preached a very remarkable sermon, the memory of which long remained in the Presbyterian Church of Woolwich, from the text, "I wish that men pray everywhere, lifting up holy hands, without wrath and without doubting."

" You are aware that I saw it to be my duty to leave our Establishment at the time of the Disruption, and I well recollect that, when he first came to see us afterwards, he appeared not to be quite sure whether we would welcome him as cordially as in former years : but his doubts, if they really existed, were soon dispelled, and our hearts went out in adoring grateful praise at the Lord's marvellous dealings with us both.

" I considered it to be, on one occasion, no less my privilege than my bounden duty to state, from the floor of the General Assembly of the Free Church, that, in my opinion, not only the Presbyterian Church, but the Church of Christ at large, owed a debt of gratitude to my beloved friend for raising the moral standard of the Christian ministry in Canada, which ¡was certainly, at the time, much required."

In December, 1831, Mr. Machar wrote to an intimate friend in Scotland :—

"Since I last wrote to you, there have been many sudden deaths among us, and under very painful circumstances. Three persons known to me have died from excessive drunkenness ; one of them belonged to our congregation. A Christian man also died suddenly about the same time. I have tried to turn the attention of my people to these events, and to make them of use. Oh that they may hear the gracious Saviour saying unto them, "Behold I stand at the door and knock." Alas, there is much practical indifference at present ; few seem to have ears to hear what the Spirit saith unto the Churches ! When I wrote to you last I was just setting out for York (Toronto). I preached there several times, and assisted Mr. Rintoul at his sacrament. Mr. Rintoul is a truly pious man. I preached, on my way from York, at the induction of the Rev. James Ketchan, to Belleville. He is now my nearest neighbour, and I have a very favourable opinion of him. It was a solemn season ; the church was new, and scarcely finished, and never had it echoed to the voice of prayer or praise before. Its site was lately the wild wood, and where now is heard the voice of sacred melody, nothing disturbed the deep repose but the wild cry of the ravenous beast, or the cry, almost as wild, of the Indian, as he pursued his prey, in search of a precarious subsistence. I had much conversation with Mr. Ketchan regarding our own dear Scotland, and felt much pleasure at the way in which he spoke of many things. In regard to the work going on at home which you mention, I would not think it right to disbelieve it, lest I should be found fighting against God. But there is danger on either hand, either in the way of a too easy credulity, or in the way of hardened unbelief. Pray that in these eventful times, we may judge what is right! Pray for the spirit of a sound mind, and let us ever feel, in respect of judging of such things, as in every other, particular, that 'the way of man is not in himself'—that 'it is not in him that walketh to direct his steps.' Let us ever look to God for guidance, and we shall not be permitted greatly to err."

In March, 1832, Mr. Machar wrote to his sister :—

" I have not been able to answer yours sooner, having been very much occupied. The Sacrament of the Lord's Supper was dispensed to an unusually large number of communicants on the last Sabbath of February. The Lord's gracious presence was with us. I was assisted by my worthy neighbour, the Rev. James Ketchan, of Belleville. His arrival and settlement here are events in which I greatly rejoice. We have had an unusually cold winter here, but I have, on the whole ,enjoyed good health, having never been a week without preaching twice, and sometimes three times. I have increasing pleasure in my work, and though I have difficulties, and look for them, I have some success too. There is just one way to be successful ; it is to be dwelling in the light of God's countenance, and ever seeking in simplicity to know His will in all things, that we may declare it to those to whom we are sent. My dear sister, look simply to Him. Do not distrust the loving-kindness of the Lord. Do not think it presumption to believe God's gracious assurances to you ! 'He will never leave thee nor forsake thee.' Go on your way in the strength of this assurance"

In May, 1832, he writes : " I am deeply grieved to hear of the troubles in the Church. The judgments of the Lord are evidently abroad ; may the inhabitants of the earth learn righteousness ! May we be earnest in prayer that the Lord would yet revive His own work in the midst of these years. I have been sometimes very poorly this spring, but never laid aside from the work of my ministry. The Sacrament of the Lord's Supper was dispensed on the last Sabbath of February. It was a precious season to not a few. I felt more liberty than usual on that occasion, but I have felt great dulness and heaviness often during the two months past ;—sometimes as if

I could not speak a word. I have not been at all strong however, yet even in this respect the Lord has dealt very graciously with me. May He enable me to be faithful to do His will in all things! I think we have been wrong in the place we have given to our Confession as a Church, I have looked into our Confession, sometimes, during the past season, and I have been thankful to have seen so much pure truth there, but it is not truth to us unless we see it to be the truth of God's word. Where the true Church of Christ is, it will hold forth the truth ; the priests' lips will keep knowledge.' When that cannot be said of a Church, it will be destroyed at all events, and even a confession will not long retard the evil day. But let us pray for our Church ; let us earnestly pray that the Lord would sanctify to her those judgments which may soon be sent upon her, in common with other Churches ! We are quiet here at present ;—no commotion—no division. Two days ago the national fast was observed, at least with great outward decorum. I was able to preach twice to large congregations. I have much to do, and sometimes health and strength seem to give way, but if I trust in the Lord, 'as my day is, so shall my strength be.' A word of Scripture was brought home to me lately, and I have sometimes tried to bring it home to others. It is, ' *All things are of God.*' "

In January, 1832, he writes—" A period of much mental suffering, about the end of 1829, with a larger portion of bodily labour than I ought to have undertaken, brought on physical weakness, from which, through the great goodness of God, I am in a good measure recovered ; yet I feel that I shall never be wholly delivered from it till I am laid in the grave."

This ominous prediction was too truly verified. These over-exertions left effects from which he never fully recovered, often suffered severely during all his after life ; and they laid the foundation of illnesses which brought upon him premature old age and shortened his life. His physical constitution was never robust, and the strain upon it of preaching three times a day in the hot summer weather, during the time when he officiated as chaplain to the Highland regiments,—although the interest he felt in his work bore him on at the time,—was more than it could bear without injury. His strength was much exhausted also, by the long and fatiguing land journeys, performed on wheels, over rugged and almost impassable roads, through marshes, across streams, over *corduroy* bridges, and tree roots. Two of these formidable journeys in particular he long remembered as especially trying ; one being a journey to Perth to perform a marriage ceremony, and the other to Ottawa, to induct the Rev. John Cruikshank. To assist his widely-scattered brethren at their sacraments, he was often obliged to go to Montreal, Martintown, and York, as Toronto was then called ; and the tedious and fatiguing travelling of those days, which in our age of railways and steam-boats can scarcely be realized, was a serious tax on both time and strength.

At that time also, as well as at every subsequent period of his ministry, he had a great deal of engrossing mental labour. There was much correspondence to be carried on concerning the temporal business of the Church, with the Governor, and through him with the Imperial Government. Then, owing to the circumstance that ministers were so remote from each other, they could have no reciprocal assistance or relief in their Sabbath duties. For a number of years he preached regularly every Sabbath without intermission, except during his visit to Scotland in 1830 and during the severe rheumatic fever already referred to. He used to express his great thankfulness that though often unwell during the week he had never been prevented from preaching by illness, for several years, except during that single illness. He was at that time, as well as during his absence in Scotland, most kindly assisted by his brother ministers. They were a cordially united and loving brotherhood, bound closely together in the common object of

E

seeking the spiritual growth of their church and the salvation of their people. Dr. Machar, in after times, often spoke affectionately of those times and of the fellow-labourers who had early passed away—especially of the Rev. A. Connel, of Martintown, a pious and most genial and estimable man, much beloved and much regretted by all who knew him.

CHAPTER V.

1832–1836.

MARRIAGE.—GROWTH OF THE CHURCH.—MINIS-
TERIAL AND PUBLIC LABOURS.

THE year 1832 opened amidst pleasant anticipations of at last realizing—after a protracted
period of patient waiting—the hopes of domestic happiness and the ideal of *home*, which
had long been an object of greater longing than
any other earthly blessing.

These anticipations were happily realized. On
the eighth of October, 1832, Mr. Machar was united
in marriage, after an engagement of several years,
to one who still survives him, and who, herself
the daughter of a Scottish manse, was well fitted
to be in every respect a helpmeet in his increasing
ministerial duties. They were married by the Rev.
Dr. Mathieson, at the house of his friend Captain
Anderson, R.A., who was then stationed on the
beautiful island of St. Helen's, opposite Montreal.

Solemn scenes, awakening solemn thoughts, were, however, strangely interwoven with the personal happiness of
the time. That summer of 1832 was sadly remarkable for
a terrible visitation of cholera, which was fatally prevalent
in Canada as well as throughout Europe. In Kingston,

where it was very severe, many widows and orphans were left. Mr. Machar thus wrote of it towards the close of the year :—We were visited with cholera in the summer and autumn to a fearful extent. I had much to do in visiting the sick, and witnessed many intensely painful scenes. While many have been cut down around me my life has been spared. May I ever remember that 'no man liveth to himself,' and seek more diligently to fulfil the ministry which I have received of the Lord Jesus Christ !"

In January, 1833, he writes, in answer to some enquiries from Scotland concerning emigration :—

" There are several classes whom I would not encourage to emigrate. Those who do emigrate should be able-bodied, ready to go at once into the woods and to settle upon land. The young labourer who has just a little to begin with will do well here ; in a few years he would be independent, though of course to reach that he would have a good deal of fatigue to undergo. Professional men and scholars had better not come ; it is no land of promise to them."

In the autumn of 1833 the shadow of a deep sorrow overclouded his domestic happiness and darkened his dwelling. He had just rejoiced in the birth of a first-born son, and given thanks for this good gift from the Lord, when he was called to resign it. He thus writes to his sister about this keenly-felt bereavement, in December, 1833 :—" Our darling boy throve well for the first fortnight, but he drooped and sank very rapidly after that. You may conceive his mother's sorrow and mine, as we watched him day after day and night after night, and saw that we must resign him. He was a very engaging child, even in his suffering. We felt the blow very deeply, but were enabled to say, when he drew his last breath upon my knee, ' The Lord gave and the Lord hath taken away ; blessed be the name of the Lord !' I laid my first-born in the grave in the middle of November. I was accompanied by the young Episcopal minister here, who is a good man, and his sympathy was most soothing to us. Our dwelling has again resumed its wonted stillness. We feel very sad sometimes, but we have consolation too. We have not a doubt that the arms of our Redeemer are around our departed child, and that we shall yet see and know him. He will not return to us, but we shall go to him."

The "young Episcopal minister" alluded to, was the Rev. Robert Cartwright, minister of St. George's Church, Kingston, (Episcopal) in whom Mr. Machar early found a congenial friend, and with whom up to the time of Mr. Cartwright's premature death, he enjoyed much delightful Christian fellowship.

In the mean time the church had been receiving a considerable accession to its strength, very cheering to the few and widely scattered labourers already in the field. The Rev. Matthew Miller was the first missionary sent out by the Glasgow Colonial Society in 1832, and in 1833 the same Society, of which the late Dr. Burns was the active and zealous secretary, sent out ten others; the Rev. Messrs. Smith, Romanes, Roach, Stark, Mair, McIntosh, Roger, Fairbairn, Gordon and Leach. The first named, the Rev. John Smith, came out specially to the congregation of Beckwith, which had applied for a minister. It was very honourable to these gentlemen that they entered at once into the missionary field, instead of waiting or canvassing, like many others, for churches at home. All were speedily called and settled over congregations of which they were the first ministers. Only the four last named now survive. The rest, with the exception of Dr. Romanes, died the ministers of the congregations over which they were then settled.

The first missionary sent out, the Rev. Matthew Miller, who was a young man of much energy and zeal, and whose arrival had been hailed with joy, was, however, prematurely and mysteriously called away before he had been two years in his new field of labour. He had been settled at Cobourg, and in the latter part of 1833, Mr. Machar had much pleasant intercourse with him, recognising in him a steady growth of piety; but the spring of 1834 was saddened by his sudden death, under very affecting circumstances. In February, 1834, he had travelled from Cobourg to Ramsay, a distance of nearly two hundred miles, with his own horse and cutter. The sleighing was good as he travelled downward, but on his return a thaw had set in, and the snow was rapidly disappearing. He arrived at Mr. Machar's house in Kingston about noon on Friday, and remained only for luncheon. His mind seemed much occupied in contemplating some portions of the Gospel of St. John, of which he delighted to speak, and it was remarked after his departure how much he was growing in spiritual-mindedness. He was feeling undecided whether to travel homewards by the ice, (the frozen waters of the lake,) or by land. The ice was beginning to be insecure, and the roads were in many places bare, so that sleighing by land was tedious and difficult, and he had to be at home on Saturday, in order to preach on the Sabbath. Just before leaving, he said, with a shrug, "I am *eerie* about that ice, I shall go by land." But as he was starting, he was met by a person who had travelled on the ice and who told him it was safe. This information caused him to change his plan, and he accordingly took the route up the Bay of Quinte by the ice. He remained all night in Fredericksburg, with the Rev. Mr. McDowall, a venerable missionary pioneer in Canada. Mr. McDowall gave Mr. Miller a chart for his guidance when he started on his way next morning, hoping for a prosperous journey. But a violent thunder storm set in, accompanied by torrents of rain, a most unusual occurrence at that season, and Mr. Miller seemed to have lost his way, and to have been making for the shore, when his horse and cutter broke through the ice and went down in ten feet of water. When found, his watch was standing at nine A.M., the moment at which the accident must have happened. A severe frost set in the same afternoon, and on Sunday some boys, skating near the spot, observed the shaft of the cutter protruding from the ice, and discovered the lifeless form of Mr. Miller lying underneath, with his horse beside him. The sad event was a cause of profound grief to his own congregation, to his brethren in the ministry, and indeed to the whole Church in Canada.

In the summer of 1834, the scourge of cholera prevailed again to a fearful extent in the cities of Canada, as well as throughout Europe. In November, Mr. Machar wrote to his sister; " I do not remember the date of my last. It was during the prevalence of the cholera in this place. It has been very fatal in many places in Canada, and in none more so than in Kingston. Out of a population of 5000, there have been, I should think, nearly 300 deaths. On the second day it prevailed, there were eight funerals in the Scotch burying-ground alone, and as in this country ministers attend all the funerals of their people, I waited nearly all that day to receive the various funeral trains as they arrived, and at one time three bodies were laid side by side in their narrow resting-place. We have been preserved through the whole season in health. Although it was to me a time of great additional labour and distress through sympathy, yet my bodily strength continued unabated. You will be thankful for this. Many have lost their nearest and dearest relatives. Families apparently prosperous have been broken up. Many are widows and many are orphans now. Some of the most prosperous and most beloved in my congregation died; for the disease, this past season, was not confined to the lowest and most intemperate,—did not take the path which men have sometimes, in their presumption, fixed for it. What the effect of these visitations will be remains yet to be seen. There was great seriousness and solemnity for a time. The community, with one consent, set apart a day of fasting and humiliation before God, and the Governor appointed a day of thanksgiving to God for having in mercy withdrawn His heavy hand. We know what we are, with such visitations, but we know not what we should have been without them. We have had during the past two years extensive fires, and many other calamities, and it would appear as if the Lord were striving with us, and hedging up our way from going away from Him any farther."

The autumn of 1834 was a sad season of desolation in Kingston. The heads of a number of large families were cut off by a stroke, and several of those suddenly removed were most estimable members of St. Andrew's congregation, whose loss was severely felt. One of those whose loss was deeply felt by Mr. Machar, was a gentleman of great warmth of heart, and kind and genial disposition, who was rising rapidly in his profession as a lawyer. He was a Scotchman, warmly attached to his native land, but his genial friendliness made him much beloved by all who knew him, though there may be few now surviving who remember George Mackenzie. He attended Divine service on the forenoon of the Sabbath, an excessively hot day. By midnight his spirit had departed, and his remains were laid in the grave at ten next morning. There were many cases equally sudden, and some even more so.

There was much emigration that season, and many widows, fatherless children and orphans were left strangers and destitute in a strange land. But through the Christian sympathy of the inhabitants of Kingston, they were not left uncared for. The minister and members of St. Andrew's congregation did much to relieve the existing misery. One sad case may be given as a sample of many. A mason, who had come from the Highlands of Scotland, had sent for his wife and children. In the meantime he died of cholera, the week preceding the arrival of his wife and four boys, who found themselves alone and destitute in a strange land, where even the language was unintelligible to them, as they understood only Gaelic. They were supported for a time by St. Andrew's Church, instructed and cared for till places were procured for them in the country where they became useful and industrious men.

Mr. Machar, in common with other ministers, passed through many sad experiences during this afflictive season. He was called to attend the sick and dying at all hours of the night as well as the day, being often aroused from sleep to minister at a dying bed, and he never shrank from promptly obeying every call. He was himself delivered from all fear of contagion; and often went to the sick, when near relatives were afraid to venture into the infected atmosphere, going fearlessly even into the wretched abodes where foul air and want of cleanliness were most likely to breed contagion. The calm possession of the mental faculties and consciousness of approaching death, which he thankfully noticed as a striking feature of cholera, made him more especially anxious to visit those dying of that disease, and speak to them the words of eternal life. He willingly went, also, to sympathise with the beraved families, in cases where it was difficult to procure assistance for laying out the corpse, and he and his beadle were sometimes the only persons, besides the newly-made widow or widower, or the childless father, to follow the coffin to the grave. One aged man, decent and respectable in his appearance, had just arrived from Scotland on his way further west, with his daughter, his only child — when she was seized with cholera and died. He came in Scottish fashion to " the minister," who, deeply sympathising with him, made arrangements for the funeral, when he accompanied the sorrowing father to lay his child's remains in a stranger's grave. The desolate old man departed the next day, bowed down by his bereavement, but still grateful for the kindness and sympathy he had received. Such demands upon Mr. Machar's time and sympathy were incessant during that trying season.

In June 1835, he thus wrote to his friend Dr. Simpson: "You would wonder why I did not answer your kind letter. At the time, I was much hurried with church business. Then followed a severe visitation of Asiatic Cholera,—then our meeting of Synod, so that for many months together I was necessarily occupied. It is from no lack of affection, I assure you. I do not forget by-gone days; I never *can* forget them. I heard with great interest and pleasure of your appointment to Kintore, and I cease not to pray that you may be the honoured instrument of bringing many to Christ. Why have we so little success in our Master's work? Even because we do not *look for it with confidence*, because we are of little faith. The great bondage from which we should sigh and cry for deliverance,—the great power of the enemy lies here. He tempts us to doubt;—he cries—'there is a lion in the streets,'—and listening to him we become weak,—weak both in the individual and ministerial warfare. I hope that you are enabled to go forth with greater vigour than I often feel, and are meeting with tokens of encouragement among your people. Here we grow in numbers, and in some cases also, I trust, in faith and love of the Saviour, but the barrenness that prevails around us is very great. The church does not seem in these days to be reviving anywhere. Said a Romish priest to me the other day, on hearing of the recent change of ministry, and of the spoliation of the Irish Church, leading to that of other churches;—'well now, you see the reigns of your Luthers and Calvins and Knoxes have had their day, and all things promise well for the establishment of the truth of the ancient church,'—meaning the Roman Catholic Church. My labour is considerably increased since I left Scotland last. Our church is now too small for the congregation. I hope we shall get an addition to it this summer or autumn."

Although Mr. Machar's time was necessarily so much engrossed with the duties of his own congregation, and the affairs of his own branch of the Church at large, he took a deep and active interest in promoting the efforts of the various general religious societies in Kingston and the surrounding country. In this work he took a special delight, as it brought into union and co-operation both the ministers and members of the various denominations of Christians in the city, who could meet in brotherly fellowship in labouring to advance the blessed work of their one Lord and Master in the salvation of souls. He was Secretary to the Religious Tract Society, at least from 1830 to 1840, and probably for a longer period, and he continued always to attend its meetings and take a deep interest in its prosperity. The Kingston Auxiliary Bible Society was to him an object of special interest, and at the time of his death he had been for several years its President. It had been originally instituted about the year 1820. A number of ministers and Christian laymen had been aroused by the great scarcity of Bibles to the need for forming a Society to bring the Word of God within the reach of all, and especially to distribute Bibles gratuitously among the poor who could not afford to purchase them, for at that time they were both comparatively scarce and very expensive. The Society was carried on for a time with zeal and activity, the Venerable Archdeacon Stuart taking a prominent part in it, along with other members of his church, and becoming himself a collector. The Rev. John Barclay, then the young minister of St. Andrew's Church, was its Secretary. But owing to the death and departure of some of its most zealous promoters this Society, so auspiciously begun, languished and died. However, after the revival of the Religious Tract Society, under circumstances of much hopefulness, the friends of the Kingston Bible Society took courage to revive it with much anxiety and after many prayers. A public meeting was held in January, 1830, and the Society was anew organised. His Excellency, Sir John Colborne, then Governor of Upper Canada, assented to the request of the

Society that he should give his influence as Patron. From the first report of the revived Society's proceedings, drawn up by Mr. Machar as Secretary, are taken the following extracts, interesting as showing the spiritual condition of the country at that time :—

" The friends of the Bible in this place feel that Upper Canada is to be their field of labour. While they contemplate its still partially unsettled state, and look at the width of surface over which its population is scattered, they see that many years must elapse before ministers are likely to be settled in places where spiritual labourers are greatly needed, and they foresee that a fearful growth of carelessness and ignorance must mark the dreary interval.

    *   *   *   *   *

Must they be left in hopeless abandonment to the natural consequences of their unhappy circumstances? Though we may not do all for them that we might desire, may we not do something? May we not give them the Bible— that book of whose contents it is said : ' These are written that we might believe that Jesus is the Son of God, and that, believing, we might have life through His Name.' "

Three branch societies are mentioned as having been organised to co-operate with the Kingston Auxiliary at Gananoque, Waterloo, and Napanee, and a large number of copies of the Scriptures are mentioned as having been distributed to families who previously had not a Bible in their possession. A most pleasing feature of the operations of the Society, besides the earnestness and zeal with which they were carried on, was the spirit of union with which the members of the different Christian denominations engaged in them. The list of the Committee and office-bearers contains the names of the ministers and most respected members of the Churches of England and Scotland, as well as of other bodies, as also those of several British officers of high rank, stationed in Kingston, whose hearts were truly in the work. The results of these Christian exertions cannot be estimated now, but the Word of God was by their means scattered throughout many destitute localities, in faithful trust in the promise that it should not return void, but should accomplish that whereunto it was sent. Of those who then took part in the work only Dr. Armstrong, now of Rochester, survives, but the others did not become weary in well doing, so long as they were spared to labour in the field below. Mr. Machar acted as Secretary from 1830 to 1845, when the younger ministers who were then members took up the more active part of the work, but he always retained a hearty interest in its welfare.

In the cause of education he took a deep and active interest, willingly giving a portion of his time to visiting schools, and encouraging the comparatively few teachers who were then labouring in this important work. One school in particular, taught by a lady belonging to his own congregation, who had been for many years, and still is, an efficient teacher, he had great pleasure in visiting and examining, and in testifying to the thoroughness and and accuracy of the teaching, and to the great attention bestowed on the moral and religious training of the children. His annual visits on these occasions afforded reciprocal pleasure, and the few simple words of exhortation which he always addressed to them, were attentively listened to and often long remembered.

Free schools were in those days unknown, and the poor suffered from the want of any provision for educating children, whose parents could not afford to pay high school fees. Two schools taught by female teachers, at which the fees charged were very small, were supported for a time by the voluntary contributions of ladies, but it was found difficult to keep them up by subscription. Several years previously a society had been formed and incorporated, called the Midland District School Society, having for its object the providing a cheap education for the children of the poor. It was intended to conduct a school on the Lancasterian plan, by which a greater number could be taught than in any other way, but they had been disappointed in the teacher employed, and from this and other causes the school had been discontinue for several years. In 1837 it was determined to resume operations, and to devote the property they had acquired and from which they realised a small yearly interest, to the original object in view—that of providing, at a moderate rate, education for the children of the working classes. A committee was appointed to obtain teachers and to take the general direction of the school, consisting of the Venerable the Archdeacon Stuart, the Hon. John Macaulay, T. Kirkpatrick, Esq., John S. Cartwright, Esq., the Rev. Messrs. Cartwright and Machar, Alex. Pringle, Esq., and some others. The choice of teachers was committed to the Archdeacon and the Rev. Messrs. Cartwright and Machar. In the discharge of this most important and responsible trust they acted in perfect harmony, none of them having any party bias or separate interest to serve, but seeking with one heart and mind the good of the object entrusted to them, and exemplifying in this, as in other things, the truth of the words, " Behold how good and pleasant it is for brethren to dwell together in unity." Their object was to secure efficient Christian teachers, and in this aim, under the Divine guidance, they were singularly blessed with success.

These efforts, carried on in so pleasing a spirit of of Christian harmony, seemed to be prospered in an especial manner. In a short time the committee had three flourishing schools in operation, at which more than three hundred children were in attendance. The expenses of the third school were subscribed for by the trustees themselves, their funds not being sufficient to maintain more than two. The schools were not free, but the fees charged were very small, and in cases where even these could not be afforded, they were paid by benevolent individuals, so that not even the very poorest were excluded. By this means there was a constant reciprocal benefit to givers and receivers, education was more valued, and the attendance was more regular than they are under the present system of free schools. No poor child in Kingston, so far as was known, was then left without education ; their moral training and Scriptural instruction was carefully attended to by their teachers ; and there are many now occupying useful and influential positions, who have reason to look back with gratitude to the thorough teaching they received in these schools.

The time of the completion and opening of these schools—about 1843—was, however, saddened by the premature death of one of those who had been most interested and active in labouring for their establishment. In the Rev. Mr. Cartwright, cut off in the prime of his life and the midst of his usefulness, Mr. Machar lost a faithful and attached friend, and a beloved and devoted fellow-labourer in the Lord. His labours as a pastor had been abundant and incessant, overtaxing a naturally fragile constitution ; his hand and heart were ever open to the poor, and his deep sympathy with the sick and the afflicted led him continually to seek, by every means in his power, to alleviate their suffering. He was large-hearted and truly Catholic in spirit. Though warmly attached to the Church of England, and zealous for the advancement of her spiritual interests, he was always ready to sympathise and take part in every Christian work, whose object was to promote the kingdom of Christ in the hearts of men, so manifesting that where the spirit of Christian love truly exists, it is stronger than those outward walls of separation that so sadly divide Christians from each other, and cramp and fetter the expansive force of Christianity. Mr. Machar deeply felt his loss and sincerely mourned for one with whom he had ever walked hand in hand in every Christian and philanthropic effort for the public good. A little incident which took place towards the close of their earthly intercourse will show how strong is the bond of Christian love, and how it will resist the pressure of strongly conflicting opinions. On a much disputed point, regarding the claims of their respective churches on the State provision set apart for religious purposes, Mr. Cartwright and Mr. Machar held very different views, and had expressed them strongly in a private discussion. Fearing lest their decided difference of opinion might, in any degree, chill the warmth of their Christian friendship, Mr. Cartwright wrote, immediately after their conversation, a warm brotherly note, in which he says : "We cannot afford to be alienated. We know not how soon either of us may require a brother's sympathy and a brother's prayers upon a dying bed." It was not long before this foreboding was fulfilled in his own case ; and his friend, in visiting him in this last illness, enjoyed much sweet and solemn Christian communion with his departing brother. In one of their last conversations, Mr. Cartwright said, "The nearer I approach to eternity, the more I see those veils rent asunder which separate Christians from one another." Shortly afterwards he was gently removed during sleep,—without tasting death,—to the "rest that remaineth for the people of God,"

CHAPTER VI.

LENGTHENED VISIT TO SCOTLAND. ESTABLISHMENT
OF QUEEN'S UNIVERSITY.

DR. MACHAR, during all his ministerial life,
deeply felt his responsibility, as a pastor, to
the chief Shepherd, and the value of the
souls committed to his care. In his pastoral
work he laboured faithfully, to the utmost limit of his
strength, not only from a sense of duty, but also because he delighted in his work. To regular visitation
from house to house he usually devoted one and
frequently two afternoons in the week, embracing in
his pastoral circuit long and fatiguing country rounds.
These visits his kindly and genial manner always
made pleasant as well as profitable to his people, and
he took especial pains to make them both interesting
and useful to the younger members. The following
particulars of the extent of his charge at an early
period, are taken from the answers sent in by him to
certain official queries. The date is not given, but it was
probably at an early period :—

" The number of souls whom I visit pastorally, and to whom
I regularly minister, are one thousand five hundred souls ;
besides about four hundred others, whose children are baptized
by me, and to whom I occasionally preach. Of communicants

the number is three hundred and fifty. Besides the number of souls under my regular ministry, there always has been a portion of Her Majesty's troops (sometimes an entire regiment) stationed at Kingston, who have not only been provided with Church accommodation, gratuitously, by the congregation, but have in the same way had the benefit of the minister's services. During all the time that the 79th Regiment·was stationed at Kingston, a separate service was necessary for them—the church being too small to contain them with the congregation."

He always took a lively interest in the troops stationed at Kingston. When the 71st Regiment was there, a deputation from the Presbyterians who belonged to it waited upon him, requesting him to baptize their children, and expressing their earnest desire to attend the Scotch Church, if permitted to do so by their commanding officer. Mr. Machar applied to the Colonel of the regiment for the desired permission, but it was refused, on the ground that it had been the invariable practice of the regiment to attend the Church of England, and he did not feel at liberty to depart from it. Mr. Machar laid this correspondence before the Commander of the Forces, who issued an order that the soldiers should be allowed to worship according to the dictates of their consciences. From that time there was no interference with their religious liberty, and the officers and soldiers who were Presbyterians always attended St. Andrew's Church. This result afforded Mr. Machar much satisfaction, although it added considerably to his labours, without adding at that time to his income; and he had often much enjoyment in his ministerial intercourse both with officers and soldiers, among whom he frequently met with excellent Christian men. At a later period, however, when an entire Scotch Regiment, stationed at Kingston, required a separate service, he was acknowledged officially as their Chaplain, and received an occasional allowance. Except in such cases, however, his military labours were gratuitously performed, until the last year of his life, when he was recognized by the Government as Presbyterian Chaplain, and received an allowance in proportion to the number of Presbyterians attending the church, which was continued to his successor until the final withdrawal of the British troops from Canada.

In January, 1836, he thus wrote to his sister in reference to an invitation from a friend to return to Scotland to a vacant parish then in view :—

"We are by no means clear that it is our duty to leave this. I might never again have a more important station, nor a more affectionate people than I now have, and if we merely pleased ourselves in changing our place, what happiness could we expect, and what evidence should we have to ourselves that the glory of God and the good of souls were objects of dear interest to our hearts ? One thing that has sometimes inclined me to think of returning to Scotland is my occasionally feeble health. Should this increase, and I be less able to discharge the numerous and arduous duties connected with my charge, I might think more seriously of returning. If we look to God, He will make our way plain in due time."

On March 29th he wrote again :—

"It gave me great concern to hear of the death of my old and excellent friend, the Rev. James Burns. When I think of the changes that have taken place since I was at home in 1830, both the ministers of Brechin having been called away, and many more that I knew, I feel deeply how uncertain is life. Be it then ours to die daily, to die to sin and to live unto righteousness, that death may be to us what I feel assured it was to my beloved and highly esteemed friend, Mr. Burns—the portal to our better, or rather our only life."

And, referring to a second invitation to return to Scotland, he says :—

"I love my native country, and there is much to draw me back to it, but it is not inclination but duty that we must hear. It would, I believe, be felt as a heavy blow by my congregation were I to leave them, and when the parting came, I believe that sore would the trial be, both to minister and people. The Church of Scotland in this colony is as yet in what I might call a suffering state, and it would be an unkindly thing to leave it still suffering."

67

On November 10th, '37, he again writes on the same subject :—

"I am willing that my continuance in this land or removal from it should be entirely in the Lord's hands. I know that no change without His blessing would be anything but misery. The addition to our church is almost finished. It is pleasing in itself, and has been accompanied by some gratifying circumstances. I have got a new vestry-room neatly finished, which the young ladies of the congregation have fitted up for me. I only mention this to show that it is doubtful whether I might be happier among any people than those I have been among in this country. Do not suppose, however, that I am without troubles. No minister who has the spiritual welfare of his people at heart can be without trouble in these days of the church, when so much of a spirit that is not of Christ prevails among nominal Christians." `

A letter dated January 17th, 1838, contains the following account of the so-called " Rebellion " of '38 and '39:—

"Upon most people in Canada, the Rebellion came like a thunder-clap, and if we were unprepared for the outbreak of rebellion in the Lower Province, still less were we prepared to see it break out in the Upper Province, and especially under such a leader as Mackenzie. The conspiracy was well laid, and had well-nigh succeeded. Believing it impossible that in this Province any number of persons could be so mad as to rise against the constituted authorities, the Governor had sent all the troops to Lower Canada, and Toronto, the capital, was altogether without defence, and its inhabitants dwelling securely without apprehension of danger, but God saw meet in His great mercy to extend His protecting arm over those who were without the means of protecting themselves. A friend of mine in Toronto writes the following account :—' In this instance the interference of God has been so marked as to draw forth a spontaneous acknowledgment from those not used to mark the hand of Providence. Had Mackenzie come in on Monday evening, as he originally intended, there is no doubt that he would have possessed himself of the city, and as a successful opening on his part would have attracted many to his standard, it is very probable that the sacrifice of many lives would have been the consequence. The reason why he did not come in that night is understood to have been the death of a man of ferocious character,—a leader of the rebellion,—who, that very afternoon, fell from his horse and broke his neck; and his death made the others irresolute. At the Government House there were only four persons to defend, and, I believe, not ten at the fort;—and in the town all was confusion. The extraordinary mildness of the season was another remarkable circumstance, as it admitted of our obtaining speedy assistance from many quarters, and gave us confidence. For forty-eight hours all was gloom. M. and myself were under arms. My heart almost sickened as I loaded a musket, and I could not help something like a prayer that it might do no injury.' The citizens of Toronto awaking from their panic, and having armed, soon attacked the rebels in their post, totally dispersed them, and but for the sympathy and underhand aid afforded to Mackenzie by mobs of Americans on the frontier, he and his associates would have been totally crushed. He was able to make his escape across the lines to the State of New York, and by his misrepresentations succeeded in obtaining, among the worthless and unprincipled, both arms and soldiers. He subsequently took possession of Navy Island, situated on the Niagara river, a little above the Falls, and there he still is, but it is impossible he can hold out much longer. About Kingston all is loyal, almost *all* are soldiers, and all points are now in a state of complete defence. According to the secret plan which has been discovered, a day was appointed for taking Kingston, but the dispersion at Toronto prevented that, as well as other attempts which would have caused destruction and bloodshed. We trust that, under the good hand of God, we shall soon be enjoying peace and quietness."

The rebellion was then supposed to be suppressed, but in the following winter it again broke out,—ending in the well-known battle of Prescott,—when the leaders of the *émeute* were taken, and the sad spectacle was witnessed at Fort Henry of the execution of ten of them, including an unfortunate Polish exile named Schulz, for whose untimely fate, as he had been the dupe and tool of others, much commiseration was felt. Mr. Machar, however, did not personally share in the agitation of that renewed excitement, as he was in Scotland during that winter, having gone thither in the summer of 1838. He was then in delicate health, having had threatenings of a complaint which he feared might lay him aside from preaching for life. The advice of an eminent American physician was blest to his recovery, although he never completely recovered his strength, and his health continued fragile during the rest of his life.

On landing at Glasgow, he and his wife were met by Dr. Mathieson, of Montreal, who was then in Scotland, and at that time suffering from depression of spirits, and hardly intending to return to Montreal. Soon, however, the aspect of things was changed, and he set sail in October, in excellent spirits, to return to his charge. The Rev. Robert Neill, of Seymour, who had supplied Dr. Mathieson's place during the greater part of his absence, came to Kingston soon after Mr. Machar's absence, and supplied his place and pulpit with much acceptance until his return. This was delayed longer than had been at first expected, on account of the dangerous illness of a near relative, but having Mr. Neill to minister in his place, Mr. Machar had no anxiety about the welfare of his people.

During his stay in Scotland, he did all in his power to advance the interests of the Church in Canada. He had been commissioned by the Synod to meet the Committee of General Assembly of the Church of Scotland, to give them information regarding the state of the Presbyterian Church in Canada, and to co-operate with the Committee in representing to the Imperial Government their just claims to be recognised, and to participate in the support which had been appropriated for a Protestant Clergy in Canada. The Clergy Reserves were then, as they had been for many years, a matter of dispute, and had aroused much heart-burning and hostile feeling between the members of the Churches of England and Scotland in the colony,—the former claiming the right to monopolise the whole endowment. These disputes were finally settled a few years afterwards, by the equitable decision of the Twelve Judges of England, including the different Protestant denominations in a participation of the Clergy Reserves. But the matter was not allowed to rest here by those who were determined not only to maintain the "voluntary" principle themselves, but to enforce it upon the whole country, and an agitation on the subject was kept up, until the whole of the liberal provisions which had been set apart for the support of religious ordinances, and for the religious instruction of the people of a large and spiritually destitute colony, was swept away from the cause of both religion and education, and applied to merely secular uses.

The Edinburgh Committee, with whom Mr. Machar had several meetings, took a very warm interest in the affairs of the Canadian Church. One of those most deeply interested was Dr. Welsh, who, with some others of their number, accompanied by Mr. Machar, went to London to lay the matter, with full explanations, before her Majesty's Government. But it was not the temporal affairs of the Church that Mr. Machar deemed most important. He felt most deeply the need of labourers, and he travelled from place to place enquiring about young preachers, who were not yet employed in the ministry. Several of these, who had been recommended to him, he visited personally, urging the spiritual needs and the urgent claims of Canada as a missionary field,—but without success. He also addressed, with great earnestness, a meeting of the Divinity students of Edinburgh, but in all his efforts in that cause he was disappointed, and sadly felt the great lack of a missionary spirit in the Church. It was during the prevalence of the *Quoad Sacra* Act, when there were many new charges, and young preachers were not disposed to leave their native country while they had hopes of employment at home. The only one who came to Canada in that year was the Rev. W. Reid, now residing in Toronto,

Moderator, during the present year, of the Canada Presbyterian Synod.

The controversy between the Established Church and the advocates of "voluntaryism" was then raging fiercely. Great efforts had been made by the Established Church in the cause of church extension, as the population had so much outgrown the church accommodation that multitudes were left unprovided for; but the voluntary bodies strongly opposed the granting by Government of any aid for this purpose. Dr. Chalmers was then in the midst of his zealous labours in the cause of church extension,—travelling from town to town, earnestly pleading its cause with his warm characteristic eloquence. Mr. Machar met him at Brechin, and in the course of conversation asked him if he could not do something for the Church in Canada, in using his influence to obtain labourers for it. He replied, almost impatiently,—" There must be division of labour! Church extension is the work to which I have devoted myself, and when it is finished I shall retire from public life for a time, for while I am addressing the public, and going from place to place, my own soul is withering!" Seeing Mr. Machar look disappointed, however, his generous heart seemed touched; he enquired very kindly about Canada, and expressed his regret at his inability to do something for the Church there.

The Synod of Canada was at that time feeling the urgent necessity for having a University and Theological College of its own. In the extreme difficulty of procuring from Scotland ministers to supply the fast growing needs of Canada, they felt they must ultimately depend upon a native ministry, for the education of whom a college was absolutely indispensable. As they were then projecting plans for the accomplishment of that object, Mr. Machar conferred with the Assembly Committee in Edinburgh respecting it,—finding in all of them, and especially in Dr. Welsh, a warm interest in the scheme, and an earnest desire to afford all possible aid towards its accomplishment. It originated with them at that time, to bestow on the college an annual grant of money, which has been continued to the present time, and for which the Church in Canada owes a deep debt of gratitude.

After a very pleasant sojourn in Scotland, during which he exceedingly enjoyed visiting the scenes of his child-hood and youth, and the renewed intercourse with his old friends, Dr. Simpson, of Kintore, Dr. Guthrie, Dr. Brewster, of Craig, Dr. Clason, and several others, to whom he was much attached, he sailed again for Canada in August, 1839, and arrived at Quebec early in September. On January 1st, 1840, he wrote from Kingston, referring to his return :—

"On a Saturday we reached Quebec, and, after I had preached there on the Sabbath, we proceeded on our way on the Monday, reaching our home at Kingston on Thursday night. On Sabbath I preached twice to my people : it was exactly twelve-years on that day since I first preached to them, on my arrival among them as their minister. Many changes had taken place among them since then, but during my last visit to Scotland, comparatively few. I have sometimes said to you that, should I ever in Providence be called to minister elsewhere, I could scarcely hope to meet with a people like my flock here. Very kindly did they receive me again on my return. Soon after my arrival the Sacrament was administered, and a large number of communicants added to the church. The new part is now filled, and it is difficult to get pews. Though these things look favourable, there are important lacks among us. Alas, alas ! we may have much of the *form* of godliness, and yet be wofully deficient in the *power !* Since my arrival I have preached twice every Sabbath, and occasionally on a week-day. I have also resumed my visiting and catechising from house to house, and am endeavouring to get as much as possible done while the cold frosty weather lasts. It is terribly cold ; at night every liquid thing becomes solid.—My health is better for my voyage. I have, however, too much work for my not strong constitution. The work of my parish, alone, would be almost too much for me, but week after week I am two or three days occupied with other business, especially with correspondence on the

73

general affairs of the Church in this land, which has many difficulties to contend with. We are about to establish a College or University here, chiefly for the education of ministers. *One* thing is needful—to sit with simplicity at the feet of Jesus, and, hearing Him, to follow wheresoever He leads the way."

On March 18, 1841, he again wrote respecting his work :—

" I have been much longer in writing to you than I intended, but my avocations have been so numerous and so pressing that I have scarcely had a leisure hour, and have often gone to bed utterly tired and worn out. Yet I have enjoyed a considerable measure of health, nor have I ever been unable to preach twice every Sabbath. The population of Kingston is on the increase, and since my return I have had new families to attend to. I have also been endeavouring, by visiting and otherwise, to awaken and gather in many others who, from various causes, have become careless and indifferent. It is here with us, as in many places in Scotland. Many are sunk into a state of spiritual death, and yet not so dead but that they may be revived again, if only they are sought after, and dealt with in earnestness and tenderness. I am happy to hear from your last that intemperance is on the decline, and I rejoice to hear that the Kirk Sessions are exerting themselves against it. It has been a great evil here, and I fear it is not diminishing. In this country the progress of the drunkard, or I should say of the drinker, is very rapid, and seldom does a man take to occasional tippling, who does not soon become a lost creature. Lost to everything good, he is not long in finishing his course under disease which is produced by the use of ardent spirits."

During the close of the year 1839, the Synod set vigorously to work to raise funds, and to make arrangements for the establishment of Queen's College. Feeling the great necessity for providing a theological and also a literary institution for higher education in a new country, which was then almost destitute of general facilities for the latter, both the clergy and the laity joined very warmly in promoting the object. The most influential members of the Presbyterian Church throughout the

Province took a deep interest in it, and aided it both with judicious advice and pecuniary aid. The late Hon. William Morris was especially serviceable to it by his legal counsel and his political influence, as well as other gentlemen whom the world now knows no more. Those ministers, too, who were so earnest in furthering the work and in devoting to it their time and labour, among whom may be mentioned Dr. McGill, Mr. Gale, Mr. Rintoul, Dr. Mathieson, Dr. Urquhart and Dr. Cook, have nearly all passed away.* A very united and enthusiastic meeting was held in St. Andrew's Church, Kingston, and many earnest heartfelt addresses were given by voices now long silent in death. Of the speakers at that meeting and the committee who were appointed to collect funds, two only survive. When, twenty-eight years after, the very existence of the College was threatened by the withdrawal of the Government grant, the meeting then held vividly recalled, to those who still survived, the one just mentioned, in being characterised by the same spirit of union, enthusiasm and hope.

In 1841, the seat of Government was established in Kingston, as it was then thought, permanently; but its continuance proved to be of very short duration. As its location there was very sudden, and there was great want of accommodation for the many strangers it brought to Kingston, every house was occupied and rents were doubled. It was just at that time that Mr. Machar received a letter from Dr. Walsh, dated October 27, 1841, from which the following extracts are taken :—

"The Royal Charter for Queen's College having at last passed the Great Seal, the Colonial Committee, at their meeting on Wednesday last, appointed the Rev. Mr. Liddell, of Lady Glenorchy's Church in this city, to the office of Princi-

---

* The Rev. Henry Gordon, of Gananoque, should not be forgotten among those who took a warm and efficient interest in its establishment. A very liberal donation from him was called at the time the " nest-egg " of the fund for the College endowment.

pal. Official notice will be given by the Secretary of the Committee to the Hon. W. Morris, Chairman of the Board of Trustees, but from your situation in Kingston, and your official connection with the University, I think it right that you should have the earliest possible notice. The necessary steps towards loosing Mr. Liddell from his charge are in course of being taken, and we hope he may be able to sail in the steampacket for Halifax on the 3rd of December next, so that you will have some idea when you may expect him in Kingston. I have written to Mr. Morris as to the anxious efforts made by the Committee, and I have no hesitation whatever in saying that of all the individuals thought of as likely to accept the situation, Mr. Liddell is entitled to the first place. Drs. Gordon, Buchanan, Candlish, Cunningham, Clason, Paul, and other ministers of Edinburgh who were present at the committee meeting when the election took place, all express themselves to the same effect, and from his talents and acquirements and habits and principles, I should be disappointed indeed if he does not prove a blessing to the Institution."

From some erroneous information which the Colonial Committee had received, they were under the impression that everything was ready for commencing operations, and that the trustees were only waiting the appointment of a Principal, whereas the trustees had no idea that the appointment of a Principal would take place so promptly, but expected that they would be apprised in time to make due preparation for the opening of the college. Accordingly they were quite unprepared for this announcement; nothing was ready—intending students had not been apprised, and they had not even a house in which the classes could be commenced. Mr. Machar and the other trustees were placed in a situation of great perplexity. They felt the extreme awkwardness of the situation, and the disappointment which Dr. Liddell must feel when he arrived, which he did in the end of December, coming directly to Mr. Machar's house. It was exceedingly painful to Mr. Machar to meet Dr. Liddell, knowing the disappointment he must feel in finding things so different from what he had expected, and to have to inform him, as he immediately did, of the situation of affairs, expressing his regret that it should be as it was. Dr. Liddell's disappointment was very great. He had left Scotland hurriedly, leaving his family behind, lest the interests of the college should suffer from any delay. But he bore it in a noble and Christian spirit, uttering no reproach, but rather sympathising with the trustees in their difficulty, and expressed himself as being willing to commence immediately with whatever students they could collect, however few they might be. A house—such as they could get—was immediately taken and fitted up with class-rooms, the opening of the college immediately announced, and the Rev. P. C. Campbell, of Brockville, who had been elected Classical Professor, was summoned to his post. The trustees had decided, in their present circumstances, to begin with two professors—the Principal to take the theological department, and Mr. Campbell the faculty of arts. The college was opened with seven or eight advanced students who intended to study for the ministry, and some ten or twelve who were to commence their course in arts. But the extremely low state of education in Canada at that time was revealed by the fact that even of that small number of students, very few were fitted to be matriculated. Professor Campbell did all in his power to remedy the deficiency, and even gave two hours a day to ground the students thoroughly in the elements of classical education. That the state of education in Canada is now so different, is owing, in no small degree, to the good work done by Queen's College, for, besides many useful members of the other professions who have done ample credit to their Alma Mater, she has sent out not a few efficient teachers, who have been of great service in diffusing thorough Grammar-school education throughout the Province.

The additional duties which the affairs of the college and the presence of the seat of Government involved, occupied Mr. Machar's mind and time to such an extent that he was often oppressed with work, and interrupted in his meditations for the pulpit. This was a great trial to him, as he ever felt deeply his responsibility as a minister, and his pastoral duties were always the most congenial and delightful part of his work. He wrote to his sister in October, 1842 :—

"I should have written to you long ere now, but I have always been occupied with many more matters than it is possible for me to attend to. Formerly I used to think my situation a laborious one, but the labour then was nothing to what it has been since the transferring of the seat of Government to Kingston, and the opening of the college. The Presbyterian population here has in consequence been greatly increased, and our church accommodation is now inadequate to meet the wants of the people. A new church and minister must be thought of, but in the meantime the whole burden of the pastoral office lies upon me. The duties of our church courts, too, are more burdensome than they used to be. This is Friday, and this week I have attended a meeting of Presbytery a hundred miles distant, where we had a whole day's business. Such incessant, varied and often difficult employments are wearing, nay, *very* wearing, but here, in the course of Divine Providence, is the post assigned me for the present, and as long as I am continued here, the promise will not fail, 'As thy day is, so shall thy strength be.' I hope, my dear sister, you will look to this promise, and have faith in its fulfilment. Our second session of Queen's College has just commenced, with a promising increase of students. The Parliament of Canada is now sitting here, and during its meeting we have had a good many political changes. We know not what the results may be."

But other changes than political ones were at hand, more immediately affecting—and that in a very painful manner—his own ministerial work. A sad ecclesiastical change was, ere long, to take place, and another Presbyterian congregation was to be formed in Kingston, under circumstances little thought of when the foregoing lines were penned.

CHAPTER VII.

1844.

DIVISION OF THE PRESBYTERIAN CHURCH IN CANADA.

PREVIOUSLY to this time, although Mr. Machar had had much wearing labour both of mind and body, he had yet enjoyed outward peace, peace in his congregation, and union with his brethren. But a painful trial was now to be felt. The Controversies between the Church of Scotland and the Civil Courts had then been stirring the heart of Scotland to its core. It is unnecessary here to enter into the merits of the questions in dispute, or their results. Many faithful ministers, rather than submit to a state of matters of which they conscientiously disapproved, were willing to suffer the loss of all things and trust in God, towards whom they desired to maintain a conscience void of offence, and their trust was not disappointed. A disruption became inevitable ; all found themselves obliged to espouse one side or the other. The Church of Scotland had long enjoyed much liberty to be faithful to Christ, but she had settled on her lees and been at ease ; and her unfaithfulness had brought upon her from the Lord the heavy chastenings of divisions and separations, —brother separated from brother,—no longer able to see

79

eye to eye, but misconceiving and condemning each other. To his own master, each man standeth or falleth. There were, and are, still, on both sides, many whose consciences are clear in this thing, and in the present time the spirit of bitterness and division is giving way to a spirit of peace and the desire for union. Love is of God, and the love of God alone can truly unite and prosper the Church. The following admirable sentiments on this subject are extracted from an address by Lord Ardmillan, a consistent and conscientious Free Church man, and one of the Lords of Session, given at a Conference of elders on the Union question, at which he acted as Chairman :—

"Now, I most distinctly state and emphatically declare, that I am not actuated by any hostility to the Established Church. I cherish no such feelings, and am influenced by no such motives. The experience of the many years which have passed since the Disruption, has tended not only to allay the irritations and smooth the asperities incident to such a struggle, but to satisfy me that many harsh words, in these times of conflict and severance, were unmerited and unbecoming ; that good men remaining within the Established Church acted as honestly and faithfully, according to their own views and on their own principles, as I hope I did upon mine ; and that there are now within the Established Church a number —I hope and believe a great number—of pious and worthy men, ministers and laymen, who are faithfully devoting themselves to labours which God owns and blesses in proclaiming the Gospel message, and in many ways striving to advance the kingdom of our Lord and Saviour. Those who know me will, I am sure, give me credit for saying this in all simplicity and sincerity. I have uniformly acted in accordance with this declaration, and I do most heartily wish success to every Christian work within the Established Church. At the same time, it was for no trifling reasons, and on no light grounds, that I quitted the Establishment. I have always felt, and now again declare, that that step was a very grave and solemn proceeding, which nothing could justify but clear grounds and deep convictions. On these grounds and convictions I acted."

It is refreshing to hear, from one in so influential a

position, a testimony so Christian, so large-hearted and so candid, which, while decidedly avowing and adhering to his own conscientious views, admits the equal conscientiousness and honesty of those who hold views and principles opposed to his. It may be hoped that there are many men of this type in both sections of the Church.

The disruption of the Church of Scotland was deeply felt by the Presbyterians in Canada, but it could not have been anticipated that it would cause a disruption of the Church there. There were, indeed, strong opinions and sympathies on both sides, and a good deal was done to excite and intensify them ; but in Canada the causes in *no degree existed* which produced the disruption in Scotland. There was no patronage, and there could be none. There never was nor could be any interference, jurisdiction or control attempted by the State over the Church, even in her temporal affairs. No voluntary Church in the world could be more *free* than she was. It is painful to linger over this unhappy period of the Church's history, but in justice to the memory of one who was ever consistent and conscientious in the course he pursued, and who was at the time much misconstrued by those opposed to him, it is right to give his own views, as expressed in his private letters to his friends on the subject. The following letter was wrttten to his friend Dr. Simpson, of Kintore, in January, 1844 :—

" MY DEAR FRIEND,—I have been much longer in writing to you than I intended, but it was not from forgetfulness, nor backwardness in sympathising with you under the trouble through which you have passed, or may now be passing. It has arisen partly from the continual and urgent pressure of ministerial duty, which has of late been heavier than I can well bear, and partly, too, I must confess, from a shrinking from adverting to some topics of present overwhelming interest on which I hold views different from yours.

" You say you do not exactly know my mind upon some of the great questions that have agitated the Church of late years,

I have, in a great measure, abstained from entering upon the question in my letters to my friends. I very long,—indeed almost to the last,—cherished the hope that the storm would blow over, and I was willing to shun controversies, for which, while I could, with great difficulty, find time for them, I fondly hoped there would be no necessity. Had I been a minister in Scotland, I know not how I should have acted at the late eventful crisis. I could not, however,—with my present light, —were I called upon to take a side,—make up my mind to desert the Established Church, or take one step for its over-throw. I have not been indifferent to those great principles for which you have contended. I think them deeply import-ant, and because I do so, I would yet contend for them within the walls of the establishment. My very dear friend, I scarcely intended, when I began, to say so much upon this subject. I view the matter with no violent, but with deeply sorrowful feelings.

" You may suppose that I have been sounded as to whether I would return to Scotland to occupy a post in the Established Church. My brief reply has been,—I would *not*, in my pre-sent circumstances, take one step to be brought home. I have been labouring to promote peace here, by entreating those of opposite views to bear with each other upon points having no bearing upon our ecclesiastical condition in Canada, and to prevent the introduction of what would only divide those who cannot afford to be divided ; but how far we may succeed in promoting peace I cannot foresee. We are in a very ticklish state, both as respects political and ecclesias-tical matters. Dr. Cunningham is now in New York, and should he visit us and seek our separation, there is no saying what may happen. A church which, weak though it was, was beginning to do some good, and might have done more, may be rent asunder, and that for no reason ; for, as you are aware, our connection with the Established Church implies no jurisdiction or control or interference whatever. The storm here *may* blow over, but it may not, and you may hear of our passing through the same scenes which you have passed through."

In March, 1844, he wrote to his sister :—

" Yesterday week was our Spring Communion Sabbath. We had fine weather and large audiences on all the days, as well as a large number of communicants. Twenty-five young communicants and twenty-eight strangers were added. Peace has hitherto reigned among us, but attempts are being made to bring about a disruption. Those who know the relation of the Presbyterian Church in Canada to the Civil Courts, may well wonder how this should have entered the minds of persons at a distance. Here we have no patronage, no interference of any kind from the State or the Civil Courts. We possess the most perfect freedom as to spiritual jurisdiction. In vain, however, do we state these things. It is yet to be hoped, however, that better counsels will prevail. In such a place as Kingston, there might be two congregations, but in many other places, where the Presbyterians are thinly settled, divisions would in all likelihood put an end to the administration of Divine ordinances for many a day. Those among us who are for peace in regard to matters where there is no call to go to war, must lay our account to be condemned as enemies to Christ and His Kingdom. All this matters very little if we are enabled to preserve consciences void of offence towards God and towards man. The Synod meets here in July, and here, we are told by the newspapers, the battle must be fought. The meaning of which is just this ;—the poor Presbyterian Church of Canada, her ministers and people, who have not a single reason for separation, but every reason to preserve union, must, for some days, oppose each other, and then separate, to hinder each other's work, instead of unitedly advancing the Kingdom of their common Lord. Drs. Cunningham and Burns are in the United States, but neither of them has yet paid us a visit. We must, however, be prepared to receive them. Receive them kindly we shall some of us assuredly do, but as we are yet in a Church in connection with the Established Church of Scotland,—to be honest, we must be determined to act consistently with that title in our intercourse with them. I have never agitated about the controversies at home, but have just continued to preach the Gospel and attend to my pastoral work."

To the intention he thus expressed, he firmly adhered. He would gladly have welcomed the Free Church Deputation to his pulpit to preach the Gospel in brotherly kindness. But he could not admit the controversial discussion of the questions at issue, until they had first been regularly disposed of by the highest Court of the Church.

On June 11th, 1844, he writes again :—

"The Deputation has been here, and the consequences are just what was anticipated. It is easy to excite strife among brethren ;—far easier than to unite them in the bonds of love. A storm has been raised which may not soon be laid. Wounds have been inflicted upon a Church ill able to bear them, and which half a century may not heal. Alas! these bitter contentions are wounding things. They try us sorely, and few there are that, passing through them, escaped unhurt. I desire deeply to acknowledge the kindness of Mr. ——, in desiring to forward my being brought to Scotland, though unknown to him. Were I ever to return to labour in the Church of Scotland, I would strive for her purity. I should contend for much that many of the Free Church ministers sought, but I should, so far as I see matters, contend for them *within* the Church. There would be many difficulties, however, in the way of my returning. The very attachment of my people at this time would render it far more difficult to leave them than at any former time; and again, I would not go into any parish unless I were particularly called by the people, and were to receive a cordial welcome. I love my people here, and could not easily part with them, and, even if I were positively called, I do not say that I would return home. Let us seek in this, as in all other matters, to look to God, and He will direct our steps. I am much concerned about the college. The Professors are excellent and able men, but what can such an institution do under difficulties which would have been next to insurmountable, had the Presbyterian body continued united, but which are rendered much more formidable by our wretched divisions ?"

The division of the Presbyterian Church in Canada was felt by those most deeply concerned for its welfare to be the greatest evil that could befall it. It is unnecessary to enter into the circumstances connected with that sad event permitted by God in judgment, but also for correction. By many it was lightly regarded, and even thought to be a good thing by some who quoted the words of our Lord,—

"I come not to send peace on earth, but rather division;" as if they conveyed a sanction for divisions, whereas they were spoken of those who should oppose the Gospel wherever it was preached, causing divisions even among families; as our Lord foretold. The seed of the serpent is ever persecuting the seed of the woman, but the rending asunder a Church of Christ, which is one body, is a very awful thing. The worst fears of those who longed for peace were realised by the disruption which took place at the following Synod; and the Presbyterian Church of Canada, which had been formed under such hopeful auspices, was broken asunder. Brethren in the ministry who were united, and worked heart and hand with each other, were separated, and thrown into a position of almost antagonism. Many congregations who had been united under one minister, who was quite sufficient for their needs, were now divided under two ministers, who, with their people, were subjected to the strong temptation of competition and unholy rivalry, while the poor and thinly settled localities of the country were left spiritually destitute;— evils sad enough, yet only symptomatic of deeper evil,— the quenching of the love of Christ in the Church. Had this not been so, a better way would have been found than separation. There may be activity, there may be zeal, there may be numbers in the Church; but, if the love of Christ is not there, the real union of the Head to the Body, and of the members to one another, the *life*, is wanting, for the love of Christ is the true and only life of the Church. "As the Father hath loved me, so have I loved you; continue ye in my love." "This is my commandment, that ye love one another as I have loved you. By this shall all men know that ye are my disciples, if ye have love one to another."

Nor is it only the division in this particular case that is so deplorable. The many divisions in the Church of Christ—the many isolated sections into which it is broken— are a stumbling block to the unconverted at home, and a hindrance to missionary efforts among the heathen. It can hardly indeed be hoped that the Church, in its present divided state, can be greatly blessed in her missions to the heathen, or that she can manifest Christ as the Light of the World, while she is so far from accomplishing the design of her Lord, the Head of His Church, whose prayer is,—and that prayer shall yet be accomplished,—" that they all may be *one*, as Thou, Father, art in me, and I in Thee ;—that they also may be one in us, *that the world may believe that Thou hast sent me.*"

The meeting of Synod at which the Disruption was accomplished took place at Kingston in July, 1844. Had the separation not been hurried on at a time of great agitation and excitement, it might, in all probability, never have taken place. Had the office-bearers and members of the Church delayed, in the spirit of love, another year, for calm and prayerful consideration, the Lord would have given them light in those things in which they were "otherwise minded," and they would have remained united. Brother would not have been rudely severed from brother ; pastors would not have been severed from their flocks, nor families rent asunder,—nor the unseemly spectacle presented to the world, of a Church holding one doctrine, government and form of worship, torn into two parts working against each other, in a spirit of rivalry and emulation. There can be no doubt that the deputation sent out by the Free Church of Scotland, and the influence of the secular press, by agitating and exciting the people, had much to do with accelerating the movement. In the beginning of that Meeting of Synod, two much esteemed ministers, who afterwards threw all their energies into the interests of the Free Church, were asked whether they thought a disruption would take place. " Oh, no !" said one, " the minority will exonerate their conscience by entering their dissent, as John Willison did." " But," said the other, if there is not a disruption of the *ministers*, I fear there will be one of the *people;* for the pressure from without is great at present."

Here, for the sake of truth, must be noticed a mistaken statement occurring in a letter by a minister of the Canada Presbyterian Church, which appears in the Life of the late Dr. Burns. The passage is as follows: " When the Synod met at Kingston before our disruption, I remember going with Dr. Burns to the Governor to ascertain his mind in regard to the Government grant, should our Church carry out our resolution to follow the example of the Free Church at home. He told us that if we were unanimous, all our privileges would be confirmed, but that if any remained, *they* could claim them. We told this to the Synod, but some of them were afraid of losing *the loaves and the fishes.* Now there was no need of disruption in this country; all we had to do was to drop the words—' in connexion with the Church of Scotland.' "

In regard to this statement it may be observed in the first place, that Dr. Burns was *not* present at that meeting of Synod at all, having left Canada some time before. But the late Chief Justice McLean, who was present as an elder, explained the position of the Presbyterian Church in Canada, and her right to enjoy her temporal privileges as a branch of the Church of Scotland in Canada. It was not however the words—" *In connexion with* "—that caused the difficulty. Many in the Synod would have been willing to drop that designation, though they did not wish that their doing so at that time should have the effect of condemning and repudiating the Mother Church. A resolution to drop the designation, while at the same time continuing on terms of " fraternal intercourse not only with the parent Church, but with all other Presbyterian Churches holding the same standards," was moved by the Rev. Robert McGill and seconded by the Rev. John Clugston, but it was, unfortunately, not adopted by the Synod. Those, again, who seceded at that time, considered " that the designation—' *In connexion with the*

Church of Scotland,' after having been distinctly explained, *might without any compromise of principle be retained,* as it did not, of itself, irrespective of the actings of the Synod, imply connexion with the Established Church, or limit their freedom of action in regard to her." * What they *did* seek was, to repudiate that Church, to separate from her communion and withdraw from the fraternal intercourse they had hitherto held with her. This the majority of the Synod would not do, nor would their people have done so, even had it been done by all the ministers there assembled, who would thus have left many of their people, over whom they had been ordained, to be scattered as sheep without a shepherd.

It is worthy of remark, that, while the withdrawal of the Synod from connexion and communion with the Church of Scotland was strongly urged by the seceding party, there was, however, with them, *no opposition in principle* to receiving the endowment. It was even urged by one who was most urgent for separation, that the words *" in connexion"* might be preserved *in order to save the endowment,*—provided that the Synod separated from the communion of the Established Church of Scotland.

Mr. Machar, it is hardly necessary to say, felt the disruption intensely. It grieved him to the heart to be separated from his brethren in the ministry, with whom he had hitherto walked in love and in unity of spirit and purpose, and to see some of his flock, over whom he had carefully and lovingly watched, alienated from him, and even brought to believe that he was an enemy to the kingdom and the glory of Christ. He was also much grieved on account of Queen's College, in originating which the Church had been so united, and which they had established with so much labour and care. *Now,* the energies of some who had been active in founding this

---

* Quoted from resolution of the Rev. Dr. Bayne, in the minutes of the Synod of 1844.

much needed Institution were to be employed on a rival one, a state of things in which, as it seemed, neither could prosper.

But the disruption was now a *fait accompli*, and it was useless to waste time in unavailing regrets over what had become a thing of the past. Feeling this, Mr. Machar, now that the excitement of the struggle was over, found a solace for the painful feelings it had occasioned, in applying himself quietly and faithfully to the pastoral work which he had always loved. He now felt himself more truly than ever the pastor of his flock, to whom it seemed to form a fresh bond of union, that they had, as it were, chosen him a second time, manifesting their confidence in him by remaining under his ministry, while others had left it. It was remarkable that, with one single exception, all the trustees, elders, and Sabbath-school teachers of his congregation had continued staunchly to adhere to their old church and their beloved pastor.

CHAPTER VIII.

1844-1849.

PRINCIPALSHIP OF QUEEN'S COLLEGE. THIRD VISIT TO SCOTLAND.

NOT long after the disruption, the Rev. W. C. Burns, son of Mr. Machar's old friend, the minister of Dun, afterwards the ardently pious and devoted missionary to China, visited Kingston, where he remained for some time, earnestly preaching as an evangelist in and around Kingston. He came as identified with no Church, but simply as a Christian evangelist, endeavouring to win souls to Christ. He visited the manse, where he was gladly welcomed, and the Scripture readings and Christian intercourse which he held with its inmates were especially delightful to them at a time when the bitterness of division was still deeply felt. Mr. Machar was at that time visiting pastorally in the country, and Mr. Burns requested him to intimate to the people at the week-day service held by him, the time of his own coming to preach in that locality, so ready was his Catholic spirit to co-operate with a brother in Christ.

Mr. Machar's people had recently built for him a sub-stantial and commodious manse, close to the church, which, as it was somewhat of the old Scottish type, was sometimes playfully styled by visitors a "model manse." Into this he had recently removed, and he much enjoyed planning and laying out the grounds—a most congenial recreation to him at all times.

In the autumn of 1845, the Church of Scotland sent a deputation to Canada and the Lower Provinces, consisting of Dr. Simpson, of Kirknewton ; Dr. John Macleod, of Morven ; and his nephew, the late lamented Dr. Norman Macleod. The latter came simply as the minister of Dalkeith, his name being then scarcely known in Canada, but all who came in contact with him were fascinated by his genial, loving, philanthropic spirit, and large-hearted catholicity. On the Sunday of the deputation's visit, he gave a most impressive and practical address to parents and children, in St. Andrew's Church. He earnestly exhorted them to fulfil the parental duty of Christian home training. He warned them against trusting to the Sabbath-school alone for the religious education of their children, since upon *them* was laid this responsibility, and unless the Scriptural instruction received at the Sunday-school were impressed on the heart and conscience in its application to the duties and relations of daily life, it would, in all probability, remain a dead letter. This impressive and useful exhortation was long remembered by the parents who heard it.

Never had Mr. Machar been more happy in his pastoral work than he was after the troublous and agitated disruption times had passed away; and never had there been more life and spirituality in his preaching. It was at this time that he commenced a most useful congregational work, carried on by the ladies of his congregation, the history of which will be more fully narrated in succeeding pages. New and unforeseen trials were, however, at hand. The Principal of Queen's College, the Rev. Dr. Liddell, now minister of Lochmaben, Scotland, and the Rev. Professor Campbell, now Principal of the University of Aberdeen, to both of whom the disruption in Canada had been a very severe trial, resigned their professorships in Queen's College, and returned to Scotland. Their departure was felt to be a heavy blow to the college. Both were gentlemen of high principle and profound scholarly attainments ; and thoroughly acquainted with collegiate training, as well as fully equipped for the duties of their respective posts. They had deeply felt the difficulties and discouragements they had had to contend with from the very low state of education in Canada, but they had been willing to devote themselves to the work of moulding and training the minds of the youth committed to them, and of raising education to a much higher standard, thus diffusing its elevating influence throughout Canada. But they now felt their position so much changed, and the difficulties of doing the good they desired to do so much increased by the division of the Church into two rival sects, that they determined to return to their native country. The Rev. Dr. Williamson, Professor of Mathematics and Natural Philosophy, was the only professor now left to the college, to which he has adhered through all the phases of its history, a much esteemed and beloved professor, devoted to the interests of the University. The loss of Principal Liddell and Professor Campbell was deeply felt by the whole Synod, but by none so much as by Mr. Machar, who had walked side by side with them in unbroken friendship and harmony, and who entertained for them a high esteem and a warm personal regard.

In 1846, the Synod took into their most serious consideration the question—what was to be done with Queen's College? They could not think of letting it go down, needed as it was, both for the sake of higher education in the country, and, in a special manner, for the ministry of the Church. Mr. Machar was solicited to become Principal and Professor of Hebrew, for the present, at least ; and the Rev. George Romanes, then minister of Smith's Falls, and a man of vigorous ability and thorough scholarship, was appointed Classical Professor. As a provisional arrangement, also, for the theological department, Dr. Urquhart, of Cornwall, and Dr. George, of Scarboro', were requested to become Professors of Theology, dividing the session between their respective courses of lectures. These arrangements took effect during the following session.

Mr. Machar thus wrote to his sister in October, 1846:—

" In consequence of the greatly lamented resignation of my friend Dr. Liddell of his office of Principal of Queen's College, I have yielded to the solicitations of my brethren here, to become Principal for a time. You may wonder at this, that, having already so much to do, I should take upon myself *more*. But it was unavoidable. I was unwilling to see an Institution go down that we need so much, and after all, as I am to have colleagues in the Divinity department, and as the number of students is not great, my duties in the University will not add very greatly to my labours, and will not interfere with my pastoral duties. All I have engaged to do, at present, is to preside over the Institution, to assist in its government, and meet twice in the week with the Divinity students. I really feel overworked here, however, and at times long for rest. I have now been in the harness ever since my last visit to Scotland,—I may say without intermission, and a pause from labour has become in some measure necessary. Whether I may be able to visit Scotland next year, I cannot yet tell. I have not yet got a missionary assistant, but may perhaps succeed in getting one before Spring, and if so, I may be over, if it please God to spare me. We must look to God more in all our affairs. He is our true portion in the land of the living, and I am more and more convinced, however toilsome and distracting I feel my labours here, His blessing and presence alone can make us happy anywhere. Oh ! let us seek to realise this, for, without our *realising* it, our religion is really nothing. My chaplaincy to the 71st Regiment, which has just terminated, (that regiment having just been removed from Kingston,) has been pleasant, though it added a good deal to my labours. I have always much comfort among my own people, with whom I dwell in peace, and that makes up for many other disquiets. Our Missionary Association scheme prospers, and all my people are anxious to get me an assistant, as they are all persuaded that I have more to do than one man ought to have."

To his friend, Mr. Alexander, Brechin, he writes :—

" Life, with me, has been a scene of unceasing toil, since we parted in 1839. I do not murmur at this, for I am never happier than when engaged in the duties of the ministry. It has been our hap to light upon strange times in the Church. We have seen sad things in our day, for surely it is one of the saddest things to see brother warring with brother, and destroying one another's work for differences of opinion in matters which do not practically affect them. With you, there might have been cause for division, but, *here* division took place without a cause. This is now beginning to be felt, but the conviction comes too late. Wounds may be inflicted in a moment which many long years may not heal. It has been my lot, in these sad times, to stand upon one of the high places of the field, and I, of course, have had my share of attack, but I am thankful that I have been enabled to hold on the even tenor of my way. It was not difficult, indeed, for me to do so, in my circumstances. Having an attached people, who (with some exceptions, however,) approved of the course I adopted, and thus being peaceful within, it was comparatively easy to remain undiscomposed by the storm without. Many of my brethren have had far more trial than I have had. I enjoy, on the whole, good health, but the work I have is far too much for me, and this winter it is somewhat increased, from my having had to accept the Principalship of Queen's College, for the time, in consequence of the much regretted resignation of Dr. Liddell."

In the summer of 1847 occurred a severe visitation of typhus fever, called " ship fever " from its origination, in many cases, in the overcrowded ships that brought over Irish emigrants ; too often, only to die in a strange land. This epidemic caused serious additions to Mr. Machar's labours, as well as called him frequently into scenes of deadly infection from which he never shrank. He thus wrote to his sister in July, 1847 :—

" Though very busy just now, I sit down to write you a few lines this morning, knowing that you will be anxious about us in this time of prevailing sickness. There has been an immense emigration from Ireland this summer. Poor people, many of them will never be settled here ! Hundreds of them,

—I might say thousands,—have been cut off by that malignant fever, either brought from Ireland, or generated in the over-crowded vessels which have brought them over. At every town on the St. Lawrence, on their way to Upper Canada, multitudes of them are lying sick. Here, at present, the number of the sick in the hospitals, in tents and in private dwellings, is between three and four hundred, and there have been sometimes upwards of twenty deaths in one day. The fever is now spreading among the people of the town also. Hundreds who were in attendance upon the sick have died of the fever. Several Roman Catholic priests and ministers of the Church of England have died in Lower Canada, and a Roman Catholic priest died here yesterday. By the mercy of God, we have all been preserved in health hitherto, although I have been much occupied in attending upon the sick and the dying ; but the events around us are very solemn, and say to us 'Be ye also ready.'"

On December 10th of the same year, he wrote again to the same :—

" By a newspaper I sent you, you will see that my people, after waiting long, and seeing no prospect of a missionary assistant from Scotland, have given an invitation to Mr. John B. Mowat, a son of one of my elders, who is now in Edinburgh. Should he accept the invitation, as I think it likely he will, I shall much rejoice, as I have a very high opinion of him personally, and also of his qualifications, and am persuaded that he will prove an efficient as well as an acceptable labourer in the Lord's vineyard."

He had, in March, 1847, received from the University of Glasgow the degree of Doctor of Divinity. The diploma, at the request of his congregation, was first transmitted to them, and by them presented to their pastor, in a very gratifying manner, together with an affectionate address and a handsome pulpit gown. The honour was quite unexpected, as it was unsolicited. He refers to his feelings in regard to it in a letter written to his friend Mr. Alexander, October 10th, 1847 :—

" I cannot tell you, my dear friend, how happy it makes me to receive your account of Mrs. A. I feel assured that should

95

she and I be spared to meet once more on earth, we shall be able to hold fellowship together in the same spirit of kindness which ever marked our past intercourse, and that when we revert to the sad rendings asunder that have taken place, we shall be disposed, instead of blaming one another with bitterness, to mourn over the iniquities on all hands, which provoked these heavy judgments, and to pray that He who can bring order out of confusion, and good out of evil, would, after showing us all our sins, and humbling us under them, graciously heal our breaches and restore peace to our Zion. You refer to the grief and trouble I must have had in these evil days. Of this I have no doubt had my share, but in the midst of it all I have had my consolations too, and I am thankful that I have never suffered my spirit to be embittered by what was sufficiently trying to flesh and blood.

" Last year when Dr. Liddell resigned the principalship of Queen's College, I accepted the office temporarily, and this year again, at the urgent request of the trustees, I have consented to continue ;—with much reluctance, however. Much as my brother-professors do to lighten my labours,—and they do all in their power for me,—the college takes from me more time than I can spare for it ;—not that my people have ever made this remark in reference to my engagements in the college, for I am very happy with them. Indeed few ministers, perhaps, have been happier with a people than I have been with mine. Still I wish to give myself wholly to the pastoral work, and whenever I can, rightly, lay down the principalship, it will be a great deliverance.

" You congratulate me on receiving the degree of D.D. I thank you for your congratulations, but if I refer to this event at all, it is to say that you heard of it long before I did—that I never dreamed of receiving such a distinction, and that my feelings on hearing of it were rather of depression than of elevation, remembering that there were others more entitled than I to such an honour. Yet there was one thing in regard to it which was pleasing ; it was, that as it was bestowed upon me utterly without my knowledge or privity,—so was the announcement of it conveyed to me in the most gratifying way, and in terms specially referring to my labours as a pastor of Christ."

In May, 1848, Dr. Machar was enabled to fulfil a desire which he had for some time cherished, of revisiting Scotland;—the state of his health, after so many years of arduous and unremitting labour, very much requiring rest and change. His place was supplied, until the arrival of his assistant, by his friend, Professor Williamson.

On the voyage, he experienced a very trying disappointment. Upon the arrival of the steamer at Halifax, he went ashore, and having been misinformed by one of the officers that the vessel would remain in port for *three* hours, returned,—at the end of *two*, to find, to his great disappointment, the vessel steaming out of the harbour. In a letter from Halifax, he thus writes about what seemed at the time to be a great misfortune.

"I thought, as I had so much time, I would call upon the two ministers, Messrs. Martin and Scott, which I did; and at the end of two hours I was returning slowly to the vessel, in company with Mr. Scott, when casting my eye towards the harbour, I saw the *Acadia* already under weigh for England, and found that I was left behind. You know I am not easily turned from an object;—I was, for the moment, overwhelmnd, but I immediately proceeded to do everything which was possible, in the circumstances, with the view of reaching the vessel. I got signals from the citadel, I procured a boat, &c., but all was in vain. I was too late! This, you will easily conceive, was a severe trial;—left a stranger, without money, separated from my luggage,—having no hope, as I thought at first, of reaching Scotland in time for the meeting of the Assembly, &c., &c. My disappointment and anxiety threw me for a day or two into a high fever, and Friday night, and Saturday the 6th were days I shall not easily forget. On Sabbath, however, I was better, and in the great mercy of our Heavenly Father, I am again restored to my ordinary state of health. I am staying at the house of the Rev. Mr. Scott, and nothing could exceed the kindness of both Mr. and Mrs. Scott to the stranger. If ever the Lord shall bring me back to my habitation, we must be kinder to strangers than we have yet been!

"This thing was evidently in the Providence of Him who ruleth over all; for wise and gracious reasons, I can have no doubt, I was not permitted to go in the *Acadia*. This is the view of the matter which I know you will take, and instead

H   97

of being cast down, will praise the Lord for His so mercifully restoring me. I have at times, during these days past, been very sorrowful, and have felt very lonely. Oh, that all may humble me, and bring me nearer to God. Mr. and Mrs. Scott have sympathised with me, and cheered me much. They think there is every probability of my reaching Scotland during the time of the Assembly. This day, Friday, we are looking out for the steam packet *America*, and as she is a fast sailing boat, it is thought she may reach Liverpool in eight or nine days, and so I may be in time. The people here have striven much to cheer me, but oh how slowly these seven days have passed !"

This hope was fulfilled. He had a short and prosperous voyage to Liverpool,—meeting the *Acadia* in the Mersey, and reclaiming his baggage in time to prevent its being carried out again to America, and reaching Edinburgh in good time for his special business at the Assembly ;—but after passing through a very solemn and striking experience, which he thus describes :

" Last night it was just four weeks since we parted. Oh, it has been an eventful four weeks to me ! May I learn wisdom from its events ! It is altogether of the preserving mercy of the Lord, who held unworthy me in the hollow of His hand in the hour of danger, that I am now writing to you :—that I am yet in the land of the living. On Tuesday, I left Liverpool for Edinburgh by the train. It happened that I joined the express train from London at Preston. This train reaches Edinburgh at half-past nine or ten o'clock. We were within twenty miles of Edinburgh when the engine-car to which the carriages for passengers were attached, ran off the rails, and by its force, buried itself deep in mossy ground. We were running, I understand, upwards of fifty miles an hour. In a moment, I found myself lying in the carriage amidst broken glass and yawning spars, for the strongly-built carriage was rent asunder at various places. The shock was over and I rose from under the other passengers, and, escaping through one of the rents caused by the concussion, stood upon the ground uninjured, except that my left shoulder was slightly hurt. Three men belonging to the engine were killed ; — two of them instantaneously, and the third died soon afterwards, but, wonderful to relate, all the passengers escaped comparatively unhurt, with the exception of a French lady whose face was a good deal scratched and disfigured.

"I reached Edinburgh on Tuesday, in time to visit the Assembly, and it so happened that I entered the House at the very time they were proceeding to the Colonial Church matters. I was asked to say something in regard to Canada, and although my nerves were a good deal shattered, and I was otherwise much fatigued, I thought it better at once to proceed. I spoke under considerable disadvantage, but perhaps I should not have done much better, had I had more time. I was obliged to be very short, as the reports of the Committee and of the Deputation were very long. I am attending the meetings of the Assembly, but I cannot say I have much pleasure in being there, and I long to get down to Forfarshire, and to try a thorough rest and care to recruit my health and strength."

Shortly afterwards, he wrote to his children, expressing the delight he felt in the beauty of Scotland in the "leafy month of June:"

"Hitherto our Heavenly Father has been very gracious to me,—bringing me in safety over the sea, and preserving me in the hour of danger on land. Scotland is at this time very beautiful. The fields are clothed in the brightest green—the grass is every where bestrewn with the mountain daisy, and the lark sings beautifully in the mornings. . . . . You have read about Mary, Queen of Scots. I dined on Saturday at the Palace of Holyrood, in a room where probably she once sat, and just opposite to me there was a picture of her grandson, Charles I., who was almost as unfortunate as herself. . . . When she embarked in the vessel that was to carry her away from France, it is said that she kept her eye upon it, and apostrophising it, called it '*belle France*,' (i. e. beautiful France,) in a way that overcame her attendants to tears. I remember leaving Scotland once with similar feelings. But, happiness depends not upon place and outward circumstances, —happiness depends on the state of our minds, and if we are only the children of God, delighting in Him, He will make us happy, no matter where we may be. Think of this, and let it be your great concern to be the children of God. Think, too, that, however, beautiful and sweet to us our country *here* may

99

be, there is a *better* country, even a Heavenly, to which we must be looking."

During this visit to Scotland, Dr. Machar did his utmost to excite interest in the Church in Canada, and in the college. He had opportunities of addressing the Students' Missionary Societies of several of the Universities, in whom was awakened a warm interest in the students attending Queen's College. They proved their active interest by the bursaries or scholarships, which, during the years between 1848 and 1854, were regularly sent from Edinburgh and St. Andrew's, while one or more were also contributed from Aberdeen. The first one from Edinburgh had been sent in the spring of 1848, and in the letter of the Treasurer of the Association to Dr. Machar, he says :—" The Association has been led to give this bursary, mainly on the recommendation of the Rev. Dr. Fowler, of Ratho,* who formed one of the Deputation from the Church of Scotland, and gave a most heart-stirring account of what he had seen and heard,—as a means of showing their interest in the spiritual welfare of their countrymen in America, and in the hope that the students of your college might be encouraged by receiving this small token of friendship from the students attending the University of Edinburgh." This kind Christian interest so manifested by the students of the Scottish Universities, was very gratifying, not only to the students but to the professors of the college, and it should be remembered that the Church in Canada does indeed owe a deep debt of gratitude to the Church of Scotland for her continued liberality,— during many years,—both to the College and the Church.

During Dr. Machar's short sojourn in Scotland, he met with what occasioned him some mental trial, in being strongly advised to move in regard to a prospect of a set

---

* Dr. Fowler was a member of a second deputation from the Church of Scotland, which visited Canada some years after the first one.

tlement in a Scottish parish. His always strong attachment to his native land had often led to inextinguishable
longings to return eventually to Scotland as other ministers in Canada had done; and the state of his health,
which was far from strong, and which suffered from the
continual strain on his mind, had led him sometimes to
think with a wistful regret of the quiet and retirement of a
country parish in Scotland. But these feelings were always
counteracted by his attachment to his own congregation,
his sincere desire to walk in whatever path the Lord should
mark out for him, and his jealousy over himself, lest he
should be actuated by mere self-pleasing. In reference to
this, he wrote, during this visit to Scotland :

"Desires I thought I had got above have been more than
once revived. But I have, on the whole, been able to conquer
them, and the longer I stay here, the stronger is my longing
to come back, and labour—if it be the Lord's will to give me
strength, among my beloved flock at Kingston.——I shall
have temptation, but it is my earnest prayer to be preserved
from error. Our happiness, I am persuaded, does not depend
upon place, nor on any other part of our external circumstances. I am far from being in that state in which I sincerely
desire to be, but of this I am most fully persuaded, that I
could have true peace only in the consciousness of being a
follower of Christ;—that I was doing His will, and not seeking
to please myself. I think I am now escaping from an incubus
that has been pressing upon me for weeks. I think only of
being soon back, and of resuming my labours, if it be the Lord's
will, among the flock committed to my charge. Oh how
dangerous it is to let *feeling* carry us away in any matter !"

He spent a month or two of beneficial rest very plea-
santly, among his relatives and friends in Scotland. His
voyage and respite from labour had already done him
much good. "My friends here," he writes, "must have
expected to see me bearing the marks of age,*—Says

---

* Dr. Guthrie at this time expressed to Dr. Machar his regret that
there should have been a disruption in Canada, for which, he remarked, "there was no need."

Thomas Guthrie to me—'How young you look! You seem to me to have grown years younger than when I saw you last.' "

Blended, however, with his enjoyment of old home-scenes, there was always in his letters a strong undertone of regret and yearning for the dear home and family from which he was so far separated, and for the time of his return to them and to the flock, whose concerns, general and individual, were seldom absent from his mind.

In July he visited London, and on board the steamer in which he proceeded thither from Scotland, he wrote in July 6th, 1848:

" To-morrow afternoon, if all is well, we shall be in the great city. I intend to sojourn in London for ten or twelve days. As to France, in the terrible condition of affairs just now, I shall leave it unvisited. It may seem somewhat strange to go to such a place as London, in the hope of being able to study in it; especially during a short visit like mine ; and yet I am promising myself some time to read and think, when there. I need this much, for notwithstanding many good resolutions, I have not been able to spend my time so profitably as I could desire. One and another visit has to be made, and anything like protracted study and contemplation has been impossible."

From London he wrote pleasant letters to his children, describing in simple language the various objects of interest which he saw, particularly those of historical interest, such as the Tower of London, with its national associations, and especially his having seen, in Hyde Park, the Queen and Prince Albert, driving with some of their children.

From London he wrote, later in July :

" The time of my being at the Assembly was my only opportunity for doing anything in the way of awakening attention towards Canada. I feel I can do but little to get ministers, the preachers and students being at this time scattered all over the country. I shall soon be in Edinburgh and Glasgow, and shall make all the enquiries I can there. What a wondrous place this is! But I am so heartily tired of its incessant bustle and din,—that I shall be glad to get out of it to go down to Woolwich, to see Colonel Anderson. I am tired of wandering and long to be at home. It is one of the heaviest parts of the curse of the evil spirit that he has no home, but goes to and fro in the earth! I hold to my purpose of sailing from Liverpool by the packet of the 26th of next month. There is much that is beautiful and interesting in England and Scotland, but I feel that my abode is in Canada. The Lord does all things well. How gracious has he been to us!"

His return voyage was safely accomplished, and with a thankful and happy heart, he found himself once more in his beloved home, and amidst his warmly attached flock, who rejoiced to welcome him back in renewed health and strength. With fresh zest, also, he returned to the pastoral work that he loved best, as well as to the more arduous labours in connection with the college, which still, for a time, devolved upon him.

In a letter written to a friend in October, 1848, after referring to his short passage out, of twelve-and-a-half days, —presenting such a contrast to his first voyage of *fifty-two* days—he says:

"Yesterday we had our Communion;—a beautiful day— and a large number of communicants. I am likely to have much to do this winter, as my brethren have insisted on my retaining my connexion with Queen's College,—but I am very happy with my people; happy too, in my relations with the professors,—while this session, our students have considerably increased, and these circumstances are strengthening to me; and most of all, I have for my assistant and missionary, an excellent young man, Mr. J. B. Mowat."

To another friend he wrote, in January, 1850:.

"I am very busy this winter,—having along with my pastoral duties, the government of the college, besides teaching Hebrew and Divinity. I am assisted, however, by an excellent missionary assistant, who divides the pulpit duties with me, and is otherwise very laborious in visiting and catechising. It is a great pleasure to me to have good and peaceable, as well as eminently qualified colleagues as professors in the college ; and to find that the institution is more prosperous than in former years. This year we have about thirty students."

The interests of the college were always very near his heart, and his anxiety for its welfare was intense, not only during the period of his more active connexion with it, as Principal and Professor, but also when he was connected with it only as a trustee. In this latter capacity, as one of the few resident trustees, he had, at all times, a full share of the care and responsibility of its management, which, as the institution passed through several seasons of great perplexity and trial, was often felt by him to be a heavy burden.

CHAPTER IX.

PASTORAL AND PERSONAL TRAITS.

DR. MACHAR'S zeal and faithfulness as a pastor have been already referred to. He never ceased to feel most deeply the sacredness and responsibility of the ministerial office, and the value of the souls committed to his charge; and as he had been entrusted by God with the precious message of the gospel, it was his earnest aim to speak, not as pleasing man but God, who trieth the hearts. He was well aware of the tendency of the natural heart which says, "Prophesy not unto us right things—speak unto us smooth things;" but while he highly valued the favour of his people, and keenly felt the pain of being in any case deprived of it, he was much more anxious for the welfare of their souls, although he felt strongly the truth of the Apostle's regretful saying, that the "more he loved them, the less would he often be loved."

His pulpit expositions of Scripture were earnest, clear and practical. Though often tenderly and affectionately impressive, he avoided such appeals to the feelings as were calculated to excite merely sentimental emotions. He ever exhibited the gospel of Christ in its freeness and fulness, and its adaptation to the deep needs of the souls of fallen men. And while the constraining love of Christ, and the riches and freeness of His grace to perishing sinners, were the themes on which he most delighted to dwell, such doctrinal statements were always accompanied by earnest appeals to loving obedience and godly living as followers of Christ, "who suffered for us, leaving us an example that we should follow His steps." It was his custom also frequently to compare Scripture with Scripture, and to elucidate the meaning of a passage in the best way, by placing it in the light of another.

In his preparation for the pulpit he was faithful and conscientious, never leaving it to be hurried through at the last moment, but spending upon it as much time as he could spare from more active duties, and only regretting that he was often prevented, by the multiplicity of calls upon his attention, from devoting to it as much time as he would have wished. His prayers as well as his sermons were carefully considered beforehand, for he would not carelessly or inconsiderately engage in any portion of the service of the sanctuary. His tastes, as well as his early habits, were studious, and it was his regret that the distractions and interruptions of a city minister's life left him so little leisure to carry on private study, and so much curtailed the time that he loved to spend in what he was wont to call his "pleasant library," surrounded by the familiar faces of the large and valuable collection of books that covered the walls.

But the duties of his pastoral office were not among the interruptions that he regretted. They were his delight, and none of them would he ever omit on any account whatever. From the commencement of his ministry, it had been his habit to visit pastorally from house to house, and he continued to do so during the whole course of his ministry, as long and as far as his strength permitted. During a number of years he generally devoted two evenings in the week to pastoral visitation, going over the whole congregation in the course of the year; but in the later years of his ministry he was unable to accomplish this, though he continued to the last to visit as much and as often as he was able. He attached great importance to family visitation. It enabled him to know more personally and individually his people, their difficulties, trials and temptations,—to sympathise with them in their troubles and anxieties,—to adapt his counsel and instructions to their need; while it also gave him the opportunity of ascertaining how the children were trained and taught at home. He was most earnest in his exhortations to parents to instruct their children in the knowledge of the Scriptures, and to accustom them early to attend church and the Sabbath-school—while at the same time he warned them to beware of casting the responsibility of the religious instruction of their children upon the latter. The Sabbath-school he regarded only as intended to aid and co-operate with parents in bringing up their children for the Lord, and felt that it would do evil rather than good, should it lead parents to devolve upon it the duty committed by God to *them*,—the religious training of their children. He deeply felt and earnestly inculcated the importance of this training, both by precept and example, and especially of the loving instructions of a mother, impressed upon the mind and heart, even in infancy. He strongly believed in the influences of the early home-life, as moulding the character of the individual, and in the influence of the way in which the youth of a people are trained individually, as forming the national character. The duty and the benefit of daily family worship he always earnestly impressed upon his people, never failing to inculcate it upon parents when administering the ordinance of baptism. On his return from his evening visitations, fatigued though he often was, the cheerfulness of his face and voice would betoken the encouragement he had felt in visiting families who were prepared for his visit, and met him with a cordial welcome, where the children had been carefully instructed, and were consequently delighted to answer his questions. He would mention each child by name, dwelling especially on the *youngest*, who had learned a few verses of a psalm or hymn to repeat to him. But he was proportionately depressed on returning from visiting families where the children were ignorant, indifferent, and neglected by careless parents. These he heartily pitied, and often invited them to come next day to the manse to receive a little book and a few words of kindly exhortation. He always carried with him on his visit a supply of attractive little books for presentation to the children, and in days when children's books were not so abundant as they are now, these were much appreciated.

In the Sabbath-school connected with his own church Dr. Machar always took a deep interest, regularly opening it himself, and visiting each class individually that he might enquire of the teacher regarding its progress, and notice any absentees. He also addressed the children from time to time, and encouraged them in missionary efforts, in which he was, for a number of years efficiently aided by his friend John . Paton, Esq., so long Secretary of the Juvenile Mission of the church. It was always Dr. Machar's practice to prescribe, himself, carefully selected lessons for his Sabbath-school, and in the last years of his ministry he had prepared and printed, for the use of the children, a double series of a "Scheme of Lessons," which was pronounced by Principal Leitch, long connected with the supervision of Sabbath-schools in Scotland, to be a "Model Scheme," and which has, since his death, still been in use in the Sabbath-school of St. Andrew's Church.

His country visitations he reserved for the winter, when good sleighing made travelling over rough roads easier. He had eight or ten stations, or centres of visitation, some of them eleven or twelve miles distant from town; and his custom was, first to visit separately each family in that vicinity, catechising the children and exhorting the parents; and then to meet all the families in the School-house of the district, where he addressed them collectively. Even the sleighing did not always make the rough circuitous roads very pleasant for travelling, and he occasionally met with such accidents as being upset by a stump and thrown over a bank into the ditch below. On one intensely cold day, when his sexton was driving him, a traveller who met them called out, "I guess, friend, your nose is frozen!" The driver's nose was indeed quite white, and was only saved by a timely application of snow by the kind stranger. Notwithstanding his frequent exposure, however, Dr. Machar never met with any injury from his country visits, with the exception of an occasional cold, owing to the sudden change from the heated rooms within to the bitter cold without. These remote stations are not now, however, destitute of spiritual privileges as they were then—the people having churches of their own, and enjoying the ministrations of the gospel in their own neighbourhoods.

One of the annual reports given in by the session to the Presbytery, dating from July, 1840, to July, 1841, shows the numerical condition of the congregation at that time. The statistics are as follows :—Average attendance at church, 800; number of communicants, 350; infants baptized, 77; marriages, 30; families visited, 400; amounting, perhaps, to 1,600 souls. In another annual report to the Presbytery, dating from July, 1844, to 1845, the year following the disruption, the numbers are as follows :—Average attendance at church, 650; number of communicants, 300; infants baptized, 61; marriages, 20; families visited, from 250 to 270, amounting, perhaps, to from 1,200 to 1,400 souls. The formation of a second congregation after the disruption was felt by Dr. Machar as, physically, a relief, his charge having grown to a size considerably exceeding the limits of his individual strength to overtake its needs.

In regard to baptism, he often felt much difficulty, believing as he did, with the Westminster Catechism, that it should be administered only to "the children of those who are members of the visible Church." But when applied to by the ignorant and careless to administer this ordinance to their children, he endeavoured to make it a means of drawing the parents to look to the Saviour for themselves, and of instructing those who were ignorant from the neglect of others, for whom he always felt much sympathy and compassion.

His faithfulness in visiting the sick and dying, not shrinking, even in seasons of sweeping and contagious epidemics, from penetrating to the wretched and miserable abodes where infection has its strongest hold, has already been adverted to. In those early years, when the immigration was extensive—bringing during several seasons, fatal epidemics in its train, and when the preparations to meet it were very inadequate, there were frequently more burdens in connexion with it laid on the one Presbyterian minister in Kingston, than properly belonged to his office. At a time when there was no hospital in Kingston, he was sometimes obliged to go out in the heat of a noon-day sun in July, in search of an asylum for a sick and destitute stranger, not resting until he had found one. On one occasion a young man, an emigrant from Scotland, was brought to Dr. Machar, in the delirium of a brain fever. As no suitable place could be found for him, and as the doctor said he could not recover unless he received great care, the invalid was received into the Manse and taken care of for several weeks, until he was perfectly recovered, and able to proceed to his destination.

The short addresses which he usually gave at funerals were regarded by many who listened to them as peculiarly impressive and touching, his quick sympathies enabling him to enter strongly into the feelings of the mourners, and to speak from a deep sense of the solemnity of the occasion. It need hardly be said that his consolatory visits in time of trial were keenly appreciated, and sorely missed by many, when the time came that they must cease.

He always took a warm interest in missionary objects, abroad as well as at home. Once a month, from a very early period of his ministry, it was his custom to hold, instead of the usual weekly meeting "for prayer and the reading of the Scriptures," a missionary meeting, "for the communication of missionary intelligence," and although such intelligence was then far from being so abundant as it is now, he was able to make these meetings both interesting and profitable, a collection being made at its close for some foreign missionary object. Missionaries from abroad, when they visited Kingston, were always warmly welcomed to his pulpit and received his cordial sympathy.

Dr. Machar's disposition was naturally cheerful, genial and sociable, and he possessed a strong vein of playful humour, which, when not overborne by the pressure of ministerial or public cares and responsibilities, often enlivened his familiar conversation, though it never degenerated into anything like *levity*. He enjoyed social intercourse, especially *Christian* intercourse, though it was a pleasure which he had to deny himself in a great measure, owing to the constant occupation of his time with duties which he felt he could not neglect. The frequent occasions when some of his brethren in the ministry were with him at the Manse, were seasons of pleasant relaxation, and often profitable interchange of thought and feeling ; and it was always a source of regret to him when, on such occasions, the more external matters of Church organization crowded out more spiritual and important subjects of converse. He often wished that he were able to have more frequent personal intercourse with his brother clergymen of other denominations, in Kingston, but from his enfeebled health, chiefly caused by frequent attacks of erysipelas in the head, which very much affected his nerves, his ordinary avocations were often interrupted, so that an accumulation of work had to be overtaken on his recovery.

But while keenly alive to simple social pleasures, he never countenanced, either by example or influence, amusements or social meetings which partook so much of the spirit of this world as to be, he believed, unfit for those who have undertaken to follow Christ, and to "love not the world." In regard to such things his opinion was well known, and he was faithful in expressing it when the occasion arose. He strongly disapproved, also, of meetings in connexion with churches, which mingle amusement with sacred things, and introduce the spirit of the world into the Church. He felt that they fostered a taste which must grow with its gratification, and that they must increase the natural love of excitement, and the equally-natural distaste for spiritual things, especially in the young, to whom he believed that they must be most injurious.

He was naturally careful and accurate in everything he did, and on this account found it impossible to *hurry* through any part of his work. He used to say that he could not do nearly as much work in the same time as some were able to do, and that it was only by attention to method, to doing everything in its own time, and never leaving till to-morrow what should be done to-day, that he was able to accomplish what was given him to do. Whatever he undertook he was most faithful and conscientious in performing, whether it was the duties connected with his own congregation or the more public ones imposed upon him by the Church, or in connection with the college. None were ever forgotten, neglected or carelessly performed, and every appointment was punctually kept, unless some very unusual and sufficient cause occurred to prevent it. He was as conscientious, also, in his judgments, as in the performance of active duty, earnestly seeking, at all times, to keep his mind from being unduly biassed by feeling or prejudice—a characteristic that made his opinion especially valued in Church courts, and in the other boards of management with which he was connected.

Always strictly upright, accurate, just and honest, both in speech and in transactions, and careful to obey the Apostolic injunction to "owe no man anything," he was liberal in giving, either to public or private objects, and he was always ready to help those in need of his aid, especially in cases for which he felt particular sympathy, where extreme poverty was, with difficulty, hidden under a decent and respectable exterior. "The Lord has been very kind to us," he would say, when directing some such gift, "and we should not forget to be kind to others."

Neat and orderly in all his arrangements, he was at all times scrupulously so in regard to his outward attire, both from a right self-respect and a due regard to the sacredness of the ministerial office. He believed that a Christian minister should always be, both in mind and in externals, a *Christian gentleman*. In counselling another in this particular, he wrote :—

"I have said to you, *dress well*—besides this, cultivate a courteous, graceful and kind manner. My father died when I was a student, and my funds were not always abundant, but, somehow, I managed to purchase many useful books, and, besides, to dress well."

His temperament was a highly sensitive one, acutely sensible of either mental or physical pain, and after an attack of erysipelas, he was sometimes liable to a nervous irritability which was a source of great trial to him. But when, under its influence, he had spoken impatiently or unkindly to any one, it made him most unhappy, and he could not rest till he had acknowledged or made compensation to the individual. On one occasion, when he particularly desired to be left to study without interruption, a stout able-bodied vagrant arrived and insisted on seeing "the minister." When the latter came down and saw the vigorous applicant for charity, he was rather impatient, and dismissed him summarily. A little while after, he came down saying he could not study. He had sent away the man without enquiring particularly into his case, and, after all, he *might* be a person requiring relief—a stranger too, so he must go and try to find him again. He went, accordingly, but, much to his regret, he could not find the dismissed beggar. Kind and genial, as he habitually was to all,—to the poor and helpless, to children, and to dumb animals, he was always especially kind.

Except on his occasional visits to Scotland, he rarely left home, unless when called by duty to attend meetings of Synod and Presbytery. During the last few years of his life he yearly spent a week or two at springs or at the sea-side, his delicate health absolutely requiring such a change ; but he always rejoiced in being at home again. His chief recreation was in superintending the care of the garden and grounds of the manse, which it gave him much pleasure to lay out and cultivate. It was a great enjoyment to him to see the trees and plants growing and flourishing from year to year, on a spot which his care and taste had converted from a piece of bare common into shady and beautiful grounds, both the beauty and extent of which have, however, by recent alterations, been considerably impaired. His always delicate health suffered much from the extreme cold of a Canadian winter, and he greatly rejoiced in the opening buds of spring. The first white narcissus—one of his favourite flowers—which opened its snowy petals and golden crown, was always brought in with delight to grace his study-table, and refresh him with its perfume ; and he, every spring, enjoyed anew the beauty and appropriateness of the sacred words— "Lo ! the winter is past, the rain is over and gone ; the flowers appear on the earth ; the time of the singing of birds is come, and the vines with the tender grape give a good smell.".

He had great delight in genuine poetry, both sacred and secular, and some of his own early attempts at writing it still exist. Especially he loved the poetry of his native Scotland, with its simple and touching ballads, breathing to him so many cherished early associations ; and he was wont to say that "there was nothing for pith and pathos like Scottish poetry."

Iuto his happy domestic life it is not necessary to enter, farther than to say that he was a devotedly affectionate husband and father, never so happy as when at *home.* Always watchful for the welfare of his children, he found time even amidst his numerous avocations, to take frequent personal supervision of their studies, and even at times to become their preceptor himself, and a more careful and accurate one they could not have had. Of the tenor of his counsels to them the following passage taken from a letter addressed to one of them when absent from home, will give an example :—

" I feel the time long that you are still to be away from us. But God, who has hitherto preserved us, may again bring us together. We will follow you with our earnest prayers, morning by morning, and evening by evening. You will remember us, too, at a throne of grace, praying God to be with you in the way that you go. You will, necessarily, see much more of the evil of the world, than you have seen before. May you see it, only to abhor it, and if ever temptation to join in it overtake you, look to God for strength to enable you to overcome it. Intellectually, you will enjoy many precious opportunities for improvement—morally, you may do so too. Oh, seek to improve them ! Read your Bible regularly,—keep the Sabbath,—think of us daily, and of what our hearts would wish you to be,—pray for the blessing of God. Do this, and all will be well."

In regard to temporal matters he was ever unselfish and unworldly. His expenses were always growing, and in later years, from increased prices and the many claims on a city minister's resources, much exceeded his stipend, but of this he never asked any increase. Having some private income, he was not entirely dependent upon what he received from his people, and this being the case, he was more anxious to see the congregation freed from the debt which had long lain heavily upon it, and which before his death he had the satisfaction of seeing entirely liquidated, than to add to his own emolument. He was wont to say, "I shall soon need an assistant, and my people will support one for me ;" and in this expectation he was not disappointed.

CHAPTER X.

IT was in 1845 that an important undertaking was first entered upon by the ladies of St. Andrew's Association, connected with the object of procuring an assistant for their minister, and with another consideration which had long weighed heavily on Dr. Machar's mind,—the spiritual destitution of the country around Kingston. His periodical pastoral visitations among the people, his visiting the sick, and baptising the children were as much as he could possibly do ; but this was in no degree adequate to their need. Those who *could*, came long distances on the Sabbath to attend St. Andrew's Church, but those who could not seldom heard a sermon from one year's end to the other. Dr. Machar, after much thought on the subject, had formed a plan whereby an assistant missionary might be supported, and had communicated the project to several others, who warmly approved of it. The ladies of this congregation, in particular, took it up heartily, and sent the following requisition to Dr. Machar, with a hundred and three signatures attached :—" We the undersigned ladies, members of St. Andrew's Church, feeling that your many and unceasing labours in this place demand a united effort on the part of your people to afford you relief, hereby request you to call a meeting of the congregation on an early day, to take into consideration the best means of procuring a missionary for the congregation, and to aid you in ministering to the spiritual wants of the population in the town and neighbourhood."

By the trustees and others, this was felt to be a very serious undertaking. The congregation lay under a heavy debt, which, after the disruption, fell more heavily on those who remained, as those who left the church no longer held themselves accountable. With £1900 of debt on church and manse still unpaid, it was thought by some that it would be preposterous to begin any new scheme, until that liability had been fully liquidated. But the faith and energy of the ladies prevailed. " Fear not," said one, " to enter upon a work for God ; He will prosper it, and the money for the debt will come in all the more on that account." This hope was strikingly realised, as the hope which springs from faith in God for the support of a good work ever will be. The scheme was at once put into execution. The ladies, who had formed themselves into a Missionary Association, carried out the work most energetically, collecting monthly from house to house for the support of the missionary and the liquidation of the debt, simultaneously. The people most willingly contributed for this Christian object, which prospered beyond their most sanguine expectations, and at a general meeting of the congregation on April 10th, 1846, Dr. Machar was authorized by the congregation to write to Dr. Norman McLeod, requesting him to look out for a young preacher of piety and zeal, who would be fitted for the work of missionary assistant. Owing to the difficulty of obtaining ministers at that time, both in Scotland and in Canada, the application was unsuccessful, and after vainly looking to Scotland for some time, Dr. Machar, with the cordial consent of thr congregation invited Mr. J. B. Mowat, now the Rev. Prof. Mowat, of Queen's College, who was at that time completing his theological studies in Edinburgh, to undertake the work. He, however, was not able to enter upon his duties until July, 1848. Both minister and congregation had cause to be thankful for the selection to which they had been guided. The appointment was a most happy one, and gave unanimous satisfaction, both as regarded the preaching and the abundant and devoted pastoral labours of the missionary. It was a cause of much regret that his stay with them was of such short duration, as he accepted a call to be minister of Niagara before he had completed the second year of his labours in Kingston.

The Missionary Association, however, continued steadily to carry on its work, and the Rev. Duncan Morrison, now of Owen Sound, was appointed in May, 1850, as the second missionary, and continued to labour devotedly and with much acceptance until December, 1851, when he accepted a call to Beckwith. In his Report of July, 1850, he mentions ten stations which he regularly visited, either on Sundays or week days, preaching at the more distant and important ones on the Sabbath, and holding week day services at those nearer to the city. Two of his stations were at Pittsburg, one in Glenburnie, one at Bally-na-hinch, and one on Wolfe Island. He also visited from house to house, reporting one hundred and thirty families belonging to the church, outside the limits of Kingston, while, every week, new ones were discovered. The Rev. Kenneth Maclennan, now of Peterboro', Ont., was his successor, and was also a most faithful and laborious Missionary, and an acceptable preacher. He continued the regular preaching and visitations, devoting much of his time and attention to instructing and catechising the young ; and reported a hundred and ninety families, who all, in some degree, received the benefit of his services. On his removal to the charge of Dundas, the late Rev. John Campbell, of Nottawasaga, took his place. He followed in the steps of his predecessors in faithfulness, diligence and devotedness, but he was called away from the mission field at the end of six months, to the charge in which he laboured up to the time of his death, eleven years after. The regret felt at his death, and the affection still cherished for his memory by his late congregation, is particularly referred to in Mr. Croil's* published Historical and Statistical Report of the Church in 1866.

The extreme scarcity of ministers in proportion to the number of vacant charges, made it impossible, after Mr Campbell's resignation, to procure a licensed preacher as his successor. The monthly collections were therefore suspended, and the Professors of Queen's College undertook to visit and preach in the most distant and important stations, as often as they were able. The Ladies Missionary Association, however, could not remain idle while they still saw so much spiritual destitution unprovided for. Wolfe Island, from its isolated situation had been particularly destitute of religious privileges, and its people, often without regular Sabbath services, had little to remind them of the sacredness of the Lord's Day, which was, in a great measure, devoted to visiting, amusement, or idleness. Many of the young were growing up in intellectual and spiritual ignorance, and consequently were sunk in a state of religious apathy. The Presbyterians brought their children for baptism to Dr. Machar, to whom they looked as their pastor, and he, knowing their circumstances, felt a very deep interest in them; visiting them as often as he was able, and comforting or counselling them in troubles or difficulties. His missionary assistants had also

---

* Contemporaneously with Mr. Campbell, laboured in the mission field of Stirling, also in the Presbytery of Kingston, another promising Queen's College student, who was also called away in the midst of his usefulness,—the Rev. John Lindsay, whose untiring zeal and devotion to his Master's cause made his early death a severe loss to the Church. By his zealous missionary labours, Stirling was prepared for being, as it now is, a settled charge, with neat church and manse, under the ministry of the Rev. Mr. Buchan.

visited the island occasionally, in common with other stations; and their ministrations had awakened, among the people, an earnest desire for the preaching of the Gospel. At Dr. Machar's suggestion, the Ladies Missionary Association most willingly agreed to send a student of Divinity, as catechist, to Wolfe Island during the summer months, whom they were to support, not by collections, but by the work of their own hands disposed of quietly at small monthly sales. The first labourer chosen for this important mission was the Rev. Donald Ross, now of Dundee, then a student of Queen's College, whose zealous and devoted labours in the mission field gave the Association reason for thankfulness for the Divine guidance that had led them to appoint him. Entering upon his work with his whole heart and energy, he soon won the hearts of the people, who gladly attended his ministrations. As they had no suitable place for holding Divine service, he felt strongly the necessity of having a church, and energetically set about having one built. The people, feeling that he was disinterested in seeking their good, gave their hearty co-operation, and when Mr. Ross, after labouring there for two seasons, left the island amid the general regret of the people, who were warmly attached to him, he had the happiness of seeing a commodious Presbyterian Church in course of erection; the funds for it being provided almost solely by the willing contributions of the people, assisted only by the Ladies' Missionary Association in Kingston. The Rev. David Camelon, now minister of London, Ontario, who became successor to Mr. Ross, was also a zealous and earnest evangelist, preaching, visiting and superintending the Sabbath-schools, and having about four hundred and eighty souls attending his ministrations. He visited a hundred and twenty families, some of whom consisted of Episcopalians as well as Presbyterians, as there was then no minister of the Church of England on the island, and the missionaries were gladly received by all, although there still existed, to a considerable extent, a discouraging religious apathy, which the Holy Spirit alone could quicken into life.

Mr. Darrach, also a student, who was subsequently minister of St. Matthew's Church, Montreal, where he died in 1865, deeply regretted, was the next missionary to Wolfe Island, where he followed the example of his predecessors, earnestly seeking to proclaim the Gospel of Christ. Subsequently the Rev. George Porteous, now of Matilda, was settled as minister on the island, where he remained, for twelve years, the much esteemed pastor, and during whose ministry was erected a neat and comfortable manse. The charge is at present vacant, a catechist, however, labouring among the people ; but the Ladies' Association have had the pleasure of seeing their efforts much blessed and the Lord's work prospering through their instrumentality. In an address sent in to the Association by the trustees of St. Andrew's Church, Wolfe Island, after gratefully expressing their sense of the moral and spiritual good which the Society had been "the instrument in the hand of God of accomplishing," they added :—
" The change produced in the moral and spiritual sentiments of the people since your missionary came amongst us, is much greater than we ever expected to witness. Thanks be to God, the open desecration of the Sabbath is fast disappearing, and a higher tone of morality, accompanied by a general disposition to attend the means of grace, is strikingly manifest ; so that we now begin to thank God and take courage, hoping that there are yet greater spiritual blessings in store for this people."

The charge of Pittsburg is another which has grown up through the efforts and fostering care of the Kingston Ladies' Association, having for a number of years had a neat church and manse and settled minister of its own. Nor did the Association, while continuing their efforts for the support of the Gospel in the destitute places around them, neglect the debt which lay upon their own congregation, and which was liquidated by their instrumentality also, in collecting and working for it until it was wholly paid off. The blessing of the Lord indeed rested visibly on their quiet, unobtrusive and cheerfully self-denying labours for the spiritual welfare of others. They were blessed in the harmony of spirit in which they worked with each other and with their pastor, whose heart was gladdened by witnessing their labour of love. They were blessed, also, in the missionaries given them for the work, whose faithful labours prepared the way for the permanent ministrations of the Gospel in these formerly destitute localities. It is but just that this slight tribute should be paid to the memory of an Association which was the means of accomplishing a much needed and useful work, and so many of whose most active members are no longer connected with the congregation, some having removed to other places, while a number have gone home to their rest and their everlasting reward.

CHAPTER XI.

RESIGNATION OF PRINCIPALSHIP—LABOURS IN CON-
NEXION WITH THE COLLEGE—FOURTH VISIT
TO SCOTLAND.

IN the summer of 1849 Canada, was again
visited by Asiatic cholera. In Kingston it
brought death and distress into many a happy
home, and Dr. Machar had again the sorrow
of seeing several of his most attached people removed
by a stroke. In the course of this and the following
year also occurred other changes which affected him
deeply. One of these was the removal to another
sphere of labour of his assistant, the Rev. J. B.
Mowat, to which reference has already been made.
In the spring of 1850 the late Dr. Romanes resigned
his Professorship in Queen's College and left Canada,
—an event which Dr. Machar felt as both a personal
and a public loss, for Professor Romanes was not only
an excellent teacher and thorough classical scholar,
possessing high powers of mind and a correct literary taste, but also a man of kind and amiable disposition,
and a steady and faithful friend. Dr. Machar and he had
held much harmonious fraternal intercourse, seeking
unitedly the good of the University, for which they
laboured in fellowship.

To another trial, which he experienced in 1850, in the

death of an old tried friend, which he felt as a personal bereavement, Dr. Machar alludes in the following extract from a letter written towards the close of 1850:

"You will see that I am still in the Principalship of the University. I had resigned, and it was only at the earnest request of the Trustees that I consented to remain in the office for some time longer. It adds a good deal to my cares, and although my people have given me a missionary, who relieves me much, I have still too much to do. I have often felt wearied and over-worked of late. One thing is pleasing, the Institution has been steadily progressing. How our years are passing on, and soon we shall reach the end of ou journey! But let us not mourn because of this, if only we are striving, through the grace given us, to finish it well. I have lately lost a highly valued and beloved friend who assisted me in many things, especially in regard to the College. He was a good man, and while I deeply feel my own loss in his removal, I cannot but rejoice in his unspeakable gain."

This friend was the late Alexander Pringle, long well-known in Kingston as a man of sterling integrity and of most truly disinterested and unselfish benevolence. To his house, Dr. Machar had been warmly welcomed as a guest on his first arrival in Kingston, and he had been, ever since, one of his most faithfully attached friends. The Church and the College were objects most dear to his heart, and to them he sacrificed much of his time and his personal comforts. To promote the welfare of the latter, he gave up the quiet of his own home, and resided in the College-building for several of the last years of his life, in order to take the supervision of the domestic life of the students, who then boarded within the College walls; and many of those who were then students there, will remember with what almost paternal interest he watched over them, seeking to promote their moral and spiritual, as well as their physical welfare.

In reference to "difficulties and trials," which Dr. Machar was feeling at this time, he wrote:—

"The worst thing about a trial is, to be impatient under it, or unthankful for it, for trials are best for us of all the things our Heavenly Father sends us. I most firmly *believe* this ; however, I may fail in being consistent with the creed. *We* know not what is good. Most truly do you say, ' God knows how to dispose of all His creatures,' and something more is true, too, that He will make ' all things work together for the good of them that love Him'—not *some* things only, but *all* things, and among them the very things that, in our haste, we may speak of as having no good in them.—

> " His children thus most dear to Him,
> Their Heavenly Father trains,
> Through all the hard experience led,
> Of sorrow and of pains.' "

While deeply regretting the loss of some of his valued colleagues in the University, Dr. Machar was thankful that his friend, Dr. Williamson, still continued to fill his important post, and that Dr. Urquhart and Dr. George, both old and valued friends as well as colleagues, still co-operated with him in the theological department. Both have now followed him to the better country ; but they have left an ever enduring testimony in the hearts and memories of all who were privileged to hear their valuable lectures, and to receive their wise instruction and fatherly counsels. The blank caused by the removal of Professor Romanes was filled by the appointment of the Rev. Malcolm Smith, then minister of Galt, and an accomplished scholar, to the classical chair.

In 1853, Dr. Machar resigned the office of Principal. Some circumstances attending his resignation were to him exceedingly painful, but into these it is unnecessary and inexpedient to enter. Although he at that time resigned decidedly and finally, yet as another Principal had not been appointed, he was induced, out of consideration for the good of the College, to perform the office of Principal during the following session of 1853–54. He had never desired or expected to retain the office permanently, and had accepted it, and continued to hold it, solely on account of the exigencies of the University, and only until a permanent Principal should be secured, who should be able to devote his whole time and energies to the government and the work of the College, with a salary adequate to his position and office—Dr. Machar accepting only a nominal salary, from which he defrayed the expenses arising out of his College work, and presented contributions to the Bursary-Fund. But he would never have resigned the pastoral office for such an appointment. His delight was in his ministerial labours, and it was often a source of deep regret to him, that the many interruptions and distractions to which he was exposed prevented him from giving his whole mind and time to the work he loved best. On this account he often regretted his connexion with the College, although, having, from a sense of duty, undertaken the important office he held, he was most faithful and conscientious in performing all its functions, and he had the great satisfaction of seeing the institution prospering under his care. His teaching was marked by the thoroughness and accuracy characteristic of him in all that he did,—and in his public addresses to the students at the opening and close of the sessions, he ever sought to impress them with a sense of their responsibility in preparing for the serious duties of life—to inculcate faithfulness, diligence, accuracy in study, and, above all, to urge upon them the inexpressible importance of cultivating personal religion and making it their chief aim to love and serve Christ. He took a deep interest in the students personally, often conversing with them privately at his house, encouraging, admonishing, or counselling them as occasion arose, and not a few have, in after days, gratefully recalled the kindness they received from him. Many who were students during the period of his connexion with the College, are now able, zealous and useful ministers of the gospel in Canada, while others are useful and distinguished in secular professions ; as indeed in all the different stages of the history of the University, there have been students whose after life has reflected honour upon their *Alma Mater*, and done ample credit to the ability and faithfulness of their Professors, not only in their several professions, but also in the various British Universities to which some of them have gone.

An extract may here be given from an address of the late lamented Principal Leitch,—delivered on the day of the first meeting of Convocation after Dr. Machar's death, when a fine portrait of him had just been placed in the Convocation Hall,—which bears a just tribute to his memory :—

" I cannot but allude to that event which has deprived this University of one of its most distinguished ornaments, and Canada of one of its most revered and honoured clergymen. Though, for many years past, Dr. Machar has acted only on the Board of Trustees, the College at a former time enjoyed the benefit of his prelections and superintendance. The Institution, in its early history, had many difficulties to contend with, and it is in a great measure due to his wisdom and devoted zeal that it has surmounted them, and now presents a complete University equipment in all the faculties of Arts, Theology, Law and Medicine. While his congregation have resolved to erect a costly monument where his ashes lie, you have deemed it a fitting tribute to his memory to grace the walls of the College with the portrait which has been to-day hung up in the hall. Long may his influence as a felt presence live in this College ! His scholarly tastes, practical wisdom and genial disposition gained for him the respect and love of many. While others mourn for him as a friend, we, as a University, cannot but deplore his loss as a public benefactor."

These words gain an additional and touching interest from the circumstance that the speaker, only a year later, was also taken home to his rest,—his premature death being a heavy blow to the University, to which his services, during his short tenure of office, had already been so useful, and of which his distinguished talents promised to make him so bright an ornament. An admirable portrait of *him*, also, graces the Convocation Hall, side by side with that of the friend whose loss he then deplored.

Although Dr. Machar ceased to be Principal of the University, he never, during the remainder of his life, ceased to take a warm interest in its welfare, rejoicing in its prosperity, and grieving, as for a personal calamity, when the dark clouds of adversity overshadowed its course. Owing to changes which occurred in the professorial staff in 1853 ;—Dr. George being appointed to the chair of Moral Philosophy and Logic,—in which his glowing prelections will long be remembered by those who were privileged to be his students, and Professor Smith being transferred to the Hebrew chair,—while Professor Weir succeeded him in the classical department ;—Dr. Machar was relieved from the labours of the Hebrew Professorship. He was now able once more to devote himself to the work of the pastorate ; but his strength had been a good deal overstrained, and he often felt himself impedes in the labours which he loved, by the weariness and exhaustion from which he frequently suffered.

The summer of 1854, was marked by another visitation of cholera,—the last occasion on which that scourge has been permitted to extend its ravages to Canada ; and again several beloved and attached members of his congregation were suddenly removed. In the autumn of that year he wrote to a friend in Scotland :

" It is long since I heard *from* you, but I have the pleasure of hearing often *of* you, and of your being able to continue your useful labours ; and while God gives you health and strength I would not counsel you to resign them, for I believe it would not be for your comfort. I have a large congregation, and I am happy to say an increasing one, and I have now no assistant. I feel a good deal oppressed at times, yet I am thoroughly persuaded that I am better as I am than I would be if I were to be set free from the exertions of the ministry. My life is one of toil, but I would not have it otherwise. I have little news that would be interesting to you. The progress of " reform," is at last to deprive us of the Clergy Reserves. Let them go ! We need a spiritual revival, and had we this, though I am not an admirer of Voluntaryism, I believe that energies would be awâkened within the Church which would do more and better for us than any mere temporal support coming to us from without.

" So we have war, alas ! a bloody, and it may be, a protracted war. We got the authentic report of the Alma victory a few days ago. Our people have proved themselves brave, eminently so ; but if glory has been gained for our nation, dear, dear has been the price ! We are in a state of expectation now,—hoping to hear that Sebastopol has really fallen."

The secularisation of the Clergy Reserves, above referred to, took place the same year, 1854. A *commutation* was made with ministers then having claims on the Fund, which placed at the credit of sixty-eight ministers of the Church of Scotland in Canada, the sum of £127,448. This sum these ministers, of whom, of course, Dr. Machar was one, agreed to invest in a common Fund, for supplementing the stipends of ministers of the church in all times to come, and this formed the nucleus of what has been called the Home Mission Fund. These ministers also agreed to deprive themselves of a portion of the yearly allowance they had hitherto received, in order that eleven other ministers, whose claims had *not* been admitted by the Government, might benefit by the Fund, to the extent of, at least, £100 per annum.

In 1855, Professor Smith left for Europe with his amiable young wife, who was threatened with pulmonary consumption, and ordered to a warmer climate for the ensuing winter. He was therefore absent during the session of 1855–56, and died suddenly at Gareloch-head in the autumn of 1857, a few months after the death of his wife, and just before his intended return to Canada,—leaving the Hebrew chair vacant. In the absence of a regular professor during the sessions of 1855–56 and 1856–57, Dr. Machar again, at the request of the trustees, undertook the duties of the chair in the emergency. As he declined to receive any pecuniary remuneration for his services, the trustees of the college, in recognition of them, presented him with a beautiful copy, in eight large folio volumes, of Walton's Polyglott Bible with the, " Lexicon Castelli." This rare and costly gift, which was procured from London, he always valued as his choicest literary treasure.*

As has been already mentioned, the late Rev. John Campbell, of Nottawasaga, was the last of the four excellent regular assistants, whose aid Dr. Machar had successively enjoyed since 1848. From the scarcity of ministers at the time, and the number of congregations requiring them, it was vain to look for another assistant in Canada, and equally difficult to succeed in procuring one from Scotland, so that Dr. Machar, though receiving occasional pulpit assistance from the professors and others, remained without the regular assistance which he so much needed, until the autumn of 1860. Although feeling this want very much, as regarded himself and his work in Kingston, it was still a great satisfaction to him to feel that during these years, Wolfe Island, the most destitute of the country stations in the neighbourhood, was enjoying the ministrations of the zealous and estimable catechists already mentioned.

In September 1858, he thus wrote to one of the friends in Scotland, to whom he had vainly applied to endeavour to procure for him a suitable assistant :

" I feel how much it would contribute to my comfort, if I had only the right kind of man for an assistant ; yet, on the other hand, I cannot be blind to the painful things that might arise from getting a person of a different stamp. Indeed, so much have I, at times, shrunk from what might have been the result of my negotiations, that when they have failed, I have thought ;—' Well, if I have not got an assistant, I have at least escaped the misery of being tried with a bad one,'—and

---

* The Hebrew Chair was at this time permanently supplied by the appointment of the Rev. J. B. Mowat, who still continues to fill it.

I have felt that if I could only go forth, and shake myself as at other times, I should be strongly inclined to go on yet for a time as I am, or at least with such aid as I might obtain here. As I have told you, my congregation are anxious to give me an assistant, and are disposed to make him comfortable, and I look upon the situation as an inviting one for an earnest, good man, and as sure to lead to promotion in the Canadian Church, my previous assistants having all of them been called to fill important charges. I may hear from you again, soon, and if only you can hear of a man of missionary spirit whose preaching is average, and who would be likely to prove an acceptable fellow-labourer, you will not fail to let me know."

No one, however, could at that time be heard of, willing to come, and in all respects suitable, so that, until 1861, he was obliged to dispense with other assistance than what the professors and others, temporarily near him, were able to afford him. In a letter to his sister he says :

" I am generally very busy, but I shonld not be so busy as to prevent me from writing to you. As you remind me, it cannot be long that you will be here to receive a letter from me.* We know not *how* long ; our times are in God's hands. There let us be willing to leave them, as well as all else that concerns us. I have often a strong yearning to revisit Scotland ; too strong, at times for my comfort. A voyage across is not now very formidable, and we may yet meet in the flesh. I often think of you—indeed I may say, I never forget you. I remember very early things, when you carried me across the stream to the wood, to get to which was the summit of all my wishes. My dear sister, the attachments of time will surely be revived in eternity ! Only let us be united in Christ, and though divided for a while, there will be a re-union in which there will be no regrets, no fears. This is Saturday, and I have no assistant. The whole duty is too much for me. I hope yet to get a permanent assistant ; you will easily see that this is a matter which causes me some anxiety."

Early in the year 1860, Dr. Machar received from his people a most gratifying evidence of their affectionate

---

* This sister, considerably his senior, survived and still survives him.

regard and appreciation of his labours, in the presentation of a very beautiful silver tea-service and salver,—designed, as the inscription testified, "as a token of their sincere respect, and an expression of their heartfelt gratitude for his unwearied and faithful ministerial services among them, during the long period of thirty-two years." Costly as the gift was in itself, it was valued far more for the love which prompted it than for its intrinsic value. It was accompanied by an affectionate address, and the meeting at which the presentation took place was one of the pleasantest which can occur between a pastor and his people.

In March, 1860, occurred one of the severest trials of a long pastorate, that of witnessing the death of an old and tried member of his congregation. In this case it was the last survivor but one of the nine elders who had welcomed their minister among them on his first arrival, John Mowat, Esq. Strongly attached to the church of his fathers, the rending asunder of which, at the Disruption, was a great grief to him, he had been an active member of St. Andrew's congregation from the commencement of its existence, and had taken an energetic part in the organizing of the congregation and the building of the church. The College, also, was an object of deep interest to him, and he was, up to the time of his death, one of its most efficient and active trustees. He was a man of large heart and steady principle, intensely loyal and patriotic in his feelings, benevolent and kind to the needy, especially to emigrant strangers, to whom he was always ready to afford, to the utmost of his power, the best kind of assistance, that of procuring for them employment which would make them self-supporting and self-reliant. He died as he had lived, a sincere and humble Christian, leaving sons who worthily perpetuate their father's name.

The six years of incessant and arduous pastoral labour which Dr. Machar had had since the departure of his last assistant in 1853 had told very much upon his strength, which was still farther reduced by rather severe illness early in the summer of 1860. He had had for some time an earnest longing to cross the Atlantic and revisit his native country, not only for the improvement of his health, but also in order to see once more his relatives and friends; for the last time, as he thought, and as the event proved.

In the beginning of July he was able to sail for Europe, and on his arrival in Great Britain he proceeded almost directly to Germany, where was then residing his old friend Dr. Romanes, who had sent him a kind invitation to visit him. He wrote, on Aug. 8th, from Mauheim, near Frankfort on Main :—

"I suppose you will be somewhat anxious about me, while I am away on the continent. I am dwelling here with Mr. Romanes and his family. After passing through so many strange places, and seeing so few persons to speak to, it is most delightful to be once more with this family. I cannot now enlarge upon the many interesting things and places I have seen in my travels. Notwithstanding the hurry and excitement incident to such rapid travelling as mine must necessarily be, home is oftener in my thoughts than anything else, and I long to be back again with you and the flock committed to my keeping. I hope all is going on well in the congregation, and that the pulpit is regularly supplied. Give my kindest regards to the elders and to Mr. Paton, who, I know, will neglect nothing. Tell Mr. Paton to remember me most affectionately to the children at the Sabbath-school, and to assure them that I often think of them. He can tell them that the churches here are not like our plain churches in America, but are full of ornaments, images and pictures. But religion consists not in these things, but only in meeting the gracious command, ' My son, my daughter, give me thine heart.'"

In his next letter, dated Aug. 14, he says :—

As the time I could give this tour on the Continent was so short, I left for Heidelberg on the Thursday, and reached that beautiful place quite in time to visit and inspect the castle, with its singularly beautiful environs. Next morning, early, I went to the University, a building in no way remarkable, but having immediately behind it St. Peter's Church, containing the simple tomb of the beautiful and learned Olympia

Morata, of whom interesting mention is made in one of Mr. McCrie's volumes. Mr. Romanes left me here, and I was again among a people whose language I did not understand. I journeyed on to Mannheim, feeling more lonely than at any time I can remember. I had some difficulty in getting forward, as all were Germans, speaking what to me was an unknown tongue. However, by signs and otherwise, I managed to get on the train for Metz—the capital of the Moselle in France; and now, being among French people, I could make myself understood.

" Metz is beautifully situated at the confluence of the Seille and the Moselle, and rising early on Saturday, I went over the interesting places in and around it, visiting, especially, its Cathedral and Museum. Leaving it on Saturday afternoon, I proceeded to Paris through a beautiful and interesting country, passing many places celebrated in history, and arriving in that great city just before midnight.

" Aug. 15.—Yesterday I went to Versailles, and through its miles of paintings, etc., wandering over its galleries till I was thoroughly tired and footsore. But I must not attempt any description of this wonderful place, so full of dazzling splendour and magnificence. On Tuesday I visited *Notre Dame*, the Madeleine, Pere-la-Chaise, the Hotel de Ville, St. Roques, etc., etc. Paris is a city of brightness and gaiety, but there is always sorrow somewhere. Coming in my round to the Seine, I passed a small house which I was told was the *Morgue*, of which you have heard. I thought I would look in, and I saw a sight which I will not soon forget. There were four bodies, all seemingly under forty, and with each, no doubt, was connected a thrilling history, unknown, it may be, to man, but all of it naked and open to the eye of Him with whom we all have to do. There is but one London, it is said ; there is also but one Paris in the world. It is a strange place, containing much that is evil, but also, much that is good. The English Church has a chapel here, and there is also a Scotch church with a regular service twice on the Sabbath.. Last Sunday Dr. Jamieson, of Glasgow, preached, and I had an opportunity of hearing two edifying' discourses. I have now only to see the Louvre, and I shall be off from Paris. To-day was the annual *Fête de l'Empereur*, and the variegated lamps and fireworks at the Tuileries were of the greatest splendour. What a wearisome thing, after all, is this travelling ! How long to be back with you all again, and how dreary seems the interval before that can be !"

From Lochmaben, August 21st, he writes :—

" I am very sure that you will be glad to find that I arrived in safety, from that fatiguing journey on the continent. I came from Paris to London on Friday last, and had an opportunity of hearing Mr. Spurgeon and seeing several friends there. After having been on the Continent, I am delighted to be back again on Scottish ground, and am thankful for the gracious Providence that watched over me in my wanderings and brought me back in safety. I came down from London yesterday, but, unfortunately, Dr. Liddell is not at home, and I shall not see him this time. I am sorry for this, but Mrs. Liddell has given me the warmest welcome, and this is pleasing and refreshing to me after my wanderings among strangers. I shall endeavour to call upon the friends you wish me to see in passing through Edinburgh, but really, it is difficult to see all the people I would like to see, or who would like to see me, and I must now try to get some rest and quiet for study and thought."

From Edinburgh he writes, August 23rd :—

" I arrived here the night before last, and yesterday and part of this day I spent at Ancrum Manse and its beautiful and romantic neighbourhood. I met with a most hospitable reception from Mr. and Mrs. Paton. Altogether, my visit was very pleasant, and gladly would I have prolonged it, had my time permitted."

From Brechin he writes, September 6th, 1860,—and after describing a visit to the house in which he was born, which was formerly quoted, he says :—

" The village is greatly changed ; it yet contains one old woman who lived there when we did. I found out the session clerk and read the record of my *baptism*, December 16th, 1794. On Sabbath I preached here in the old church. I thought I should be fatigued, but I was not so, and large as the church is, I preached in it with great ease. There are some of my old acquaintances here,—not many, however, and with them my visit is an event. You have referred to the matter of my getting an assistant here. I am getting information as I can, but I fear that such men as I could desire, and as might fill the situation well, may not be disposed to come out,—there is now so much more demand than formerly for really good preachers. I am going to day to Montrose, and afterwards to proceed to Aberdeen and Kintore, for a short visit, however, for I must be at Maulesbank on Monday, the 10th, to meet with our Principal-elect (Dr. Leitch). I long to get a few days at Maulesbank after all my weary wandering. It is very unprofitable in many points of view, but I find it impossible to avoid it. Dr. McCosh is here just now. I had a long conversation with him yesterday. He is really an able man. On the 29th of this month, if not before, I have decided to sail from Liverpool. How I long to be with you all again."

From Maulesbank, September 1860, he writes :

" Penelope wrote to Ulysses, when he had been long at that weary Trojan war. 'Write nothing back to me, but come yourself!' Well, I trust that the letter of next week will be my last to you from this side of the Atlantic, and then I will 'come myself.' Most earnestly now do I long to return to you, and to resume, if it be the will of our heavenly Father, the duties of the work committed to me ! On Thursday evening I went to Aberdeen, and next morning I called on Principal Campbell, who was much disappointed that I had not more time to spend with him. I went on to Kintore, and it was very pleasant to meet with my old friend Dr. Simpson, and to enjoy the opportunities for profitable conversation which we had during the afternoon of that day, and the forenoon of the following one. I returned to Maulesbank on the Saturday evening and have been there since."

About that time he had a severe and alarming attack of illness, probably caused by over-fatigue, from which, however, he was soon mercifully restored. The numerous journeys and rapid travelling during the short time he was at home had been too much for his strength, causing his frequent complaints of *weariness*, but he had such an earnest desire to see his old friends once more, that he went beyond his strength to accomplish this object.

His last letter from Scotland was written from Glasgow, September 27th, 1860. He says:

"I left Maulesbank on Monday for Edinburgh, and, after spending a-day-and-a-half there, came on here yesterday with the view of proceeding by rail to Liverpool, to sail thence on the 29th, in the *Africa*, for New York. I was not successful in my attempts to see the Edinburgh ministers, most of them being out of town at this season. I saw Dr. Glover, however, and had some pleasant conversation with him. I also saw General Anderson and held some pleasant converse with him about the late revivals, in the reality and extent of which he expresses great confidence. This is the week of the meeting in Glasgow for the promotion of Social Science, and as Mr. Bryce, as well as all other persons with whom I am acquainted are attending these meetings, I am not able to have any private conversation with them about Canada. I am sorry that I mentioned to you that I had been ill. In the great goodness of God, I am now restored to my usual health. I have no heart to enter upon the most unhappy events in Kingston, in regard to the * Prince's visit. They have been permitted, and doubtless for some wise purposes, though we cannot see them at present. I am anticipating a pleasant voyage, and hope to be in Kingston by October 15th or 16th, if not earlier."

* The visit of the Prince of Wales to Kingston, where, on account of difficulties with the Orangemen, he did not land.

CHAPTER XII.

1860–1863.

CLOSING YEARS.

IN October 1860, Dr. Machar arrived once more at home, after his last prolonged absence. The voyage out had not been, as he had anticipated, a pleasant one—but very tempestuous. He reached home, however, on the very day on which he had expected to arrive, and though his health and strength were not so much improved by this visit, as had been hoped, he was enabled to resume and continue his ordinary labours, although often weighed down by fatigue and weariness.

He wrote to his friend Dr. Simpson, in January 1861

"I hope it is not too late to wish you a happy New Year. May this year be to you a happy one in the best sense of the word,— a year of rich blessing from the Lord, and diligent labours in His service! You and I —my old and dear friend—have spent not a few years of the space allotted to man, and many happy returns we may not expect to have; but since our Master, in His long suffering, is still permitting us to continue at our several posts, may He give us grace to redeem what remains of our time, by a more diligent and earnest improvement of those opportunities of usefulness, with which it has pleased Him so abundantly to favour us both! The earthly tabernacle must by and by come down, and we shall have warnings from time to time. Soon after I parted from you last, I had an attack of illness

139

which shook me much,—one which, I thought, might have prevented my future usefulness. He in whose hands I am, has, however, been better to me than I feared, and I am again, —if not vigorous,—yet able to go about my ordinary work as before. At our last Synod, a retrograde step was taken in regard to the Union among Presbyterians, and perhaps it was as well, as it plainly appears that they are not yet ripe for amalgamation. As you can easily understand,—there is nothing here to keep us asunder, and let only the spirit of love be cherished towards each other, and in no long time, we may be one, forming a compact body, and able to effect far more for the progress of the Gospel and the conversion of souls, than is possible in a divided state."

As will be seen from the foregoing sentences, Dr. Machar earnestly desired the re-union of the Presbyterian Church in Canada, heartily believing that it is " a good and a pleasant thing for brethren to dwell together in unity," and at one time he hoped that, as he had seen the division he so much regretted, he might live to see the Union so much to be desired. But it was not so to be.

In October 1861, he again wrote to the same friend :

"I did not think I should have been so long in replying to your welcome letter, but during the last few months I have been without the assistance in my work, which is now so necessary to me, and each day has brought with it duties often demanding more time and exertion than I was well able to give. I am thankful that I have now the near prospect of an assistant,—a young man who will, I hope, be a comfort to me, as, in addition to powers of mind which will, I think, render him an acceptable preacher, he is, I also think, a young man of piety and of amiable dispositions. Our Autumn Communion is just passed, and I was able to go through the usual exercises with almost as little fatigue as on former occasions. It was a pleasant season to many of us, and I would hope, not an unprofitable one. I have recently lost the senior elder of my congregation, the last of my first ordained session, who met to welcome me on my first arrival in Kingston, and who were at that time a numerous staff."

It was evident, during the last years of his life, that his health and strength were gradually failing,—although he had rallying seasons of improved health, which some-times gave him for a time some of his old buoyancy and hopefulness. Often, however, he was weighed down with great languor and depression. He was still as care-ful as ever not to leave any duty undone, though his necessary work was often a burden to him now, and he would sometimes come down from his library, saying sadly, "I went up to study, and I fell asleep and have done nothing. I cannot 'go forth and shake myself as at other times!'" The experience of another faithful and laborious minister towards the close of his ministry, is here transcribed, as truly expressing what his condition and his feelings often were: "There is an unceasing mar-tyrdom,—a life of self-sacrifice under the pressure of a decaying body and the languor of a breaking mind, in the endurance of weakness and infirmities, during months and years of pain, weakness and toil, in the unvarying details of regular ministerial work!"

For a short time, in the beginning of 1862, he enjoyed better health than he had done for some time before. In his last letter to Dr. Simpson, Jan. 27, 1862, he says:—

"While many of our contemporaries, and of men much younger than you or I, from the palace downward, have been recently removed from their places, it has pleased God to spare us, notwithstanding my apprehensions of failing health of which I told you during the autumn of 1860. I have been pretty well of late. Now, however, I seldom preach more than once on the Sabbath, having at last got an assistant, an excellent young man, of good talents, pious and laborious, and withal, very amiable. He is very young, and was licensed to preach only in July last, but he promises well, and, in my private duties, is a great help to me."

The satisfaction, so long desired, of having an agree-able assistant, was thus at last given him, and in the sea-son of his greatest need ; but it was for a short time only, for, little more than a year after the date of the foregoing letter, he had entered into the eternal rest.

During the year 1862, he was frequently oppressed by

failing health and strength. Sometimes, indeed, he would rally, and have a few bright days, but his usual state was one of weakness and weariness, which, as he said, indicated "the gradual coming down of the earthly tabernacle." He attended the meeting of Synod at Toronto, in the summer of 1862, but, while there, felt far from well, and came home very much exhausted. In August, he went to his favourite sea-bathing resort, near Portland, The bracing sea-air and the bathing very much invigorated him for the time, and he enjoyed, almost as much as ever before, the rambles on the sands and in the pleasant woods.

But, on his return, there was a decided reaction, and from that time, the disease, which was to terminate in death, made steady progress. Towards the end of October he suddenly and rapidly grew much worse. He suffered from great and painful nervous excitement, and thought that death was close at hand. At this time he wrote the last letter which he was able to write to the aged sister, to whom he knew that his removal would be a heavy blow, and whom he thus endeavoured to prepare for the stroke, and to direct to the only source of consolation.

"You must not be very much grieved when you receive this, but think with great thankfulness of the mercy I have experienced in having been spared to reach my sixty-sixth year, though of a constitution far from the most vigorous. I may be mistaken about my state; those around me think I am, and you may, ere long, receive better tidings about me. But such is not my own impression. Lately all the symptoms have become much aggravated, and my nights are poor and my strength much wasted. Towards the end of August, I visited the sea-side, spending there upwards of a fortnight, and during that time, I was remarkably well, so much so as to return, with renewed strength, to the discharge of my duties. Our Communion was to be on the 19th of October, and on the previous Sabbath, the 12th, I was able to preach. During the week, however, I became considerably worse, and, on the Communion Sabbath, all I was able to do, was to take the first Table Service, and I have scarcely been out of the house since. I think I can say from the heart,—*my lips* often say it, ' The will of the Lord be done!' If it be His will to spare me yet a little longer, I would fain live to serve Him better than I have ever yet done, for oh! I have been a most unprofitable servant, and I feel now how awful a thing it is to have undertaken to be a minister! As I retrace my course, I see sin everywhere,—sin, sin! Truly, the sting of death is sin! But we may conquer. There is one that can give us the victory— Our Lord Jesus Christ. I see no comfort anywhere but in this, 'The blood of Jesus Christ cleanseth us from *all* sin!' Dear sister, this is my comfort, so far as I am able to receive it. Oh! see that it be yours, and that you and I may, ere long, meet where there is no sin and no sorrow. Now don't be much distressed about me. I have just written to you as I feel to-day. Those around me tell me I am more depressed about my condition than there is need to be. You will tell Mr. Alexander what I have written, and ask him to speak to you particularly about the atonement of Christ,—how there was a necessity for it, and how He met the necessity, so that now the chief of sinners,—the very chief, may look to Him with confidence for salvation. Is not that comfort both for you and for me? 'This is a faithful saying, and worthy of all acceptation, that Jesus Christ came into the world to save sinners, even the chief!'"

The Communion season to which he refers in the foregoing letter was the last occasion on which he was able to be out. His addresses at the table service which he conducted were particularly earnest and impressive. The notes of them which he had written out previously, in a hand tremulous from illness, were afterwards printed for the benefit of his people, as being the last words they ever heard from his lips, and are added at the close of this volume. At the close of the table services, he waited, according to his usual custom, to watch the long train of advancing and receding communicants, according to the old Scottish custom, presenting, at one moment, nearly the whole body of communicants to his view. It was the last time he looked upon his congregation, or was seen by them, and the wistful sadness with which his eye rested upon them was noticed at the time. Doubtless the presentiments he was feeling so strongly weighed upon his spirit, as well as the keen sense of the defects he saw in his ministry, which oppressed him during his illness. Perhaps, too, he was thinking of that large portion of his congregation who had passed before him into the service of the upper sanctuary. But, though neither pastor nor people knew it at the time, it was a farewell look, and a more appropriate closing scene for a long and faithful ministry could not have been devised.

The increasing coldness of the weather seemed to have an aggravating influence upon his disorder, and the painful nervous excitement from which he had suffered was succeeded by an entire prostration of the whole system, accompanied by great depression, while his condition, owing to the action of the disease upon his peculiar temperament, was one of such morbid sensitiveness and nervousness, that during his whole illness he was unable to see any one, even his most intimate friends. With the rarest exceptions, no one except his family and his medical attendant ever entered his library, where he lay during the long confinement to bed that followed a severe shock which his nervous system seemed to have received about the beginning of November.

The veil would hardly have been withdrawn from the personal experiences of his inner life during the three months of painful and protracted illness passed in such seclusion, but that it is felt right to record his dying testimony to the divine truths which he had believed and taught, and which he now personally realised with a vividness and intensity greater than he had ever before known. It is, unfortunately, too common in our day to speak slightingly of the truths of Revelation, which have been the strength and comfort of so many souls, in sickness and suffering and death, when all other stays were passing from under them—as now obsolete and unworthy the credence of an enlightened and scientific age; but he, when drawing near the unseen world, and consequently feeling the near presence of God, felt more intensely than ever that they were no "cunningly devised fables," but the very Truth of God. While he lay in a state of bodily weakness and helplessness, his mind was deeply exercised in spiritual things, and he saw, as he had never done before, the holiness of God,—the depth and spirituality and purity of the divine law, as taking cognizance of every thought and motive, and of every desire and inclination of the heart. He saw it to be truly good, and the transgression of it to be evil, not in word and action merely, but in the thoughts and imaginations,—in the secret movements of the inward spirit. He saw that God must condemn and punish sin, since He would not be the righteous God if He did not; but it was not the *punishment of sin*, but *sin itself*, that he felt to be such an evil and bitter thing. It was holiness for which he longed, meetness for heaven, and conformity to the mind of Christ. He had a deep sense of the loving-kindness of God shown to himself during all his life, and felt the keenest anguish for having been, as he counted himself, such an unprofitable servant—adopting the language of Job, "Wherefore I abhor myself and repent in dust and ashes." Lying low at the feet of Jesus, he accounted it "a faithful saying and worthy of all acceptation, that Christ came into the world to save sinners, even the chief;" and his only hope was in Him in whom there is complete redemption, and whose blood "cleanseth from all sin."

From the time he became so much worse he felt that "this sickness" was "unto death," and in the derangement of his nervous system, and the acute sensibility of every feeling, he felt intensely the pressure of the disease. But he meekly received the suffering, even in its most aggravated form, as a Father's chastening. "He will do right," he would say; "He knows what I need, and He will do right. Father, I accept Thy chastening; I know

K   ·145

it is in righteousness and love ! O preserve me from ever murmuring against it, but enable me to say from the heart, 'Not *my* will, but *thine* be done,' and let Thy loving purpose of discipline be accomplished in me !"

He would often engage in audible prayer, asking his Heavenly Father to "look down upon his suffering child," to "save him when flesh and heart fainted and failed," to be "the strength of his heart and his portion for ever." He would repeat the word "*Father*," as if the very name were his comfort and stay. He would also audibly beseech his Saviour to "cleanse him from all sin,—to leave him not, and let his faith not fail ;" and the Holy Spirit, to "be not grieved away from him, to purify and make him meet for the inheritance of light," to "enable him to see the glory of God in the face of Jesus, that he might be changed into the same image." It being remarked to him how suitable were the words of Scripture for prayer, he assented to the remark, but added—"*words* are not prayer !"

He often spoke of his congregation with warm feeling, repeatedly dwelling upon the kindness which they had always shown him. He seemed to remember every special act of kindness which he had received from any one of them, and he grieved that he had not been more faithful and devoted in his ministry,—that he had not more earnestly and solemnly warned them. He sometimes expressed his desire, if it were the will of the Lord to restore him, and to prolong his life, that he might yet more urgently warn and plead with his people. He could tell them how unfit was the mind, on a death-bed, to learn the knowledge of God, and repentance toward Him. In his short and earnest prayers for himself and his family, he prayed earnestly for his flock, that there might be a revival of true religion, a real turning to God, among them. He felt that he had spoken *the Truth* to them, though in weakness, and he desired them to remember and give good heed to what he had taught them, longing that they should all come to Christ *in earnest ;*—that they should be satisfied with nothing short of a *real* conversion of the heart to God, a personal partaking of the salvation of Christ. The young, especially, he would have exhorted to seek early conversion, and not to live in peace while alienated from God.

During the whole period of his illness he manifested the deepest humility and self-abasement toward God, and also great meekness and humility toward his fellow-men. "I am sure you forgive everyone," it was said to him, thinking of an injury which he had received, and which it had been at the time difficult for him to forget. He emphatically replied, "I have nothing to forgive."

There were a number of passages which his mind dwelt especially upon, as giving him much precious help and comfort. The fifty-third and fifty-fifth chapters of Isaiah he particularly prized. As the forgiving love of God and the cleansing from sin by the blood of Jesus were his constant theme, he delighted in the parable of the Prodigal Son and the hundred and third Psalm. He would frequently repeat the words, "He knoweth my frame." "*You* cannot understand my state or my feelings," he would say, "but *He* knoweth them." Psalms xxv., xxxv., lxxii., cxvi., cxxx., cxxxix., li., and the twenty-second paraphrase were often quoted by him as expressive of his feelings. He spoke of a verse of Psalm xciv. as most comforting: "Blessed is the man thou chastenest, O Lord, and teachest him out of thy law, that he may have rest from the days of adversity." He was wont to repeat one short text at a time, and dwell upon it. The following were among his last meditations: "Oh, Israel, thou hast destroyed thyself, but in me is thine help found ;" "A man shall be an hiding-place from the storm, and a covert from the tempest ;"—"He that believeth in me, though he were dead, yet shall he live, and he that believeth on me shall never die ;"—"I am he that liveth and was dead, and behold I live for evermore, and have the

147

keys of hell and death." The latter part of Matthew xiv. being read to him in a time of deep depression, he repeated most earnestly the words, " O thou of little faith, *wherefore didst thou doubt?*" and they seemed to revive and comfort him. He had much consolation in thinking of the verse in the Epistle of Jude, " Keep yourselves in the love of God, looking for the mercy of our Lord Jesus Christ unto eternal life ;" of which he said, on the day before his death,—"That text I laid up for *this time.*"

The thought of death was familiar to him during his whole illness, and he often calmly spoke of it, giving directions about the things he wished to have done. Some matters of business he felt it needful to arrange lest others should suffer, and as he was feeling so unfit for dealing with business affairs, they were a great burden upon his spirit until they were settled. After they had been finally arranged, he said, " I have now done with the world ;" and he never again referred to any worldly matter. " Oh, what madness it is," he would say, "to have the heart engrossed by the world as its portion, and that spiritual and eternal realities of such infinite importance should be obscured by worldly things ! Some might say that this is just the effect of weakness of mind, caused by bodily disease, but, oh, it is *not* so ; it is only a clearer view of eternal realities."

Though surrounded by his books, which he had so enjoyed and valued, he never, during his illness, seemed to care for reading or hearing any book but the Bible, except that at one time, when feeling temporarily stronger, he read a little of a favourite book—Milner's " History of the Christian Church." Passing events, too, had lost all their interest for him. It seemed that the Lord had taken him aside for a season, dealing with him closely and personally, teaching and chastening him " as a father chasteneth the son whom he loveth," and deeply impressing him with a sense of the holiness of God ; the intrinsic evil and corruption of sin ; the darkness, bondage and misery that it brings into the soul, separating it from the life of God and His blessedness. He was also deeply impressed with a sense of the ",love of God, that passeth knowledge," in the redemption of his soul by the death of His own Son ; in delivering it from the bondage of sin and Satan, and restoring it again to his favour and fellowship. The power of upholding Divine grace was remarkably manifested in him during the whole of his illness, in his entire submission of spirit, and the meekness and patience with which he bore a dispensation of suffering that pressed most heavily upon his acutely sensitive temperament. Through it all he was upheld by the abiding conviction that the suffering was sent by a Father's hand, and sent in love to purify and make him a partaker of His holiness.

Towards the close of January he became very weak, and it was evident that the end was near. When he felt his strength sinking, he said, " I am not able to pray now, but He who knows my frame will not impute this to me. I have commended my spirit to the keeping of my Saviour, and He will never leave me nor forsake me." When very weak and suffering much, he said, " My Father is working out His own purpose with me." " You believe that that purpose is love?" it was said to him. " Oh, yes," he said—" ' He that spared not His own Son, but delivered Him up to death for us all, how shall He not with Him, also, freely give us all things?' " *

It was a bitterly cold and dreary season, and he said one day, when the snow was falling thickly, " I shall go away in a cold time. Had it been summer, when everything was beautiful and the trees in leaf, I might have felt more at leaving. I wish to go away very quietly. If

---

* These and the other sayings here recorded are given, not from memory, but from memoranda taken down soon after they were spoken.

it could have been, I should have wished my funeral to be a very private one, but that cannot be."

It was always a trial to him to hear the church bell ring on the Sabbaths and the Wednesday evenings, calling his people to the house of prayer, where he could no longer meet them. The last time, during his life, that the weekly evening service was held, he said, "I shall have a trial to-night; the bell will ring for the prayer-meeting." He fell asleep, however, about the time that the bell should ring. On awaking, he remarked, "The bell has not rung." He was told that it was rung while he was asleep. "He has mercifully spared me that trial,"—he said. Owing to his extreme weakness and sensitiveness, things unimportant in themselves sometimes assumed a special importance to him, but he always felt God's dealing in them all.

On the day before his death he was suffering much from extreme weakness and dreadful spasms of pain which recurred very frequently, but his mind was remarkably clear to the last. He thought, though very weak, that life was still strong within him, and he had a great dread of what he might have to suffer in the last struggle. He would say, in allusion to Bunyan's Pilgrim's Progress— "The river is not smooth; it looks stormy." But his Heavenly Father, who knew his frame, and who would not permit one pang beyond what was needful, smoothed the last billows into a perfect calm. Conscious suffering was all over before the last indescribable "change" took place, and when death indeed came he did not know that it was death. He lay for the last hour or two apparently insensible to all external things, while his breathing became gradually weaker, with longer intervals between the respirations. All unconsciously, he was passing through the "dark river," and it seemed as if his Saviour was bearing him up, that its waters "should not come nigh unto him." The moment of departure could hardly be told, and when, at last, those beside him watched in vain for any succeeding respiration, it was less like *dying*, than simply ceasing to live this mortal life. " He was not, for God took him."

He left many besides his own family to sorrow deeply for his loss. The mournful tolling of the church bell in the early winter morning, announcing to his people that he was at length at rest, carried sorrow into many a home, and weighed down many a heart with personal grief, not for *him*,—for they knew that he had only passed from long-continued pain and weariness into the rest which is eternal gain,—but for themselves, and the loss that was theirs. Many of those who had anxiously watched the progress of his illness, though, owing to circumstances already mentioned, they had not seen him since that last Communion Sabbath, now came to take a farewell look of his remains, "sorrowing most of all that they should see his face no more."

His death took place on the 7th of February, 1863. On Wednesday, February 11th, his body was carried to the grave. His remains were carried by his elders to the church, which, solemnly draped in black, was filled with an overflowing audience ; and before the long funeral train proceeded on its way, his old and esteemed friend, Professor Williamson, read the solemnly hopeful passages from the fifteenth of 1st Corinthians and the fifth of 2nd Corinthians, and delivered the following funeral address :

" I might, my friends, content myself with reading these solemn and affecting passages of Scripture; or I might make some remarks generally suitable to an occasion like the present. I feel, however, that I can neither remain wholly silent, nor bring myself to dwell merely on such general observations as might be appropriate in another case. I must speak, however little and imperfectly, of him who is gone from among us, leaving it to him by whom, by his dying request, his funeral sermon will be preached, to offer a more fitting memorial to his worth.

" We are now about to accompany to their resting place the mortal remains of one who, although quiet and unassuming in demeanour, was indeed a Master in Israel, and whose loss is deeply felt, not only by his bereaved family, but by his congregation, by the Church, and by the community around us. An attendance like this, on the present mournful occasion, is attribute to his memory which could have been called forth only by the universal respect for his character, as that of the good pastor, friend and citizen. I might speak of him as a friend, ever judicious in his counsels, and affectionate in his sympathies;—as a member of society, peaceful and pleasant in his manner, firm, yet gentle, hospitable and kind, and taking an active and prominent part in every work of public benevolence;—as a member of the Synod of our Church from its very commencement, who, although speaking seldom, exercised, by the few and wise words which he spoke, an influence inferior to that of none other there;—and as a member of the Church of Christ, who, while strongly attached to that portion of the visible church with which he was connected,—I think I may say it without fear of the truth of the statement being doubted by any who have long resided here,—did more than any other to promote and maintain a spirit of unity and brotherly kindness among all, of whatever name, who love the Lord Jesus Christ in sincerity. I might speak of him in all these respects, and while I should have no desire to do so in the language of fulsome and unmeasured panegyric, to which no one had a greater aversion than our dear departed brother himself, I could say nothing in his praise that would not find an echo in every heart. I forbear, however, to enlarge on these sad yet pleasing themes ; and shall merely briefly touch upon his character as pastor of this congregation, and as for a number of years the Principal of Queen's College.

"As a minister of a congregation he was pre-eminently distinguished—I might almost say he was the model of a Christian pastor. Year after year, after his settlement in Kingston in 1827, as successor to his esteemed predecessor, the Rev. Mr. Barclay, his congregation increased until it was found necessary to enlarge the church in order to accommodate the growing number of its worshippers. For many years he toiled on almost alone, receiving very little help from any of his brethren, who were then comparatively few and distant. While he faithfully observed the Apostolic practice of visiting his people from house to house, and was ready at every call of the sick, the poor and the afflicted, his work for the pulpit was incessant ; and when we consider the admirable nature of his discourses, which his high sense of duty always constrained him carefully to prepare, we can have no doubt that he laid the foundation of that ill health with which he was often visited in later years, in his early sacrifices of his own ease for the good of his flock. We do not, my friends, sufficiently consider the arduous nature of the work of preparation of two sermons every week for the pulpit. I have little doubt that he wrote for the benefit of his people in the first fifteen years of his ministry, as much as some of the most voluminous authors have written in their whole lives. His discourses were uniformly excellent in arrangement and matter, sound in doctrine, scriptural and searching in precept, and affectionate in exhortation ; and as a preacher, taking him all in all, he was excelled by few clergymen in the Church of Scotland, or in any other church. And when to this I add his no less valuable ministrations in private, his consistent walk in his intercourse with his flock, illustrating that faith and love which he endeavoured to carry home to the hearts of his hearers, his weekly prayer-meetings, and the flourishing Sabbath-school over which he so long presided, it is not to be wondered at that he continued to the last in the enjoyment of a degree of respect and affection on the part of his people which have rarely been exceeded.

" One other part of his character and life I must advert to. At a great sacrifice of time and labour he undertook, at the solicitation of the Board of Trustees of Queen's College, to act as Principal of that Institution, and with what advantage to the College and to the Church is known to all. Some of the most valued ministers of our Church were trained under his care and that of his colleagues, one of whom was the friend and the companion of his younger days, the Rev. Dr. Urquhart. This office he held for six years ; and I shall never forget the wisdom and aptitude for business with which he administered its duties, as indeed he did those of every other station which he occupied, and the uninterrupted harmony which existed between him and his colleagues. Yet for all this, which would otherwise have cost the College a very large sum, he refused to receive any but a very inadequate remuneration ; and even that he gave towards the payment of the debt of the church in which we are met, and other public objects.

" One word more and I have done. Some may have found

fault with him who is gone, and if he had been free from fault he would have been more than human. When, however, we consider his position, and the arduous duties which he had to perform, there will seldom appear an instance in which there was less fault to be found, and more to praise. See then, my friends, that you 'remember him who lately had the rule over you in the Lord, who spake unto you the word of God ; whose faith follow, considering the end of his conversation, Jesus Christ, the same yesterday, to-day and for ever.'"

A very impressive funeral sermon was preached on the following Sunday by his former assistant and valued friend, the Rev. Professor Mowat, before a profoundly attentive and deeply moved congregation, many of whom were attired in mourning, out of respect for the memory of their departed minister.

His remains lie in Cataraqui Cemetery, near Kingston, in a pleasant spot, commanding a lovely view across an undulating country, towards the distant lake, on which he always loved to look. A costly and beautiful granite obelisk has been placed there by his congregation and other members of the community, in memory of his ministerial usefulness and consistent Christian life, and bearing the appropriate text : " The memory of the just is blessed."

PREFACE TO THE SERMONS.

CONSIDERABLE difficulty has been felt in making a selection from the large number of MS. sermons left by Dr. Machar. Many of his sermons and lectures were delivered in course. During his ministry he lectured regularly through St. Matthew, St. John, the Acts of the Apostles, and the Epistle to the Romans. It was, besides, his practice in the morning service to give a short exposition of the chapter read, on which account the sermon was shorter than it would otherwise have been. The sermons selected for publication are not those which would be considered most profoundly theological, but rather some of his more simple and practical pastoral sermons, such as might be most useful to those who may read them, as those who heard them have, in numerous cases, testified that they had conveyed to their souls precious words of life, and sustaining consolation.

SERMON I.

ISAIAH liii. 6.—All we like sheep have gone astray ; we have turned every one to his own way ; and the Lord hath laid on Him the iniquity of us all.

AN inspired Evangelist teaches us to find Jesus in this Scripture. The whole of the chapter refers to Christ ; these words, to His substitution and sacrifice for us. The speakers, who are plainly believers of the House of Israel of the Pentecostal day, were familiar with the transference of guilt to a victim. When Israel was in the wilderness, the High Priest was directed to take two kids of the goats for a sin-offering, one of which he was to slay, and sprinkle its blood upon the mercy-seat, while concerning the other this was the law, " Aaron shall lay both his hands upon the head of the live goat, and shall send him away by the hand of a fit man, into the wilderness, and the goat shall bear upon him all their iniquities into a land not inhabited ; and he shall let go the goat in the wilderness." Let us imagine ourselves witnessing these impressive and significant rites—types to the Church of that day of the good things to come, when Christ should appear to " put away sin by the sacrifice of Himself." The animals have been selected. The sins of Israel are typically transferred to them. The priest has laid upon them their fearful burden. All is silence and awe throughout the congregation, while they who are enlightened worshippers, and can look through the shadow to "the body which is of Christ," exult with holy joy, for, as the offering is completed,—as the one animal bleeds upon the altar that its blood may be carried within the holy place, and the other disappears for ever from their view, as it is led away into the wilderness with its burden of curse,—the adoring language of their hearts—hearts now purged from dead works to serve the living God—is this : " He who is promised to us, who only can put away sin, surely He is stricken for our transgressions ; and surely He bears our transgressions away from us, to be seen no more."

Even such is the scene which seems to have been present to the minds of the early converts, who had found Him of whom Moses in the Law and the Prophets did write ; and we cannot but see how natural it was for them, with the full light now thrown upon this scene by the death of Christ, to pour out their hearts in language like that in our text,—" All we like sheep have gone astray ; we have turned every one to his own way ; and the Lord hath laid on Him the iniquity of us all." Two points here present themselves to our minds, which it will be of the highest importance for us to consider, especially on this day of solemn commemoration by us of our Redeemer's sacrifice. They are the nature and misery of our condition as sinners, and the blessed means provided for our restoration.

I. Let us first consider the nature and misery of our condition as sinners. Sin is wandering from God. We go astray when we transgress the Divine law ; and this we have all done. It is not the way of God in which we naturally walk ; we turn every one to his own way, casting, each in a manner of his own, the commandments of God behind our backs. The Divine law is a law of love, requiring love to God and love to man. But we have not this love. We have not the love of God in us, but are alienated from Him, none of us understanding and seeking Him as our soul's treasure, but each of us turning away from Him to walk in the sight of our own eyes, and in the way of our own hearts. And alienated from God, we are alienated from one another. Selfishness is the leading principle of unrenewed men ; they live for themselves ; they seek their own. A common union to God had united them, had made them a band of brothers ; but, this union having been severed, instead of loving one another, their proper description is, "hateful and hating one another." Such is our condition as sinners, and it is compared to that of strayed sheep. "All we like sheep have gone astray ; we have turned every one to his own way." What is here presented to us is a flock of sheep that have wandered from the fold and pastures of their shepherd into the howling wilderness ; and that, separated from their shepherd, are scattered from each other, straggling each on a path of its own ; and in this object we are to find a picture of the misery of our condition as wanderers from our God. It is a lively picture, revealing the destitution, the danger and the hopelessness of the state into which we have come.

Our condition as sinners is a condition of destitution, of want. Survey the strayed sheep in a barren wilderness—away from the green pastures where once it fed, and the still waters from whence it drank ;—it is starving there, it can find no nourishment, nothing to stay its hunger, to quench its thirst. Such is our condition in our estrangement from God. The lower appetites of the body, indeed, may have something to satisfy them, but our souls hunger and thirst ; there is a craving void in them that we can get nothing to fill. Where is the wanderer from God who is satisfied, nay, upon whom, amidst all his enjoyments, there does not press a heavy and corroding sense of want? If we could feed upon the husks of this world, if we could be satisfied from the cistern of carnal gratification, we should not be thus in straits, we should not feel this weariness and destitution. But we were born for higher enjoyments, and therefore these cannot satisfy us; and let us have all of them that our hearts could wish, and still, if without God, we must be in want;—" As when a hungry man dreameth, and behold, he eateth, but he awaketh, and his soul is empty; or as when a thirsty man dreameth, and behold, he drinketh, but he awaketh, and behold he is faint, and his soul hath appetite."

The picture before us reveals, too, the danger of our condition as wanderers from God. The safety of sheep depends entirely upon their continuing under the shepherd's care; let them wander beyond the protection of his arm, and they become an easy and unresisting prey to every ravenous beast of the wilderness. And so with us in our alienation from God. We are menaced by danger on every side; we are already in the hands of numerous and formidable enemies, who are ever seeking the life of our souls. Our own lusts draw us away and entice us on to our destruction. The world spreads all its fascinations before us, to allure us within its fatal circle. Our "adversary, the devil, as a roaring lion, goeth about, seeking to devour" us. Still, all this were little if God were our friend, but the wrath of God abideth upon us while we abide in sin; and we may at any moment fall into His hands to be "punished with everlasting destruction from His presence, and from the glory of His power." To aggravate this danger, we are insensible to it; we will not believe that it exists; we look upon those who warn us of it as gloomy visionaries, conjuring up phantoms of alarm that have no real existence. This makes our state dangerous indeed. We provide against a danger we believe in, but who provides against one that he deems imaginary, the fiction of a diseased mind?

The picture here given also speaks to us of the hopelessness of our condition. As far as depends upon ourselves it is utterly hopeless. A sheep that has once strayed from the fold never returns to it. The dove could find its way back to the ark. There are some other animals that have a certain power of retracing their steps—of regaining a situation they have left. But no such power is possessed by the wandering sheep ; once astray, it goes astray for ever,—it never comes back. And so with us. Once alienated from God, we do not of our own accord return to Him. He may seek us, but we never seek Him. The truth is, we cannot seek Him. Our wills carry us in the opposite direction. " The carnal mind in us is enmity against God ; it is not subject to the law of God, neither indeed can be."

Such are the views of the misery of our condition as sinners, to be gathered from the figure in our text. It is a condition of destitution, of danger, of hopelessness. But there is one view of it where the figure does not hold, where the case of strayed sheep fails to represent our situation. " We have turned every one to his own way." Our own way is the way of our choice, the way we select, and determine to pursue. Such is that way of alienation from God and from man, into which, under many diversified forms, we all naturally turn. It is not through external force, or in obedience to blind instinct, that we are in it. We come into it through our own voluntary choice. We remain in it through our own voluntary choice. We are in it because we will to be so. This it is that gives its darkest shade to the picture. We are not so much objects of pity, though we are to be pitied, as we are of blame. Here our case differs widely from that of straying sheep. When they wander, they are not objects of blame. Their straying is their misfortune—they cannot help it. Not so with us. When we stray, it is our iniquity, our wickedness ; we stray wilfully ; we stray because we love to stray. Our errors are wilful errors ; our transgressions are wilful transgressions. We are moral wanderers,—wanderers who have said, " We will not have the Lord to rule over us ; we have loved strangers, and after them we will go."

L   161

II. Let us now, secondly, consider the blessed means provided for our restoration. There *are* means provided for this, and we may well wonder at this grace. With right views of our state, we could not have anticipated it ; previously to its bestowment, we could not have hoped that it would be bestowed. How shall creatures such as we are, be dealt with ? Can it be that there may be hope for us ? When we think of the dark features of our case, as moral wanderers from our God—with what wilfulness and determination we have broken that law of love which would have linked us to God and to one another,—how vile, how hateful we have made ourselves by our iniquity, would it have been wonderful if God had forgotten to be gracious to us, and in anger shut up from us for ever His tender mercies ? Suppose that there could still be in His heart movements of compassion towards us ; that in His mercy He might yet long to recover us from our fatal wanderings, and set us again within the shelter of His fold,—how can pity be shown in circumstances like ours ? How can mercy ever find its way over those barriers which our sinfulness has placed in its way ? The law of God is a righteous law, and cannot be broken with impunity. Sin is an evil thing, and there is a necessity that the righteous Ruler of the universe should treat it according to its nature, and execute the righteous curse pronounced upon it. But how, then, can mercy reach us ? If our iniquity must be dealt with according to its desert, —if condemnation and punishment must follow transgression, how shall we be pardoned and saved ? Here is a question at which the highest created intelligence must have stood aghast, which only He who is infinite in wisdom and boundless in resource could have answered. It it is a question which—blessed be His name !—He has answered and taught us to answer. A mediator has been found, one able and willing to stand in the breach for us, "and the Lord hath laid upon Him the iniquity of us all."

This mediator was no creature, but "the fellow of the

Lord of Hosts,"—" God's own Son,"—" the brightness of the Father's glory, and the express image of His person ;" and the burden wherewith he was burdened by the Father, as the holy Governor of the universe, was the iniquity of us all,—that is, as is evident from the nature of the case, as well as from express declaration, not our sin itself, our guilt, but its burden and punishment—the curse, the wrath, the woe due to us for it. It is a mysterious, overwhelming thought, that one of such dignity—one " in the form of God, and thinking it no robbery to be equal with God"—should have had such a burden laid upon him. But He who would become our Deliverer must take it upon Him, and so bear it away, and bear it to the uttermost. In any plan of restoration for us that can be conceived, the law must be magnified and made honourable, the perfect righteousness of Jehovah must be declared, and the Restorer must suffer for our sins, " the just for the unjust," before He can bring us to God. He must take upon Him our nature—be "made of a woman "—" made under the law," as making Himself one with us, and entering into our very place ; and then he must drink the sinner's cup ; He must taste death for us ; He must even descend into the very depths of our curse, and by exhausting it to the full, realizing all its horrors of thick darkness, and all its sore amazement, and all its exceeding sorrow, carry us through it, and beyond it, into the light of the divine countenance, and within the range of a reigning grace. Accordingly, all this has been realized in the history of our Deliverer. The Eternal "Word was made flesh ;" and He, " the man Christ Jesus," the representative, the head of the race, "tasted death for every man." Oh ! it is no fiction, but a blessed reality, what He will this day tell us at His table,—"This is my body, broken for you ;—this cup is the New Testament in my blood, shed for many for the remission of sins."

The mighty emergency has been met. It was met from eternity. The counsel of peace was between the Father and the Son, and in pursuance of that counsel the Father laid upon the Son—caused to meet upon Him, the iniquity of us all. He was bearing it when He said in Gethsemane, " My soul is exceeding sorrowful, even unto death." He was bearing it when He cried on Calvary, through that preternatural darkness which had at length stilled every tongue, and awed every heart : " My God, my God, why hast Thou forsaken me?" The Father laid upon Him our sins, bruised and put Him to grief as He stood for us. And let us not suppose that the Son was less willing to bear it than the Father was to lay it upon Him. " It pleased the Lord to bruise Him and to put Him to grief." He bore our burden with a ready, a delighted mind. The victim must not be dragged to the altar, and Christ's was no compelled, reluctant sacrifice. Dark as were the scenes He knew He must pass through, He entered upon them with cheerfulness and resolution ; overwhelming as were the woes He must endure, He shrank not from one of them. Though He had to "tread the wine-press of the wrath of God," and to tread it in loneliness and desertion, uncheered by one look of encouragement, or beam of light from earth or heaven, He trod it with firm and unflinching step. In the full view of His dying agonies, He said—" I have a baptism to be baptised with, and how am I straitened until it be accomplished ;"—" I lay down my life for the sheep ; no one taketh it from me, but I lay it down of myself." " He is led as a lamb to the slaughter, and as a sheep before his shearers is dumb, so he openeth not his mouth."

Oh ! what did this willingness to drink the full cup of our sorrow bespeak ? Even that He was the righteous Lord, loving righteousness and hating iniquity. He thus " condemned sin in the flesh." In thus willingly submitting himself to the suffering of death for sin, He declared that He judged it worthy of death,—a thing so hateful, so abominable, as to render it right that the vials of God's holy indignation should be poured out upon it. And herein lay the reason why the sufferings of Christ were a sacrifice of a sweet-smelling savour to God ;—they were endured in the spirit of holy, sin-hating love. They were acceptable to God, not merely because they were sufferings, but because they were holy sufferings, endured through the Eternal Spirit,—the sufferer, by His patient bearing of them, continually declaring the righteousness of God in their appointment as the portion of iniquity. This gave His sacrifice its value, its excellency. When God saw this sight in our nature,—when He saw sin thus condemned, and His name thus glorified, in that flesh in which sin had hitherto reigned,—then was He "well-pleased towards us for His righteousness' sake," —then did He see the sacrifice for sin in which His soul could delight,—and then did He acknowledge Jesus His "beloved Son, in whom He was well pleased ; "—" anointing Him with the oil of gladness above His fellows," and " exalting Him with His own right hand to be a Prince and a Saviour, to give repentance to Israel and forgiveness of sins."

Such are the means provided for our restoration to God, and they are no vain means. Christ crucified is the power of God, and the wisdom of God, to every one that believeth. The sight of the holy sin-hating love manifested in the sufferings of Christ, slays the enmity of our hearts to God, and brings us back from our wanderings to dwell under His shadow, and in the shelter of His fold. In those who receive Christ to dwell in their hearts by faith, and know that love of His which passeth knowledge, the fire of divine love is again rekindled on the long cold altar of their hearts. They love Him who first loved them ; and loving Him, they love, too, them that are His. They thus become a flock, a united body,—one fold under one shepherd ; one family under one Father ; a multitude having one heart and soul,—all in communion with God, and all walking in love, one towards another. But mark, brethren, mark carefully, only in those who receive

Christ,—who rest upon Him as their atoning sacrifice, and know Him as their Life,—is this blessed change effected; only they who have the blood of Christ really sprinkled upon them through faith, have this love, which is of God, dwelling in them. Only with them is the darkness past, the true light shining. See, then, that ye receive Christ; see that ye have His blood sprinkled upon you by faith. You are this day, many of you, coming to His table, to receive the memorials of His dying love, in token that you receive Himself. Oh! let this be a real thing with you! All things are ready, you have only to appropriate. Christ, the great Sacrifice, has been offered; He has been " wounded for our transgressions, bruised for our iniquities;" He has had that heavy burden of iniquity laid upon Him, which He only, who beareth up the pillars of the universe, could support. Come, then, and do in regard to Him what Israel did in regard to the scape-goat—confess all your iniquities over Him, putting them upon His head, and trust in Him to bear them away, as into a land not inhabited. And He *will* bear them away, never again to appear to condemn you. • His blood will " purge your consciences from dead works to serve the living God;" and thus, having boldness into His presence, you shall be made nigh to Him, nor shall you be any more " strangers and foreigners, but fellow-citizens with the saints and of the household of God."

We can only, in conclusion, press upon you two lessons from what has engaged us; one for those who are rejecting the counsel of God respecting our great sin-offering, and the other for those who deem that they have embraced that counsel. You who will not rest your dependence upon the provided Sin-offering, may see the utter hopelessness and awful danger of your condition. You despise the sacrifice of Christ, you will not lay upon His head your iniquities, choosing, rather, to carry them yourselves; but how can you do this when you think of Gethsamane, when you remember Calvary? Behold what Christ endured when He took on Him the burden of our expiation ; and how then shall they escape who reject His great salvation, brought to them at such a price? " If these things were done in the green tree, what shall be done in the dry ? " Let the thought of this impel you to an immediate close with offered mercy while it is yet near. " Kiss the Son lest He be angry, and ye perish from the way. When His wrath is kindled but a little, blessed are all they that put their trust in Him."

They who deem that they have received Christ as their salvation may see from what has been said whether it be so or not. If it be that you are made nigh to God, and are within the fold, you will be walking in love. Our straying is our alienation from God, and from our fellowmen ; our being brought home is our re-union to God, and, through re-union to Him, re-union to our brethren. A true "faith worketh by love ;" "we know that we have passed from death to life because we love the brethren." As, then, we would have confidence towards God, let us love,—love "not in word or in tongue, but in deed and in truth." Let us "bear one another's burdens, and so fulfil the law of Christ." To replace love in hearts from which it had utterly departed,—this was the object for which Christ "endured the cross, and despised the shame ;" and when He sees it glowing in these hearts, He "sees of the travail of His soul and is satisfied." The greatest of all the graces is Love. As there is nothing so dark and revolting as hatred, there is nothing so bright and beautiful as love. The more of love, the more of heaven. It makes us nearer to God, and liker to Him than all things else. Oh! had we love, the evidence of our being in Christ would not be doubtful ; it would be clear that the dark season of our wandering was past ; that we had exchanged the wilderness for the fold ;—that the far country was forsaken ;—that we were in our Father's house ;— no more "as sheep going astray, but returned unto the Shepherd and Bishop of your souls."

Is it wonderful that it should be said of love,—" Hereby we know that we are of the truth, and shall assure our hearts before Him?" Many calling themselves Christians, so far from having assurance, look upon it as a heresy and error to have it. But strange indeed is this! Is he who, after a long and weary absence from the paternal dwelling, has been welcomed within its longed-for bosom, doubtful whether he be in it? Does he who, after many sad and lonely wanderings through a far-off cold world, basks once more in the sunlight of a father's or a mother's smile, require to be informed that that smile is beaming upon him? Does he from whose heart love is tenderly emanating upon the dear inmates of a long-lost, but regained home,—as from their hearts love is as tenderly emanating upon him,—need to be told that he is in the midst of them? Surely that, at least, he knows. He may need to be told many things, but he needs not to be told *that!*

SERMON II.

St. John, vi. 15–21.—"When Jesus, therefore, perceived that they would come and take him by force, to make him a king, he departed again into a mountain himself alone," &c.

OUR Lord, who was now in a desert place near Bethsaida, had just healed a multitude, consisting of several thousands, with five barley loaves and two small fishes. We read at the fifth verse, "When Jesus then lifted up his eyes, and saw a great company come unto him, he saith unto Philip, Whence shall we buy bread, that these may eat? And this he said to prove him"—that is, to try the faith of Philip—"for he himself knew what he would do. Philip answered him, Two hundred pennyworth of bread is not sufficient for them, that every one of them may take a little." Then we have the account of their being fed with the five loaves and the two small fishes ; and the command to the disciples, "Gather up the fragments that remain, that nothing be lost. Therefore they gathered them together, and filled twelve baskets with the fragments of the five barley loaves, which remained over and above unto them that had eaten." What a striking miracle was this ! No wonder that the men who saw it recognised Jesus as the expected Messiah, saying, "This is of a truth that prophet that should come into the world." But this was not the only effect produced upon them by the sight of this miracle. In the enthusiasm of the moment, they wished to come and forcibly place Him at their head, as the king and liberator of their nation ; and in the first of the verses now read for lecture, we have related to us the course adopted by Him in this emergency. "When Jesus, therefore, perceived that they would come and take him by force, to make him a king, he departed again into a mountain himself alone." That no commotion might be excited, and no occasion found by those who sought His hurt for interrupting Him in the peaceful prosecution of His ministry, He immediately withdrew to a mountain, and, as will be observed, he withdrew *alone ;* His disciples were not with Him. These, as Matthew and Mark relate, He had already sent away—a thing which it might be the more necessary to do, as they, from their yet carnal conceptions respecting His kingdom, were likely enough to join with the multitude in their present design. Indeed, the word "constrained," which is employed in reference to His sending them away on this occasion, would seem to indicate a strong reluctance on their part just then to leave Him—a reluctance most probably arising from a disposition in them to second the views of the multitude who wished to make Him a king.

Whether the proposal to exalt Him to regal dignity and power was a temptation to our Lord Himself, we are not informed. We know that Christ could be tempted, yea, that He "was in all points tempted like as we are, yet without sin." Satan had already assailed him with a temptation of this very nature, showing Him the kingdoms of this world and the glory of them, and offering Him possession of them under a sinful condition ; and it might be that at this time the Tempter was presenting to His mind the dark scenes of suffering through which He was to pass—the mockeries of Herod and his men of war—the spittings, and buffettings, and scourgings, and tauntings ; the apparent forsaking by God and man that should accompany His decease at Jerusalem, and asking Him why He improved not the present favourable moment for not only escaping all these evils, but for reaching a pitch of earthly greatness and glory to which the mightiest potentates of the world had never approached. If, as is not improbable, the Prince of this world did at this time come to our Lord in this way, he found nothing in Him. Our Lord immediately escaped from the snare of the enemy, and escaped from it by betaking Himself to prayer —" offering up prayers and supplications, with strong crying and tears, unto Him that was able to save Him from death." Not listening for a moment to a proposition ordinarily so dazzling to flesh and blood, He immediately got Him away from the admiring multitudes, and went up into a mountain apart to pray, continuing in that exercise, as Matthew and Mark inform us, until three in the morning.

Are we, brethren, when in society, exposed to any strong temptation? We should immediately escape from it by going into some lonely place, and there offering up, as Jesus did, " supplications and prayers, with prolonged and strong crying and tears, unto Him who is able to keep us from temptation and save us from death." We do not well, nay, we act presumptuously, in looking for deliver-ance, if, when assailed by a temptation, we linger in a posi-tion where it has advantage to work upon us, instead of instantly making our escape from such a position ; and we are equally wrong, and equally presumptuous in our expecta-tions of deliverance, if, when we have made our escape from that position in which a temptation has most advan-tage to work upon us, we do not follow up this escape by earnest and persevering prayers for strength to endure. Why is it that so many of those who profess themselves the followers of Jesus, are overcome of the temptation by which they are assailed, and so often and so grievously fall? Just because they neglect these precautions— because they neglect what their Master did not think it safe to neglect ! Just because, when tried with Satan's devices, they either do not promptly shun their entanglements by removing from them, or, having removed from them, do not follow up the movement by earnest supplication to the Omnipotent Helper. Did we attend to these things, we should never fall—we should "be heard in that we feared;" and He who has Himself known what sore temptations are, would come to our relief in every hour of danger,—"making a way of escape for us, and not suffering us to be tempted above that which we are able to bear."

Whatever be the complexion of our circumstances, whether exposed to temptation or otherwise, we ought frequently to retire apart for private prayer, nor should we allow any hurry of business or feeling of weariness to lead us to postpone or neglect this practice. Our Lord watched unto prayer in secret. The day had been with Him a day of incessant occupation, and we may well suppose that weariness and exhaustion had unstrung His bodily frame as well as His mental powers; yet when the evening is come, it is not for repose that He seeks the mountain top, but to pour out His heart in solitary supplication to His Heavenly Father. And even thus should it be with us. However occupied or fatigued, prayer in solitude should never be omitted by us, and daily as the evening comes, escaping from care and rising above languor, should we seek the secret place of communing with God, "praying always with all prayer and supplication in the Spirit, and watching thereunto with all perseverance."

"And when even was now come, His disciples went down unto the sea, and entered into a ship, and went over the sea toward Capernaum. And it was now dark, and Jesus was not come to them. And the sea arose by reason of a great wind that blew." Here we observe the disciples of Christ in jeopardy from the storm. If, brethren, we are disciples of Christ, we must expect storms. If we have not natural storms to meet, we are sure, if we are true disciples, to encounter spiritual storms. "In the world," said Jesus to His disciples, "ye shall have tribulation;" and this is more or less true of them all. Some may be vexed with fewer tempests than others, and He who holds the blasts in the hollow of His hand may stay for them much of their fury; but none have ever entered the haven of eternal rest upon whom the winds have not blown and the waves dashed themselves, and who have not frequently had the sentence of death in themselves, fearing that they should perish. The Christian needs storms, otherwise they would not be sent. Such events, in fact, subserve the most important purposes to him. They show him his own weakness and insufficiency; they endear to him his God and Saviour; they awaken him to more fervent supplication; they, in a word, lead him to self-distrust and dependence upon God—the most blessed posture of soul in which a child of God can be. The night, it will be observed, was dark; and added to this, the disciples had not Jesus with them in the ship, as on a former occasion. This was to lead them up to a higher lesson than they had learnt before; it was to teach them to walk by faith and not by sight. It is comparatively easy to trust in the Lord in the light; the difficulty is to trust in Him in the darkness, and when we are cut off from all visible support; but if this is harder, it is the more blessed. "Blessed," said our Lord, "are they that have *not seen*, and yet have *believed*."

"So when they had rowed about five-and-twenty or thirty furlongs, they see Jesus walking on the sea, and drawing nigh unto the ship; and they were afraid. But he saith unto them, It is I; be not afraid." The Evangelist Mark speaks of their toiling in rowing, from the wind being contrary to them; and he says, also, that it was about the fourth watch of the night that Jesus came to them, walking on the sea. Such difficulty did they have in making any way, that even when the fourth watch of

the night was come, they were only a few miles from the
place whence they had sailed. Among the Jews the
night was divided into four watches, each consisting of
three hours. The first began at six and continued till
nine; the second was from nine to twelve; the third
from twelve to three; and the fourth from three to six.
In the last of these watches—that is, in the watch between
three and six in the morning—Jesus went to His disciples,
pacing over that tempestuous sea, with its raging billows,
as if it had been a carpet spread under His feet. The
lesson we here learn is one of the highest importance.
However difficult and dangerous our circumstances may
be, we need not be greatly alarmed if we have come into
them in obedience to a clear command of our Heavenly
Master, seeing that in such a case He will think upon us
and come to our relief. It was in compliance with their
Lord's constraint that the disciples had embarked, and
were now in jeopardy on the sea of Galilee on a dark
and tempestuous night; and we see that they were not
forsaken by Him in their hour of need. If He delayed
to deliver them, yet He at length brought them deliverance; if he allowed the second and third watches of the
night to pass, and still appeared not for their help, yet
they saw His familiar form and heard His cheering voice
in the fourth watch, when, as it would seem, the storm
was at its height and their danger was most imminent.
Herein lies our safety—that we keep the way of the
Lord! Only let us be where Christ would have us to be,
and acting under His directions, and we may be calm
whatever tempests rage, and whatever billows swell around
us. He will come and save us out of all our troubles.
He may not immediately appear for our relief,—he may
leave us for many a weary hour to struggle through the
darkness, alone, and without any sensible assistance,—
"afflicted, tossed with tempest, and not comforted;" but
He will not so leave us *always!* When it shall be best
for us, and most glorifying to Himself, He will give us

help, proving to us His faithfulness to His promise, "I will not leave you comfortless ; I will come unto you."

When the disciples at first saw Jesus walking on the sea, and drawing nigh unto the ship, they were afraid. We cannot wonder that they should have been thus affected. The sight of a man walking over the tumultuous billows in the darkness of night, was a sight to strike them with awe and terror. As it was the belief of the Jews that hurtful spirits walked abroad in the night, they accounted for the marvellous appearance they saw in this way. As is elsewhere stated, " They said, ' It is a spirit ; an evil demon come to work us mischief.' " And so great was their alarm from this their conviction of what they saw, that they cried out for fear, evidently apprehending some great and sudden calamity. Thus, often, is He mistaken still. When He comes to His people in some unaccustomed form, by some unwonted way, in the shape of some heavy affliction, in the way of some painful cross, they are troubled at His presence, they think of Him as an enemy and cry out for fear. Under this impression, however, He cannot suffer them to continue, and He lifts up His well-known voice in their ears, saying, " ' It is I ; be not afraid !' My hand is in this very event which agitates and perplexes you, and why should you be afraid? Can you suppose that I would lay upon you one needless sorrow? Say not of anything which I send you, ' It is against me.' It is not so ; it is *for* you. If I come to you in this form, it is to do you good, and to put a new song in your mouth, even praise to your God ! ' It is I ; be not afraid.' " These are gracious words. They mark the tenderness of Jesus towards His own ; His eagerness to calm their fears, to reassure their minds. They should have known better than to be so overcome of the imaginary horrors which now haunted them ; they should have remembered that if they were followers of that which was good, nothing would *really* harm them. Yet even this foolishness of theirs, this slowness of heart in them to believe, does not hinder Him from hastening to them with the words of consolation. Let us see from this what a loving and gracious friend we have in Christ, and seeing this, be comforted in all our troubles.

But let us observe, too, whence Jesus had just come when He spoke to His disciples the cheering words before us. It was from that lonely mountain top where He had spent many hours of sweet communion with His Heavenly Father. It is important to remark this, as emphatically showing how untrue is the supposition that the retired habits of him who gives himself much to secret prayer, tend to separate him from sympathy with his kind, and so to deaden his active benevolence. The supposition could only be made by those who altogether misconceive the manner in which the man of secret communion with God is employed. His prayers are not all for himself. Many of them consist of earnest intercessions for his brethren of mankind, especially for those of them with whom he is more especially associated. Now, must not such an exercise on their behalf have a directly contrary effect to that of either deadening his sympathies with them, or the activity of his benevolence towards them? Must not the habit of spreading the woes and necessities of others before God, and of beseeching His gracious interposition on their behalf, tend to kill the bitter root of selfishness within us, and, in the most powerful manner, quicken our sympathies with others, so that we shall come to their relief whenever we have it in our power to help them? We can conceive an ascetic Pharisee, who prides himself on the number or the length of his prayers, issuing from his retirement, hard-hearted, to pass another day unredeemed by one kind word : no ear that hears him " blessing him," and no eyes that see him "giving him witness ; " but we cannot conceive this of the man whose fellowship is truly with the Father and with his Son, Jesus Christ. Moses and Paul were, both of them, men of long-continued fellowship with God in secret. Were their sympathies less tender, their labours of love less abundant on that account towards those with whom they were associated? Did Jesus, in the privacy of the lonely mountain top, forget His toiling and endangered disciples, or show Himself slow to come to their aid? That very night He walked upon the raging waves to their rescue. That very night He stood beside them in their extremity, and they heard from Him the words of tenderness and power;—"Be of good cheer: it is I; be not afraid."

If, therefore, men who are living without God in the world, and who would fain have others so to live, labour to bring disrepute upon habits of secret prayer, by representing such habits as deadening to active beneficence, they thereby only betray their own enmity to God. The man who dwells most with the God of love, is ever the most loving man. Those in the present day who are willing to see things in the Church as they really are, think that the practice answers not to the profession. What can be the cause of this? Perhaps we should not err if we mainly ascribed it to the little seeking unto God in secret. Of all who ever lived, the man Christ Jesus continued most in prayer to God. Well, *this* was *His* character, that "He went about continually doing good." Be ye like Him in your piety towards God, and like Him ye shall be in His benevolence towards men! Where there is a praying heart there is an open hand— a soul of large and well-directed benevolence.

Of the account of this voyage of the disciples, this is the conclusion: "Then they willingly received Him into the ship: and immediately the ship was at the land whither they went." "Then they willingly received Him." When He had come to them on the sea, and when He had calmed their terrors by these words of kindness, "It is I; be not afraid," then it was that they willingly received Him. We do not of ourselves willingly receive Christ. We do not seek Him until He seeks us. Though He is the chief among ten thousand, and altogether lovely; though He is the fountain of all blessing and the source of all strength, so that without Him we enjoy nothing, and can do nothing, yet are we slow of heart to receive Him; and He has to bring down upon us the dark night, and to rouse around us the angry storm, and to manifest Himself to us in these, before we will make Him our refuge, and say to Him with a willing heart, " Lord, I am thine; save me." The bark of the Church of God is now upon the stormy sea, and it is there by His bidding; but how small is the way which it makes! Though the rowers seem to be rowing hard, they advance not; the opposing storms and surges of the world are too much for them. Why is this? Is it that He sees them not, or is unwilling to come to them? No; but because they are not yet made willing to receive Him. But they *shall* be made willing! It is said to Christ, " Thy people shall be made willing in the day of thy power," and that day is nigh at hand. Infidelity asks, " Where is the promise of His coming?" But come He shall—come quickly. The night of toil and weeping will soon be over for the tossed rowers, giving place to that morning watch, when they shall welcome the King in His beauty, and shall, under His guidance, immediately reach the haven where they would be. Let it be our concern, brethren, that we may be found of Him in peace at His coming. Let the attitude of our souls be that of waiting for Him; nor let us be unwilling, should He appoint, to meet the dark night, and to encounter the beating storm. It is but a little while that trouble can be upon us. We sorrow not as those who have no hope. Our redemption draweth nigh. " Blessed be the God and Father of our Lord Jesus Christ, which, according to His abundant mercy, hath begotten us again unto a lively hope, by the resurrection of Jesus Christ from

the dead, to an inheritance incorruptible, and undefiled, and that fadeth not away, reserved in Heaven for
you who are kept by the power of God through faith
unto salvation, ready to be revealed in the last time.
Wherein ye greatly rejoice, though now, for a season, if
need be, ye are in heaviness through manifold temptations; that the trial of your faith, being much more
precious than that of gold that perisheth, though it be
tried with fire, might be found unto praise, and honour,
and glory at the appearing of Jesus Christ."

SERMON III.

ST. JOHN, vi. 66 to the end.—" From that time many of his disciples went back, and walked no more with him. Then said Jesus unto the twelve, Will ye also go away?" &c.

IN religion, the enlightenment of the mind and the purification of the affections are, both of them, things of indispensable necessity. There must be love in the heart, but there must be, no less, light in the head. We must be well instructed in the things pertaining to the kingdom of God, and so able to give to ourselves and to others "a reason of the hope that is in us;" nor without this shall we be able to maintain our steadfastness in trial, and cleave to the Lord through evil report and through good report. The time at which many of our Lord's disciples are here said to have gone back and walked no more with Him, was the time when, instead of continuing to feed them, as they had hoped, with bread for their bodies, He spoke to them of that better bread which their souls needed—the bread of spiritual life—telling them that He Himself was "the living bread that came down from heaven,"—that, as the Son of man, he was to "give His flesh for the life of the world," and that it was they and they only that should "eat His flesh and drink His blood," "that should have eternal life, and be raised up at the last day."

Now, these things at once dissolved the charm which

had drawn after Him the vast proportion of His present followers. "Ah!" said they in their hearts, "this is not the Messiah, after all; this is not the Prophet we look for; He is not to give us the meat which we desire;" and so saying, and finding a pretext for leaving Him in the hardness and offensiveness of His sayings, they went back from Him, and went back, as far as appears, to return to Him no more. Our Lord was not unprepared for this desertion; He knew that in their carnal state they could not enter into the kingdom of God. He had told them that no man could come to Him except the Father which had sent Him drew him; and He knew that, intent as they were on earthly things alone, they were in no disposition to hear and learn of the Father. But though prepared for their desertion, it did not the less grieve Him. They were His own—the people whom He came to save; and, to use His own loving language, he would have "gathered them together as a hen doth gather her chickens under her wings."

We may imagine, then, the sorrow with which He saw them forsaking Him; nor only forsaking Him, but perverting the most gracious words which sinful men could hear, into a justification of their course. And how far will this desertion proceed? Carried away by the contagion of general example, will His own familiar friends, too, go back from Him, and leave Him "as a worm, and no man," among those who were to Him objects of a love stronger than death? "Then said Jesus unto the twelve, Will ye also go away?" This question was the language of ardent affection; it came from the depths of a loving heart. It would have grieved our Lord more than He had yet been grieved, to part with His beloved disciples; still He will have them serve Him willingly and without constraint. He will not keep them with Him against their will; and if they remain with Him, it must be from a conviction that it is good for them to remain—that it is their blessedness and salvation to cleave to Him, and that it would be their misery and destruction to go back. He spoke to try them ; and on this occasion, as the words of their spokesman, Peter, evince, they were not found wanting. " Then Simon Peter answered Him, Lord, to whom shall we go ? Thou hast the words of eternal life. And we believe and are sure that thou art that Christ, the Son of the living God." This reply showed that the twelve had not been so long with Him in vain ; it showed the depth of their attachment to their gracious Master, and that it was no blind attachment, but one for which they had the strongest and most satisfactory reasons. Our Lord, it is evident, was pleased with this answer, yet, as a salutary check to the confidence with which it was delivered—to put them upon their guard, to lead them to take heed to themselves, and to fear always, He added the awful words—" Have I not chosen you twelve, and one of you is a devil ? He spake of Judas Iscariot, the son of Simon ; for he it was that should betray him, being one of the twelve."

Without offering any explanation of a passage which, it will be observed, is so plain that it needs none, we will now consider it in its application to ourselves. In the first place, it reminds us of a temptation to which we are all liable ; and, secondly, it points out the way in which we shall be best prepared to overcome this temptation.

I. The temptation of which this passage reminds us, as a temptation to which we are liable, is that of departing or going away from Christ. We have come to Christ ; we profess to be His disciples, and to be walking with Him ; and what we profess in regard to these things may be true. But yet we may depart from Him ; we are liable to the temptation to do so ; and we are all liable to it. To whom was it that our Lord put the question, " Will ye also go away ?" It was to the chosen twelve—those whom He had selected to be with Him, and to share His daily and hourly intercourse ; and who, with one sad exception, walked in a manner becoming so high a privilege. Yet He says to them, "Will ye also go away?" while on another occasion His words to them were, "Watch and pray, that ye enter not into temptation." And if *they*—that chosen little band—were exposed to the danger of forsaking their Master—and if they did, afterwards, for a little season, forsake Him, who of us shall venture to say that this is a temptation to which we are in no danger of yielding? It is a fearful thing to go away from Christ—how fearful, is emphatically marked in the words, "If any man draw back, my soul shall have no pleasure in him;" but fearful as the thing is, even the most advanced Christian is not exempt from the possibility of falling into it. Listen to the words of St. Paul: "I keep under my body, and bring it into subjection; lest that by any means, when I have preached to others, I myself should be a castaway." We are not forgetting the doctrine of the perseverance of the saints; we know that "He who hath begun a good work in any will perform it until the day of Christ;" we know that Christ has said—"My sheep hear my voice, and I know them, and they follow me; and I give unto them eternal life; and they shall never perish, neither shall any pluck them out of my hand." But this is not to render us secure, to puff us up with a vain confidence that we are not liable to temptation. We are never in more awful danger than when we deem ourselves secure, and we are safe only when, setting before us the possibility of the saddest spiritual declensions, we fear always, and look, even from moment to moment, to Him who is "the strength of our life," and who alone can "hold up our goings that our footsteps slide not."

The danger of our apostatising from Christ will be especially great if we were led to follow Him at first without sitting down to count the cost—without a careful consideration of the sacrifices which the taking such a step must involve. Many like the joys of religion, but shrink from its self-denial and sacrifices. They want a religion without trouble, reproach and suffering; and when they find that not such is the religion of that Saviour—when they see that they can be His disciples only by "denying themselves and taking up the cross and following Him," they are offended. It now seems an evil thing to serve Him, and their "goodness is as the morning cloud and the early dew, which soon pass away." The thronging multitudes had still pressed around our Lord, and deemed of Him that He was their long-promised Messiah, if only He had continued to feed them with the loaves and fishes—it was only when He exhorted them to "labour not for the meat that perisheth, but for that meat which endureth to everlasting life," that they said, "This is a hard saying; who can hear it?" and "walked no more with Him." It is even thus that we may be in danger of apostatising. When we find that, so far from having our carnal desires satisfied, we must "mortify our members which are upon the earth," "loving not the world, nor the things of the world"—when we find that we must not be of the world as Christ was not of the world, it will be a great temptation to us to let go our profession and to return to our former course. And especially will the temptation have power if we see others falling away. The leaven of evil spreads with astonishing rapidity; and when, of those whose faces were once set heavenward, we see one and another turning back, and bringing an evil report upon the good ways of the Lord, it will be difficult indeed to resist the contagion of their example, and to stand faithful, like the chosen twelve, in the midst of the faithless. Only, indeed, as we have root in ourselves, as we have a spiritual mind, a divinely enlightened judgment, shall we be preserved from falling from our steadfastness, and bringing disgrace upon the doctrine of God our Saviour.

II. We consider, secondly, what is stated in this passage as to the way in which we shall be best prepared to overcome the temptation to depart from Christ. It is to be thoroughly persuaded of the importance of the blessings which we have in Christ. When our Lord says to the twelve, "Will ye also go away?" this is the reply of Peter, "Lord, to whom shall we go? Thou hast the words of eternal life ; and we believe and are sure that Thou art that Christ, the Son of the living God." This reply shows the high place which eternal things held in the estimation of Peter and his fellow-disciples. It was the meat that perisheth that absorbed all the concern of the multitudes that at this time came thronging around the Saviour ; but it was not so with His chosen twelve. It was the life of the soul, not of the body, that was in their eye, "the one thing needful." To be redeemed from the power of iniquity, and to have "fellowship with the Father and with His Son, Jesus Christ,"—this they had learned to account as their best heritage, and for this they were willing to suffer even the loss of all things. In comparison with the blessing of eternal life, all other things, in their view, shrank into utter insignificance ; and this blessing they knew that Christ could bestow upon them. They understood Him, in part at least, when He said, "I am the living bread which came down from Heaven. If any man eat of this bread, he shall live for ever ; and the bread that I will give is my flesh, which I will give for the life of the world." They knew that, by nature, they were alienated from the life of God, their only true life ; but they knew that Christ was come to restore them to this life, and that, by receiving Him, they should be redeemed from their state of alienation and death, and made blessed in the presence and in the fellowship of God. They saw not as yet so clearly as they afterwards saw, what He meant by "eating His flesh and drinking His blood ;" but they knew that to have Him was to have life, to be renewed in the spirit of their minds, to taste that God was good. And thus it was that they stood fast when the multitudes around them fell away. Thus it was that when their Lord put to them the question, "Will ye also go away?" they were able to reply, "To whom shall we go? Thou hast the words of eternal life. We seek eternal life—that life which consists in restoration to the presence and fellowship and image of God; and who but Thou can give us this blessing? Shall we go to the wisest of the heathen? They have become 'vain in their imaginations,' and in the matter of eternal life, their foolish minds are utterly darkened. Shall we turn to our own scribes, the Masters in Israel? They are 'blind leaders of the blind.' We see our only hope of obtaining eternal life in Thee, and we know that it is a sure hope. We recognize in Thee our long-looked-for Prince and Saviour; we believe and are sure that 'Thou art that Christ, the Son of the living God,' having life in Thyself, and that life for all of our perishing race who believe in Thy name." Such persons, it is evident, would not be easily induced to forsake Christ. Their faith in Him was no blind faith. They knew whom they believed, and they had reasons for believing in Him—reasons, we see, of the very strongest kind.

Now, brethren, is *our* faith in Christ of this kind? Are we rooted and grounded in His love, as these early disciples were? Are we persuaded that we have life, even the very life which our souls need, in Him, and that it will be vain for us to seek that blessing in any other? With this persuasion dwelling in our minds, it will be no light trial that will lead us to go back from Him. We shall not indeed go back from Him, but shall be able to say, in the midst of our trials for His sake, "What things are gain to me, those I must count loss for Christ; yea, doubtless, and I count all things but loss for the excellency of the knowledge of Christ Jesus my Lord." We have need, then, to consider whether we have this root in ourselves. If we have, we shall stand fast and flourish; if we have it not, we shall soon wither and perish.

Brethren, the high calling of God in Christ Jesus is,

surely, something worthy of our pressing after, even though it should be through many trials ; and if we have really come to Him, and seen His preciousness, oh ! what is there that should reconcile us to the thought of leaving Him ? We may be tried : nay, it must needs be, if we are His, that we shall often " be in heaviness through manifold temptations ;" but what then ? Where but in Him shall we and what our souls need ? If we go not to Him, then whither shall we go ? Shall it be to the world ? It will certainly deceive us. Shall we return to sin ? It will inevitably destroy us. Shall we listen to those who call religion a lie ? What can they give us in its place ? Can they comfort us in sorrow and in death ? Shall we go to the scene of unhallowed revelry, where the drunkard quaffs his cup of death, and blasphemes his God ? What should we do in the end thereof ? " No !" says he who has been once enlightened, and tasted of the heavenly gift, " I can go nowhere but to Christ. Lord, let me never leave Thee, the fountain of living water and go and hew out for myself cisterns, broken cisterns,' that can hold no water." Does the Devil suggest to the believer that he is too unworthy, too sinful, to come to Christ ? Still the answer is, " To whom else can I go ? Jesus Christ came into the world to save sinners, and He has said that He will in no wise cast out any that come unto Him. I dare not, then, keep back from going to Him. The more unclean and guilty I am, the more need I have to go to Him, whose blood alone can cleanse, and whose grace can strengthen me. No other can do for me what Christ can. I must cleave to Him, and if I perish, I will perish at His feet." This, brethren, is to have on the shield of faith—that shield behind which we shall stand unmoved in the evil day, since it quenches all the darts of the wicked one.

But, secondly, that we may overcome the temptations to depart from Christ, it is needful that we be actuated by a constant fear lest we should depart from Him. That they might learn not to be high-minded, but fear, it was, doubtless, that Jesus on this occasion answered His disciples, " Have I not chosen you twelve, and one of you is a devil ? He spake of Judas Iscariot, the son of Simon ; for he it was that should betray Him."   And this was not the only time that our Lord made to them the same statement, for we find Him, at a later period, thus expressing Himself : " Verily, verily, I say unto you, that one of you shall betray me."   Now, to what end did He thus speak to them ?   Plainly, that He might put them upon the most earnest self-examination, that He might lead every heart to make the trembling enquiry, " Lord, is it I ?"   Nor only this, but that He might render them fearful of being led astray ; that He might teach them to watch and be sober, to take heed of themselves, and to see what spirit they weer of.

And these, brethren, are things which we, equally with the chosen twelve, need to do. We need to examine ourselves, and to examine ourselves with the deepest earnestness, and we need to fear always.   There is nothing so dangerous for us as the taking up of the persuasion that all is well with us, without carefully examining whether all is indeed well.   We must never be secure in an enemy's land ; and such is this house of our pilgrimage.   Here, as every one might know, our own hearts are ever ready to deceive us ; here, wherever we go, the world spreads snares for our feet ; here our " adversary the devil goeth about seeking whom he may devour."   Here, then, to be off our guard, is to be undone ; to allow ourselves to cease to " be sober, be vigilant "—is to court destruction—is to expose ourselves to influences, the operation of which will drown us in perdition.   " There remaineth a rest for the people of God ;"—if we are· Christ's true people we shall, ere long, enter a land where all will be quietness and assurance ; but here we cannot be in quiet, for here Satan will not let us alone, but will ply us with his devices—meeting us where we least expect him, and

188

tempting us through objects the most innocent and the most unlikely to furnish occasions of falling. Let us, then, fear always ! Knowing that dangers lurk around us, let us "watch and pray that we enter not into temptation." Knowing that the heart within is treacherous and may admit the foe, let the attitude of our souls be that of waiting upon Him whose "grace is sufficient" for us, and whose "strength is made perfect in weakness." Thus, even in the attitude of "looking unto Jesus," shall we be kept from falling, until the perils of the wilderness are past, and we reach that holy mountain, where "there is nothing to hurt or to destroy !"

SERMON IV.

St. John xii., 20–26.—And there were certain Greeks among them that came up to worship at the feast : The same came therefore to Philip, which was of Bethsaida of Galilee, and desired him, saying, Sir, we would see Jesus.

EVENTS of a most important character were now thickening in Jerusalem. There was a movement in men's minds respecting Jesus of Nazareth, such as had not been seen at any previous period of His earthly history. There was a growing conviction that He could be none other than the promised Messiah. Multitudes had gone forth to meet Him as He approached the city, carrying triumphal palms, and crying, as He drew near, " Hosanna ! Blessed is the King of Israel that cometh in the name of the Lord ! " In a word, there were so many that now believed in Jesus, and so many others who were inclined to believe in Him that the Pharisees, who were watching all that took place with the keen eye of jealousy, said among themselves, " Perceive ye, how ye prevail nothing ? Behold, the world has gone after him." It is nothing surprising, then, to find persons who had come up at this Passover from distant places of the earth, and who might previously have heard little of Jesus, sharing in that universal interest concerning Him, and taking steps to obtain an interview with Him.

Among these, we find there were Greeks—" And there were certain Greeks among them that came up to worship at the feast : The same came therefore to Philip, which was of Bethsaida of Galilee, and desired him, saying, Sir, we would see Jesus." Some question has been made who these Greeks were ; whether Jews speaking the Greek language and living among Greeks, or proselytes to the religion of the Jews from heathenism. It may incline us to adopt the latter opinion, to remember that the Greek and the Jew are generally spoken of in Scripture as two distinct classes of men, and to find, as we do, that, at the subsequent feast of Pentecost mentioned in the second chapter of the Acts, there were present from various lands persons called Jews and proselytes. Besides, their being of Gentile race seems to be glanced at in our Lord's language in the thirty-third verse of this chapter, obviously spoken in their hearing—" And I, if I be lifted up from the earth, will draw all men unto me." However this may have been, it speaks much for the piety of these men—it might shame others under a clearer light—that they had come up to worship at the feast— that, in their desire to worship God in the way appointed in His Word, they had incurred the expense and surmounted the difficulty and danger of a long journey. It is known how easily many are prevented from coming up to worship God in His house by their having even a short distance to come, or by some other slight inconvenience attending their coming. Might not such persons do well to say to themselves, " Is my interest in spiritual things such as it ought to be ? Is there no cause for apprehension on my part, that when I am weighed in the balances I shall be found wanting, and that, among those who shall rise up in the judgment to condemn me, will be found those Gentile proselytes who came so far, and encountered so much, that they might wait upon God in His temple ? Let me judge myself in this thing that I may not be judged ; and let the future witness in me a far different interest in keeping God's ordinances than that which has marked the past."

It further speaks well for these proselytes that they approached our Lord in the manner they did. Real piety is never bold and presuming in its bearing towards those with whom it seeks intercourse ; it is modest and retiring. It shrinks from taking a high place, and loves a low one. In their eagerness to have an interview with our Lord, these Gentile proselytes would, no doubt, have desired at once to approach Him, but they were held back by the apprehension that it was not for them, since they belonged not originally to the favoured race, to claim such a favour. Accordingly, they came to Philip of Bethsaida, expressing to him their desire to see Jesus, and perhaps asking him, if he could not venture himself upon such an application in their behalf, to confer about the propriety of it with some of his fellow disciples. At all events, we read that immediately on their preferring their request to Philip—" Philip cometh and telleth Andrew ; and again, Andrew and Philip tell Jesus."

It is not stated in so many words that the Greeks were successful in their application to be admitted to see Jesus. We cannot doubt this, however, as they were not of a class to be cast out by Him, and as, besides, there is evidence in the discourse of our Lord which follows, to satisfy the attentive reader that they were among its hearers, and especially in His eye when He spoke it. The Evangelist neither notices their introduction into our Lord's presence, nor the personal salutations that took place on their being introduced. Passing over these things, as not entering into his design, or as what the brevity which he had to consult required him to drop, he comes at once to the discourse spoken by our Lord in consequence of the coming to Him of these Gentile strangers.

"And Jesus answered them, saying, The hour is come that the Son of Man should be glorified." This seems to be a reply either to something that had been said by these Greeks, or to something which our Lord saw was passing in their mind. "He knew what was in man;" and most probably he took up the thought that was most occupying them, and addressed Himself to it. They had witnessed His triumphal entry into Jerusalem. They had seen Him come to Zion as it had been predicted by Zechariah that He would come : they had heard, perhaps joined in, the exulting shout, "Hosanna, Blessed is the King of Israel, that cometh in the name of the Lord!" Now, these things, it is evident, were calculated to excite expectation. They were calculated to excite the expectation which had been formed on another occasion, that the kingdom of God should immediately appear. Surely, they must have thought, this man, whose works proclaim him to be the Son of God with power, and who has, at length, permitted himself to be publicly acknowledged as the King of Israel, is no longer to continue the obscure and lowly man he has hitherto been. Surely, as has been foretold of him, he is now to " sit as king upon the holy hill of Zion," and to have " given to him dominion, and glory, and a kingdom, that all people and nations and languages," and we in the number, "may serve him."

And how does our Lord meet these thoughts? Even by telling them that what they expected was at hand—that the time of His humiliation was hastening to its close, and that His exaltation to the right hand of power was near. "The hour is come that the Son of Man should be glorified." The word "hour" here is not used in its strictly literal sense, but in one in which it is very often employed, namely, the season, the time, the period. The season, the time for the Son of Man being glorified is come, and glorified He shall now be ; the Father loses sight of none of His purposes, and all that is written of the exaltation of the Son shall be fulfilled. Such was the import of our Lord's words at this time ; and we know that they were accomplished, as He said they would be ;

N

—that, at that very season, He was received up into glory, and sat down on the right hand of God, "from henceforth expecting till His enemies be made His footstool." Brethren, let it comfort our hearts that the counsel of the Lord standeth fast, that though heaven and earth may pass away, His words pass not away. The Son of Man was glorified at the time to which we are referring; the heavenly gates then lifted up their heads to give Him entrance as the king of glory, and as the king of glory He did enter within them. But we look for a season, a period, in which the Son of Man will be glorified as He has not yet been, and we shall see, what we do not yet see, all things put under Him, every knee bowing to Him, and every tongue confessing, of things in heaven and things on earth, and things under the earth. We look for this, because it is written, and we look not for it in vain. At the appointed time "His glory shall be revealed; He shall come to be glorified in His saints, and to be admired of all them that believe." Let us wait upon Him from heaven, and we shall have part in that glorious coming; "for when Christ, who is our life, shall appear, then shall we also appear with Him in glory."

It was true, as these Grecian strangers supposed, that the season had arrived when the Son of Man should be glorified; but how little did they understand of the way by which alone He could enter into His glory. This He now proceeded to tell them, making use, for this purpose, of a most striking and significant figure. "Verily, verily, I say unto you, except a corn of wheat fall into the ground and die, it abideth alone; but if it die, it bringeth forth much fruit." The expression "verily, verily," marks the certainty and importance of the declaration which it ushers in; and surely, if ever there was a declaration needing to be thus introduced, it was this of our Lord. He tells the Greeks that the hour for His being glorified was come, but He could only be so through His dying. What a damp this must have thrown over their highly

raised expectations! How strange, how incredible must
it have seemed to them that the way to His glorification
should be through death! But it was even so. They
were familiar with the fact of life coming through death.
The riches and glory of harvest were the result of a
previous death. A corn of wheat that did not fall into
the ground and die, produced nothing, but abode alone;
it was only when it died in the earth that it was quickened
and germinated; and brought forth fruit. This, said Jesus,
is an emblem of me. Like the grain of wheat, I must be
laid in the earth, I must die; but out of this death there
shall come life; it is thus that I shall spring up, and become the fruitful source of a new and imperishable seed.
You are disappointed and grieved to hear me speak of my
death, but if you understood your condition and need
aright, you would rejoice, for you would see that the only
hope for a lost world lay in my suffering and dying.

Have you understood this, my friends? It should not
be so difficult for us to understand it as it was for these
Greeks, since our position is so much more favourable
than theirs. "The good seed of human nature which God
had planted had become corrupted in the earth; it failed ·
to yield the return of righteousness. God looked over
the successive generations of men, but found not a single
individual among them all whom He could reserve as the
new root, or seed, of another and righteous succession.
At last one man was found,—one only,—a man perfect
and without spot. One single grain of human nature was
obtained, and God took that, nourished it carefully, and
planted it in a fruitful soil. That one instance of human
perfection was Jesus Christ, the second Adam, 'the Lord
from Heaven.' He was wholly a good seed; and God
took Him and brought Him into the dust of death, that
He might become the stock and source of a new and
godly seed."* It was only by dying that he could become

* From Stevenson's "Christ on the Cross."

the stock and source in respect of corrupt man. It was only thus that He could take the prey from the mighty; it was only thus that He could receive "power over all flesh, to give eternal life to as many as the Father had given Him;" the perfections of God and the necessities of their condition equally demanded that if He should deliver them from death, it should be by His voluntarily dying for them, and His offering Himself, without spot, to God for them. And thus it is that He becomes a source of life to them. This was the very purpose of His dying; not that He might abide alone, but that He might have a numerous seed, that He might "see of the travail of His soul and be satisfied." And this He has already seen, and shall yet see more and more. They who receive Him in the exercise of a lively faith live through Him. They are crucified together with Him, yet they live, and yet not they, but Christ lives in them. "They are buried with Him by baptism unto death; that like as Christ was raised from the dead, even so they also should walk in newness of life."

This prepares us to understand what our Lord proceeds to address to these Greeks in the twenty-fifth verse. "He that loveth his life shall lose it, and he that hateth his life in this world shall keep it unto life eternal." He was Himself to die, that He might become the stock and source of a new and divine life to those who were dead in sin. This was His sacrifice, but there must be a sacrifice, too, on the part of all to whom He was to bring life. They also must die, in order to have life. To enter fully into our Lord's meaning here, it is necessary to bear in mind that there are two things in Scripture called life; that there is a carnal life and a spiritual life. There is a carnal life; there is a happiness, an enjoyment in the things of the world, apart from God, for which we have a capacity through the flesh; and this carnal life all men have in their natural state. Now, this carnal enjoyment without God is evil; it is so, because God is shut out of

196

it, and the whole charm of it is that self is exalted and
worshipped. Though the natural heart is unwilling to
think so, this interest in earthly things is evil now ; for
" there is no peace," no real peace, " to the wicked,"
to those alienated from God, even here ; and it will be
shown to be evil hereafter, when this state of things, in
which men can have an enjoyment in the flesh and away
from God, is brought to an end, and all that is evil—all
that is not of God—" is cast into the lake of fire." Again,
there is a spiritual life—a life which consists in knowing
God and being made like to Him, and so having a capacity for partaking of those joys which are in His presence
—a life which, begun on earth, will be perfected in
Heaven, when " that which is in part shall be done away,
and that which is perfect shall be come." Now, keeping
these two kinds of life in view, we shall see our Lord's
meaning in the words before us, and we shall be sensible,
as we discern their meaning, of their deep interest to
every one of us. He that clings to that interest and enjoyment in present things, which is through the flesh, as
his portion—he that loves his life in this sense, shall lose
his life—shall lose that which alone deserves to be called
life, the life of God, and shall die the second death. He,
on the other hand, that hateth his life in this world—he
that rejects as evil all that ungodly enjoyment in present
things for which he has a capacity through the flesh—he
that " crucifieth the flesh with its affections and lusts"—
he that hateth his life in this sense, shall keep what alone
is worthy of the name of life, shall be " blessed with all
spiritual blessings in heavenly things in Christ Jesus ;"
shall even now taste a blessedness which " eye hath not
seen, nor ear heard, nor heart conceived," and at the
resurrection of the just shall be made perfectly blessed
in the full enjoying of God to all eternity. Such is our
Lord's meaning ; and surely there is matter here for deep
and earnest self-examination. Have we been brought to
this point, even the being made willing to lose our own

life that we may find the life of God? It is this that shows that we have been grafted into the new stock, that Christ has been formed " in us the hope of glory ;" and with what earnestness should we seek that this may be so with us! We should even travail as in birth, that this spiritual quickening may be realised in us, for without this we have no lot nor part in the second Adam, " the Lord from Heaven," but are "dead while we live," destitute of that which alone constitutes the true and proper life of our souls.

Our Lord continues, " If any man serve me, let him follow me ; and where I am, there shall also my servant be : if any man serve me, him will my Father honour." The Greeks, who had desired to see our Lord, had in all probability pressed their desire to be His servants ; here He instructs them how only they could serve Him, and points their view to those unspeakable rewards which awaited His servants. " If any man will serve me, let him follow me." He had been speaking of suffering and self-sacrifice, and the following Him here evidently respects these things. Those whom He was addressing might have borne a palm-branch at His triumphal entry into Jerusalem ; they might have shouted on that occasion, "Hosanna to the Son of David!" These were easy things ; there were harder things awaiting all that should serve Him. He, as He had intimated to them, was to be a sufferer ; it was through suffering that He was to be glorified. So, too, with all His servants. They must be sufferers. They must suffer with Christ here, before they can be glorified with Him hereafter, before they can be with Him where He is, and be crowned, as His servants, with glory and honour by His Father. " They," as He tells them, " must drink of His cup, and be baptized with the baptism that He was baptized with." Here there are two views of Christ's sufferings, which must be carefully distinguished from each other. On the one hand, His sufferings were propitiatory—were His atonement for sin ; on the other hand, they were the road by which He passed to glory. In the first of these we have no part ; we cannot partake of the sufferings of Christ in the sense of making with Him an atonement for sin ; for to atone for sin was a work in which no creature, and surely no sinful creature, could possibly have any share. But in the other view of His sufferings, He is the pattern of our condition. While, in treading the wine-press of the wrath of God to obtain our eternal redemption, we have no participation ;—in treading the steps of holy suffering by which He, as our Forerunner, entered into His glory, we have and must have a participation,—in *this* we must follow His steps ; we must be made conformable to Him. A participation of the sufferings of Christ in this view of them, is, in fact, our high and blessed calling in this present time ; nor unless we thus suffer with Him now, shall we reign with Him hereafter.

" If any man serve me, let him follow me." Do we wonder at this, that with us the way to the crown should be by the cross ? When Christ, " though He were a Son, yet learned obedience by the things which He suffered ;" is it strange that we, if sons, should be called to learn obedience by the things which we suffer ? There is a blessed need for our being " partakers of Christ's sufferings." They are from our Father's love, and are His merciful and gracious discipline to conform us to Christ's image, that we may be prepared for Christ's glory. Our suffering with Christ is, in fact, a part of the acting of that new life which every Christian lives in the flesh by the faith of the Son of God, and which he must live, and which alone it is blessed for him to live, until the body of sin and death in him is finally destroyed, and he is " clothed upon with his house from Heaven," and hence those pantings and aspirings of the Apostle, " That I may know Christ, and the power of His resurrection, and the fellowship of His sufferings, being made conformable unto His death, if by any means I might attain unto the resurrection of the dead."

Brethren, does it pain you to hear the Christian life thus represented ? Does it grieve you to be told that, to be servants of Christ, you must follow " the Captain of your salvation ;" that you must be conformed to your Lord ; that you must " drink, indeed, of His cup, and be baptized with the baptism that He was baptized with ? " And is it so hard, then, that God should " deal with you as with sons ;" with you, as He dealt with His own beloved Son who never offended Him, while you have constantly grieved and provoked His Holy Spirit ? And is there no present blessedness in thus suffering with Christ ? This is no joyless calling ; the sorrow that attends upon it is no sorrow of the world working death, but a Divine sorrow working life. They who have most suffered with Christ have rejoiced with a " joy unspeakable and full of glory." They who suffer with Christ, putting, by their willing and ready suffering with Him, His condemnation upon their sin ; they whose sufferings are of this holy character, have even now a joy which no man taketh from them ; and " as the sufferings of Christ abound in them, so their consolation also aboundeth by Christ."

And then, what a hope is theirs when this brief season of conflict and tribulation is over ! " Where I am, there shall my servant be." " If we suffer with Him, we shall also reign with Him." " If so be that we suffer with Him, we shall be glorified together." " Our light affliction, which is but for a moment, worketh out for us a far more exceeding and eternal weight of glory." And shall we then think it grievous that we should be called to suffer with Christ ? Might we not well grieve if we were not called to suffer with Him ? For would it not be a token to us that our state was evil ; that our spirit was not the spirit of Christ ; that we were still out of the way, and had never known the path to life and immortality?

SERMON V.

St. John xiii., 1 to 7.—"Now, before the Feast of the Passover, when Jesus knew that his hour was come, that he should depart out of this world unto the Father,—having loved his own which were in the world, He loved them unto the end."

IN the preceding chapter we have an account of the close of our Lord's lessons to the people at large. The curtain had now fallen around the scenes on which He had appeared as a public teacher; and here the Evangelist conducts us into the sacred circle of the chosen disciples, and makes us hearers of the sublime and consoling instructions which He gave them previously to His departure out of the world. The transaction here related, in which He gave His disciples such a touching proof of His condescension and love towards them, took place in an upper room in Jerusalem in which He and they were assembled for the purpose of eating the Passover. "Now before the feast of the Passover, when Jesus knew that His hour was come that He should depart out of this world unto the Father, having loved His own which were in the world, He loved them unto the end." We have here a mark of the time or occasion of our Lord's giving His disciples the striking illustration of His self-sacrificing affection which follows. It was before, and, as we find, immediately before the Feast of the Passover,—that feast which, while it commemorated the deliverance of Israel from Egyptian servitude, typified a far greater deliverance than that—even the redemption, by the blood of Christ, of a world enslaved to sin and Satan. It was the last Passover that Jesus was to keep; and He knew that it was. He was aware that His hour was come, when he should depart out of this world unto the Father. He was just to pass into His glory through the gates of suffering and death, but His disciples were, for a time at least, to be left behind. They were to follow Him to His glory afterwards, but they could not do so then; they must yet continue for a season in the world, and it was a world in which they were to be hated for His sake, and where they were to have great tribulation. How does he now act towards them? They were "His own,"—given Him by His Father, chosen by Himself; His constant companions, His familiar friends,--the objects of his peculiar affection,—the subjects of His saving benefits. They were thus His own; and He had "loved" them as His own. He had cherished and manifested towards them, in all his past connexion with them, a tender and peculiar affection. And it was so still. He thought of them as in the world, and as, therefore, standing in need of His love as much as ever; and He did love them. The near contemplation of His sufferings, calculated as they were to engross His human soul, neither diverted nor diminished his affection; "He loved them unto the end;" He felt and He manifested towards them the depth and the tenderness of His regard down to the very close of His being with them in the world;—thus showing them that "He rested in His love," that He would never withdraw it from the soul on which it had been set.

We know not, brethren, who of you are Christ's own; who of you have received Him. *We* cannot tell, for appearances are deceitful, who are the Saviour's friends, the objects of His love, the subjects of His grace; *that* is known only to God and your own hearts. If you are

Christ's own,—if conscience now gives its testimony that you love Him, and are loved by Him, let me speak to you of the rich consolation which is here given you. You are in the world, and while in the world you must needs have sorrow. "In the world," the Saviour says to you, "ye shall have tribulation." But behold the consolation that is yours. Whatever may be your circumstances, you have in Christ a fast and unfailing friend—a friend that "that loveth at all times," that will never leave, never forsake you. If He were to withdraw his love from you, you might well be cast down; but He will never withdraw it. "The mountains shall depart, and the hills be removed, but my kindness shall not depart from thee, neither shall the covenant of my peace be removed, saith the Lord that hath mercy upon thee." "Who shall separate us from the love of Christ? Neither death nor life, nor angels, nor principalities, nor powers, nor things present, nor things to come, nor height, nor depth, nor any other creature shall be able to separate us from the love of God, which is in Christ Jesus our Lord."

"And supper being ended, the Devil having now put it into the heart of Judas Iscariot, Simon's son, to betray him."—The expression here rendered, "supper being ended," should rather have been translated, "In the course of supper," or "while they were at supper." It was during the meal that the circumstance about to be mentioned took place. By the Devil's "putting into the heart of Judas" to betray his Lord, is meant his tempting him to commit this fearful act of treason. This, we know, he did by means of his avarice. Satan is the great tempter, but Satan has no power to tempt any one except through some corrupt inclination or passion of the mind which he can make use of. Where there is such an inclination or passion, he artfully addresses himself to it,—he presents to it the objects fitted to arouse and inflame it; and thus gets the advantage he seeks. What he found to work upon in the case of Judas was his love of money; and we know with what success he did work upon this passion in him. Oh, brethren, let us beware how we lust after any evil thing—how we cherish any corrupt propensity in our hearts. Let us especially recall to our remembrance here the danger of indulging a covetous, worldly spirit. The love of money has been the ruin of multitudes. "They that will be rich fall into temptation and a snare, and into many foolish and hurtful lusts, which drown men in destruction and perdition."

"Jesus, knowing that the Father had given all things into His hands, and that He was come from God, and went to God; He riseth from supper, and laid aside His garments; and took a towel and girded Himself. After that He poureth water into a bason and began to wash the disciples' feet, and to wipe them with the towel wherewith He was girded." There had been, at this time, a most unseemly contention among the disciples which of them should be the greatest; and one object of the lowly act here performed by our Lord was to show them what constituted true greatness, and how mistaken they were who supposed it to lie in lording it over others. Our Lord at this time knew that He was just about to be betrayed into the hands of His enemies; He had fully before His mind the sufferings and death which He must undergo. But He had before Him, too, the glory that lay beyond these. He knew "That the Father had given all things into His hands;" that He had come from God as the Redeemer of a lost world; and that through the appointed way of a complete expiation of the sins of man by the suffering of death, He was going back to God to be "crowned with glory and honour," and to receive the rich reward of His sufferings. In these circumstances, when the intensest inward suffering, and the near prospect of unparalleled agonies, united with the most undoubting anticipation of triumph and recompense in "seeing of the travail of His soul," discovered Him, in the most sublime manner, the union of the human and the divine natures—in these circumstances did he stand up to show to His disciples, and to all succeeding generations of men, in an emblematic action, as remarkable for its beautiful simplicity as for its profound significance, the mystery of true human greatness—to teach what it is to be " great in the kingdom of God." " He riseth from supper, and laid aside His garments ; and took a towel and girded Himself. After that He poureth water into a bason, and began to wash the disciples' feet, and to wipe them with the towel wherewith He was girded." Wonder, O heavens ! Be astonished, O earth ! He into whose hands the Father hath committed all things : He who came from God, and is going to God : He who is fully aware of all this, in the guise of a servant washes the feet of men—of simple men—of publicans and fishermen ! He tells us elsewhere, that " He came not to be ministered unto, but to minister, and to give His life a ransom for many " ; and in what He here does, He gives us an exhibition of His saving work on our behalf. " Being in the form of God," robed in the glories which He had with the Father, He " emptied Himself ; " laid aside these glories as far as they could be laid aside; " took on Him the form of a servant," and in that form " humbled Himself," stooping to the lowest offices, yea, " even to death, the death of the cross ; " and all this that we, being washed by Him, might have part in Him, being made sharers of is Hholiness, and so of His happiness."

"Then cometh he to Simon Peter ; and Peter said unto him, Lord, dost thou wash my feet ? Jesus answered and said unto him, What I do thou knowest not now ; but thou shalt know hereafter." The conduct of Peter on this occasion is in the highest degree characteristic. The disciples must have witnessed our Lord's act at this time with amazement, but their wonder must have been mixed with shame ; for imperfectly as they might apprehend the meaning of the act, they could not but feel that it rebuked their worldly ambition, their desire for preeminence and self-exaltation. Still they spoke not, suffering, if reluctantly yet unresistingly suffering, their venerated Master to perform towards them the part of a servant. Simon Peter alone brooked not to see his Lord so servilely employed ; with characteristic impetuosity, he refused to submit to what he thought it was a degradation to Jesus to do for him, asking, " 'Lord, dost thou wash my feet ?' Dost thou, the Son of the living God, perform such an office towards me, a sinful man, a worm of the dust? This be far from thee ! " It was to receive the reply, at once so meek and so full of majesty, " ' What I do, thou knowest not now ; but thou shalt know hereafter.' The design of My action is at present mysterious and unexplained ; full light will soon be thrown upon it. Meanwhile, it is thy duty to submit to My will, trusting that thou shalt receive the fullest satisfaction in regard to it, in due time." And this was written, not for the instruction only of the disciples then, but for the instruction of all disciples. It was written, brethren, for our instruction. The Lord's dealings with us are often mysterious ; in vain do we try to penetrate their meaning ; we cannot think what their end will be. What in such circumstances is God's language to us? It is this : "What I do thou knowest not now, but thou shalt know hereafter." Meantime submit thyself calmly and joyfully to my appointments ; possess thy soul in faith and patience, awaiting the time when all that is dark and perplexing shall be made plain to thee, and thou shalt see that I did all things well.

Consider, brethren, that in the Lord's present dispensations towards us, there will often be things which are mysterious to us. This He prepares us to expect ; He says, " I will bring the blind by a way that they know not, I will lead them in paths that they have not known." The disciples knew not, at this time, what the Lord was doing ; His providence was involved in an obscurity which they could not penetrate. And the same has been the experience of the people of God in every age. His judgments to them have been unsearchable, and "His ways past finding out." It was so with Jacob, with Joseph, with Israel in the wilderness, with Job, with Daniel ; with what feeling would all these in their day have entered into the language of the Psalmist :—"Thy way is in the sea ; and thy path in the great waters, and thy footsteps are not known."

And it is the same with the people of God still. If we are His people, we shall often be led in a way that we know not. His dispensations will be perplexing and mysterious to us. The reason for their being sent,—the course they are to take, the means whereby we may be relieved of them, the purposes they are to answer—all these things will be hidden from us. But shall we stumble at these things ? Shall we permit them to give rise to dissatisfaction and murmuring in our hearts ? Because the crooked thing is not all at once made straight, because the dark thing is not immediately made light, shall we be offended, and say, "Why should I wait for the Lord any longer ?" It should be enough to still all such thoughts that whatever be the path in which we are led, it is the Lord who is leading us ; that whatever is done with us, He is doing it. "Trouble," my brethren, "springs not out of the ground," nothing has come,—nothing can ever come to us, but what He appoints. "Without Him a sparrow falleth not to the ground—by Him the very hairs of our head are all numbered"—how much more may we feel that this must be so, in regard to things which affect us more deeply ! Let us never lose sight of the great truth that the Lord reigns, and that, therefore, whatever befalls us, He can say, "I have done this," even He who cannot err, and who loves us with a love stronger than death. We become impatient only when we forget that Jesus goes before us in the way, and measures out to us in infinite kindness the troubles that befall us ; when we realise His nearness to us, and His interest in us, and how, by all His dealings, He is working out with us His gracious purposes, we are impatient no longer ; the storm is all quieted ; and we are still, knowing that He is God, and that He is right in all that He does.

But consider farther, that what we know not now, we shall know hereafter. It must needs be that the dispensations of God towards us now will be often dark and mysterious. There must be much in the movements of of the leader of an army which the common soldier cannot understand ; there must be much in the conduct of a parent towards a child, the meaning and purpose of which will be unseen by that child. So it must be with us in respect of our Divine Leader, our Heavenly Father. In that Leader's arrangements concerning us,—in that Father's treatment of us, there must be much that we cannot comprehend ;—much that only a little more knowledge and experience would convince us that it would not be well for us that we should all at once comprehend. But the knowledge which is now of necessity, and in mercy to us withheld, will not always be withheld ; there is a time coming when what is now dark and mysterious in God's ways will have the fullest light thrown upon it. That time will be, if not in the present world, certainly in the world to come. Often it will be in the present world. Think of Joseph. The ways of God to him were long dark ; but how clear to him did they at length appear, when made second in the kingdom of Egypt, he became not only the instrument of " saving much people alive," but the " nourisher of his father, and his brethren, and of all his father's household." Think of our Lord's disciples at the very period to which the passage before us refers. Much as he had done to make known to them the mysteries of His Kingdom, there were many things of which He spake to them which they could not understand. His sufferings, of which he forewarned them, were altogether a mystery to them ; when He told them that He should " be delivered into the hands of sinful men," and of what should be done to Him, they were offended in Him. But in a few days all was made plain to them, and they were glorying in the very truths at which they had stumbled, and of which they had been so impatient.

Thus, often, will much that is dark and perplexing to us in God's ways, be cleared up, even in the present world. In the coming world *all* shall be explained to our perfect satisfaction. Here it is still night with us ; but there is "no night *there !*" *There*, no cloud will rest upon the Divine dispensations ; *there*, we shall discern that infinite love directed every one of those things which once so perplexed and confounded us ; *there*, as we retrace all our course, and see the need for every maze and winding in it, and how each particular trial worked out the glorious consummation we have arrived at, our language will be, " He did all things well!" Dear friends, let these things repress in us every tendency to hasty and irreverent objections to the doctrines of Scripture, on the ground of the difficulty and mystery that clings to them. Few things are more common than the indulgence of rash and irreverent cavils in regard to things in the Bible which appear difficult ; but there is nothing so nnbecoming,—nothing of which the cavillers, if they at all reflected, should be so much ashamed. How many things are there, my friends, which were once dark and perplexing to us, which are now clear and satisfactory ? How many things, once deemed foolish by you, are now seen to be the highest wisdom ? And may it not be so in regard to what now may seem difficult in the Scriptures ? May it not in a little while have such a light thrown upon it, that it shall be the ver thing in which you discern the greatest beauty and excellence ? And is it well then, to be in haste to judge in these things ? And albeit there are things difficult to be understood in the peculiar doctrines of Christianity, is it honourable to reject them, saying, " These are hard sayings—who can bear them ?" Surely the sober-minded will have no difficulty in seeing that there is a more excellent way than this.

O

Let us learn, also, from these things never to charge God rashly in regard to any of His dispensations towards us. Some heavy trial has come upon us, and we cannot see how it is to work for our good, rather we see, as we think, that it must operate injuriously upon us. In such seasons, we are tempted to murmur at what has been dealt out to us, to call in question the wisdom and goodness of the Lord. But let us resist such a temptation ! Let us remember how little we know of God's ways, and how much more likely it is that we should be wrong or mistaken than that He should err. There is a common but significant proverb which we would do well to remember here,—" Fools and children should not see things half done,"—for, in contemplating the Divine manifestations, the wisest of men are but in the place of children who gaze on the intricate operations of some profound mechanician, or skilful artist. Something of what is done, they may see, but into its reasons they cannot enter, or if they can, it is only a little way. Far, then, from us be the disposition to find fault with any of the Lord's doings towards us ! Let it be enough for us that it is His hand that directs all things. Let this produce in us a calm, unquestioning, joyful submission. He loved us in our low and lost estate ; —He loved us then, so as to lay down for us His life ;— He has gone, with all that love to us, within the holy place, and can He then appoint us one thing which has not for its object the advancement of our highest good ? It cannot be ! His kindness never departs from us ; and those trials which He sends us, even those of them that are the darkest and most perplexing, are but varied expressions of His goodness. There is not one of them all, which we shall not one day recognise as a token of love, and which, when we come to contemplate it in the light of Heaven, will not furnish us with a theme of gratitude and praise, as having formed part of that plan of grace by which we were fitted and matured for glory.

SERMON VI.

Acts xx., 35.—I have shewed you all things, how that so labouring ye ought to support the weak, and to remember the words of the Lord Jesus, how he said, It is more blessed to give than to receive.

IT should give a peculiar interest to the words here recorded to have been spoken by our Lord, that they should have been preserved while so many others of His sayings were suffered to pass into oblivion. This saying is not found in any of the narratives of the four Evangelists, but they do not profess to record all His sayings. Every word uttered by Him, of whom it was so justly said, " Never man spake like this man," was precious, was worthy of being handed down to coming age, but to preserve them all was impossible ; and it was thus that John, who wrote last, closes his gospel—" And there are also many other things which Jesus did, the which, if they should be written every one, I suppose that even the world itself could not contain the books that should be written." It would thus happen that many of the things which Jesus spake, being not committed to writing, but left to the uncertainties of oral tradition, would soon be irrecoverably lost. Here, however, was a saying of His too precious to be suffered to share the common fate, and the great Apostle of the Gentiles was over-ruled, on the occasion to which he here refers, to gather up and preserve the precious fragments for the Church's use in all generations. During his ministry at Ephesus, as he here reminds

the elders of that church, he had not neglected to inculcate the duty of giving to the destitute, to those unable
to provide for themselves, as is signified by the term "the
weak ;" he had particularly instructed them in this important duty, and bound it upon them by a consideration
of all others the most affecting to the heart of a Christian,
" I have shewed you all things, how that so labouring ye
ought to support the weak, and to remember the words
of the Lord Jesus, how he said, It is more blessed to give
than to receive."

These words remind us of the duty of supporting the
destitute, but yet, as will be observed, present to us the
matter of giving to the needy more in the light of a
privilege than of a duty. There is a blessedness in giving.
He who withholds not his compassion from the destitute,
but opens for them his heart and hand, has a happiness,
a delight in what he does. There is a *peculiar* blessedness attendant on giving. It was said by our Lord, "It
is more blessed to give than to receive." There *is* a
blessedness in receiving, and a great one. Unless, where
the hearts of the distressed have become utterly cold and
dead to human sensibilities, a deed, or word, or even a
look of sympathy in the day of their calamity, always
awakens emotions of pleasure. Such manifestations of
concern for them draw forth their gratitude, and gratitude
to a benefactor is always a sweet sensation, especially
when we contemplate the hand of God in raising him up
to relieve us. But if there is a high blessedness in
receiving, there is a yet higher in giving. He who bestows is happier yet in bestowing than is the object of
his bounty in receiving ; and sweet as are the emotions,
he awakens in the bosom of another, yet sweeter still are
those he feels within his own. And this high blessedness
we may know *now*—here in this present time. It is not
only that, upon the whole, and taking our coming eternity
into the account, it will be found thus peculiarly blessed
to be givers—but even now, and regarding man merely

as a denizen of this present world—this great blessedness
waits upon the exercise of giving. There is a day
approaching when the truth of the Saviour's sentiment
will be impressed upon every heart that ever beat within
a human frame, and when it will not be needful to prove
to a single individual of all the countless myriads that
shall have lived and died upon the earth, that "it is more
blessed to give than to receive." It will be when all shall
stand at the judgment seat of Christ, and when He, the
King, shall say to them on His right hand, "Come, ye
blessed of my Father, inherit the kingdom prepared for
you from the foundation of the world : For I was an
hungered, and ye gave me meat ; I was athirst, and ye
gave me drink ; I was a stranger, and ye took me in ;
naked, and ye clothed me ; I was sick, and ye visited
me ; I was in prison, and ye came unto me." On such
a day there will be but one feeling regarding the sentiment in our text—that, taking the whole of man's being
into view, it states an incontrovertible truth. But it is
not in reference to its future recompence merely, that our
Lord is to be considered as having uttered this sentiment.
He speaks not of beneficence as a thing that will be found
to be blessed hereafter, but as a thing that is blessed now ;
he speaks of its great *present* reward—of the immediate
peculiar felicity which will accompany it, as often as it is
exercised. "It is more blessed to give than to receive."

There are two points to which we would now briefly
invite attention. They are, first, the peculiar blessedness
which attends the exercise of beneficence, and, secondly,
the means which we possess of exercising this beneficence.

I. There is, as is indicated by the words "It is more
blessed to give than to receive," a blessedness peculiarly
great, attendant upon giving. To establish this, there
needs no elaborate process of reasoning. Strange as it
may seem when we consider the selfishness that is in
every human heart, when we mark that passion so
universal among mankind—the passion of concentrating

upon self—the sentiment of our Lord in the remarkable words before us commends itself to almost every mind, commanding the convictions however little it may influence the practice of men. That it may command our convictions, we have only to ask ourselves one or other of these two questions—Whom of all those whom we have observed, or whom we have heard of, do we deem the happiest? What have been those seasons when we have enjoyed the truest happiness ourselves?

Whom, brethren, of all those whom you have either observed or heard of do you deem to have been the happiest? We fear not to reply for you—they have been the most self-sacrificing. You have observed the activity and devotedness of maternal love. You know how utterly a mother can forget herself in caring for her infant offspring—how she can labour for them by day, and watch for them by night—and how, if only she can shield them from harm and promote their happiness, there is no personal danger she will not encounter, no personal comfort she will not give up. Is hers a joyless existence? You know that there is not a happier being beneath the sun than that self-sacrificing mother. You know that she is thus happy just because she is self-sacrificing, and that, were worlds to be offered her in exchange for the joy she feels in devoting herself for her helpless babe, they would be utterly contemned. You may have observed the faithful and laborious Sabbath school teacher. That he may feed his young charge with the bread of life, he foregoes not a little of present ease and of direct personal benefit. He might spare himself the pain often inflicted upon him through the inattention, the rudeness, or the unthankfulness of those he labours to instruct. He might give the time he devotes to them to private reading and meditation, or to other exercises more pleasing in themselves and more immediately profitable. Is he, therefore, unhappy in thus devoting himself for his charge? He will tell you that, though he would be happy to receive the spiritual benefit he misses, it yet affords him a higher happiness to be the imparter of the spiritual benefit he bestows, and that in his humble walk of usefulness, he has learned of a truth that "it is more blessed to give than to receive."

We have heard of the beneficence of *Job*. In the time of his calamity, he thus sketches a scene of his former life which he only, who had been in it, could so describe—"When the ear heard me, then it blessed me ; and when the eye saw me, it gave witness to me, because I delivered the poor that cried, and the fatherless, and him that had none to help him. The blessing of him that was ready to perish came upon me, and I caused the widow's heart to sing for joy." We stop not to ask whether those were blessed on whom Job thus had piety, whether their emotions were not among the sweetest known to human hearts—but who does not feel that if they were happy in receiving, yet far happier was he in giving?

We have heard of *Paul's* self-sacrificing love. We have read how he spent himself, and was spent in seeking the glory of God in the salvation of his fellow-men. We have read of his toils, his perils, his watchings, his weariness, his bonds and affliction, and finally, his martyrdom in the cause of dying souls. Was his, think we, an unhappy lot? We have only to look upon him while toiling and sacrificing to make others happy, to know that he himself was among the happiest of men. We have only to read over his address, in this chapter, to the elders of Ephesus, to know that its warm language could have welled up only from the depths of a supremely happy heart, and to learn that those words of the Lord Jesus, of which he reminded others, he found true in his own lengthened and latest experience,—" It is more blessed to give than to receive !"

We have heard of the philanthropist, Howard. He was eminently a giver, and many in many lands, and those among the most forlorn and forsaken of our race, were the receivers at his hands. Under the impulse of a love caught from that Saviour who, he tells us, was all his hope, he gave up the charms of home, and of ease, and of a rural life, which he had the means of embelllishing with all that could minister to a taste most exquisitely refined. He forsook all this to make his way into the most noisome cells of almost every prison and hulk in Europe, that he might take the dimensions of the deep misery that was there, and force others, less actively humane than himself, to labour for its abatement; nor did he ever rest from his labours in this self-denying work until he died on a foreign shore, a martyr to the cause of suffering humanity. Did Howard, suppose we, miss the path that led to happiness, while pursuing that of constant self-sacrifice? Oh! could we have gone with him through some of those dungeons whither he took his way, and witnessed how healingly fell his words and deeds of sympathy upon the heart of the despairing captive, we should have felt that he, indeed, had power to make others blessed, but we should have felt, the while, that if they were happy who were the objects of his bounty, yet happier still was he who dispensed it to them, and we should have thus returned with another confirmation of the statement in our text,—"It is more blessed to give than to receive."

All men by nature fall under the description,—"hateful and hating one another,"—and all the self-sacrificing love ever found in any human heart has been only an emanation from that which dwelt in infinite fulness in the bosom of the Man Christ Jesus. As a giver, he left all others immeasurably behind. He "came not to be ministered unto, but to minister." He went about continually doing good. His whole life from His first assuming our nature to His taking it with Him into heaven, was one mighty sacrifice. "Ye know the grace of the Lord Jesus Christ, that, though He was rich, yet for your sakes He became poor, that ye through His poverty might be rich." Had He no joy in thus denying Himself for us? It made Him most blessed thus to give. "My meat and drink," says He, "is to do the will of my Father, and to finish His work; and who but must gather from such language that He proved in His own experience the truth of His own saying to others, " It is more blessed to give than to receive"?

But, to come now to the other question which we suggested we should put to ourselves, it might serve to bring to our minds a yet deeper conviction of the high blessedness of giving, to consult our own past experience, and enquire what have been the seasons of our life when we have enjoyed the truest happiness. Sure we are that with none of us are those the green spots of memory when we shut our ears to the cry of the distressed, and passed by on the other side. No! such spots we would blot out from the past, if we could, for they never present themselves to our view without giving us pain; and if ever we have been truly happy, it has been at those times, if such there have been in our history, when, like Job, "the blessing of him that was ready to perish came upon us, and we made the widows' hearts sing for joy." It must needs be so, for to give is a form of love, and love is blessedness, yea, it assimilates us to the blessed God in blessedness. For "God is love, and he that dwelleth in love, dwelleth in God, and God in him."

II. But it is time to consider our second point, namely, the means we possess of exercising the self-sacrificing beneficence of which we have been speaking. We trust none will be found to say, "What matters it that the blessedness of giving is so great, when I have nothing to give, and must consequently be shut out from such blessedness?" You must be poor, indeed, if you have nothing wherewith to minister to the necessities of the destitute. Even the poor may have the means of doing much for those who are poorer still than they. If silver and gold they have none, yet out of what they have, they might give what would bless a neighbour that is near, while yet more richly blessing themselves. But even

217

money they might give far oftener than they think, and so reach a brother far off. You will remember the two mites of the poor widow, and the gracious recognition it met with from Him who justly weighs each deed we do. You will remember what is said by Paul of the churches of Macedonia,—" How that in a great trial of affliction, the abundance of their joy and their deep poverty abounded unto the riches of their liberality." But your complaint, perhaps, is not so much that you are poor, as that your expenditure exhausts your income, and so precludes your giving to the needy. But could you not practise a stricter economy, and thereby have the power to give to them? Could you retrench nothing on dress, on food, on furniture? Surely there is no one who looks at the actual state of things among us but must see that much might be saved on each of these things, and that, if only what is squandered among us on expensive entertainments, and in gay and gorgeous assemblies, wholly unbefitting a Christian, were henceforward to be redeemed, many who have now no disposable revenue for the disbursements of charity, would find themselves amply furnished for this work, and enjoy, in doing good, a higher luxury than any yet tasted by them.

But, if you neither have wherefrom to give, nor could save in order to give, could you not labour in order to do so? Listen to Paul in our text,—" I have showed you all things, how that so labouring "—that is, labouring with their hands, as he had done—" ye ought to support the weak." And listen also to another exhortation of his to the Ephesian Church, " Let him that stole steal no more ; but rather let him labour, working with his hands the thing that is good, that he may have to give to him that needeth." Oh, complain not, my friends, that you have not the means of giving to the destitute, when by labour you might acquire the means of giving to them. Will you say,—This is too lofty a benevolence for Christians to practise? Who will say this, who remembers how little it comes up to the example of His beneficence, who, to relieve our sore misery, not only laboured but died ; and who remembers, too, that Jesus has said,— "This is my commandment, that ye love one another, as I have loved you"?

From this subject you may see, brethren, how greatly we, who are ministers, should err, if, while we testified to you that you are saved by faith, we did not lift up our voice like a trumpet to warn you that never is a saving faith unaccompanied by good works ; but that it is, on the contrary, a "faith that worketh by love," that must needs be doing good, and that will never be found deaf when approached by the cry of a genuine distress. Let this be borne in remembrance. Let none account of faith, as if it could be disjoined from good works, as if it could exist where there was no showing mercy on the poor, no dealing of one's bread to the hungry ; for this can never be. "Faith without works is dead,"—is, in reality, no faith at all, and only proves that the man who has it, instead of being, as he may think, in the way of life, is, to this hour, abiding in death. "What doth it profit, my brethren, that a man say he hath faith, and have not works? Can faith save him? If a brother or sister be naked, and destitute of daily food, and one of you say unto them, Depart in peace, be ye warmed and filled ; notwithstanding ye give them not those things which are needful to the body, what doth it profit? Even so, faith, if it hath not works, is dead, being alone."

And to what do we invite you, when we invite you, this day, to draw forth your souls to the needy? We invite you to what the excitements of ambition could not do for you,—to what neither the accumulations of avarice nor the pleasures of dissipation could do for you. We just invite you to be blessed. By your liberality to those who need it, you may communicate happiness to their hearts, but you shall surely bring home a higher happiness to your own. May you, then, give to the

needy, adoring Him who hath made it bliss to love,—
humbling yourselves in His sight for all your departures
from this love, and casting yourselves upon His mercy to
forgive these departures from it, and upon His strength
to enable you henceforth to dwell in it ;—may you give
with these views and feelings ;—then, surely, you shall
have your reward ; yours shall be a blessedness known,
among all the dwellers on the earth, only to the self-sacrificing ; yea, yours shall be a very foretaste of that blessedness which is theirs with whom faith is changed into
sight, and hope hath risen into fruition, but with whom
perfect love, even the love that is of God, remains to
constitute their overflowing and everlasting well-spring of
felicity ! *

---

* This was the *last sermon* preached by Dr. Machar—October 12,
1862.

SERMON VII.

ROMANS, viii. 23.—"And not only they, but ourselves also, which have the first-fruits of the Spirit, even we ourselves groan within ourselves, waiting for the adoption, to wit, the redemption of our body."

BY a bold and beautiful personification common in Scripture, the Apostle, in the preceding words, represents the whole creation as groaning and travailing in pain, under its subjection to vanity, through the sin of man, and yet, nevertheless, losing sight, as it were, of its pains and anguish in the ravishing contemplation of its deliverance from the bondage of corruption at the manifestation of the sons of God. Here he refers to the feelings of believers in their present circumstances as being analogous to those of the suffering creation. And not only they,—that is, the inanimate and unintelligent creatures of this lower world,—not only do they eagerly look onwards to that period when the curse under which they now suffer shall be removed, and they shall again rejoice before the Lord, and under His approving smile ; but we, the children of God,—we ourselves also, which have the first-fruits of the Spirit, " even we ourselves groan within ourselves, waiting for the adoption, to wit, the redemption of our body."

Dear friends, is this language, as we think, plainly descriptive of the state and feelings and expectations of true Christians? If it cannot be doubted that it is, then how momentous for us to mark it well, that, discerning from it the true features of the children of God, we may see whether we belong to this number, or are yet "strangers and foreigners," "without God and without hope in the world!" May we have given to us the hearing ear and the understanding heart while we now address ourselves to the consideration of what is here written for our learning!

In the first place, the Apostle speaks of himself and his fellow-believers as having the first-fruits of the Spirit. The first-fruits of the Spirit are the love, the joy, the peace, the holiness which the Spirit brings with Him when He enters the believing heart; they are the likeness to God which this Divine Agent works in believers, and the communion with God to which He calls them. It will be remembered by those who are familiar with the usages under the law, that the first-fruits of the field were offered to God,—they who brought them thus glorifying God as the God who gave fruitful seasons, and filled their mouths with food and gladness; and in allusion to this, may those graces which the Holy Spirit now confers on believers be called first-fruits, as redounding to the glory of that God by whose blessing and energy only do they spring up and grow in the soil of any human heart. The idea chiefly intended, however, seems to be that the love, the joy, the peace, the holiness, the various graces which the Holy Spirit now confers upon believers, are a pledge and earnest to them of their coming felicity and glory. Believers, as we have seen, are the children of God; and, as being children, they are heirs, "heirs of God, and joint-heirs with Christ." But they are not yet come to the inheritance which the Lord their God giveth them; they have yet to wait for this inheritance for a little season. But He who gives them all things richly to enjoy, as far as their present circumstances admit, gives them

‿omething of their inheritance in hand ; He communicates to them many a blessed foretaste of their Heavenly portion in confirmation of their hope of it, and to stimulate their desires and endeavours to reach it. Such are the gifts and graces of the Holy Spirit,—the love which he sheds abroad in the heart of the children of God,—the joy and peace which He imparts to them,—the " righteousness and goodness and truth" by the way of which He leads them ;—these first-fruits He now puts into their hands, that they may judge of the approaching harvest, and that they may be comforted and upheld until the reaping time shall come round.

Brethren, do we know what it is to have received these first-fruits of the Spirit ? The Apostle, observe, represents it as distinctive of believers that they have the first-fruits of the Spirit. His language shows that they who have not these first-fruits of the Spirit cannot be believers. Well, then, have we these first-fruits ? Has God given us His Holy Spirit to dwell in us in enlightening, renewing, and consoling power ? Have we ceased to draw our felicity from the muddy cisterns of earthly enjoyment, and does our joy now flow to us from a Divine source ? Is it of the same nature with the joy of the Lord—a foretaste of the glory which will one day be revealed to His people ? Does conscience answer " No ? " Then, brethren, see your true state, that you are not yet the children of God, and go and beseech Him that He would have mercy upon you,—that you be not destroyed with the world. But are there some who have tasted that the Lord is gracious,—some into whose hearts He has put a gladness which the world could never have communicated ? See that ye glorify God with what you have received. As the first-fruits of the harvest were consecrated to God, so do ye, who have received the first-fruits of the Spirit, offer yourselves to God as a kind of first-fruits. As the first-fruits of the field were offered publicly, so do ye present yourselves openly to God as living sacrifices,

—never concealing through cowardice, nor clouding through inconsistency, the profession of your faith, but "letting your light so shine before men that they may see your good works, and glorify your Father which is in Heaven."

In the second place, the Apostle speaks of true believers as now groaning within themselves. He says, " Ourselves also, which have the first-fruits of the Spirit, even we groan within ourselves." He is referring to the feelings and emotions which, by a figure of speech, he represents as actuating universal nature, under her present blight and distress, and he says—"not only they"— the whole creation—groan and travail in pain, looking forth in eager anticipation for the coming deliverance : but *we* also, with all the advantages which we possess, even *we* groan ; the time with us is a time of oppression and suffering and sore burthening. Even now, indeed, the child of God is not without his consolations ; he is made to feel that "godliness has the promise of the life that now is ;" and it is of his present portion that it is said that "Eye hath not seen, nor ear heard, neither hath it entered into the heart of man to conceive it." Even now, the believer knows how true it is that "wisdom's ways are ways of pleasantness, and all her paths peace," nor, however poor in this world's goods, would he change his lot with the richest of the earth who know not "the only true God, and Jesus Christ whom He hath sent."

But still it is true of the believer, that in the world he has tribulation ; that now he must "needs be in heaviness through manifold temptations." We which have the first-fruits of the Spirit, even we groan." It cannot be otherwise with those who have the Spirit, as long as they carry about with them a body of sin and death ; for the flesh, that is in them, still lusteth against the Spirit, and while they "delight in the law of the Lord after the inward man," they see "a law in their members warring against the law of their minds, and bringing them into captivity to the law of sin and death in their members." Under these restless stirrings of indwelling corruption, they are frequently in heaviness and sorrow ; and hence it is that we find the Apostle himself, in the preceding chapter, pouring forth that complaint which bespeaks so much anguish, " O, wretched man that I am, who shall deliver me from the body of this death?" and in another passage making use of the same doleful language, " For we that are in this tabernacle do groan, being burdened." Such is the present experience of all the children of God. The sin that is in them is not to be kept under but by a sore and incessant struggle ; and hence, though they have their abounding consolations, they have at all times their disquiets and their groaning and travail. It would seem that in no other way can those who have fallen so far be matured for glory. It would seem as if such a painful experience were needful to detach us from all dependence upon ourselves, and make us see that in God alone must be all our boast. It would seem as if only through the humiliation and bitterness of our felt corruption can self be dethroned within us, and God come to occupy his rightful place in our hearts. But this experience of corruption will make believers groan ; and the more they are renewed after the Divine image, the more painful to them will be the workings of the indwelling sin, and the more earnestly will they look and long for the period of their full deliverance from " the bondage of corruption into the glorious liberty of the sons of God." " We groan," says the Apostle, " within ourselves." This distinguishes the groaning of the believer, that, unlike that of the hypocrite, which is outward, it is inward. It is a thing not for the ear of man, but for the ear of God ; it is a part of the hidden life of believers,—known only to themselves and to God. But it is an important part of their life. Bound to a body of death, whose loathsome ness they cannot but feel, they mourn in secret to God, saying, with the Psalmist, " All my desire is before thee, and my groaning is not hid from thee ;" and this secret mourning in them, God regards well pleased. He puts their "tears into His bottle ;" He writes their secret groans in His book.

This groaning of theirs is, indeed a fruit of the Spirit of God in their hearts ; and " blessed are they who thus mourn, for they shall be comforted." Brethren, do we know nothing of this secret groaning? We may well tremble for ourselves, for the absence of this distress shows that, as yet, we have not received that heart of flesh which God gives to all His true children, and which alone can render us precious in His sight. While we feel no distress because of the sin that is in us, God cannot draw near to dwell with us, or bestow upon us one token of His regard, for it is to Him only of the sons of men who is of a poor and contrite spirit, that God will look. " The proud He knoweth afar off ;" He " dwells " only " with those who are of a humble and contrite spirit,—to revive the spirit of the humble, and to revive the heart of the contrite ones."

In the third place, the Apostle speaks of true believers as "waiting for the adoption, to wit, the redemption of the body." The adoption here meant, and of which the Apostle gives the explanation, is the same thing with what is, in the preceding verses, called " the manifestation of the sons of God," and " the glorious liberty of the children of God." Believers have a present adoption, but there is also an adoption which they wait for. God has now taken them from the family of the wicked one, and placed them among His own children ; nor has He given them the rank and title of children, only ; but also the nature and disposition of children, as is evident from the manner in which they are addressed in the fifteenth verse of this chapter :—" For ye have not received the spirit of bondage again to fear ; but ye have received the spirit of adoption, whereby we cry, Abba, Father." But this adoption is secret,—it may be known only to themselves ; but there is a time coming when it will be fully manifested, and they will be glorified together with Christ, their Elder Brother.   Now are they sons, but as yet they are sons in a state of expectancy ; and great and glorious as their present privileges are, yet as their bodies are corruptible and mortal bodies,—bodies which are not yet conformed to the glorious body of Jesus Christ, they still wait for the entire accomplishment of their adoption, when, at the resurrection, they shall appear with Christ in glory, and " shine forth as the sun in the kingdom of their Father." Accordingly, our Lord denominates the resurrection " the regeneration," because then, not only the souls of believers, but also their bodies, shall bear the heavenly image of the second Adam. Then they shall enter fully upon the possession of their inheritance ; then, fitted for their high dignity as children of the Highest, their souls having been purified, their bodies having been changed from natural into spiritual bodies,—then will Christ grant them the fulfilment of the promise to receive them unto Himself, that where He is they may be also ; then will He say to them: " Come ye blessed of my Father, inherit the kingdom prepared for you from the foundation of the world."   This is the adoption for which believers now wait, and it is so called, because it is the accomplishment to them of what their adoption imports,—the blessed and glorious consummation of that grace which the Father exercises towards them when He takes them into His family, and along with the name, communicates to them the nature of children.

This adoption, which believers now wait for, is, in fact, the glory spoken of in the eighteenth verse of this chapter,—the " glory which will be revealed in us." It is what St. Paul had in his view when he says, " For we that are in this tabernacle do groan, being burdened ;—not for that we would be unclothed, but clothed upon, that mortality might be swallowed up of life." It is what St. John refers to in the passage, " It doth not yet appear what we shall be ; but we know that when He shall appear, we shall be like Him ; for we shall see Him as He is." We shall be like Him,—conformed to Him in image, and made partakers of His blessedness. We shall walk with Him in white, and with Him we shall drink of that "fulness of joy which is in God's presence, and of those rivers of pleasures which are at His right hand for evermore."

Lest, however, we should fall into any error regarding the meaning of the term "adoption" in this place, the Apostle himself explains it, calling it "the redemption of the body." The spirit or soul of the believer is now redeemed. "The law of the Spirit of life in Christ Jesus" has made his soul free from the law and the slavery of sin, and though his conflict with his indwelling corruption is often so strong as to extort the complaint, "O wretched man that I am ! who shall deliver me from the body of this death ?"—yet can he add :—"I thank God, through Jesus our Lord." His soul is thus free ; His spirit is life because of righteousness—it lives to God, and it constrains, too, the members of his body to do service to God. But still, that body is a body of death, and death has power over it because of sin. It is a mortal body, and it will soon fall under the stroke of temporal death. While the spirit of the believer at death goes to God, his body for a season returns to the earth as it was. There exists, we are told, a necessity for this. The body must thus perish for a space, in order to be prepared for incorruption and immortality. It must go down to the grave, there to leave behind it its corruption, its weakness, its dishonour. But it shall come again from the land of its captivity—it is under a charter of redemption, and redeemed it shall be from the power of the enemy. As the seed which we deposit in the earth dies not there utterly, but passes through death in such a way as to overcome death, and to revive and fructify on the other side of death, so with the bodies of believers. They die but to live. They are buried in the earth, but to spring up as the corn and grow as the vine, and to reappear in the possession of an incorruptible and endless life, and a perfect vision, and an undecaying beauty. " They are sown in corruption ; they are raised in incorruption. They are sown in dishonour ; they are raised in glory. They are sown in weakness ; they are raised in power. They are sown a natural body ; they are raised a spiritual body." These glorious things will be realised to the believer at the day of the resurrection ; and hence is that day called the day of redemption, as in that word, " Grieve not the Spirit of God, by whom ye are sealed unto the day of redemption." We are redeemed even now, nor, unless our souls are now purified through the belief of the truth, shall we ever be partakers of redemption hereafter. But it is only hereafter that we are to attain the last and highest degree of our redemption ; it is in the day when the body shall be reunited to the soul, that we shall know the completeness of that redemption which Christ obtained for us. But then we shall know this. Then, " this corruptible having put on incorruption, and this mortal having put on immortality, there shall be brought to pass the saying that is written, Death is swallowed up in victory," and each child of God shall raise this triumphant strain, " O death, where is thy sting? O grave, where is thy victory?"

In conclusion, we would address ourselves, first, to the man whose heart is in the world. You are not "waiting for the adoption, to wit, the redemption of the body;" you are not looking forward to it with desire and with expectation. So far as you understand it, you cannot desire the inheritance of the children of God, for you know that it is an inheritance which you could not enjoy ; you know that to give it to you would be in effect to rob you of all that now constitutes your happiness, your life, since it has nothing that can minister to " the lust of the eye, the lust of the flesh, and the pride of life." It is

treasures on earth that you are laying up for yourselves—
not treasures in heaven. But where will these treasures
be in the day when God taketh away your soul?
Is it well, is it wise, to be bartering away the hopes and
expectations of eternity for the things with which you
must so soon have done, from which you may even be
forced to part ere to-morrow's sun shall arise? Reflect on
what you are now doing. Let the voice of Christ yet be
heard by you. Consider His awful, His thrilling question—"What is a man profited if he shall gain the whole
world and lose his own soul ; or what shall a man give
in exchange for his soul?"

But we would speak also to those who are waiting for
the adoption, the redemption of the body ; and we would
put to them two questions. We would ask them—should
you not be heavenly-minded? And should not you be
joyful in your tribulations? With such glorious prospects
as yours, having the hope of being with Christ, and being
like Him, ought you to be found caring for earthly things
as the children of this world care for them? Surely conformity to the world befits not your circumstances. The
worldling may have some apology for his devotion to the
pleasures of an ungodly world, for *he* knows of nothing
better ; but *you* have no apology for devotion to them,
since God has shown you a better portion. And have
you no mercy upon your own souls, and upon the souls
of your fellow-men, that thus you strive to defeat the very
purpose for which Christ gave Himself for us—that thus
you countenance and uphold a system which drowns so
many souls in irretrievable destruction? " Grieve not
the Holy Spirit " by this worldliness of spirit and conversation. " Be not conformed to this world, but be ye
transformed by the renewing of your mind, that ye may
prove what is the good and perfect and acceptable will
of God."

Again, we ask you—with such glorious prospects as
yours, should not you be joyful in all your sufferings?

Suffering, if you are Christ's, you must needs have in this present time; nor shall any reign with Christ hereafter who do not suffer with Him now. But what then? Shall we not rather rejoice to find ourselves upon the very path by which our brethren who have gone before us have reached the glory which they now inherit? Why should we faint at any trial? What is present suffering to be accounted of, when a hope so blessed, and so soon to be realised, is set before us—when every cloud that now darkens our condition is so soon to be scattered before the effulgence of the day of redemption—when there awaits us, only a little way in advance, "a far more exceeding and eternal weight of glory,"—when He with whom our life is hid will, ere long, appear to say to us, "Come, ye blessed of my Father, inherit the kingdom prepared for you from the foundation of the world?"

SERMON VIII.

ROMANS viii. 26, 27.—"Likewise the Spirit also helpeth our infirmities : for we know not what we should pray for as we ought," &c.

BELIEVERS in the present world have to wait for their full redemption ; and the Apostle is speaking of the provision which has been made for our being saved, or preserved, amidst our present troubles and afflictions. An important part of this provision, as the Apostle tells us in the preceding context, is *hope.* " We are saved by hope." God gives us a most precious and sure hope of coming glory ; and such is the power of this hope, that while we hold it fast, we are preserved amid what would otherwise prove fatal to the life of our souls—we are not overwhelmed by our sufferings, nor do we fall under our spiritual enemies, nor do we faint at our appointed labours. We look onwards to that blessed inheritance which our Heavenly Father has told us He will give us, and we realise the blessed entrance upon it which we shall soon have ; and the effect of this is a present joy and animation, under which we are lifted above our depression, nor are shaken or moved by any of the trials through which we have to reach the glorious resurrection that awaits us.

In the verses now read, the Apostle presents another part of that provision by which we are preserved unto God's heavenly kingdom. " Likewise the Spirit also helpeth our infirmities." The word "infirmities" has respect to that state of weakness and helplessness into which we have been brought through sin. It is the same word with that which is translated "*without strength,*" in the fifth chapter and sixth verse of this epistle : " For when we were yet without strength, in due time Christ died for the ungodly." In our natural and unconverted state, our oppression by the devil is complete ; we are all weakness, we have no spiritual strength, and even when we are brought back to God, we have still no strength in ourselves, but our whole sufficiency is of God ; nor could we stand a single moment but for the forth-putting of His almighty power. The Apostle well knew this, and hence that remarkable expression of his, "When I am weak, then am I strong." It was only when feeling his own weakness, and when, under that feeling, driven to take hold of Divine strength as his help—it was then only that he felt he had strength. And so it is with all the true children of God. So it is with us, if we are His true children. Others may dream of a sufficiency in themselves, and think that their mountain stands strong, but we have done with all such vain thoughts. We know that we are all infirmity, unequal to the doing anything of ourselves, and this in a scene of difficulty and trial, where the greatest strength is needed by us. But what then ? Shall we be overwhelmed at the thought of this ? Surely not, when we hear St. Paul saying, in the name of himself and his fellow-believers, " The Spirit also helpeth our infirmities." The Spirit is the third person of the glorious Trinity—is God ; and, as God, He is infinite in understanding to know our infirmities ; infinite in compassion to pity us under them ; infinite in power to help them. In previous parts of this Epistle, the Spirit is spoken of as performing most important offices for them that believe. We read that by Him " the love of God is shed abroad in our hearts ;" that " He dwells in us ;" that we " are led by Him ;" that He is in us a spirit of adoption, whereby we cry "Abba, Father;" that He "beareth witness with our spirit that we are the children of God." In addition to all which, it is here said of the Spirit, that He helpeth our infirmities. The word in the original, rendered "*helpeth*," is a term of singular strength and significancy, and plainly conveys the idea of *effectual* help. It refers to a case of this kind. One is vainly striving to carry a burden which is too heavy for him. Another observes this, and placing himself on the other side of the burden from the struggling man, lifts it up, and carries it forward along with him, making that easy to him which was before impossible. It is thus that the Holy Spirit—even He concerning whom the Saviour says that "He shall dwell with us, and shall be in us;" —it is thus that He acts towards us. He sees us struggling under our heavy burdens, and vainly attempting to bear them in our own strength, nor does He see this unmoved. As might be expected of Him who is, pre-eminently, the *Comforter*, He comes to our relief. He strengthens us inwardly. Nor only so, but He takes up the burden along with us, so that we sink no more under it, but, strong in the co-operation of our omnipotent Helper, we go lightly and cheerfully forward. Let it be observed that we are still the bearers of our burdens, and that it is our part not to relax our exertions in bearing them, but to stir up, and to put forth to the utmost the grace already given us. The help vouchsafed us by the Spirit of God is not to *supersede*, but to *call forth* our activity; "he that hath, to him shall more be given;" and just then when, in simple obedience to the Divine command, and in simple dependence upon Divine strength, we are addressing ourselves steadfastly to the work of bearing the burdens which must be borne by us, just then it is that the God of all grace giveth more grace; just then it is that the Holy Spirit is with us as a never-failing and all-sufficient helper.

Do you, brethren, feel your many infirmities? Do you

see that in your heavenward path you have many a heavy
burden to carry, while in yourselves you are wholly without strength? Yet be not cast down because of these
things! Think of "the love of the Spirit;" you are not
without a resource. It is true that your burdens are as
weighty as you regard them, and that your strength to
bear them is utter weakness. But there is *One* ever near
to you—*One* who knows every step of the way that you
take, and all the pressure that lies upon you; all your
conflicts, and trials, and difficulties, and all your insufficiency to meet them. There is such an One ever near
to you, and He is ready to help your infirmities, to
strengthen you with all might in the inner man. He will
strengthen you. He will help you. Only go forward,
shrinking from no trial, and declining no labour to which
you are appointed on the path of duty, and you shall be
holden up, neither shall anything be too hard for you. It
is no vain word, "The Spirit helpeth our infirmities;" and
if He help, what is there that should for a moment move
you? "He giveth power to the faint, and to them that
have no might He increaseth strength. Even the youths
shall faint and be weary, and the young men shall utterly
fail. But they that wait upon the Lord shall renew their
strength; they shall mount up with wings as eagles, they
shall run and not be weary, they shall walk and not
faint."

"The Spirit," says the Apostle, "helpeth our infirmities;"
and to illustrate his meaning in this declaration, he gives
us a particular case. "For we know not what we should
pray for as we ought; but the Spirit itself maketh intercession for us with groanings that cannot be uttered." In
prayer, which is so needful to us, we labour under great
infirmity—infirmity in regard both to the *matter* of our
supplications, and to the *manner* of them. As to the *matter*
of prayer, we know not what to pray for. Such is our
ignorance of ourselves, and of the things which are really
good for us, that we need the constant illumination of the

Holy Spirit to show us what we should ask of God. We are, in a great measure, blind to our wants, and therefore it is not wonderful that we should not know what to ask in supply of them. We know not where to begin in prayer, or what particular things we should make the subject of our supplications, and we are, consequently, in danger of asking amiss—of asking what is unsuitable, or what, if bestowed, would be hurtful to us.

And then, again, as to the *manner* of prayer, we know not how to pray as we ought. We ought to pray with the deepest awe upon our minds, as remembering that we are drawing near to the great and dreadful God; but how often is our spirit a light and careless spirit! We ought to pray with holy fervour and importunity, like Jacob, who wrestled with God, and said, "I will not let thee go until thou bless me;" but how cold and lifeless often are our petitions! We ought to pray with a deeply humble and contrite heart, but with how much of secret pride and self-consequence are we apt to approach God! We ought to pray with an entire resignation to the will of God, and humble faith in His promises—with a holy sincerity of soul, with an ardent desire for spiritual blessings, and a simple reliance on the mediation of the Saviour; but how often does a repining, unbelieving, insincere, cold and selfish spirit steal upon us! And even when our frame of spirit is better than this, and we are conscious that we are really lifting our souls unto God, how frequently are we so oppressed, so agitated, so borne down by our afflictions and trials, that we can neither properly conceive nor properly confess our complaints and requests to God.

Now, under this infirmity in prayer, the Spirit helps us. "The Spirit itself maketh intercession for us." It is still we that intercede or pray, but the Spirit is present with us, so to illuminate our minds that we may know what to pray for, and so to cleanse our thoughts and excite our desires that we seek God in fervent, effectual intercession. This is, obviously, the meaning of the Spirit making intercession for us. When the Spirit directs the *matter* of our prayers, teaching us to pray for right things, and when, also, he directs the *manner* of our supplications, enabling us to ask for right things as we ought to ask for them, then the Spirit maketh intercession for us. This language concerning the Spirit is thus not to be understood of his acting the part of a mediator between God and us, but of his performing a work within us, even the work of helping our infirmities in our supplications at the throne of grace. Christ is our advocate with the Father above ; the Spirit directs and effectually aids our own pleadings here below. Christ intercedes for us and the Spirit is given ; the Holy Spirit intercedes for us—that is, takes hold with us of the work of intercession in which we engage, and we implore the benefits of the Saviour's death. By the intercession of Christ, all the obstacles to our salvation are removed, as they respect our offended God ; by the intercession of the Spirit, all the difficulties are taken away which arise from our weak and corrupt hearts. Through Christ, the Intercessor in heaven, our prayers are accepted—through the Spirit, the Intercessor on earth, we have light and ability to pray. The Holy Spirit was of old promised as a Spirit of grace and of supplication, and He becomes such in our hearts, *not* by taking the work of supplication out of our hands, but by *enabling us* to perform it. The meaning of the Spirit's making intercession for us will be at once seen to be such as it has been described to be, if we turn to Galatians iv. 6: " Because ye are sons, God hath sent forth His Son into your hearts, crying Abba, Father ;" and compare this with the language employed in the fifteenth verse of this chapter, " Ye have received the Spirit of adoption, whereby we cry Abba, Father." It will be plain, we think, that by the Spirit's crying in our hearts, "Abba, Father," is meant His enabling us so to cry. In like manner, then, by the Spirit's making intercession for us, is meant His enabling us to make intercession, or to pray for ourselves.

"The Spirit itself maketh intercession for us," it is said, "with groanings that cannot be uttered." If you will look back to the twenty-third verse, you will find true believers represented as groaning within themselves—waiting for the adoption, to wit, the redemption of the body. Believers sigh or "groan within themselves." They have desires towards God which they cannot utter. The Holy Spirit gives them such views of their necessities, and of the excellency of spiritual blessings, that their hearts go forth in supplication to God for these blessings, with pantings and longings which no words can ever adequately express. They cannot put these pantings and longings into articulate speech, and all they can do is to lay themselves down in the dust before the Hearer of prayer, saying, with David, "All my desire is before Thee, and my groaning is not hid from Thee." The Psalmist, at the time when he uttered this, was so feeble and sore broken and disquieted, that he could not embody his desires and aspirations in articulate language; his tongue could not frame what he felt into audible sounds; but this was his consolation, that God knew all, that his every desire was before God, and that no groaning of his was hidden from Him. Brethren, it is not for naught, or for a purpose of small moment, that we are here told of the Spirit's drawing forth and aiding and directing those groanings in our hearts which cannot be uttered. If we are the children of God, we shall meet with many an occasion when we shall feel the strong consolation arising from this particular operation of the Spirit of God in our hearts. We shall surely meet with such an occasion when we come to die. As our outward man decays, the tongue will refuse its office, and all our prayers will be confined to groanings that cannot be uttered. How precious, at that season, will the assurance before us be! To feel, at that hour when prayer is so deeply needful to us—when Satan is making his last and fiercest onset upon us—when he is coming like a flood upon the soul,—to feel that then the

Spirit of the Lord is helping our infirmities—is lifting up within us a standard against our strong enemy, and strengthening our faith in God, and drawing forth deeper and more ardent aspirations for the light of the divine countenance than could be expressed in words, even had we the power of uttering them—with what peace, and even joy, shall this fill our hearts in our departing hours !

The Apostle goes on to say, in the twenty-seventh verse, " And he that searcheth the hearts knoweth what is the mind of the Spirit, because He maketh intercession for the saints according to the will of God." It belongs to God to search the hearts which He has made, and they are all naked and open to Him, without any outward expression to indicate their state. He knoweth what is "the mind of the Spirit "—that is, those feelings, or that state of mind and affection which the Holy Spirit produces in us when we are engaged in prayer. The believer, perhaps, cannot give any adequate expression to his deep, heartfelt emotions ; he can only sigh and groan within himself—unable to utter a word before God. But his inward emotions and aspirations are not therefore lost —they are most fully known to Him who searcheth our hearts, who is privy to all the intricacies of the hidden man within us. When the Holy Spirit enters into any heart, and enables that heart truly to pray, He who is God over all knows this. His eye is upon that heart, and whether it breaks forth into audible supplication, or only heaves the secret sigh, He knows its desire. Whatever longing in our hearts is of His Spirit, *that* He, as it were, pre-eminently knows, for that He delights more to look upon than upon any other object in our sinful world. And hence the expression "*knoweth*," in this place, is inseparable from *approving*, from delighting in. He knoweth, and knoweth with approbation, what is the mind of the Spirit—what desires His Spirit teaches us and sanctifies us to form, because He "maketh intercession for the saints according to the will of God." There

239

are three considerations here stated why God regards with such interest, or knows with so peculiar a knowledge, the supplications we make in the Spirit. First, they are supplications dictated by the Spirit—by Him who is one in essence and mind with the Father; they are supplications, therefore, which the Father cannot but approve. Secondly, they are supplications, not of the wicked, not of the unconverted; but of the saints, of persons regenerated by the Spirit—renewed in the spirit of their minds. Thirdly, the supplications we make in the Spirit are supplications according to the will of God. The Spirit is God, and He creates no desires in us towards God but such as are in perfect harmony with the Divine will. It follows that these desires will not pass unheeded by God, but will be all treasured up by Him as precious things. So far as we pray in the Spirit, there is not a sigh or a groan in us which He does not note and remember, and to which He will not give an answer of peace. "This is the confidence that we have in Him, that if we ask anything according to His will, He heareth us."

And now, brethren, perhaps I speak to some here who do not pray at all. What can I say to you who are prayerless? Plainly, you are without God in the world; plainly, you know not God; for if you did know Him, you would be holding communion with Him in prayer; His Spirit would be helping you effectually to pour forth to Him, if not the expressed desire, yet the secret groan. But you are a stranger to everything of this kind; perhaps it is even a subject of mockery to you. You know not God, nor are seeking to know Him. But is it not sad that this should be the case with you— that, contending as you are with the burdens and sorrows of life, you should have no hope in God for time or for eternity, but should be of those

> "Who will not look beyond the tomb,
> And cannot hope for rest before?"

But we speak to others who make their "infirmities" a reason for their not praying, or, at least, for their sparingly engaging in the exercise. But are not you who do this altogether inexcusable? True, your infirmities in prayer are great—greater, perhaps, than you yet well conceive; and when you go to the throne of grace, you neither know the things you should ask, nor the right manner of asking them. But should you therefore faint in prayer, or grow weary in the exercise? Surely not, when the Holy Comforter—the infinitely compassionate and all-powerful Spirit of God—is with you to guide and uphold you in all your communications with the Hearer of prayer. This leaves you wholly without excuse in restraining prayer before God, because of its difficulty to you; it makes your conduct as unreasonable as would be that of the man who, having the treasures of the world laid at his feet for his taking up, should say, "I must still continue poor and destitute of all things."

But we may be speaking to others, again, who, knowing well that they are not God's holy ones or saints,—knowing that they retain a carnal, worldly heart,—knowing that they are not doing, and that they have *no real heart-felt concern* to do the known will of God, are from time to time going through a form of prayer, and perhaps making this a confidence—a refuge. To you, my friends, we would say, Remember that "if we regard iniquity in our heart, the Lord will not hear us." "The sacrifice of the wicked is an abomination to the Lord."

But there are those who, though they pray, yet being unable to order their pleadings before God as they would, or being ofttimes unable to find any language at all to utter forth their spiritual longings, unable to go beyond sighings and groanings, are, because of these things, greatly cast down, and ready to conclude that surely they cannot be the children of God. Let such take courage, remembering that God requires not the eloquence of words in our prayers to make them acceptable; remembering that the Spirit does not always give the eloquence of words, but that often when He is working in the heart, *it* only speaks, uttering itself in secret sighs and groans, and that yet such prayer rises in sweet memorial before God. It is well to seek to have liberty of utterance in prayer; for this may be desirable in your private supplications, and is needful to fit you to engage in social worship; yet be not utterly dejected,—write no bitter thing against yourselves because of your lack of this liberty of utterance, provided only there be the outgoing of earnest desire towards God. The Lord requires not in our prayers well-arranged words, nor even always requires words at all. "The sacrifices of God are a broken and a contrite heart;" and there may be such a heart when the suppliant utters no word, nay, lifts not so much as his eyes to Heaven, "but only smites upon his breast" in token that he needs mercy, and deems himself undone if he shall not obtain it.

SERMON IX.

ROMANS viii. 28.—"And we know that all things work together for good to them that love God, to them who are the called according to his purpose."

THE connection between privilege and character must never be lost sight of, for, if it be, a door will be opened for the grossest delusion, and men will be found appropriating the consolations of Christianity, for whom such consolations were never intended. Hence the most gracious announcements to believers are always the most guarded, and the consolation they afford is so worded, that they only to whom it of right belongs, can take it home to themselves and make it a subject of rejoicing. Thus, the writer of the eighty-fourth Psalm, in speaking of those from whom no good thing will be withheld, distinctly characterises them as "those that walk uprightly." Thus, in the tenth chapter of the Gospel of John, where our Lord is speaking of His sheep, it is in immediate connection with His description of them as "hearing His voice" and "following Him," that He makes concerning them the gracious declaration, "I give unto them eternal life ; and they shall never perish, neither shall any pluck them out of my hand." And so, in the words before us, the Apostle, in making to us one of the most consolatory announcements in the whole Word of God, clearly defines

who, and who only, are they who may take to themselves
its abundant consolations ; " And we know that all things
work together for good *to them that love God*, to them
who are the called according to His purpose. We will
consider, first, the character of the children of God ; and
secondly, their privilege.

I. The character of the children of God is, that "they
love God," that they are "the called according to His
purpose."

"They love God." This was not always their character, for, as you will see on looking back to the seventh
verse of this chapter, "the carnal mind," that is, the mind
which men have in their original condition ; this mind
"is enmity against God." They once loved not God, but
hated Him, for they were evil ; and as such, the righteous
and holy character of God could not but be the object of
their aversion and enmity. But how, then, did they
come to love God ? The way was this : God first loved
them. God shed abroad His love in their hearts by the
Holy Spirit—that is, His love in giving His Son to die
for them. "Herein," it is said, "is love ; not that we
loved God, but that He loved us, and sent His Son to be
the propitiation for our sins ;" and when the Holy Spirit
reveals or sheds abroad this love of God in the hearts of
men, then is this enmity to God slain, and they cry with
a rejoicing heart, "We love Him, because He first loved
us." Previous to God's moving towards them in love, they
had no love to Him ; and even for a time after He had
begun to move towards them, and to reveal something of
Himself to them, their spirit towards Him was more a
spirit of fear than a spirit of love. They "received the
spirit of bondage, to fear ;" and it was only after knowing
the discomforts and apprehensions of this bondage that
they received the spirit of adoption, whereby they cried
"Abba, Father." But this spirit they have received,
knowing and believing the love that God hath to them,
the fear, that is, the slavish apprehension and dread of

God as an enemy, has been cast out, and they lift their hearts to Him as their Friend, yea, as their Father, with childlike confidence and affection. It was even thus, brethren, if you love God now, that you came to love Him. In your natural condition you were sinners before Him, and if you thought of Him at all, it was with alarm—with the feeling that His wrath was pursuing you.

In such a state, love to God was, of course, impossible ; it was only when He made known to you the riches of His grace, when He taught you to look to Him as a "God in Christ, reconciling the world unto Himself, not imputing unto them their trespasses ;" it was only then that you loved Him. This has been your experience if you are now of those who love God ; and if this has not been your experience, then you are deceiving yourselves if you think that you love God. Love to God, like love to man, is a most active principle, and will, wherever it exists, give evidence of its presence in a variety of ways. Where there is love to God, there will be fear to offend Him. It was the love which Joseph had toward God that led him to say, "How can I do this wickedness, and sin against God?" Where there is love to God, there will be an anxious desire to please Him ; the love which Enoch had towards God led him to "please God." Wherever there is love to God, there will be devotedness to Him ; the Psalmist's love to God led him to ask, "What can I render unto the Lord for all His benefits to me?" Where there is love to God, there will be love to His children, for "every one that loveth Him that begat, loveth Him, also, that is begotten of Him."

Real love to God, again, will show itself in a readiness to submit to all God's appointments, teaching a man to say, even of the most painful of them, "It is the Lord ; let Him do unto me what seemeth Him good." Real love to God, in fine, will appear in a cordial and unreserved obedience to all God's commands ; they who have such love in them will delight to do the will of God, and

245

their language will be, " O that there were such a heart in me that I might fear the Lord, and keep all His commandments always ! "

The children of God are further characterised as those that are the " called according to God's purpose." All who have the Gospel preached to them are, in one sense, called. They are bidden to the marriage supper of the Lamb. But not all who are thus called by the preaching of the Gospel are those who, along with the outward call of the Word, have received the inward call of the Spirit, and been made "willing in the day of God's power." They have not only had Christ preached to them, but they "have received Christ ;" they "have believed in His name." This is a blessed calling ; for all who are thus called "joy in God, by whom they have received the atonement ; " "they are filled with all joy and peace in believing." And it is a holy as well as a blessed calling ; and perhaps the Apostle had this feature of their calling chiefly in view in the words "according to His purpose." The children of God are "called to be saints ;" their calling is a holy calling. " They who are now the called according to God's purpose, were once even as others, serving divers lusts and pleasures, but now they are set apart from others, and consecrated to the service of God. They have " put off the old man, which is corrupt according to the deceitful lusts, and they have put on the new man, which, after God, is created in righteousness and true holiness." They are not perfect, indeed, but they are saints ; they are holy and advancing in holiness ; they have relinquished the course of this world, and they are more and more dying unto sin, and living unto righteousness.

II. Having seen the character of the children of God, we pass on to take a view of their privilege. Their privilege is, that they know that "all things work together for their good ;" that is, are made by Him who ruleth over all to work together for the advancement of their best

246

and highest interests; for their true good—for what they shall hereafter see to be good, when all that now clouds their vision shall be removed, and they shall, in God's light, see light clearly.

Observe, it is said, that *all things* shall work for this good to them; not only *some* things, but *all* things; all things whatsoever. By some, this expression has, indeed, been limited to *afflictions;* but these, though an important part of what is included in the "all things" of our text, are not the whole of what is included in this phrase. The context does not necessarily limit it to afflictions; and it seems preferable, therefore, to take it in all the extent of meaning of which it is susceptible, especially as in other places where it is employed by the Apostle, it is employed altogether in an unrestricted sense, as where it is said, "All things are for your sakes;" and again, "All things are yours, whether Paul, or Apollos, or Cephas, or the world, or life, or death, or things present, or things to come; all are yours, for ye are Christ's, and Christ is God's." In both these passages the expression is unrestricted in its import, and in the absence of any reason in the passage before us, or in its context, for restricting its import, it were obviously arbitrary to refuse it its full latitude of meaning in this place, even such a latitude of meaning as to include even the falls or sins of believers.

Observe farther, it is said "all things *work together* for good" to the persons of the character stated. All things work *together* for their good—not singly, not separately, but *together*. The providences of God towards them are a great whole in which not one thing is necessary, but every event is bearing its particular part in the general design, so supplying what is wanting, correcting what is hurtful, and aiding what is useful in some other event— that if only one should be left out, the design of God for their benefit could not be carried out. Some things may appear to us little likely to forward such a design; nay, it may seem to us as if such things must obstruct it ; but it is not so. As all the things that befall a believer are of God, so every one of them, even the minutest, has an important part to accomplish in bringing about that issue which God purposes in regard to him. The providences of God towards "them that love Him—them that are the called according to His purpose," are, in fact, like a chain whose use would be destroyed by the want even of one single link. They *all* "work together for good ;" but destroy the concatenation, and they would not work at all for such effect. What a striking example of this truth do we find in the history of Joseph ! His telling his dream to his brethren ; their hatred and cruel treatment of him on account of it ; the passing by of the Midianite merchantmen, to whom they sold him into Egypt ; his servitude in that country ; his being falsely accused by his mistress ; his disgrace, and his being cast into the King's prison ; his meeting there with the officers of Pharaoh, and interpreting to them their dreams ; the deliverance of the chief butler from prison, and his mentioning him to Pharaoh when the King was troubled on account of his dreams ; all these were so many steps which, under the direction of Infinite Wisdom, were made subservient to his future advancement. In this long chain of events, had but one of the links been wanting, we see not how he would have been raised to that high station in the court of Pharaoh which enabled him afterwards to become the preserver of his family, and of the whole land of Egypt ; and doubtless, in looking back on the Lord's dealing with him, he would feelingly own that " *all* things " *had* worked together for good to him.

Observe, too, it is said that the children of God *know* that all things work together for their good. It is not said that they *see* this, but that they *know* it ; they are persuaded of it ; they are sure of it. Often, indeed, they see that God's providences towards them have worked, and are working, for their good. David could say from experience, " It is good for me that I have been afflicted, that I might learn thy statutes ;" and to the same effect does an eminent servant of God of a later day express himself, "We fear," says he, " our best friends : for my part, I have learned more of God and myself in one week's extremity, than the prosperity of a whole life had taught me before." The people of God often see how afflictive dispensations operate for their benefit. They observe the blessed effect of trials and temptations in discovering to them their weakness ; in stirring up their watchfulness ; in putting life into their prayers ; in calling all their graces into action. Have they met with worldly losses and disappointments ? These things have weaned their hearts from the world ; have taught them to set their affections on things more stable and enduring ; have quickened their desires and exertions after a heavenly inheritance. Have they been laid on a bed of sickness, or visited with bereavement, or threatened with it? They have been led to a stricter self-examination, that they might see what God had had against them, and they have been led to a closer walk with God.

Have they fallen into sin? These sins, hateful as they were in the sight of a holy God, have yet, as they can see, been graciously overruled for their good ; for, by them, their self-confidence has been weakened, their self-abasement is increased, their godly zeal is renewed, and the blood of sprinkling rendered more than ever precious to their souls. It is not, however, always given them to see how it is that particular events work for their good, for God often moves in a mysterious manner to perform His gracious purposes towards them ; but still, though they cannot see what He is doing with them, and how this and the other event is promoting their benefit, they know that He is doing all things well. If tempted, in times of trial, to think that something has fallen out inopportunely with them--if tempted, in their haste, to say, with Jacob, of a series of dark events, " All these things are against me," they soon check such a disposition, for, as under a loving kindness that will not be taken from them, and as the objects of a guardianship that cannot err, they know and are persuaded that good is the hand of the Lord in all His appointments, that He is doing nothing towards them but what is necessary for their good, and what He is rendering subservient, also, to their good—that, though "His way is in the sea, and His path is in the great waters, and His footsteps not known," yet is He leading His flock, and them as a portion of His flock, "like a shepherd"—that though it is not given to them to discern the reasons of many of His proceedings, yet has He reasons, most gracious reasons, for every one of them, and is all the while, and by means of all that He is doing, "guiding them in the right way that leads to the city of "everlasting habitation," where faith will be changed into sight, and they shall see that their God did *all* things well,—that " *all* things," in His hand, "worked together for their good."

In looking back upon what has now been opened up of the Lord's doings, we may see, my friends, how enviable is the condition of the true people of God—how peaceful and happy they may be. We may now be speaking to the sons and daughters of affliction. The Lord may have seen meet to afflict you very heavily, and to send you not one trial, but many, and you may not know why it is so with you,—why God has, as it were, singled you out and set you as a mark for the arrows of His quiver. But should you, therefore, murmur or repine? Should you cherish a sorrow that refuses to be comforted? Surely not, when you know that there is a need-be for every trial, yea, and that everything in your trials, however adverse, however dark and bitter, as now seen, is a link in that chain which God holds, and by which He is drawing you to Himself; when you know that His tender mercies are ever over you, and that the way by which He leads you is surely "the right way," and the way which you shall one day see to be right.

We may be speaking to the child of prosperity. God may have given you much of this world's goods, and, contrary to what is usual among men, you may be troubled because of the dangers that encompass a prosperous state. It is well to be alive to your dangers from this source, that you may watch and pray, but your disquiet may well be removed by the thought that your prosperity is the appointment of God, and that by it He is working for your good.

We may be speaking to those who have fallen into sin, and who know something of that wounded spirit which no man can bear. Yours is a sad case, and God forbid that we should utter a word to diminish or deaden your sense of the vileness and hatefulness of your sin. But surely it should be a balm even for your wounds, that though sin is the evil and abominable thing which God hates, and His children are ever to abhor the thought of sinning because His grace abounds, yet the sins and falls of His children He most mercifully turns to their good. Oh! there is just one thing that we need to be careful to see to, and then, whatever be our circumstances, we need not be greatly moved. It is that we " love God," and that we be " the called according to His purpose." Only take heed as to this ; only keep yourselves in the love of God, by keeping in view His love to you in Christ Jesus ; only, by the diligent and unceasing cultivation of all the graces of the Christian life, "make your calling and election sure," and then you may "rejoice evermore,"—nay, then you *will* rejoice evermore, for then God will make you to feel that by all He does and permits, He is working for your good, and your language, even when all is frowning and dark, will be, The Lord is leading me in the right way ; " goodness and mercy shall follow me all the days of my life, and I shall dwell in the house of the Lord for ever."

But if the condition of those who "love God, who are the called according to His purpose," is so blessed, how unhappy, my friends, is that in which you are who love *not*

God, who are *not* the called according to His purpose. All things are not working for your good—on the contrary, all things are working for evil to you. True, God has no pleasure in your death, and so long as He spares you in this place of hope, so long does He order His appointments to you, so that they might be blessings to you. But you turn every good He sends you into poison. If He sends you prosperity, His goodness leads you not to repentance, but your hearts are hardened by it; and by furnishing you with larger means for gratifying your ungodly propensities, it proves a snare to your souls. If He visits you with adversity, even this leads you not to Him whose hands have wounded, and whose hands would also make you whole; but you rebel against Him more and more. If He puts into your hand a price to get heavenly wisdom, you trample upon the gift, and turn afresh to your folly. If He sends His Spirit to strive with you, you quench Him; if He calls you by the Gospel to the marriage-supper of His Son, you have other things to occupy you, and you cannot come. Thus is everything by which God would bless you and do you good, turned through your perversity to your destruction. And how long shall this go on? Even until you perish from the way, until you know what is meant by the awful expression, "The wicked is driven away in his wickedness." Dear friends, have mercy upon your own souls, and turn you at the reproof of your God. He is yet calling for you. He is now calling you by His Word—proclaiming to you afresh, through that Word, the riches of His grace, and that it is a grace that can reach you. Let the call be at length effectual— no more shut out the word in determined unbelief, but let it come to you, "not in word only, but in power and in the Holy Ghost, and in much assurance." And you shall yet know the peace, the blessedness of the children of God. You shall be numbered with those upon whose heads the candle of the Lord shone—shone in all their darkness; with those who can be brought into no circumstances in which they cannot feel that goodness and mercy are following them, that the way in which God is leading them is "the right way," and that "all things are working together for good to them."

SERMON X.

ROMANS viii. 3, 4.—" For what the law could not do, in that it was weak through the flesh, God sending his own Son in the likeness of sinful flesh, and for sin, condemned sin in the flesh: That the righteousness of the law might be fulfilled in us, who walk not after the flesh, but after the Spirit."

HE Apostle had just described the character of those who, being in Christ Jesus, are freed from all condemnation, to be, that they "walk not after the flesh, but after the Spirit;" and as the reason why they possess this character, the Apostle, speaking in his own person, had added, "For the law of the Spirit of life in Christ Jesus hath made me free from the law of sin and death." Some understand by "the law of the Spirit of life," the Gospel, which is indeed the ministration of the Spirit, but, as by the phrase "the law of sin and death," is meant that power or principle of corruption in us which works unto sin and death, by the phrase "the law of the Spirit of life," would seem more properly to be meant that new power or principle of spiritual life called the Spirit, in opposition to the flesh, which believers have received through Christ in believing. It is through the communication to them of this new principle or power of life that believers attain that blessed deliverance from the law of sin and death to which the Apostle so joyfully refers; and it will be seen that the object of the verses now read is to set forth more fully both the nature and the way of this deliverance. "For what the law could not do, in that it was weak through the flesh, God sending His own Son in the likeness of sinful flesh, and for sin, condemned sin in the flesh, that the righteousness of the law might be fulfilled in us, who walk not after the flesh, but after the Spirit." There are in these words two points of the deepest moment to us. There is, first, the blessed object which God has in view for us; and there is, secondly, the gracious way in which this object is to be effected.

I. Let us advert, in the first place, to the blessed object which, it is here stated, God has in view in regard to us. It is " that the righteousness of the law might be fulfilled in us." In that state into which we have come through the fall, and which is called our natural state, the righteousness of the law is not fulfilled in us. Alas! that law of God which is "holy and just and good," we have none of us kept; we are "all gone out of the way" of righteousness; and so entire is the corruption into which we are sunk, that " the carnal mind in us is enmity against God; it is not subject to the law of God, neither indeed can it be." Now, that we should be brought out of this evil state— that the righteousness of the law, which has not been fulfilled in us, should be fulfilled in us—this is the great object of God in regard to us. We are evil,—unclean;— evil, unclean in heart—yet God has looked upon us in this state, and this is His purpose concerning us, even to create a new heart, to renew a right spirit in us. Thus He says: " I will put my laws into their minds, and write them in their hearts." Thus, also, it is stated, " Christ bare our sins in His own body upon the tree, that we, being dead to sin, might live unto righteousness." And again, " He who knew no sin, was made sin for us, that we might be made the righteousness of God in Him."

Such is the object, in regard to us, of that God from whom we have so deeply revolted. We have called it a blessed object, and is it not so? Does it not prove how excellent the loving-kindness of God to us is, how deep is His concern for our good, that He should have such a design concerning us as that of raising us from the death of sin, to a life of perfect conformity to the law of God? To some, indeed, this may not be a matter so clear. With hearts rising in rebellion against the holy requirements of God's law—perceiving that obedience to it would compel them to sacrifice those fleshly lusts and gratifications in which they have all their life and joy, they can see no blessedness in such a design of God in regard to them, and they would rather that His object in respect of them had been something of a less high and holy character—something not altogether incompatible with the retaining of their worldly idols and their carnal gratifications. So must they think who live after the flesh, for the flesh loves not and cannot love that which would touch its life, which would crucify it.

But let us consider. Is this life of the flesh a life with which a creature formed in the image of God, and fitted to have its enjoyment in Him, should be so reluctant to part? To be "alienated from the life of God,"—to be "led captive by Satan at his will,"—to be under the tyranny of the law in the members,—to be impelled forward in a course against which conscience is, ever and anon, lifting up its accusing voice,—is this a state so desirable that the proposal to deliver us from it should be so grievous? Are they happy who live after the flesh—who have pleasure in unrighteousness? "Misery and destruction are in their ways, and the way of peace they have not known." "There is no peace to the wicked"—thus speaks the God of peace—He only who can tell us the way to peace. He sees that to be wicked is to be wretched ; and therefore, as He desires not our misery but our happiness, His loving object in regard to us is to rescue us from our misery by delivering us from our sin—to raise us to blessedness by raising us to righteousness.

How much, my friends, must we be overlooking the nature of the righteousness of the law, if we do not see that the way to be truly blessed is just God's way to be so—is just to be righteous according to the righteousness of the law. The righteousness of the law is love, for "love," to God and to man, "is the fulfilling of the law." But is not love blessedness? Is not enmity misery? And does not he who casts from him this enmity, cast from him that which destroys his peace, and grow in blessedness as he grows in love?

Again, since the law is a transcript of the mind of God, righteousness, or conformity to the law, is to be conformed to the mind of God—to be renewed after the divine image, and made a "partaker of divine nature." And must not this be blessedness, yea, the highest blessedness? It must be so. God, in designing that we should be made righteous, designs not only that we should have happiness, but that we should have the highest happiness. The joy which He desires and seeks that we should be brought into is His own joy. The river of which He would give us to drink is the river of His own pleasures. The blessedness wherewith He would bless us is the being made perfectly blessed, according to our measure, in the full enjoying of Himself to all eternity. Surely, then, the object of God in regard to us is a blessed object. Surely we may well be amazed at the grace which marks it. "Behold what manner of love the Father hath bestowed upon us, that we should be called the sons of God." What a blessedness is this for those to be raised to, who had sunk so low as we have done, who were children of wrath and heirs of hell!

Here, my friends, you cannot but perceive the utter groundlessness of the objection to the Gospel, that it makes void the law by destroying the obligation and necessity of yielding it obedience. How can it thus make void the law, when it so distinctly declares that the great object which God has in view in regard to us is that we should be conformed to the law, and that there can be no life or blessedness for us except in such conformity?

II. Let us now, secondly, take a view of the gracious way in which this object of God in regard to us is effected.

It is not through the law. The law could not secure from us the fulfilment of its own righteousness. Not that there was any defect in the law, for the law is "holy and just and good,"—is the same perfect rule that it ever was; and "had there been a law given that could have given life, verily, righteousness would have been by the law." The inability of the law to produce in us the righteousness which it required arose, not from any weakness in itself, for it ever demanded from us what it was right for us to render, and ever warned us of the danger of not rendering this; still, for the purpose of producing righteousness in us, it was weak through the flesh in us, that is, our corrupt nature. The flesh, or the natural man in us, is not and cannot be subject to the law of God, for the flesh, or the carnal mind in us, is, in its very essence, "enmity against God." However good, then, the law may be in itself; let its voice be as holy as it may, and let it proclaim its terrors as it may, yet, if it speaks to those who are in the flesh, it can meet with no obedience to its requirements; nay, the more it attempts to control the natural man, the more it reveals to him of its spirituality and its exceeding breadth; showing him his condemnation, the more will it irritate his corruption and bring out his deep and irreconcilable opposition to its righteousness. The law is thus "weak through the flesh" to recover us to the practice of righteousness. But, besides this, there is a further barrier to our being made righteous through the law. The law makes no provision for repentance, leaves no room for a return to righteousness when righteousness has once been departed from. The law leaves nothing for those who transgress it, "but a certain fearful looking for of judgment and fiery indignation to devour the adversaries. The law, without conveying to sinners one intimation of pardon, without casting over the gloom of their circumstances a single ray of hope, only utters in their ears the fearful language of inexorable justice—" The soul that sinneth it shall die." " Cursed is every one that continueth not in all things that are written in the book of the law to do them." It is evident, then, that righteousness cannot come to us through the law, and that if ever the righteousness of the law shall again be fulfilled in us, it must be through means which the law does not supply—in a way altogether different from the mere revelation of the law, however righteous it is in its requirements, and however awful in its sanctions.

What, then, is this way? It is thus stated : "God, sending His own Son in the likeness of sinful flesh, and for sin, condemned sin in the flesh, that the righteousness of the law might be fulfilled in us, who walk not after the flesh, but after the Spirit." The necessity of our having a new power bestowed upon us in order to the fulfilment in us of the righteousness of the law, is here recognised. This power is the power of the Spirit; and this power, which the law could not supply, is brought to us under the grace of the Gospel. "God, sending His own Son in the likeness of sinful flesh, and for sin, condemned sin in the flesh." God did this, and so we have the Spirit to lead us and guide us, the power of the Spirit to live in, " the law of the Spirit of life in Christ Jesus to make us free from the law of sin and death," and to make us righteous. Let us attentively consider the several parts of that which God is here recorded to have done, and we shall see how it follows as a consequence of what He did, that we have the power of the Spirit given to us in Christ Jesus. "God sent His Son." He sent His only begotten Son, that Son who was in the form of God, and "thought it not robbery to be equal with God."

This Son God sent "in the likeness of sinful flesh"— that is, He sent Him in form and fashion as a man, a " partaker of our flesh and blood,"—" made like unto His brethren in all things,"—sin only excepted. Further, God thus sending His own Son in the likeness of sinful flesh, sent Him "for sin,"—that is, as the marginal reading teaches us, He sent Him to be a sacrifice for sin. Having thus "sent His own Son in the flesh," and as a sacrifice for sin, God "condemned sin in the flesh,"—that is, executed upon sin the awful sentence denounced against it, and which justice demanded to be executed upon it. This was done when God laid the iniquities of us all upon the man Christ—treated Him as if He had been the offender, and made "His soul an offering for sin." When "He who knew no sin was made sin for us,"—when, in our nature and in our room, He "bare our sins in His own body upon the tree," and drank the full cup of wrath which we deserved to drink, experiencing a bitterness in it so awful as to draw from Him that mysterious cry of abandonment, "My God, my God, why hast thou forsaken me?"—then God "condemned sin in the flesh," poured upon it in our Head the curse which was its due—the curse which offended justice required that it should bear; thus making provision for a return on our part to righteousness, removing "the handwriting of condemnation that was against us," and opening a way for the divine favour to flow in upon us in healing and renewing power. And thus it was that God destroyed the power of sin in our nature, cast it forth from its dominion over us, which, as condemning has, in some instances, the sense of destroying, has been thought by some to be the meaning of the phrase,—"condemned sin in the flesh." Sin hath dominion over men in the flesh—holding them in a cruel and hopeless bondage; but Christ, having come in our nature and as our Head and Representative, and having "through the Eternal Spirit presented himself without spot to God," has brought our bondage to an end, has led our captivity captive; for He has not only removed our condemnation and opened our way into the holiest of all, but He has been made a quickening Spirit to us. He, as our Head, has even received, for the members, the fulness of that very Spirit through which He ever prevailed against all sin, and offered Himself up holy to God, and through which, descending to us through Him, we too may follow Him in the path of holiness—presenting ourselves to God living sacrifices, holy, acceptable in His sight.

In reviewing what has now been said, it cannot but strike the attentive mind how practical a thing is true religion. It is to be feared that this is greatly forgotten, but there is nothing which it is of greater importance for us to remember. We may have a name to live—we may wear a form of godliness—we may make a fair and flourishing profession, and because of these things we may regard ourselves as the true children of God ; but we may have these things, and yet not be His true children. We are His true children only as the righteousness of His law is fulfilled in us, as we are crucifying the flesh with its affections and lusts—as we are " putting off the old man, which is corrupt according to the deceitful lusts, and putting on the new man, which, after God, is created in righteousness and true holiness ;" and unless this is our character—unless we have ceased to sow to the flesh, and have begun to sow to the Spirit—though we name the name of Christ we are none of His. Oh, see that you be not cherishing any delusion in your minds in regard to this matter ! He that is really united to Christ will be bringing forth fruit unto God. "Little children," says the Apostle John, "let no man deceive you ; he that doeth righteousness is righteous, even as He is righteous. He that committeth sin is of the devil. In this the children of God are manifest, and the children of the devil : whosoever doeth not righteousness is not of God, neither he that loveth not his brother."

Again, we see, from what has been said, why it is that any are not living unto righteousness, and so not enjoying the great reward connected with so living. It is solely because they are receiving the grace of God in vain, rejecting the counsel of God against themselves. If they are not crucifying the flesh in them, it is not because there is no strength to do this provided for them, for, would they lay hold of it, there is a strength given them in Christ for this purpose, even the strength of His Spirit which He longs to bestow upon them, which He waits at the door of their hearts to give them, and concerning which He utters in their ears the gracious language, "Turn you at my reproof; behold I will pour out my Spirit upon you." Dear friends, how melancholy is our condition if, in the view of this amazing mercy, we are continuing in sin. To be perishing with hunger, while there is bread enough in our Father's house and to spare; to be keeping our deadly hurt, when the Son of God has brought a balm to heal it; to be rushing upon destruction, when the Spirit of grace is striving with us to arrest us in our course, and to pluck us as brands from the burning. What a fearful forsaking of our mercies is this! Let us escape, and escape at once, from a course so full of madness! "Kiss the Son lest He be angry, and ye perish from the way. When His wrath is kindled but a little, blessed are all they that put their trust in Him."

But we would address ourselves to those who have received Christ, and so have had the life of righteousness begun in them; and to them we would say, Behold the need which you have of a fuller and more constant union to Christ, by faith! It is only as we abide in Christ that we can have freedom from condemnation, for only in Him have we forgiveness, and boldness to come to God as children; and it is only as we are in Christ that we have power to crucify the flesh with its affections and lusts, for "our life is hid with Christ in God;" this is its only well-spring, and it can flow into us only through faith. You mourn under the remaining bondage of corruption; and you wonder, perhaps, that, after all your efforts, your old man is so little crucified—the law in your members is still so strong. But this should be no cause of wonder to you if you are not cleaving unto Christ by faith, since it is only from Him that you can receive that strength by which you can mortify the deeds of the body, and "yield yourselves unto God, as those that are alive from the dead." He is "the vine;" and as "the branch cannot bear fruit except it abide in the vine, no more can we except we abide in Him." He is "the bread of life;" and as bread cannot nourish our bodies unless we receive it into union with them, no more can He nourish our souls, unless we are joined to Him, and so receive His Spirit.

Oh! see, then, brethren, that your union with Him be a real union, and that it be constant and abiding. Having believed on Him, cleave to Him with purpose of heart. Thus shall you bring forth fruit unto God, and bring it forth in richer abundance. Thus shall the righteousness of the law be more and more fulfilled in you. Seeing that in that Christ died, He died unto sin, thereby casting it forth from its dominion over you; and in that He liveth, He liveth unto God—liveth that He may quicken you together with Himself, through the Spirit shed down upon you,—you shall reckon yourselves to be dead, indeed, unto sin, but alive unto God through Jesus Christ; neither shall ye yield "your members as instruments of unrighteousness unto sin, but yield yourselves unto God, as those that are alive from the dead, and your members as instruments of righteousness unto God."

And still, as you are made to drink more into the fulness of Christ's spirit, more of the fruits of the Spirit will appear in you—love, joy, peace, long-suffering, gentleness, goodness, faith, meekness, temperance, "against which there is no law," but which is the very righteousness that the law holds forth and requires, and which, assimilating us to the character, prepares us for the blessedness of " the inheritance of the saints in light."

SERMON XI.

ROMANS xiii. 8.—"Owe no man anything, but to love one another; for he that loveth another hath fulfilled the law."

IT is a strange, yet far from uncommon delusion, that men should confidently rank themselves among Christians, and yet that there should be scenes and departments of their every-day life into which they do not carry with them their Christianity. By many who "have a name that they live," the "putting on of the Lord Jesus Christ" would seem to be considered a thing for some festival or high season, not for ordinary and every-day life—a thing which it were exceedingly wrong to neglect or not carefully to attend to on certain solemn occasions, but which, when one of these is over, may very well be put away until another comes round. Religion, they think, should have its place as well as other things, and so they give it its place, and think that they do well in keeping it in it. It is truly marvellous that the vanity of such a course is not seen through by those who pursue it. Were they to go to the word of God to be taught their religion, they would learn that the Lord Jesus Christ, having once been put on, is nowhere and on no occasion to be put off—that "the man of God must be thoroughly furnished unto all good works;" that to be followers of Christ, whom He will acknowledge, we must follow Him at all times; that, in a

264

word, our religion, if it be worth anything, if it be not indeed an utter delusion, is an universally actuating principle with us, influencing us as much in regard to what is little as in regard to what is great—controlling us on the week-day as well as on the Sabbath, and in our intercourse with men as well as in our approaches to God.

In our last lecture we had occasion to contemplate Christianity as extending its influence over us as subjects, or members of the body politic; and looking at civil government as the ordinance of God for our good, we took notice of the duty of our being "subject to the higher powers." On the same principle—because government is an ordinance of God for the good of society—tribute or taxes are to be paid for its support. Since government cannot be supported, and its proper dignity and efficiency maintained, without expense, this, of course, should be borne by those who enjoy the blessings it procures. The payment of taxes for the support of the government whose protection we are enjoying is a debt as evidently a just one as any that can be named, and one that should be paid punctually and without evasion. And the man who, by artifice or deceit, avoids contributing in proportion to his property, is guilty of injustice and dishonesty. He not only defrauds the government, but in effect he defrauds his fellow-citizens; for if he evades contributing his just share, others must contribute more to make up the deficiency. These remarks apply with equal force to those who import foreign goods without paying those duties which the laws require—a practice involving deceit and artifice, and contrary to the rules of justice and honesty. We might add that it is little less criminal knowingly to purchase any merchandise thus illegally introduced, since we thus become "partakers of other men's sins," and we tempt them also to repeat these sins, it being evident that none would introduce merchandise in this unlawful manner if none could be found to purchase it.

On these matters, whether we be willing or not to hear, Christianity, and we might add conscience too, speak out to us in terms perfectly distinct and intelligible—"For this cause," says the Apostle, in the verses immediately preceding those now read, "for this cause pay ye tribute also ; for they are God's ministers, attending continually upon this very thing. Render, therefore, to all their dues ; tribute to whom tribute, custom to whom custom." Such precepts are sufficiently plain. But, as has been already observed, that Christianity which is of any value is an universally actuating principle, following and influencing its disciples everywhere ; and we have now to view it accompanying them into a department where many men would seem to be yet more unwilling that it should follow them, than into that to which we have just been referring. Passing with us from the duty of paying our proper proportion of the public revenue, the Apostle comes to the duty of our paying our ordinary debts, when he says, "Owe no man anything, but to love one another."

"Owe no man anything." There are two senses in which this may be taken. It may be viewed either as a prohibition to contract debt, or as a command to be prompt and honest in paying the debts we have contracted. It may mean "Never get into debt," or it may mean "Leave no debt you have incurred unpaid." The latter is probably the sense in which it was meant by the Apostle to be taken ; but looking at the many and fearful evils which, it is acknowledged, arise from the too common practice of contracting debt, and considering how many of these evils would be prevented by a system of ready money transactions, it were greatly to be desired that there were a far more general adoption of the rule—not to contract debt. And certainly, in regard to pecuniary transactions, we should never contract it without necessity. We should never contract it if industry might save us from the need of doing so, nor if we might avoid it by a rigid frugality and economy, for we need scarcely observe how utterly wrong it is to borrow from another to enable us to keep up a certain style and splendour of living, since what is more selfishly base and unprincipled than to be living in luxury and splendour on other men's means? It should be equally superfluous to remark that it is highly iniquitous to borrow of others for the purpose of embarking what we thus obtain from them on hazardous speculation on which it may be lost. To lay out what is our own in this way is to incur a heavy responsibility; how much more heavy, then, the responsibility we should incur in so acting with the property of another. We only remark further here, that it should be imperative with us not to run into an amount of debt which we have no sufficient reason to believe we shall be able to discharge at the proper time of payment. So much for the rule before us, viewing it as a prohibition against contracting debt; but taking it in the other sense which has been mentioned, regarding it as an injunction not to leave unpaid any debt which has been contracted by us, it is evidently a most important rule, and one which, as Christians, we should see that we carefully observe; since, if we neglect it, we must inevitably bring great reproach upon the doctrine of God our Saviour. We would not interpret the words before us to mean that we should never, under any circumstances, be a debtor to any one, were it but for a day or an hour. It may not be wrong, while we keep strictly within these well-understood limits to which we have referred, to contract a debt. It may be a matter of convenient arrangement that people should borrow and lend among themselves, and there may be no sin in our becoming indebted to a neighbour, so long as the sum does not exceed our means of discharging it at the period when it becomes due. In this way we may have contracted debt without any blame being imputable to us; but even then, having got into it without blame, we should be concerned also to get out of it without blame. It should be a matter of solemn obligation with us to pay what we owe. For this purpose, we should, previously to the day of paying, be frugal in our living, and economical in our expenditure, that our creditor may not fail to receive his own through any waste or mismanagement on our part. And when the day of payment comes, we should pay fully. There should be no attempt to escape from any part of our obligations, or endeavour to beat down our creditor, and to get him to accept less than is his due. We should pay promptly and cheerfully as well as fully. We should not need to be called upon again and again by our creditor. We should never force him to have recourse to compulsory measures to obtain payment from us. We have been told that many in this land who even wear a Christian name, think little of doing this, and can coolly and unblushingly set at defiance the man who asks from them but his own. If it be so, it is a disgrace to our land. It is an iniquity to be punished by the Judge of all. What shall we think of those who will remorselessly put a creditor to all the trouble and vexation and annoyance of legal proceedings before they will satisfy his just claims? The Word of God leaves us in no difficulty as to how to estimate such persons. It is the " *wicked* that borroweth and payeth not again." "Thou shalt not defraud thy neighbour, neither rob him." "Let no man go beyond and defraud his neighbour in any matter; because that the Lord is the avenger of all such." Oh! brethren, let not your hands be stained with this iniquity! "Render unto all their dues." Do this "not only for wrath, but for conscience' sake." Remember that though your evading payment of just debts may not expose you to the obloquy of breaking the eighth commandment, it is really as truly a breach of that commandment as many other things which are more emphatically condemned and more summarily dealt with among men.

In the remarks that have been made, we have referred principally to pecuniary debts; and we have done so because of the great practical importance of this matter.

The injunction, however, embraces every other kind of debt that we may owe. Thus, if we have given any one a promise, we owe him the fulfilment of that promise; and we should sacredly stand by it. Then, again, if we have received a kindness from one of our fellow-men, we owe him a debt of gratitude; and we should not fail to repay it as we have opportunity. No one who fears God as the God of truth, will be untrue to his promises, and no one who regards God as "the righteous Lord, loving righteousness and hating iniquity," will be guilty of the dark and hateful sin of ingratitude.

But this may, perhaps, be rather struck at in the words that follow. The injunction, you will observe, is, "Owe no man anything, but to love one another." "*But to love one another.*" Love is a debt which cannot be discharged. It is a debt which we owe all men, and which, after ten thousand payments, will yet be due. It is a debt, my friends, that we should always be paying, and yet feel that we always owe; for it is true now, and it will be true for ever, that "if God so loved us, we ought also to love one another." We are to love one another *always*, and when we have done for one another all that love can do—still never to have done loving, "because he that loveth another hath fulfilled the law." That the "law of God be fulfilled in us," is our highest blessedness; it was the very end for which Christ died for us upon the accursed tree. "He loved us, and gave Himself for us that He might redeem us from all iniquity, and purify us unto Himself a peculiar people, zealous of good works;" or, in other words, that the law might be fulfilled in us. Now, "love is the fulfilling of the law." The lack of righteousness among men is entirely owing to the lack of love; and were perfect love to be implanted in any heart, then there would be a perfect observance of all God's commandments.

This the Apostle goes on to show in the verse that follows: "For this,—Thou shalt not commit adultery,—

Thou shalt not kill,—Thou shalt not steal,—Thou shalt not bear false witness,—Thou shalt not covet ; and if there be any other commandment, it is briefly comprehended in this saying,—namely, Thou shalt love thy neighbour as thyself!"   The meaning here is plain.   It is as if the Apostle had said, " I have observed that he that loveth another hath fulfilled the law."   Let this be considered. If there were perfect love of God, there would be a perfect fulfilment of the first table of the law, since the sum of what it contains is this,—"Thou shalt love the Lord thy God with all thy heart, and with all thy soul, and with all thy mind."   Then, to take the second table,—its injunctions are summed up in the command,—" Thou shalt love thy neighbour as thyself."   This will be at once evident to all who give the matter a thought.   Nothing is more clear than that, if this command,—" Thou shalt love thy neighbour as thyself," were within the heart, it would lead to a perfect fulfilment of the fifth commandment, nor would the duty owing to parents, and to our other superiors, be ever left undone.   And it is equally clear that to banish all fraud, injustice, oppression, falsehood, adultery, impurity, murder, hatred, theft, evil-speaking, covetousness, and overreaching, there needs only that the law of love to others be in the heart.   It is the same as the Saviour's golden rule, " Whatsoever things ye would that men should do to you, do ye even so to them."   And who does not see that if every man would so act towards others, as he would wish and think it reasonable for them to act towards himself, were he in their circumstances and they in his, — the righteousness which is in the second table of the law would infallibly be fulfilled by him.

And this is yet farther confirmed in the tenth verse. " Love," says the Apostle, appealing to our convictions, " Love worketh no ill to his neighbour ; therefore love is the fulfilling of the law."   Love never injures our neighbour in any respect.   It is not in its nature to injure him, but on the contrary to do him service.   As, then, love

never does evil to one's neighbour, but is an active principle leading to the doing him good, "love is the fulfilling
of the law," and therefore should it be our supreme desire
to increase in love, never to consider that we have enough
of this divine grace, but ever to seek to have it in more
and yet more living and vigorous exercise. It is " a fruit
of the Spirit of God ;" and only when we have "the love
of God shed abroad in our hearts by the Holy Spirit,"
does love spring up in our breasts. But then it does
spring up within us, and we learn to say in regard to God,
"We love him who hath first loved us;" and, in reference
to our fellow-men, "If God so loved us, we ought also
to love one another." In this view, of what unspeakable
value is the Gospel of Christ ! That law, the end or the
completion of which is love, we have all of us broken
times and ways without number ; and as a broken law it
worketh wrath, leaving us helpless and hopeless under the
fearful sentence—"Cursed is every one that continueth not
in all things that are written in the Book of the Law to do
them." But there is help and hope for us in Christ. " He
is the end of the law for righteousness to every one that
believeth." And this righteousness is fulfilled in us, in our
believing. "The law is not made void through faith—on
the contrary, it is established through faith." It is established because, through faith, the love which is the fulfilling of the law is put into our hearts ; for " faith worketh
by love," and the more that our faith increases, the more
does our love and consequently our obedience increase.
The Holy Spirit "takes of the things of Christ, and shows
them to us," and thus it is that the love which is of God
is implanted within us, for thus receiving " Christ to dwell
in our hearts by faith, and so being rooted and grounded
in love, yea, made to comprehend what is the breadth
and length, and depth and height, and to know the
love of God which passeth knowledge," — the enmity
that is by nature in us is displaced, and love occupies its
room, even the love which constrains us to walk with God

in all holy obedience — the love which is ever asking,
" What shall I render unto the Lord for all His benefits to
me ?" and which, never satisfied with any of its renderings,
still presses after a fuller conformity with the Saviour's
commandment, " That we love one another as He hath
loved us." You who have had the law of love written
upon your hearts know that even thus was the history of
its being written there. You know that if you have purified your souls unto that unfeigned love which is the
fulfilling of the law, it has been in " obeying the truth
through the Spirit." You know that, if you are walking
in love, " putting on bowels of mercies, kindness, humble-
ness of mind, meekness, long-suffering, forbearing one
another, and forgiving one another," it is because Christ
loved you and gave Himself for you. And say then, brethren, is not the knowledge of Christ Jesus the Lord a
knowledge above all price? Is there not something in
this knowledge " more to be desired than gold, yea, than
much fine gold; sweeter also than honey and the honey,
comb ? " If it be so that you possess this knowledge, be
thankful for it, and seek to grow in it, praying that " the
light of the glorious Gospel of Christ, who is the image of
God, may shine upon you, giving you the light of the
knowledge of the glory of God in the face of Jesus Christ."
You will know that the light *is* shining upon you by your
being changed into His image, even the image of Him
who is love, from glory to glory. You will know that your
religion is not vain, but a religion that will stand on that
day when God shall try it, by its having for its fruit that
love which worketh no ill, but all good to your neighbour.
And this it is needful ever to bear in remembrance ; all
the more so, that by many who have a form of godliness,
it would seem to be lost sight of. Many would appear to
forget the Apostolic declaration. " If ye fulfil the royal
law according to the Scriptures, thou shalt love thy neighbour as thyself, ye do well." But this, nevertheless, is the
test of true religion, and hereby only " know we, that we

have passed from death unto life." We may not speak of our faith if it be not working by love and leading us to love " in all righteousness and goodness and truth." " Faith without works is dead ;" and if we are not living in love, doing good works unto all men as we have opportunity, it were better for us to assume at once that we are yet strangers to the faith of the Gospel, and to go and receive Christ, even as if we had never received Him before ; for unless we do this, we shall die in our sins, and only discover when it is too late, that our Christianity was a delusion, and that with a name that we lived we were dead. " For as the body without the spirit is dead, so faith without works is dead also."

SERMON XII.

COLOSSIANS ii. 6, 7.—"As ye have therefore received Christ Jesus the Lord, so walk ye in Him : rooted and built up in Him, and stablished in the faith, as ye have been taught, abounding therein with thanksgiving."

LET us enquire, my hearers, in the first place, in what manner the Colossians *had* "received Christ." As the Apostle, in his exhortation to them to walk in Christ, refers to the way in which they had received Him, the knowledge of this way is absolutely necessary to the understanding of the exhortation. How, then, we enquire, had these Colossians "received Christ Jesus the Lord?"

They had received Him, in the first place, as their *peace*. The Apostle, in the preceding chapter, states concerning Christ, and states it as a thing which the Colossians would well understand, that He "had made peace through the blood of His cross." They had not always enjoyed this blessing, but they enjoyed it now. As sinners they were under the curse, since "cursed is every one that continueth not in all things that are written in the book of the law to do them;" but they had seen "Christ redeeming them from the curse of the law by becoming a curse for them." As sinners, they owed to the Divine justice a debt of fearful amount, and which they had nothing to pay; but they had seen Christ "blotting out the handwriting that was against them, which was contrary to them, taking it out of the way, and nailing it to His cross." They had seen these things, and in seeing them they had found peace ; they had had their guilty apprehensions removed. A sweet confidence in God had taken the place of that tormenting dread which they had felt towards Him. Their heart was healed. " Beauty was given them for ashes, the oil of joy for mourning, and the garment of praise for the spirit of heaviness."

The Colossians had, moreover, received Christ as their *sanctification;* as one who was " exalted a Prince and a Saviour to give repentance as well as the remission of sins." To this the Apostle refers in the preceding chapter, where he speaks of their " giving thanks to the Father, as making them meet to be partakers of the inheritance of the saints in light ; " and again, when he speaks of Christ's having " reconciled them in the body of His flesh through death, to present them holy, and unblameable, and unreproveable in His sight." They had been " dead in trespasses and sins," " alienated from God, and enemies to Him by wicked works," but Christ had been to them a quickening Spirit. They had heard the voice of the Son of God ; and hearing it, they had lived. From the moment that they had received Christ, they had become "new creatures ;" they had "put off, concerning the former conversation, the old man which is corrupt according to the deceitful lusts, and they had put on the new man, which, after God, is created in righteousness and true holiness." Not that the old man was fully put off, for, alas ! the law in their members yet warred against the law of their minds, so that, often, they could not do the things which they would ;—still, the victory was theirs through their Lord Jesus Christ. Through Him strengthening them, they did all things ;—through the power of His might they ceased to be conformed to this world, and they were " transformed by the renewing of their mind, proving what was the good and perfect and acceptable will of God."

The Colossians had received Christ, too, as their *hope;*

their hope of heaven, their hope of glory. The Apostle, in the foregoing part of this epistle, speaks to them of Christ as being "in them the hope of glory." Their abode was still the world where the curse had taken effect. It was a dim and troubled scene which they had now to pass through,—dimmed and troubled by sin ; but there lay beyond it a land of unclouded brightness and uninterrupted peace. The Lord of that land was their Lord, and He was maturing them for its joys. This they knew; and therefore could they exclaim,—" It doth not yet appear what we shall be, but we know that when He shall appear, we shall be like Him, for we shall see Him as He is." " Blessed be the God and Father of our Lord Jesus Christ, which, according to His abundant mercy, hath begotten us again unto a lively hope, by the resurrection of Jesus Christ from the dead, to an inheritance incorruptible and undefiled, and that fadeth not away, reserved in heaven for us."

In this manner, my friends, had the Colossians received Christ Jesus the Lord ; they had received Him as their peace, their sanctification, their hope. In this manner must all receive Him, who would have any part in Him. If you, my hearers, have embraced Him at all, you have embraced Him in the same manner that these Colossians did. You have received Him as your peace. The burden of sin once pressed heavily upon you. Well, how was it removed? It was by a believing view of the cross of Christ. Your hearts were once distracted by the terrors of the Lord. How were they quieted? They were " sprinkled from an evil conscience" by the blood of Jesus, —that blood by which a way is opened for us into the holiest, and through which we hear God addressing to us the gladdening words —" I have blotted out your transgressions as a thick cloud, and as a cloud, your sins."

Again, if you have received Christ, you have received Him as your *sanctification*. The Spirit of Christ has been given to you, and of Him you have been born again. He has taken of the things of Christ, and shown them unto you. He has led you into the truth as it is in Jesus, and that truth has sanctified you. It has written the laws of God in your hearts; it has put these laws in your inward parts. Sin has not had dominion over you as it once had; but " you, beholding as in a glass the glory of the Lord, have been changed into the same image."

If you have received Christ, you have also received Him as your hope. You have much from Him in possession, but you have, if possible, more from Him in prospect. Amidst the sorrows that now bow you down,—amidst the temptations that now assail you, you contemplate the glorious and peaceful rest which remains for you in another world;—you remember with delight the words of your Lord by His Apostle,—" Christ loved the Church, and gave Himself for it, that He might sanctify and cleanse it with the washing of water by the word; that He might present it to Himself a glorious Church, not having spot or wrinkle or any such thing, but that it should be holy, and without blemish."

And what then, my hearers, is the exhortation which I would address to you from the words of our text? It is that, even as you have received Christ Jesus the Lord, so you would continue to walk in Him; that you would abide in Christ; that you would get yourselves rooted and built up and stablished in these truths which you have been taught respecting Him. Be thankful—be very thankful for the grace you have received; for the knowledge of Christ into which you have been led; but go forward, grow in this grace, grow in this knowledge; cleave unto the Lord with full purpose of heart; there can be neither spiritual safety nor spiritual prosperity for you, but in walking in Him, knowing your completeness in Him, and living upon His fulness.

You have known Christ as your peace; you have felt the tranquillising influence of His blood; it has removed that tormenting dread with which you once contemplated your offended God; it has given you boldness to enter into the holy of holies, to come unto God as a reconciled Father and Friend. This is well; yea, it is a mercy which should call forth increasing thanksgivings to Him who bestowed it; but, my dear hearers, you are ever to look unto Christ as your peace; you are, from day to day, to become more and more acquainted with Him in this endearing character. The atonement of Christ is the only ground of a sinner's confidence toward God, and if you stand not firmly on this ground—if you allow yourselves to be moved away from it, you will lose your confidence; a strangeness will rise up between you and your God; you will cease to delight in Him as you were wont; and He will have no pleasure in you, for He has said, " If any man draw back, my soul shall have no pleasure in Him."

You are, further, to *walk in Christ* as your sanctification. You know Him as your Sanctifier already; through Him strengthening you, you have already gained many a victory over the devil, the world and the flesh. This, also, is cause for fervent gratitude; but you are still to cleave to Christ as your Sanctifier. He is revealed in Scripture as the strength of His people, and as the Giver of repentance; now you are to cling to Him continually in this character. You are to take to Him every corruption, entreating Him to subdue it; and every pollution, asking Him to cleanse you from its defilement. You are to entreat Him to "bless you by turning you away from your iniquities." This is to place yourselves on a ground where "no weapon that is formed against you shall prosper." *Off* this ground there is no safety; *upon* it there is no danger. To all who thus cleave to Jesus, God says, "He that toucheth you toucheth Me." "Even the youths shall faint and be weary, and the young men shall utterly fail; but they that wait upon the Lord shall renew their strength; they shall mount up with wings as eagles ; they shall run and not be weary ; they shall walk and not faint."

You are, finally, to walk in Christ as your hope. You still walk amidst errors and dangers and sorrows. You are still in a world where your Lord has told you "ye shall have tribulation." But a hope full of immortality is set before you ; the Lord Jesus Christ, even your Lord and Saviour, is upon the throne of the Mediatorial kingdom, and "He must reign until all enemies are put under His feet." To this prospect you are ever to cling. You are to look away from the tears and perturbations of the present scene, to the rest and joy of the heavenly world. You are to look upon the entrance of Christ into heaven as the pledge of your entrance ; His triumph over death and hell as your triumph over them, and the earnest of your admission into those joys which "eye hath not seen, nor ear heard, neither hath it entered into the heart of man to conceive." He is the Captain of salvation ; and of those who place themselves under His leadership He says, "I give unto them eternal life, and they shall never perish, neither shall any pluck them out of my hand." "He is a Sun and shield ; He will give grace and glory, and no good thing will He withhold from them that walk uprightly." He will follow them with His loving kindness through life, and He will present them hereafter "faultless and unblameable in the presence of His glory, with exceeding joy."

What a precious Saviour, my friends, is Christ Jesus the Lord ! How suitable to our condition are the blessings which He brings to us ! How amply do they provide for all our wants from first to last ! Why is it that any of us continue comfortless and desponding ? Why is it that Satan gets such an advantage over us, and that sin maintains so strong a dominion in our hearts ? The only reason for these things is, we are not walking in Christ ; we are resting our dependence elsewhere than in Him ; we are forgetting that we have nothing, and never can have anything but what we receive from Him. Oh, let us guard against this serious error, and let us henceforth walk in Christ, seeking to be wise in His wisdom, and strong in His omnipotence. As the tree takes a firmer hold of the soil the longer its roots are struck into it, so let us take a firmer hold of Christ the longer we live in union with Him. So shall we maintain our steadfastness amidst all the storms to which we are exposed, and learn to exclaim with the Apostle, "Who shall separate us from the love of Christ? For I am persuaded that neither death, nor life, nor angels, nor principalities, nor powers, nor things present, nor things to come, nor height nor depth, nor any other creature, shall be able to separate us from the love of God, which is in Christ Jesus our Lord."

Let us learn, further, in connexion with this subject, the importance of using every means calculated to strengthen our faith. Since it is by faith that we receive Christ at first, and ever after walk in Christ, everything calculated to strengthen this faith should be a matter of deep interest to us. Such is the Word read in private, and heard in public; such are prayer and praise; such are all the ordinances which the Lord has given to the Church. See, then, my friends, that ye have continual recourse to these things. Let the Word of God dwell in you richly, and in all wisdom; seek closer acquaintance with it from day to day; embrace every opportunity of studying it at home, and of hearing it in the house of God. Be like the Bereans who "searched the Scriptures daily," and concerning whom we read that the result of this search was that "many of them believed." To the reading and hearing of the Word, join prayer and praise. In every exercise with which the Lord has connected a blessing—in that engage; to every place which the Lord has promised to hallow with His blessing—to that repair. Habitually repair to the sanctuary on the sacred day. Most refreshing have been the visits of God's people to that hallowed place. There He has made them glad with the light of His countenance, and chased away their depressing fears, and revived their dying faith. And over the recollection of their enjoyments there, have they learned to exclaim in the language of the Psalmist, " A day in thy courts is better than a thousand. I had rather be a door-keeper in the house of my God, than to dwell in the tents of wickedness."

The faith which we now seek to cherish and to strengthen will, ere long, be changed into vision. Time, with all its griefs and struggles, is hastening away, and eternity is near at hand. A few days of abiding in Christ and walking with Him on earth, and we shall dwell with Him amidst the bliss and radiance of heaven. He left this promise when He left the earth ; and it is a promise that will soon be accomplished to all who look for its fulfilment : " I go to prepare a place for you ; and if I go away to prepare a place for you, I will come again and receive you unto Myself, that where I am, there ye may be also."

These things, however, are the heritage of those only who walk in Christ, and if you are not walking in Him—if you are not clinging to Him as your peace, your purity, your hope—if you are not seeking to be rooted and built up in Him, you have no reason to look for any part, either in the present, or in the future happiness of His people. Alas ! so far from your having any reason in this state to look for such happiness, " there remaineth for you only a certain fearful looking for of judgment, and fiery indignation to devour the adversaries."

And wherefore are you forsaking your own mercies ? To gain what desirable object are you losing your souls ? Does sin make you happy ? Does it promise you happiness ? You know that it does not ; you know well that " vanity and vexation of spirit " might, with propriety be written over every enjoyment you have tasted in alienation from God, and in estrangement from Christ. And why, then, will you pursue the course you are doing? Wherefore do you spend your strength for nought, "and "your labour for that which satisfieth not?"

Oh, my hearers, I would earnestly and affectionately entreat you to "receive Christ Jesus the Lord." He is yet presented to you in all the fulness of His grace, and in all the extent of His offices. He is yet knocking at the door of your hearts, and beseeching you to give Him admission. This day is salvation offered to you afresh, through the atoning blood of Jesus. "Now is the accepted time; now is the day of salvation," even this day. *To-morrow!* What have you to do with to-morrow? To-morrow you may be in eternity. "What is your life? It is even a vapour that appeareth for a little time, and then vanisheth away." Seize upon the present moment; this night receive Christ. He is *now* bidding you "taste and see that He is good," but soon may He address to you different language. "Because I called and ye refused; I stretched out my hand and no man regarded; ye despised all my counsel and would none of my reproof; therefore shall ye eat the fruit of your own way, and be filled with your own devices." Flee from His wrath. "Kiss the Son lest He be angry, and ye perish from the way, when his anger is kindled but a little. Blessed are all they that put their trust in Him."

PORTION OF A SERMON.

ROMANS vi. 21.—"What fruit had ye then in those things whereof ye are now ashamed? For the end of those things is death."

(This sermon was intended specially for the troops, to whom it was first preached.)

LOOK once more upon those things of which the Apostle speaks. Behold their *deadly end*. "What fruit had ye in those things whereof ye are now ashamed? For the end of those things is *death*." You have seen the utter unfruitfulness of sin, you have seen its shamefulness, you are now invited to contemplate its direful issue. Things do not amend with the transgressors as he proceeds; they only wax worse and worse until his doom is sealed and his misery complete. The end of his course is *death*. Death followeth sin as its *natural* consequence. "The bloody and deceitful man," says David, "shall not live half his days." How many bring themselves to an untimely end, by infringing their country's laws! How many have false feelings of honour and ungovernable pride hurried to the tomb in the very morning of life? How many have we seen, in the career of profligacy, hastening on premature dissolution, or if life be prolonged, dragging out a miserable existence, with their bodies filled with the sins of their youth—incapable of relishing a single enjoyment which this world has to bestow—enduring a sort of living death!

But it is more important to observe that death follows sin as its *moral* consequence. "They that are far from God must perish." "The wages of sin is death;" under the righteous government of God, it can earn no other recompense, it can meet with no other reward. Sin and death never have and never can be severed. "In the day that thou eatest thereof," said the Lord to our first parents, —"thou shalt surely die." And did they not die that very day? Did not the sentence of God take immediate effect? Did they not instantly die, in the most important sense of the term? Do we not behold them immediately spoiled of their original glory, driven from their lovely abode, and cut off from that communion with the fountain of life in which primarily consisted their heaven, their happiness, their life? And here we feel it important to call your attention to what death really is. Death is not an eternal sleep, or in other phrase, annihilation. This view of it is, we fear, often taken, and often exerts a most mischievous influence, where the entertainment of it is altogether unacknowledged; but no view of it could be more delusive. We are not annihilated when we die; our being may then be changed, but it is not extinguished. A day will come when the wicked shall wish that it were, and that they could cease to be, but their wish shall be vain; "they shall seek this death, but it shall flee from them." Neither does death mean the mere separation of the soul from the body, when the one "returns to the dust as it was," and the other "to the God that gave it." The term "death" has, indeed, sometimes this same import in Scripture; but it has a still more extensive and more awful meaning. The separation of the soul from the body is painful and revolting; but the death to which the Apostle refers is infinitely more terrible. It is the separation of the soul from God—the being cut off for ever from the fountain of all that is good and of all that is happy. It is "everlasting destruction from the presence of the Lord and from the glory of His power," an eternal

284

privation of His favour in whose favour is life—the being linked in wrath and woe with that dreadful being who stands at the head of the principalities and powers of darkness—the being " cast into hell-fire, where the worm dieth not, and the fire is not quenched,"—the extinction, not of being, but of all that renders being a blessing of peace, and of happiness and of hope.

This is " the second," the last, the " eternal death," mentioned in Scripture. To this issue unchecked and unrepented iniquity naturally and necessarily tends. This doom the God of truth has told us, He has reserved for it. " He shall say unto them on the left hand.—Depart, ye cursed, into everlasting fire, prepared for the devil and his angels. And these shall go away into everlasting punishment." " The wicked shall be turned into hell, and all the nations that forget God." " I saw," says St. John, " the dead, small and great, stand before God; and the books were opened, and another book was opened, which is the book of life ; and the dead were judged out of those things which were written in the books, according to their works. And the sea gave up the dead which were in it ; and death and hell delivered up the dead which were in them ; and they were judged, every man according to their works. And death and hell were cast into the lake of fire. This is the *second death*."

The practical conclusions arising from this subject are obvious.

Are the things to which you have now listened true ? Is the way of transgressors thus hard ? Is the course of sin so fruitless, and so shameful, and so fatal ? Then, *what an evil and a bitter thing is sin, and how earnestly should we seek to forsake it !* You behold multitudes around you altogether insensible of its evil. You behold them yielding without a struggle to the current of corruption, and, instead of resisting the suggestions of iniquity, lending a ready ear to its vile allurements, and plunging, apparently without remorse or regret, into its miserable and guilty excesses. But is this the course which wisdom dictates? Is this the course of which you can calmly and deliberately approve? No, my friends, you cannot. You are sensible of the madness of pursuing the sinner's path. You feel the force of the Scriptural question, Have all the workers of iniquity no knowledge? And to what should these convictions lead you? To a prompt and vigorous abandonment of sin. Cast away its yoke; be no more its slave; toil no longer for its miserable wages. Be thankful that still you have opportunity to flee from its fatal path, but let the time you have lost give wings to your speed in distancing its snares. "Let the wicked forsake his way, and the unrighteous man his thoughts; and let him return unto the Lord and he will have mercy upon him; and to our God, for He will abundantly pardon."

The subject of this discourse will teach you, too, *in what light you should regard those who encourage you in sin.* In almost every large body of men, there will always be some of more reckless wickedness than others, who will seek to corrupt their fellows. You have, perhaps, met with such; you have met with persons who, not content with being wicked alone, have laboured to bring you down to the same level with themselves—have encouraged you to profane your Maker's name, incited you to the degrading debauch, and led your steps to scenes of impurity. And all this they have done under the mask and guise of friendship, under the pretext of making you merry and happy. But, *were* they your friends? Had they your true interest at heart? Have you not found them your cruellest foes? Are you not exclaiming, as you think of the misery and shame they have brought upon you—as you tremble on the precipice to which they have led you, "My soul, come not thou into their secrets; unto their assembly, mine honour, be not thou united."

This subject should, moreover, call forth *our fervent thankfulness for the riches of redeeming love.* Though some transgressors are more vile than others, we are all transgressors. We are all, naturally, the servants of sin; and we might have been all left to reap its fearful wages. There might have been no means of deliverance from its misery and its shame—no escape from its terrible curse either here or hereafter. The God whom we had forsaken might have forsaken us and allowed us to wander and wilder in the path of our own choice, until we had everlastingly and irrecoverably perished. But God has not forsaken us; and I stand here this day to proclaim in your ears the glad tidings of a deliverance from sin—from its curse and from its power. "God so loved the world that He gave His only begotten Son, that whosoever believeth in Him should not perish, but have everlasting life." "Ye know the grace of our Lord Jesus Christ, that though He was rich, yet for your sakes He became poor, that ye, through His poverty might be rich." You have fallen almost to hell, but you may be raised to heaven. There is a hand able to lift you over the mighty interval between perdition and salvation, and there is a heart as willing as the hand is able. Shall not these things call forth your gratitude and your praise? Shall not your hearts burst forth into the song of Zacharias: "Blessed be the Lord God of Israel, for He hath visited and redeemed His people." Rest not, however, in mere thankfulness. Continue not in a state of vacant admiration. Having the way of life pointed out to you, walk therein. Seek an interest in the offered deliverance of the Gospel. Believe in the Lord Jesus Christ, that thou mayest be saved. Remember that the salvation of Christ, precious as it is, and complete as it is, and free as it is, can be no salvation to you until it is applied, and delay not to apply it—to make it yours. Why, with all to lose, and with everything to gain that is valuable to an immortal spirit, should you stand a moment longer idle? You know that the time is short. You know the uncertainties of life; or if you do not you should know them. You know how death and disease have of late thinned your ranks. How often, during the bygone year, have our streets been darkened by the solemn train, and our hearts been thrilled and melted by the solemn notes that mark the soldier's funeral! You are soon to depart from this place, but where are they who marched at your side a twelvemonth ago, as gay and as vigorous as you? They little thought that their career should so quickly terminate; and that when the summons came to remove you to another station, or to call you back to your native land, you should leave their bones to moulder on a foreign shore. But their hearts are cold and still to-day. You have fired your farewell shot over their narrow resting-place, and you shall see them no more until these heavens are departed, and you meet them, where uncounted millions meet, in the presence of your Judge. And who of you is marked next to fall? You know not; but sure I am each of you should be exclaiming, "Lord, is it I?" and pouring forth the fervent prayer that the God of grace would prepare you for your latter end. "In the midst of life you are in death." "Truly, as the Lord liveth, and as your souls this day live, there may be but a step between you and death."

Oh, improve, then, the season of your merciful visitation. Allow not a day to pass over your heads till you have supplicated the Almighty Redeemer to free you from the wretched vassalage of sin, and to make you the servants of holiness. "Whatsoever thy hand findeth to do," in this matter, "do it with thy might." Are you sensible that your most important interests have to this hour been neglected? Is God still unreconciled and sin unforsaken? Does this wrath of God still abide in you? Seek now to have it removed. "Behold, now is the accepted time; behold, now is the day of salvation." "To-day hear His voice;" to-morrow it may be too late. "Agree with thine adversary quickly, while thou art in the way with him; lest at any time the adversary deliver thee to the judge, and the judge deliver thee to the officer, and thou be cast into prison. Verily, I say unto thee, thou shalt by no means come out thence, until thou hast paid the uttermost farthing!"

✠ FRAGMENT OF A LECTURE.

St. John iii. 17-21.—"For God sent not His Son into the world to condemn the world ; but that the world through Him should be saved."

IN illustration of the declaration that "men love darkness rather than light, because their deeds are evil," our Lord continues in verse twentieth,—"For every one that doeth evil, hateth the light, neither cometh to the light, lest his deeds should be reproved." The principle here laid down is so plain that it needs no explanation. The application of the principle is this : The Gospel is *light;* it reproves the sinner ;—it does so, as showing him that his sin is exceedingly sinful. Therefore do ungodly men hate the Gospel ; it is the object of their aversion and enmity, because they see that, were they to receive it, it would condemn them for their evil deeds, it would disturb their hollow peace by arming conscience against them. And here we learn the inexcusableness of unbelief. Men of infidel minds have gone far in excusing the sin of unbelief ; nay, some have tried to make it out to be no sin at all, as being a thing which men cannot help ; and a living British senator, on a great public occasion, recently gave utterance to the sentiment—that "a man is no more accountable for his belief than for the colour of his skin or the height of his stature." But is, then, the unbelief that rejects the Gospel involuntary ? Is it indeed a thing which men can-

not help? Do we not continually see that the state of
the affections has the most material influence on our
belief? Is it not found that men easily believe what they
are inclined to believe, while they as readily disbelieve
that to which they are strongly averse? Is it not true
that when truth is against a man, a man will be against
truth, and that to this indisposition it is owing that he
rejects it? Oh! brethren, it is not from want of evidence
for its truth that men reject the Gospel ;—it is not because
they have proved to their satisfaction that it is a cunningly
devised fable, that they believe it not. The cause of their
unbelief is their love of sin; they obey not the Gospel,
not because it is untrue, but because it is holy, and would
compel them to forego the gratification of their cherished
lusts ; and thus does their unbelief bring out the wickedness of their hearts in darker colours than before, showing them to be fitting objects of that wrath which, we are
assured, will be poured upon the unbelieving. Let those
who are yet abiding in unbelief look into this matter. See
whether it be not the love of sin, in some shape or other
that prevents you from welcoming the holy Saviour ; and
if it be indeed so, think how awful must be your doom
when you shall be brought into judgment !

Our Lord, in the concluding verse of this passage, ex-
hibits a striking contrast to the evil-doer,—" But he that
doeth truth cometh to the light, that his deeds may be
made manifest that they are wrought in God." He that
doeth truth,—he that obeys the truth, and walks according to it—he that no longer clings to error, however
pleasant it may be to his corrupt heart, but sincerely follows what is truth, however painful to him may be its
disclosures,—such a man comes to the light, loves it, and
desires to be in it, that he may have evidence that his
actions are right, are wrought in God, and are therefore
such as God will approve. Here, however, it will be said
to us ;—this is the character of the regenerate man ;—but
what we would know is—how shall we be brought into

this state,—how shall that great change be effected in us without which we cannot love the light, but will cling to the darkness of our natural state? To this we would reply : Cannot you bethink yourselves how awful it will be for you if you shall live on in darkness, and at last die in darkness, and be consigned for ever to the outer darkness and the second death? Cannot you see it to be your true interest to come to the light, however humbling and painful to you it may be to approach it? Cannot you discern the awful madness of deceiving yourselves, and perishing with a lie in your right hand, when you might deliver your precious, your immortal souls? Feeling how fearfully you will forsake your own mercies, if you cast away the hope of having a part and portion in the Kingdom of God,—cannot you cast youselves upon God, and cry to Him from your hearts, " Create in me a clean heart, O God, renew in me a right spirit ? " Cannot you do this much ; yea, cannot you do yet more than this ? Seeing that it is by the Word of Truth that God sanctifies His people,—seeing that it is not by doing any violence to their moral constitution, but by adapting Himself to it, that God regenerates them,—seeing that it is by the exhibition to them of His holy, sin-hating love, as that is manifested in the Cross, that He overcomes their enmity and inclines and persuades and constrains them to become His children,—cannot you turn in deepest earnestness to the Word of Truth, and enquire into that mystery of love, " that God so loved the world that He gave His only begotten Son, that whosoever believeth on Him should not perish, but have everlasting life ? " Surely, there is nothing to hinder you from enquiring, in a spirit of deepest earnestness and prayer, into that mysterious love wherewith God hath loved us in the gift of His own Son ; and would you, in the spirit of earnestness and prayer, receive the record of God's love, the mighty step of your life would be taken, your career as sons of God would be entered upon.

Observe the dealings of our Lord with Nicodemus. First, He alarmed him out of his deceitful security,—telling him, again and again, that he could not see the Kingdom of God until he was born again; and then He preached him those heavenly things, that mystery of Divine love which we have in the incarnation and death of the Son of God,—through the knowledge of which the dead in sin are quickened and made alive unto God. And through this dealing of our Lord with Nicodemus, there is reason to believe that he became a child of God, an heir of the heavenly kingdom. And might it not be the same with you? Oh! seek that you may know the truth, remembering how much depends upon your knowing it! Ask that the Spirit of God may be given to you, to take of the things of Christ and show them unto you. Be determined in the strength of God,—that strength which was never yet denied to any who truly sought it,—that the god of this world shall no longer blind you, but that you shall escape from his delusions. And it shall be so. God shall help you. He "who commanded the light to shine out of darkness shall shine into your hearts, to give you the light of the knowledge of His glory in the face of Jesus Christ; so that you, beholding as in a glass the glory of the Lord, shall be changed into the same image from glory to glory, even as by the Spirit of the Lord."

FRAGMENT OF A LECTURE.

ST. JOHN i. 14.—"And the Word was made flesh, and dwelt among us."

WE may discern here, brethren, what should be our chief concern in reference to ourselves, every day that we live. Plainly, it should be, that we may grow in the knowledge of our Lord and Saviour, Jesus Christ. If to receive Christ, believing on His name, is the way to be made partakers of the Divine nature, sons and heirs of God; and if we cannot receive Him without knowing Him, as He is revealed in the Word, surely our desire and our prayer should ever be that God would give us His holy Spirit, to take of the things of Christ and show them unto us; that "God, who commanded the light to shine out of darkness, would shine in our hearts, to give the light of the knowledge of the glory of God in the face of Jesus Christ."

And, do we not see here, too, what, if we have known Christ, and possess any of His bowels of mercies, we should seek first, and above all things, for our fellowmen? Is it not that they too may "know the only true God, and Jesus Christ whom He hath sent—whom to know is life eternal?" What do we see everywhere around us but a world lying in wickedness, abiding in death—a world sunk in ungodliness and corruption, and, as such, sunk in vast, shoreless, fathomless misery. We see but the outside of things, and therefore see but little, comparatively, of the misery. If we saw deeper, saw the whole, how appalling would be the sight! Oh, the bitterness, the woe, the anguish looked down upon by the sun between his morning rise and his evening decline! And do we know of no cure for it? If that were so, we were excusable in folding our hands, as most do, and leaving our race to dree their dark doom in time, and their yet darker immortality of ill. But we do know of a cure for man's sin and misery. If we are Christ's we have ourselves found that cure in the Word made flesh—the thing that can dry up the *misery*, by drying up its source, which is the *sin*. And shall it, then, be no concern with us to hold forth to others that Word of Life? Shall it not be our first and last, and never-ceasing object to declare to those who are bone of our bone, and flesh of our flesh, what "we have seen and heard of the Word of Life," that "*their* fellowship, too," may be with the Father and with His Son Jesus Christ; and so their joy may be full, while Christ sees in them of the travail of His soul and is satisfied? Humble as our place in the Church may be, and limited as our field of usefulness, shall we not, at the call of mercy, at the call of humanity, at the call of God, go and work earnestly with Him in the destruction of human sin and human misery; in the multiplication, in this world of woe, of rejoicing sons and daughters of the Lord Almighty; and in the hastening of that period when the Word who once tabernacled among us in flesh unglorified, shall again tabernacle among us in that flesh glorified, and that "great voice," spoken of by St. John in the Apocalyptic visions—that "great voice" out of heaven shall be heard saying, "Behold, the tabernacle of God is with men, and He will dwell with them, and they shall be His people; and God himself shall be with them, and be their God. And God himself shall wipe away all tears from their eyes; and there shall be no more death, neither sorrow nor crying, neither shall there be any more pain: for the former things are passed away."

295

LAST WORDS TO HIS CONGREGATION—SPOKEN ON THE OCCASION OF THE ADMINISTRATION OF THE LORD'S SUPPER, ON SABBATH, OCTOBER 19, 1862, THE LAST TIME HE WAS ABLE TO BE AMONG THEM.

SATURDAY ADDRESS.

EXHORTATION TO INTENDING COMMUNICANTS.

DEAR FRIENDS,—I shall not now attempt to say much to you, and yet, as one appointed to watch for your souls, who must soon give an account, I may be permitted to advert for a few moments to the solemn and delightful circumstances in which we now stand. If spared until the morrow, we shall be once more privileged to sit down at that Table where the weary have so often been refreshed and the hungry filled with good things. The Master of the Feast has again come to us, and His voice to us is, "Behold I stand at the door and knock," and He but waits for our opening the door to "come in to us, to sup with us," and to admit us to sup with Him in sweet and reviving fellowship. And when is it that we shall open the door to Him? Just then when we most feel our need of Him—when we most clearly see the evil that is in us, and that it is an evil under which, unless He deliver us from it, we must inevitably and miserably perish. Dear friends, seek to see this evil, and see it now, that you may raise your voice to Christ, and say, " Come in to me, Lord, and make me to taste the blessedness of which Thou hast spoken ! "

These communion seasons with us recur only at distant intervals ; and it is an advantage arising from this that at their recurrence the heart is often deeply solemnized. Your hearts may now be deeply solemnized. The hand of God, which can reach us in so many ways, has touched you. You are thinking of those who have gone from among us of late years, and thinking that perhaps ere another Communion season comes round, you, too, may be gone. They are thoughts to solemnize your spirit— thoughts to awaken the enquiry, How shall I be prepared for this Communion ? it may be my last on earth, with my God and Saviour. Dear friends, you will be prepared for it just as by the Holy Spirit you are convinced of sin that is in you—of its vileness—its misery—its destructive- ness—and as by the same Spirit you are enabled to open your hearts to Christ, and to count all things but loss that you may win Christ and be found in Him. Happy those among us whose sin has found them out, and who, taking the publican's place, lift up his cry "God be merciful to me a sinner !" " The sacrifices of God are a broken and contrite spirit ;" and if such at the time shall be your sacrifices, your Communion with Him will be sweet.

Ask then the Holy Spirit, as you examine yourselves this evening—ask Him to show you all that is in your heart, to convince you of sin. I commend you to Him who casts out none that truly come to Him. I commend you every one ! " The good Lord pardon every one that prepares his heart to seek God, though it be not prepared according to the purification of the sanctuary."

" The Lord bless thee and keep thee. The Lord make His face to shine, and be gracious unto thee. The Lord lift up the light of His countenance upon thee and give thee peace."

ADDRESS

TO THE COMMUNICANTS AT THE TABLE OF THE LORD,
DELIVERED ON SABBATH, OCTOBER 19, 1862.

BLESS the Lord, O my soul, and forget not all His benefits, who forgiveth all thine iniquities, who healeth all thy diseases, who redeemeth thy life from destruction. In such language, Communicants, if you were to give expression to your present emotions, would you not now utter them, as you think of Him through whose blood you have remission, nor remission only, but *healing,*—even all that you need to make you whole of your soul's plague, and to fill you with a new and pure and Heavenly life ! If so be that you have tasted that the Lord is thus gracious, what blessedness is yours! A wondering and weeping prophet once exclaimed— " Is there no balm in Gilead—is there no Physician there?" But *you* are not left to make any such dark and painful enquiries. You know of a cure of infallible efficacy, you have found a physician infinite in pity and infinite in skill. Your hurt, like that of Israel of old, was a grievous hurt. It polluted you and made you wretched. " The whole head was sick, and the whole heart faint." And it was a fatal hurt; it baffled all human skill ; it defied all human remedies ; and you must soon have sunk under its virulence, and perished for ever.

But God had mercy upon you ; He laid help for you on One mightier to save. In Christ you have a healing balm for all your spiritual maladies. His blood is a fountain opened for sin and for all uncleanness ; you have washed in that fountain and experienced the efficacy of its healing waters. And still you desire to wash in it,—still you desire to look unto Jesus, that you may have pardon and peace and purity and eternal life. And here at His

Table you desire to meet with Him, and to put yourselves wholly into His hands, that He may give you the balm of His broken body and shed blood ; and, under the sweet experience of its cleansing and healing power, cause you to sing with exulting hearts of His power and pity, saying —" Bless the Lord, O my soul, and all that is within me bless His holy name."

Trusting that such, or similar to these, are the emotions and desires of your hearts, we now proceed to put into your hands the tokens of Christ's broken body and shed blood.

AFTER COMMUNICATING.

COMMUNICANTS !—One who had suffered long and had suffered much, once came behind Jesus in the press, and touched His garment, for she said, " If I may touch but His clothes, I shall be whole." And happy was she who thus believed ; virtue straightway went out of Him, and she was healed. Now, has your confidence in Jesus been like that of this sufferer, and has it been blessed? As you have said at His Table in your hearts, " If I may but touch the hem of His garment, I shall be whole,"—does He know, and do you know, that virtue has come out of Him to heal you? Adore His mercy and goodness ; let your soul bless the Lord ; let all that is within you bless His holy name.

Cleave henceforth to your Physician. Have no Saviour but Christ. Resort for healing to none other but Him, for all others are physicians of no value,—they could not save you, and you would again become the prey of disease and death. Having experienced the Heavenly

Physician's power to heal, perform healthy acts ; engage in healthy exercises. Go forth to your daily work in God's service until the evening. See what the Lord would have you to do in your own souls, in your families, in the Church, in the world. " To do good, and to communicate, forget not." There are many around you wounded by sin—wounded by it, as you were, unto death. Can you stand by and see them perish ? Surely if you have come to Jesus and been healed, you will bring others to Him that *they* may be healed. Did *He* refuse to come into personal contact with our wickedness and misery ? Instead of sending a substitute to be our deliverer, He delivered us Himself. " He loved us and gave Himself for us !" Communicants, remember this ; and when you see those who have none to care for their souls,—and they are at your doors,—pass them not by on the other side, but have compassion on them and hasten to their relief. Love as you have been loved ; give yourselves to the recovery of the wounded and dying as Christ gave Himself for you, when you were wounded and dying. It is not long that you will have to go about this blessed work,— this only work worth living for ! The night cometh when no man can work. Some have gone from among us since last we kept this Feast. We, too, must soon leave our places in the Church below. But what of this if we have been about our Master's business, and walked in love as Christ also loved us and gave Himself for us ? Death will then have no terrors for us ; it will only sever us from a body in which we groan, being burdened ; and whether our passage over its dark waters be rough or smooth, we shall be welcomed to the joy of the Lord on the farther shore.

Finally, submit to your Heavenly Physician's treatment. Submit to it not less when it is painful than when it is pleasant. We know not what the Lord may see meet to do with us. We know not what sore trials it may be His will to send us. But oh, Communicants, let it comfort your hearts that he will do *all* things well ; that He will, with unerring wisdom, appoint the things that are for the life of your spirit ; that He will, in love to your souls, deliver you from the pit of destruction ; and that the hour is not distant when, having perfected all that concerneth you, He shall translate you to a land where the inhabitant shall no more say, "I am sick," because the people that dwell therein shall be forgiven their iniquity ! Go, rejoicing in these things. Go now from His Table singing His praises as in the Eucharistic Psalm :—" Bless the Lord, O my soul, and all that is within me bless His holy name !"

www.ingramcontent.com/pod-product-compliance
Lightning Source LLC
Chambersburg PA
CBHW020322140726
47905CB00013B/2148